NO LOOSE ENDS

NO LOOSE ENDS

Shirley J. Shepherd

No Loose Ends is a work of fiction. Names, characters, and organizations are products of the author's imagination. In some cases, places are fictional; in others, they are real, though sometimes used fictitiously and sometimes adjusted to fit the plot of the book. Any resemblance to actual persons, living or dead (except for Vladimir Puten), business establishments, or events is entirely coincidental.

ISBN 979-8-218-30277-1

Imprint: Independently Published

www.shirleyjshepherd.com

Cover Design: Limelight Book Covers
Cover Photographer: Richard McGuirk licensed through iStock

Printed in USA

This book is dedicated to my son Michael Shepherd who has believed in my writing and in this book far longer and far more than I did. His tireless, unflagging support and encouragement as well as his sense of humor have been my support throughout the process.

Author's Note:

Apologies to the people of Morehead City and Beaufort, North Carolina, for the liberties I took with some of the locations I included in this story. As much as possible, I tried to describe the geography accurately. In some cases, to better fit my story, I made small changes. For instance, Belle's and Sandy's houses don't exist, and I located them where I needed them to be.

Choosing these coastal cities as places for Maggie to run to was not by design but by happenstance. My husband Dorin and I were bringing our boat home from Puerto Rico to Maine when we developed a problem that meant we couldn't use the motor. We were just outside the barrier islands near North Carolina and decided to make an emergency stop. In the short time we were in Beaufort and Morehead City, the people of those lovely cities were kind and helpful, and we fell in love with the area.

When I started *No Loose Ends*, Dorin suggested I use that area as a place for Maggie to hide. Many years later, when I was attempting to revive the manuscript, I realized I could no longer tell what was based on fact and what was a number of figments of my imagination. I wondered, for instance, if the beach area where Maggie is chased, ever really existed. Or, if it did, was it still the same? Or was it now filled with high-rise hotels? I said as much to my friend Pam, who suggested it was time for a trip to North Carolina.

We experienced the same cordial helpfulness from everyone we talked to. At first, as we drove around, I had trouble locating the beach in Morehead City where the above-mentioned scene takes place. We finally stopped at a Visitors' Center and mentioned my writing project. The helpful woman in charge led me to a wall-size map and said, "I think what you want is right here along these two blocks." Of course, she was right. And it was the same!

While we were there, we took a ferry ride to see the horses on Shackleford Banks, the island of wild horses. These coastal cities are loaded with friendliness and charm, and the food is incredible. I'm looking forward to another visit some day. Thank you, North Carolina.

PROLOGUE

June 1999

   San Antonio's beloved Spurs had just won their first NBA title and the city was rocking! Judge Judith Sakowitz, as a local semi-bigwig, and her staff rode in each of the river parades down San Antonio's famous Riverwalk. Call it a perk, call it respect due for a career on the bench, call it what you will, but Judge Sakowitz never missed a chance to smile gratefully and wave, reminding the public who she was. She stood now with her back against the rail of her party barge that was poised for the run down the Riverwalk.

   Throngs of fans, partying raucously, lined the walk on both sides of the river and packed the arched footbridges that spanned the river. Every time she caught someone's eye she smiled. And waved. Because voters remembered when you waved to them.

   The barge cast off and Judge Sakowitz glanced around to assure herself that Webb, her personal bodyguard, was aboard.

   There he was, talking to a black security guard she didn't recognize, but who wore the uniform of Riverwalk security. She supposed the extra exposure on this trip warranted the extra protection. The new guy swooped through the motions of a jump shot, reliving, with Webb, some glorious moment of the game. They both laughed, then high-fived. Winning was everything.

   The barge moved into the center of the stream, and they were on their way down the winding, narrow channel dwarfed by two- and three-story buildings–shops and hotels–on each side. She waved at the fans as she approached the first bridge. As her barge passed beneath the stone arch, she noticed the side of the arch was so close she could almost touch it.

   She'd said in an interview with the San Antonio Herald last week that the threat of physical violence was linked to the times in which they lived, though in truth, during the last twenty-five years on the bench, her life had been threatened twice before. Only she hadn't taken it seriously in the past– the first time it was a hostile parent, the second time, a hot-tempered husband–both caught in a windstorm of emotion after she'd rendered judgment. She'd allowed a perfunctory guard for a week and then went about her business as usual.

This time, however, the threat, coming from a cool-headed source much more powerful than a cranky individual, chilled her to the core.

The Riverwalk narrowed as the boat approached another bridge. The crowd pressed closer.

She glanced up as the new security guard joined her at the rail. He was taller than she had thought. Handsome, too. He must turn the heads of pretty girls wherever he went. His eyes were kind when he nodded reassuringly at her. Then, in youthful response to the screaming crowd, he raised both arms and yahooed back at them.

He bent toward her to point out something along the walk, but his words were lost in the roar.

"Sorry, but I couldn't hear you," she shouted. She smiled at him and gestured toward the crowds. "Too loud. Too close. What did you say?"

He leaned closer to her ear and put his arm across her back; his hand cupped her elbow. "Look, back there. Did you see those kids with that sign? Here, lean this way and you'll see it."

She stretched over the rail a bit then felt herself being lifted gently an inch off the floor of the barge. Her first impression was that the young man was helping her to see better, but the next movement was abrupt. Her head slammed into a bridge abutment. Her last sensation was intense pain shuddering the length of her body.

BOOK ONE

"Which Way Did She Go?"

Of Fox and Hound

Chapter 1

Amesbury, Maine
August, 1999
Thursday

"Hey there, Otis. How're you doing?" Maggie Wiser pumped a little extra cheeriness into her voice. She would have guessed, from his baggy eyes, mussed hair and rumpled suit, he'd been awake all last night. She wondered again why he had asked her to meet him for breakfast. Because she was his accountant, they always met in her office. She slid into the booth of her favorite breakfast diner, Hal's. Hal was also a client of hers, and he kept five flavors of coffee on tap. The pancakes weren't bad, either.

"Maggie." The word cracked over morning phlegm as Otis nodded a greeting. He cleared his throat, and his bloodshot eyes met her eyes for the first time. "Thanks for meeting me away from the office. I don't feel comfortable there, you know, talking about this."

Winifred signaled Maggie from across the counter–did she want French Vanilla coffee? Maggie nodded and looked back at Otis hunkered over his cup of coffee. She decided his business, a combination grocery store and pizza place, must be in some terrible trouble though she couldn't imagine what. He would never be a millionaire, but he'd been in business for thirty years and always made a comfortable profit.

"It's okay. Thanks for making it Hal's. I'm here a couple of times a week anyway. So, what's on your mind?"

"I need a favor."

Winifred put a cup of coffee in front of Maggie and refilled Otis's from the pot she brought with her.

"The usual?" she asked Maggie.

Maggie nodded, knowing Hal had already poured the pancake batter on the griddle. Privately, she was a little sheepish at the immense satisfaction she got from having breakfast at a place where they knew what you wanted when you walked through the door.

Otis waved his hand. "I'm all set." Winifred carried the coffee pot to another table.

"Okay," Maggie said. "You asked for a favor. I'll help if I can. Shoot."

He took a deep breath and stared into his cup. "How much do you know about the new mall thing? The proposal?"

Otis was a city councilman, and this sounded like city hall business. Definitely not client and accountant business. "Not much. Just the blurb in the paper. Why?"

"Um, see, I believe building a super mall will be a wonderful boon to this city. It will boost the economy, bring new business, provide jobs–"

"I don't know if I agree with that. Money only stretches so far. And we already have a mall. But what has this got to do with me?"

"Sam, he's being really stubborn about it."

Then it dawned on her. Sam, her ex-husband, was also a city councilman. She laughed out loud. "Otis, you can't think I could somehow influence him. Is that what you're asking?"

Across the table, the husky man she had known since grade school looked sheepish.

"Yeah, something like that. I know you two are still friends. I've seen you at the Amesbury House having lunch. And, I thought if you were in agreement with us–even the mayor is in favor of this, you know–and if you found yourself on the same page, you could either make Sam see reason..."

She started to laugh again.

"...or tell me how to approach him, change his mind. The final vote is Monday night."

Maggie shook her head. "I'm sorry. It's not that I don't take you seriously, and I appreciate your confidence in me, but I wasn't able to change Samuel Wiser's mind about a single thing in the thirty-three years we were married. If that hadn't been the case, who knows–we might not have divorced ten years ago. Not that I would change it now, for anything."

Otis slumped back in his seat and stared hopelessly out the diner window.

Maggie chewed on her lower lip, studying him. "Why is this so important to you? It's only a mall. You look like it's a matter of life and death."

"No, no. No, of course not. I, it's just...well, a lot hinges on it." He hunched his shoulders. "A lot."

"If I believed in your cause–and who knows, if I heard all the details, maybe I'd be convinced–I'd help if I could. But trust me, if Sam has made up his mind, nothing I could say would change it."

He squinted out the window as though trying to make up his own mind. Then, apparently making a decision, he shook his head and looked back at her. "It's okay. Just a long shot anyway. I shouldn't have taken your time. Breakfast's on me, of course." He pushed himself sideways and out of the booth.

"One thing…" he said as he hauled his ample bulk to his full six feet. "Don't mention this to Sam, please. I have an appointment with him, and he'd be ticked if he realized I went to you first."

She couldn't help but smile. He was so right. "That I can do for you, Otis."

At the cash register he paid Winifred, and from her smile, Maggie knew he had left her a much better than usual tip.

He turned at the door and waved. "Good luck," she said, as Winifred put a plate in front of her that was more fresh strawberries than pancakes, both piled high with whipped cream. As she took her first bite, she watched through the diner window as a dejected Otis unlocked the door of an unfamiliar car. She didn't know many makes from sight, but she was sure the cream-colored car was new and very expensive and a far cry from the old, battered Ford he usually drove. Well, well— had his business picked up recently? That much?

In spite of the August afternoon heat outside, the interior of the bar was cool. Yet, sweat trickled down Otis Oxley's sides under his plaid dress shirt. The Councilman clinked the ice cubes against his glass, swallowed the last of his scotch and soda, and signaled the waitress for another.

She put a fresh napkin and drink on the glossy wooden tabletop and picked up the empty glass. Nodding his thanks, Otis took a sip and settled back into the soft, leather seat.

At the other end of the lounge a jazz combo was setting up for the evening. Otherwise, the bar was pretty much empty–just what he'd hoped for when he had set the meeting for two o'clock. He glanced at his watch. Sam was fifteen minutes late.

He took a long swallow from his drink to quiet his nervous stomach. Jesus, he felt like a rat trying to keep afloat after the ship had sunk. He tossed back the rest of the scotch and soda. He should slow down.

He signaled the bartender for another.

3

Otis pulled the swizzle stick out of the glass and dented it lengthwise with his thumbnail. The NADCO people thought Councilman Samuel Wiser had his price. They better be right, or life, as Otis knew it, would be flushed down the toilet.

He tied a knot in the swizzle stick. The problem was Samuel Wiser, Jr. acted like a holier-than-thou Boy Scout. Otis doubted he'd even consider a bribe. Besides, the Wisers were loaded, two generations back. Sam Wiser might want for some things.

Money wasn't one of them.

His stomach felt like he'd swallowed bricks. He tossed the swizzle stick aside in disgust.

He did have an ace he could play, but it was risky because NADCO would probably have a shit fit if they found out he even knew about it. After a meeting one night at city hall, he'd returned to the council room because he'd forgotten his briefcase. He was surprised to hear the voices of the two men who'd made their presentation to the council. He thought they'd left. The sound of their conversation was confidential, secretive, so he stopped outside the door and listened. In its scope, what he heard had taken his breath away.

He was turning this over when Sam came through the door, squinting as he scanned the tables, waiting for his eyes to adjust to the twilight of the bar's interior.

Otis studied him: wavy, silver-white short hair, six-feet, three-inches tall, broad-shouldered, not even a pot belly. Otis snorted. Sixty-five and the bastard still looked like a jock.

Sam spotted him. Hauling himself out of the chair, Otis extended his hand. "Thanks for coming."

"Sorry I'm late."

"No problem. I was late myself. Just got here."

Sam looked pointedly at the melting ice cubes in Otis' empty glass.

"Well, yeah, I've only been here long enough for one drink."

Sam ordered a martini; Otis cocked an eye to the waitress. She hadn't brought his third yet.

"What's up?" Sam asked.

"Well, um, I thought we should have a little talk, Sammy."

"It's Sam. And you want to talk about the mall."

Otis fumbled with the knot of his red necktie. "Yeah, about the mall. Listen, Sam, I don't think you've really considered the welfare of the people of this area..."

Sam's face hardened. "We've been through this three times. I'm not changing my mind. Like I said at each meeting, a mall doesn't bring in any new money or jobs to Amesbury–it just redistributes what's already here. A super mall would hurt the stores that have been around for years...for generations. They're just getting by now. Many of them would go under." Sam banged the flat of his hand on the table. "They're your friends and neighbors, Otis."

"Well, yes, but there are other things to consider." Otis cleared his throat. "The rest of the council, as well as Mayor Fitzhugh, are thinking about the most good for the most people."

Sam leaned closer. "No. You are thinking of the most good for yourselves. And, the only reason the mayor is going along with the council is they are promising to name the mall after him–have I got that right? And he's too stupid to know this isn't a good idea. But you, Otis. You're not stupid."

Otis kneaded his brow. Maybe he wasn't stupid. Until...

"I'm pretty sure I've got you figured out," Sam continued. "You're already planning how to spend the bribe money NADCO has promised you. How much is it? What's the price of your so-called integrity?"

The waitress was approaching. "Sam, shut up," Otis whispered hoarsely.

Otis grabbed his drink and slurped half of it. The waitress put a martini in front of Sam, and he reached for his wallet.

Otis put his hand up. "On my tab," he said, wiping his mouth on his shirtsleeve.

Sam eyed his martini. "There's nothing you can say that will make me change my mind, and you and Fitzhugh can't swing this without me. Let me stop wasting your time." Sam pushed back his chair.

"Wait!" Otis grabbed Sam's arm. "Wait, okay? Please, Sam, will you just listen another minute? See, it's not the money. Okay..." Otis waved a hand.

"All right, yes, I will get a small thank-you bonus if this goes through. There's one for you, too, Sam. It's generous, really generous, but what I'm getting at is everyone in the goddamn city will benefit–which makes for happy voters."

Sam shifted in his seat, started to rise.

"No, wait." Otis fished a silver Cross pen out of his breast pocket and removed the napkin from under Sam's glass. He wrote a number on the napkin, turned it around and pushed it across the table. He held his breath. He had learned that the first one to speak lost, so he remained silent in the long ten seconds that

Sam studied the figure. Then Sam sighed, turned the napkin over and placed his glass back on top of it.

"Otis? If there is nothing wrong with this deal, why are they offering a bribe of this size? Why are they offering a bribe at all? It's out of the question that I would accept it. But I'm just asking–why are they offering this kind of money if everything is legit?" Sam paused. "It's only a mall, for chrissake. There are other cities."

Otis nodded. He was afraid it would come to this. "Here's the thing, Sam. Now, this is strictly confidential. You get what I'm saying? I'm not even supposed to know this. Much less tell you. So, you can't say anything to anyone..."

Sam gestured impatiently. "Get on with it."

"We're not just talking a mall. That's small potatoes. This is really a two-part project. They have plans for building multi-million-dollar houses, an exclusive golf course, and a classy, high-end hotel...really nice, upscale. You know what I'm saying? Everything will unfold over the next two years, but we have to keep it quiet for a while. Sam, nobody can lose on this thing. I can't tell you how good I think all this will be for the city."

Sam slowly sipped his drink, carefully centered his glass over the ballpoint figures, and pushed it aside. Clasping his hands, he leaned comfortably forward on his elbows. The corners of his mouth turned up a little. His eyes were friendly.

Otis exhaled slowly. Whew! He'd taken the chance, and it had paid off. He smiled for the first time this afternoon. He felt some of the tension go out of his belly.

"Where, Otis?"

"Where what?"

"Where is there land in Amesbury on which to put this fabulous, high-end project?"

"Um, well, I'm not sure." Otis' pulse jumped. "I mean, I know they have some plan, but I'm not sure–"

"Otis. Where are they planning to put the golf course, the hotel, the multi-million-dollar mansions?"

"I don't think we need to get into the details–I don't really know..."

Sam's hand clamped over Otis' wrist and dug in. "Where?"

Sam's eyes hardened. When he continued, his voice was low and intense. "There's only one place around here that I can think of that has enough acreage. It's the Archibald Estate, right?" He released Otis's arm.

Shit. He should have kept his mouth shut.

"Are you telling me there's a plan to use the Archibald Estate? For *development?*"

Otis was gripped by a mild panic. He picked up his empty glass and tipped it from side to side, watching the melting ice cubes slide across the bottom.

Sam glared at him. "Old man Archibald left that land to his grandson–ah, Ernest Archibald, I think his name is–to be used as a wildlife refuge. I've always assumed that can't be changed."

He'd blown it–royally. Sam had always been sympathetic to environmental issues. Why hadn't he remembered that? Sam would never vote for the mall now that he knew about the development deal screwing up the goddam wildlife thing.

"Can it be changed, Otis?"

It didn't much matter what he said now. The cat was out of the bag.

"Yeah, well, I guess they got a plan. They're going to take it over, I don't know the details, and, when the time is right, I guess they're going to make a killing. In a real estate development deal."

"And a mall."

Otis nodded. "And a mall."

"Can they do it? Can they get at the Archibald Estate?"

"Sam, these people can do anything they want. I don't think you realize. They get what they want–one way or another."

"What do you mean?" Sam's voice was almost gentle.

"You can go along with them and take what they offer, or they'll–well, these people will find another way."

"What's the other way?"

"What do you mean?"

"What's the other way? They bribe–or they what?"

Otis was defeated–and scared. He had said way too much, and it hadn't done any good. In fact, if NADCO found out what he had told Sam, the noose around his own neck would tighten. He wasn't going to say any more. He locked his fingers around the damp glass and hung his head.

"Otis? What do they have on you?" Sam asked. "What's hanging over your head?"

There was a long pause while Otis swallowed and blinked. He stared at a spot on the table between them and cleared his throat. "Goodbye, Sam. Thanks for coming."

"Right. See you Monday night."

Otis heard Sam's chair scrape backwards on the oak floor, but he didn't look up again until Sam disappeared through the door.

Otis lifted his glass and waggled it at the waitress. This was the first time in five years–since they'd served on the council together–that Sam had given any indication he thought Otis had any brains: You're not stupid, Otis. But Sam was wrong. He was stupid. A stupid, small-town hayseed, shaken loose by the NADCO city slickers.

He fished the phone number out of his wallet. They hadn't even given him a business card. Just a number on a piece of paper. Goddammit, he didn't want to make this phone call.

He pushed back from the table and struggled to his feet. He bumped into a table on the way to the public phone at the back of the restaurant. With a sinking feeling it wasn't going to work, he dialed the number, a New York City exchange.

Lincoln Montgomery answered before the first ring ended. "Yes?"

"This is Otis Oxley."

"I know. What's happening, Mr. Oxley?"

Otis hesitated, a knot constricting his throat. He closed his eyes. "Um," he paused. "I guess it's a no go, Mr. Montgomery."

"You failed to convince him."

Before Otis could respond Montgomery said, "Well, that is, of course, unfortunate."

Then I guess," Otis ventured, "this whole deal, this just isn't going to work. We gave it a good run, but we have to give it up. Look, I can give the money back. Most of it. If NADCO brought a formal application to the city council, Sam Wiser would vote against it. Like I said from the beginning, for a project like this, where zoning would have to change from non-commercial to commercial, the vote has to be unanimous."

"Mr. Oxley, this project will move forward. Trust me."

"But how...but you...well, okay. But what are we supposed to do now?"

"That is no longer your concern."

Otis' heart slammed in his chest. "But are you going to–I mean, will they...? Well, you know. What you said they would do if I didn't deliver?" A dial tone.

Otis went back to the table. Sam's glass was still there but the napkin was gone.

Manhattan, NY

Lincoln Montgomery replaced the phone in the cradle and stood up, thinking he seemed to spend half of his working hours in front of public telephones. Though he was in pretty good shape at the age of fifty, sitting by the phone for an hour had stiffened his muscles. Arms over head, he stretched his slender, five-foot ten-inch frame then straightened his tie and evened out his shirt sleeves by tugging on his cufflinks. He needed to walk for a few minutes.

Unfortunate about the situation in Maine. He shook his head. He'd come across people like Wiser in college–driven by idealism, they were not good candidates for a bribe or for anything else that wasn't strictly on the up and up. His boss, Royal LaCroix, CEO of NADCO, did not see it that way. Money, enough money thrown at a situation, would fix all problems. Sometimes it worked. Sometimes it didn't.

Back at the bank of public phones, he dialed his boss's private number.

"Yes?"

"The situation in Maine did not improve."

"Sorry to hear it." Roy LaCroix's sympathetic voice might have been responding to news of a head cold.

Lincoln waited out his boss.

"You already know how time-sensitive this issue is," Roy said.

"I believe this situation must be resolved before Monday."

"I don't believe, Lincoln, we need to talk in terms of a deadline on this thing." LaCroix's voice remained upbeat.

"Let's just say," he continued, "that if we're going to kick off at game time, we need the field mowed and the teams in place.

"You always know how to straighten out these annoying little matters, Lincoln. I'm sure you'll find a simple solution that will enable us to continue our endeavor in the fine state of Maine. There's a meeting of the partners tomorrow afternoon. I'll tell them that, as always, we can depend on you."

"There'll be no problem, Roy."

"Good. Have a good weekend. Oh, Lincoln. Let's play golf next week."

"Sure thing. I'll look forward to it." Grimacing, he hung up the phone. He hated golf, as Roy well knew. But the golf course was where he could report without being overheard.

He indulged in a moment of satisfaction. His contingency plans had been activated a month ago. He looked forward to making the next phone call.

Amesbury, Maine

The microwave oven beeped; Maggie opened the door and removed the mug of boiling water. The green numbers on the oven door switched back to the time: ten-thirty in the evening. She dropped in an herbal tea bag and stirred, thinking she'd rather have coffee, but, of course, then she wouldn't get to sleep until three in the morning, and she had to be up at six. She decided against adding sugar. It was bad enough she'd had the high calorie breakfast. She'd also succumbed to temptation and had fried scallops for lunch–the large platter. With a bucket of tartar sauce. She patted her hips, sure she could feel the extra fat already layered on. Time to go on a diet. She thought about the slice of chocolate cake in the refrigerator. No, damn it. Time to get a grip.

She carried the steaming mug into her home office off the kitchen and looked at the pile of income and expense reports she'd been working on for the past four hours. She was physically and mentally weary. How long had it been since she had really dug into her work with relish? She sighed and decided not to go there. Instead, she'd focus on being grateful for her assistant, Angie, who shouldered a lot of her burden. Tomorrow she'd talk to her partner Stoney about giving Angie a raise.

Benjamin "Stoney" Stonefield of Stonefield and Wiser Associates had started the business as a part-time endeavor while he was teaching accounting at Marston Business College.

With the goal of becoming independent of Sam's family money, Maggie took a couple of courses from Stoney. Her only child, Joel, was three years old at the time.

Two years later, Stoney gave up teaching and devoted full time to the business. He offered Maggie a job as a receptionist, thirty hours a week. Since the only job she'd ever had was waiting on tables as a teenager, she grabbed it. Not long after, her job evolved into becoming his assistant. At his urging, she continued to take courses and eventually became a CPA. Many years later, he had offered her a partnership.

The phone rang, and she grabbed in on the first ring. It had to be Joel calling from Chicago.

"Hi, how're you doing? Burning the midnight oil?" His voice was warm and the question genuine.

"I was just about to quit for the night. Good timing. How's the trip going?"

"It couldn't be better. You are not going to believe what happened."

She heard the excitement in his voice and settled back in her chair, smiling. "Tell me about it."

"They were so happy with the job they recommended me to the parent company, and I landed the account! This will be the biggest one yet."

Her first reaction, to be caught up in his current enthusiasm, was followed a second later by a reality check. He continued before she could say anything.

"It isn't completely final, you know, but I'm having dinner with the big shots, and if we agree on all the fine points, we'll ink the contract then. I don't think there'll be a problem. We've already discussed the major points. I can't believe it. They came to *me*."

She ached to be happy for him, but... "Does this mean you'll be working more hours?" She waited through a four-second pause before he answered.

"Well, yes, but it won't be too bad, really."

"Joel, weren't you just lamenting the other night the fact that you don't spend enough time with the kids? Your solution–*your* solution–was to cut back on out-of-state accounts so you wouldn't be gone as much."

There was another silence, shorter this time. "They're not really kids anymore, Mom. Tildie is twenty-one, no, twenty-two and Pookie is, what? Fourteen?"

She bit her lip before replying. "I guess that would be my point. If not now...when?"

"Look, I've got to go. We can talk about this later."

Maggie could tell he couldn't wait to get off the phone.

She'd always been in his corner. While his father had largely ignored him, she had celebrated Joel's every success. She wanted to be happy for him, tell him she was proud of him. But dammit, his happiness at what price to his children?

"I'm meeting with the account execs tomorrow night so don't pick me up at the airport. I'll be coming in on Saturday morning. Eleven o'clock. We'll talk then. It'll be okay. You'll see. Don't worry."

"Joel, Saturday morning you and Pookie were supposed to–"

"Oh, damn. I forgot! Can you tell him for me I can't make it? I'm so sorry."

She knew he was. She bit back the words "you are just like your father." It would've wounded him to the core.

"I'll make it up to him. Tell him I've got two tickets to a Patriots at Panthers game on September second. It's a Thursday night game, but school won't have started yet."

She nodded but didn't trust her voice to speak. She felt like crying–for Sam and all he had missed as an absentee father, for Joel and all he was missing, and for Pookie.

He used her moment of silence to make his getaway. "It'll all turn out okay. I'll talk to you Saturday. Maybe Tildie can pick me up at the airport? If you're too busy?"

She felt rather than saw, movement in the doorway as she said, "Okay, have a safe trip back," and hung up the phone.

Pookie stood framed against the darkened kitchen behind him. His thickly lashed eyes were inherited from his Thai mother, except they were deep blue, genes contributed by Joel. Now, they glittered with pain and anger. At his sides, his hands were balled into fists.

"He's not coming, is he?" Turning, he stalked toward the back door. He was headed to his refuge–the carriage house where he would work on his bike or tinker with the old motorcycle he was trying to rebuild. She knew better than to follow–he needed privacy to deal with his feelings.

Sighing, she reassembled the spreadsheets and closed the three-inch-thick file she'd been working on. But she couldn't keep her eyes from locking onto a photo that hung above her desk, a duplicate of the one which was in her bedroom. She had taken the picture herself, and it included her whole family–her ex-husband Sam, their son Joel who was holding a three-year-old Pookie, and eleven-year-old Tildie. Pookie was the only one smiling.

She sighed again. "Samuel Wiser, what have you wrought?"

Chicago

Joel sat on the fifth-floor balcony looking at the city lights. Before he phoned his mother, what he'd really wanted to do was call his father. Tell him–well, tell him, "Hey, I'm as successful in my business as you are in yours–more, probably. My company is known all over the Eastern Seaboard, and we've done a few jobs in Texas and Chicago. Now I've landed the biggest account of my life in California."

Advertising his achievements to his dad. Like I'm a little kid, Joel thought.

"Hey, Dad, I hit a home run."

"Hey, Dad, I scored a touchdown."

"Hey, Dad, I was voted class president."

Dad, Dad, Dad. Hey, Dad, look at me.

Please.

Still.

The things he wanted to tell his father in person…things that always had to be put in a note for Dad to read when he got home from work, usually after Joel's bedtime.

The race to win his father's attention and approval…a race never quite won.

Now, after his mother's rebuke, he couldn't call his father even if he wanted to. What would he say? In a struggle to get your approval, I became you?

Manhattan

Lincoln Montgomery crossed the foyer of the Milton Hotel in New York City, walked toward the bank of public phones, and selected the phone at the end of a line, farthest from the inebriated guy arguing with his girlfriend. At eleven-thirty in the evening, no other phones were in use. Convenient. And discreet.

A couple of months ago, when Charles Beauchamp, second in command at NADCO, had made Royal aware of the resistance provided by Samuel Wiser, Roy had tried enticements: Wiser's law firm would get all of NADCO's business. When that didn't go as he had expected, he tried his next go-to: a bribe—a large one. Lincoln knew Charles didn't think it would work, but Roy remained optimistic: a large enough sum would bring Wiser around.

Like Charles, Lincoln hadn't shared his optimism. So, on his own, he'd contacted Jewel to see if he'd be available sometime in the coming weeks–no longer than a month. Lincoln knew, because of Jewel's phone number, he lived in Boston. There would be little to no travel. Jewel was interested.

Two weeks ago, Lincoln had made the second call, giving a tentative window. Jewel would need the lead time to set things up. Lincoln gave him all the information he had and then advanced him the needed money for initial expenses and remuneration for time spent.

Now, tonight's call. "Yes?" The voice on the other end was deep, distant.

"You're on."

"Schedule?"

"He's leaving for Cambridge Friday night, returning Sunday afternoon. He's got a reservation at the Concorde Hotel. There's a conference at the law school all weekend. He's a speaker on Saturday morning."

"He'll be alone?"

"Yes."

Dial tone.

Lincoln smiled slightly as he tugged once at each cufflink to adjust his sleeves. He enjoyed being the director of this part of the operation.

But the star was Jewel. And Jewel never failed to deliver.

Amesbury, Maine
Friday

Maggie propped her briefcase on the ground against her leg and fished her keys to the rear office door out of her shoulder strap bag. In her other hand, she held both a to-go coffee and a bag of donuts. The donuts were threatening to slip from three cramped fingers.

And, damn, the key wouldn't turn. They were always having trouble with this lock. It didn't bother Stoney, but she threatened to have it replaced every time she was the first one at the office. She put the coffee and donuts on the ground and turned the key while pushing down hard on the doorknob with the other hand. Click. Finally.

She'd just off-loaded the coffee and donuts on her desk when Stoney came in. She gave him a few minutes to get settled before she buzzed him on the intercom.

"'Morning," his voice rumbled.

"Got some donuts here."

"You're a saint."

Ben Stonefield was tall and lanky. He had a full head of thick, white hair that waved across the top of his ears. On top it was cut shorter so that none of it ever fell across his forehead. He wore jeans and a white turtleneck under a light tan sports jacket. He carried an oversized coffee mug to her desk and began fishing in the donut bag, finding the custard-filled one that she always bought for him. He sat on the couch across from her desk.

She sipped her English toffee-flavored coffee contentedly.

"Aren't you having a donut?" he asked her.

14

"Nope. I've started my new diet today."

Stoney groaned. "Not another one. How's this one different from the *old* new one? Do you eat real food?" He took a huge bite out of the donut.

"I always eat good food. Except for that liquid diet. Or when I binge. This one includes a lot of raw greens. I need to shake this last thirty pounds somehow."

"Are you going to be grouchy on this one, like you were on the last six?"

"Absolutely. It's my PMS replacement therapy."

"Good to know there're some things you can count on." He grinned around a mouthful of donut.

She indulged in another sip of coffee and thought about the cream filled Bismark she'd bought for Angie. Except Angie liked glazed, come to think of it. Bismarks were Maggie's favorite. Amazing how she hadn't remembered that when she bought it.

There was a tap at the door and Angie stepped in. "I took a client's file home last night. Something about it bothered me. You guys got time to talk about it?"

"Sure, come in. Here," Maggie said, offering the donut bag to Angie. "I got one for you. Kind of."

Angie shut the door behind her and glided across the room. She was slender and tall, even without the three-inch heels. She wore a light blue, soft linen suit which complemented her dark brown skin. Her hair was clipped closely to her elegant head, and thin gold hoop earrings emphasized delicate ears. Watching her, Maggie thought Angie had more presence at twenty-six than Maggie had mustered in her lifetime.

Angie tucked a file folder under her arm and peered into the bag. "Uh huh. A Bismark. And whom did you have in mind when you bought *that*?" Angie said in her lilting voice.

"It's for you. I'm on a diet."

"Thank you for sharing that bit of information," Angie said. "I'll batten down the hatches."

"For the record," Stoney said, "she bought *me* my favorite." He slowly licked his sticky fingers. "How do you like them donuts?"

Angie sat beside Stoney, took a bite out of the Bismarck, closed her eyes and made a show of moaning with delight. "Mmm. *So* good. *You* should try one, Maggie."

"Thanks for your support, Angela."

"Anytime."

"Tell us, is the client mine or hers?" Stoney asked.

"Hers. Otis Oxley."

Maggie sat up straighter. "Oh, my! What did you find?"

"I went over it with a fine-tooth comb," Angie said. "Do you want to see copies of the income and expense statements?"

Stoney put his half-full coffee mug on the end table. "No, that's okay. Just give us your view of the situation for now." He stretched out his long legs, crossed his ankles, and laced his fingers behind his head.

"It looks like he's not reporting income, and he's being stupid–or at least naive–about his records. If I could find it in a few hours, it would jump out at the IRS or the state in an audit. His business is booming–we know that–but his reported income goes down each year, while his expenses stay the same or go up. It's logical the expenses would rise as his business grows, but..."

Stoney nodded. "The income isn't there to justify it. If he's really been cheating Uncle Sam and Aunty Maine, he's just been destroying one or more of the tapes. Imagine the sales tax he hasn't paid."

"The other thing is that when Mr. Oxley passed his bank statement along to be reconciled, he put in his personal statement, instead of the business one."

"Oh. Must have been an absentminded slip," Maggie said.

Angie handed three pages to Maggie. "Look at the balance."

"Over two hundred and fifty thousand. Actually, two hundred and fifty-eight thousand, nine hundred and forty-three." An astonished Maggie looked at Stoney. "And thirty-seven cents. Give or take."

"And," added Angie, "Three hundred thousand of it was a lump sum deposited two weeks ago."

"Okay. Angie, will you call him and make an appointment?" Ben asked. "Let's see if he has any explanation that holds water regarding his business."

"Sure thing," Angie replied. "Can I get you anything else? Coffee?" This was directed at Ben. She turned to Maggie. "Double fudge sundae?"

Stoney guffawed.

"Angela, Monday I'll bring you a plain donut. In fact, I don't think they even *make* glazed anymore."

Angela made a stabbing motion to her heart. "I knew you had a cruel streak in you somewhere, Ms. Wiser."

Stoney was still laughing as Angie disappeared through the door.

"She always makes me feel so colorless and frumpy," Maggie said.

Ben's smile broadened. He raised his eyebrows, quizzically.

She laughed at her own choice of words. "Well, no, you know what I mean. Not colorless that way. Just–well, she's so stylish. She looks like a model in Vogue. I feel like an Alka Seltzer ad." Maggie realigned the hem of her gray jacket over her hips.

It wasn't simply that Maggie was overweight. Though her blond hair–complete with streaks caused by a combination of Clairol and sun exposure–was fashionable in color, she hadn't changed her hairstyle in ten years, maybe fifteen. Except for the bangs, she simply pulled the top and sides back, fastening the hair with a clip at the back of her head. The rest of the hair fell to the middle of her neck.

Though people frequently complimented her on her green eyes, she hardly ever thought about makeup–didn't want to take the time. In fact, the only makeup she owned, besides the old, half-used-up stuff in her medicine cabinet urged on her by her granddaughter, was a lipstick. She examined her painted fingernails, cut short because she worked in the garden, and contrasted them with Angie's perfect manicure. Stirred by an unusual restlessness, she sighed.

"Don't sell yourself short, Margaret Wiser. You're a very attractive woman. But, yes, Angie is beautiful."

"Listen, Stoney. First, I think we should give her a raise. She busts her butt around here. Second, I think we should send her to school. Pay for her night classes. Like you did for me. She's almost finished her associates degree, but she's run out of money from her husband's insurance policy. She supports two kids. She can't pay for classes anymore. But she's so sharp, and she *loves* this stuff."

Maggie clamped her jaw shut. Had she just implied that she herself didn't?

Stoney frowned and studied her for a moment. "On the raise, yes. Overdue, now that you mention it. But you're talking about her advancing to certified?"

She nodded.

He folded his arms over his chest. "Have you talked to her about this yet?"

"Not until I talked to you."

"Is it too late to enroll for the winter trimester at MB & T?" Marston Business and Technical College was where Stoney had taught for years and where Maggie had received her degree.

She could have danced for joy, but she limited herself to softly hissing a victorious, "Yes."

"I take it that means 'no, it's not too late,'" he said dryly. His eyes twinkled.

She nodded, suppressing the desire to run out and tell Angie the news.

"How was your presentation on Y2K last night?" she asked him.

Stoney groaned. "I don't think I did a damn bit of good. I gave my little speech on everything that's being done...software companies providing Y2K compliant programs, what the government is doing, how computer technicians are successfully doing dry runs. I told them what we've done here and that I'm confident we have nothing to worry about."

"Well, that sounds good. I know some people think planes will fall out of the sky at midnight because technology will fail. Computers will change the 99 in 12/31/99 forward to 00 and computers will think it's 1900. And life that depends on technology as we know it will end. But you soothed their fears?"

"Yeah, right. They opened it for questions, and the first question I was asked was, 'Should I take all of my cash out of the bank, or just enough to last for...how many days do you think before they get the banks opened for business?' Then question and answer morphed into a survival discussion. It was crazy. I might as well not have talked. People were asking each other how much food and water they've put aside, how much more they had to do to prepare. A couple of families have built shelters in their basements. One guy said he was going to be armed because when other people ran out of food or water, they would come for his. And then another speaker, a local computer guy, offered a service to anyone who wanted to sign up. For three hundred dollars, he'd look into their home computers and make the corrections needed. People couldn't get their names on the list quick enough."

"Oh, dear. Well, a waste of your time then."

"Let's talk about something that isn't a waste of time," Stoney said. "When're you going to take over this business and let me have a decent retirement before I die?" He was in excellent health, exercised four times a week.

She shook her head. "I don't want to take it over. To be honest, I don't look forward to coming here the way I used to. When I wake up, I just want to pull on a pair of jeans and go work in the garden. Or grab my camera and go exploring. Take a train ride. Do something different, exciting. I don't know what. Something."

He settled back on the couch, hands behind his head again, eyebrows knitted thoughtfully. "Don't worry. You're just going through a midlife crisis. A little late, but you were always a late bloomer, anyway."

The corner of his mouth lifted in a crooked, teasing smile. "Do what the men do. Have an affair. Or buy a goddamn sports car...it's much less complicated."

Maggie raised her eyebrows, gave him a look, and waited for it to dawn on him.

"What?" He frowned. "*What*, for chrissake? Oh, the *Porsche*. I forgot. Well, why the hell don't you drive the thing? That's a crime no man would ever commit. Leaving a fine racing machine sitting there for...how many years? It's probably ruined by now from disuse."

"Ten years. Sam has someone start it every day or maybe it's every week. I don't know. It's in his parking garage. Joel said his father even has it cleaned and waxed every few months."

"Margaret Mary Wiser, why the hell aren't you driving it?"

Maggie shrugged and shook her head vaguely. She felt tension just thinking about sitting behind the wheel of the Porsche. "It's probably because the car was a bribe. Sam's most meaningful attempt to save our marriage."

"Yeah. A man's solution to a marital problem–buy her something."

"And in Sam's case, that damn car was something that he'd like to have for himself. I've told him he can have it, but he'll never take it back. He insists I keep the title."

"But time goes by. Get over it."

"Mmm. Well, first, I don't see myself as a Porsche-type person, and second, I don't even know how to drive the blanking thing. I will never drive it."

"Speaking of Sam. Angie says you two've been having lunch more often lately? You thinking of getting back together?"

"Not a chance." Maggie shook her head emphatically. "We're just friends. Though I'm beginning to suspect he's having thoughts along those lines. Okay, Stoney. Get out of here. I've got to get to work. Don't you have work to do?"

"No, I just come into the office every day to plan my retirement."

"I'll retire before you do. Now go."

Wiggling more comfortably into the couch cushions, he gave the message, I'm not going anywhere.

"What?"

"I'm waiting to see if you go for that cupcake you have stashed in your bottom drawer."

Chapter 2

Manhattan

Chip Upton grinned as he stepped off the elevator. He glanced at his sports watch, waterproof to sixty feet. Two-thirty...half an hour late.

He pulled open the paneled oak door to the boardroom and stepped inside. The hum of conversation stopped as he entered. Two pairs of eyes glanced in his direction, and he knew they were annoyed at his tardiness. In the dead silence, he nodded in the direction of the round table and ambled over to the cart that held a coffee carafe and refreshments. "Be right with you, gentlemen."

Welcoming the sharp aroma of coffee, he picked up the coffee mug that had been left for him. The cobalt blue cup bore the word MAINE in large white letters. Their company was currently developing a project in Maine. Good...passable ski slopes, excellent waters for sailing.

Chip poured coffee from the carafe, placed two pastries on a bone china plate, and carried his first meal of the day to the table.

"Nice of you to join us," said CEO Roy LaCroix, his eyes crinkling with amusement.

Silver haired Royal LaCroix was over six feet tall, trim and athletic, spending an hour a day in the company gym. Chip knew Roy schmoozed the lower echelons to gain unflagging loyalty and admiration, but the employees believed their boss at the top was working hard to set a good example for them. Roy had memorized names and shook hands on the way into the gym and on the way out. He was beloved by all.

And, importantly, Roy didn't care when Chip arrived at a meeting as long as he blew in from whatever part of the world he was playing in and rubber-stamped whatever Roy asked him to.

Now, Chip nodded pleasantly to him. "Roy."

Roy nodded, a slight smile on his face.

Chip nodded to bespectacled Charles Beauchamp, second in command at NADCO. "Hey, Chuck. How's it going?"

Charles stiffened. He allowed no one to call him Charlie, much less Chuck. But Chip had started calling him that when he was twelve, and Charles Beauchamp was the Upton family attorney and in no position to object.

Charles also happened to be the reason Chip had the good fortune to become involved with NADCO. Chip's parents died in an avalanche while skiing in Switzerland when he was eighteen, leaving him a small fortune. By the time he was twenty-two, he'd played his way around the world and halfway through the family portfolio. Charles had sat him down and pointed out the folly of his ways. If he wanted to continue a globetrotting life, he would have to put his money in something other than blue chip stocks.

It was Charles who introduced Chip to Roy LaCroix. In exchange for thirty-five million, LaCroix promised him a third of the company and no responsibilities. With the influx of new cash at the right time, the company had quietly skyrocketed, making the three partners quite comfortable financially.

"We were just winding up a discussion on the new project in Maine," Roy said. "Our numbers show a profit in excess of a hundred million over the next three years, if all goes as planned. I'll catch you up on it later."

Chip whistled appreciatively.

"This is the big one we've been waiting for, and Charles is to be congratulated for successfully completing the first phase," Roy said. "He has spent considerable time in Amesbury, Maine—well, I have too, but not nearly as much—and there have been very few hurdles that he hasn't easily cleared. There's still a loose end or two to tie up…"

Charles Beauchamp looked startled and glanced a question at Roy.

"No, no." Roy shook his head and patted the air in front of him. "Just a small detail came to my attention." He smiled. "But I don't anticipate any problems. And so, over twelve hundred acres, much of it along the Maine coast, will fall into our hands like an overripe apple. For next to nothing."

Roy beamed at Chip. "Your wanderlust is finally going to pay off for us." To Charles he said, "You may remember our Chippy, here, gathered up the nugget of information regarding the possibilities of that piece of real estate. On a skiing trip in Wyoming, no less. Who'd have thought it?"

Chip allowed a slow smile to spread across his face and nodded. "Always happy to pull my weight, gentlemen."

Roy chuckled and even Charles responded with a small smile.

Roy looked at the two men at the table. "Do we have a consensus, then, to continue the project in Maine?"

They nodded cursorily.

Roy looked at his notes on the table in front of him. "Okay, I think we can move on to some old business. Charles, you're wrapping up the Atlanta project. Anything more we need to know?"

Chip sat back in a slouch. His mind drifted back to the evening in Victor, Idaho–across the mountain pass from Jackson Hole. He'd met a sweet young thing, a local girl, on the slopes in the afternoon. Having high expectations of scoring that night, he'd accepted her invitation to dine with friends at a funky local cowboy bar and restaurant. Turned out she was entertaining stuffy relatives from the East. He had gotten stuck sitting next to a real estate broker from Maine. Bored him nearly to tears. Chip had been in the process of cooking up a story explaining why he had to leave early.

Then, the broker mentioned twelve hundred acres of real estate along the coast of Maine that he was considering picking up for a song, and Chip was back in the game. As it turned out, the homegrown cutie he had followed over the mountain pass had been the delicious frosting on the cake.

Roy LaCroix stood. "I think we've covered everything. Thank you, gentlemen." Charles picked up his notepad and pushed back his chair. Chip came out of his reverie, laced his fingers together, reversed his palms, and stretched his arms out in front of him. "Good meeting, Roy."

"One more thing, gentlemen," said Roy. They turned in LaCroix's direction. "The Giants are playing the Pats at Foxboro on September twenty-sixth in Foxboro Stadium. Mary and I will be taking the company jet. Please join us, bring your family." He turned to Chip. "Or girlfriend. We'll have a good time. See you then, Chip." Dismissed, they moved toward the door.

Roy cleared his throat. "Charles."

Beauchamp stopped in his tracks.

"I need a rowing partner for tomorrow morning. Six o'clock good for you?" Roy asked. Beauchamp met his eyes for a split-second, nodded and left.

Amesbury, Maine

Maggie had worked late; it was six o'clock before she pulled into the driveway, entering the house by the side door. Usually her house was cool–naturally air conditioned by the huge elm and maples that surrounded her Victorian house, but today the muggy air felt thick enough to cut with a knife. She'd shed her suit jacket earlier; now, drenched with sweat, she pulled her damp knit top away from her back.

In the front hallway, her granddaughter Tildie was on the phone. Maggie looked at her with envy. Tildie's tan slacks were neatly creased, her white cotton top looked crisp and fresh.

Tildie smiled and waggled a finger wave at her grandmother. Tildie's lovely eyes were very much like Pookie's, except they were a luminous brown that also reflected her Asian heritage.

As Maggie glanced at the blinking answering machine, Tildie put her hand over the mouthpiece. "One of them is Grandpa. He hung up before I could grab it." She pointed to the handset and mouthed "Andrew" indicating she was talking to her boyfriend. Maggie nodded and Tildie resumed her conversation.

Upstairs, in her bedroom, Maggie threw her jacket on the seat of a chair and flopped on her back across the bed. She placed the toe of one shoe against the heel of the other shoe and eased the black pump off her swollen foot. The second high heel came off more easily. She kicked them toward her closet, but they fell short, landing and skittering across the polished oak floor. She stood up, hiked up her gray skirt, and wiggled out of the panty hose that felt like sandpaper between her thighs. She tossed the pantyhose on the arm of a chair.

Flopping back on her bed, she looked longingly at the pair of well-worn jeans and faded sweatshirt draped across the back of the chair. What she would really like to do after a shower was slip into them and go for a bike ride around the neighborhood in the cooler air of the fading sunlight.

She contemplated going downstairs to listen to the dreaded answering machine first, when the bedside phone rang. She leaned up on one elbow and grabbed the phone.

"Hello."

"Hey, it's me," Sam said. "I've been trying to reach you for the past couple of hours. I've left messages."

"Should I go listen to them or do you want to just tell me what you said?"

He chuckled. "Real time is good. Are you busy tonight?"

"Well, yeah, sort of...why are you asking?" She pushed herself into a sitting position.

"Actually, I need to talk to you."

Maggie hesitated. Lunch twice a month with Sam was one thing. An evening event was quite another, especially if he "really needed to talk" to her.

"Maggie, there's no one else I can talk to." The sense of urgency in Sam's voice was palpable.

"Couldn't it wait? We can have lunch tomorrow."

"I'm leaving for Cambridge later tonight. There's a conference at Harvard this weekend, and I'm speaking tomorrow morning. How about an early dinner? Or," he hesitated, "you could come to Cambridge with me. We could talk on the way–maybe stop for dinner at, oh, say Abercrombie and Finch in Portsmouth? And–"

"Sam." There was a time, in the last ten years of their marriage, when they considered Abercrombie's "their" restaurant, not because of any starry-eyed romantic memories, but because the food was so damn good, and they loved the intimate, cozy atmosphere.

"Look, I'm not trying to put the moves on you. We can have dinner at Burger King. I don't care as long as we can talk. We'll have separate rooms at the Concorde Hotel, different floors, even. You can have the morning to stroll around Cambridge, then we can meet for lunch. I was going to stay for the weekend, but I'd just as soon skip it. If you want to shop or do the museum thing, I'll go with you. Unless you have to hurry home. Then we'll just head back..." Sam paused, "and stop at Abercrombie's."

Maggie laughed. His energy and intensity, the things that had first attracted her to him, were hard to resist.

She had planned to be home on Saturday morning, maybe ask Pookie to go for a bike ride, but she knew the diversion wouldn't really help him. Spending time with a friend who also wouldn't be going to the father/son soccer game would be a better antidote.

"Okay," she said. "Sounds like an adventure. But can we be back tomorrow night? Joel is coming home, and I'd like to be here to talk to him on Sunday."

"Yeah, sure. I'd rather do that, anyway. I have a case to review before Monday morning."

"I'll need an hour to shower and pack. Pick me up at, oh, let's say 7:30?"

"Maggie?"

"What?"

"Thanks. I really owe you."

Maggie dragged her old, olive-green carry-on out of the narrow closet and opened it on the bed. She tossed in a pair of pajamas, a change of underwear, walking shoes, two pairs of socks, navy blue slacks, and a cream-colored silk blouse.

Tildie stuck her head in the door. "Andrew and I…" Then she noticed the suitcase. "Going somewhere?"

"I'm going to Cambridge with your grandfather for the night. Well, no, not for the night. I mean we're going tonight, but we're not going to be…together. For the night."

Tildie moved toward the bed. "I gotcha. Just friends. No big deal. Uh huh." She met Maggie's eyes; her grin was teasing as usual when Maggie mentioned she'd had lunch with Sam.

"No, really. We are not…I mean this is not a *together* thing."

"Okay. I somewhat believe you." Tildie pulled the tumbled clothes out of Maggie's suitcase and carefully folded Maggie's underwear and pajamas. "You really need a new suitcase. Something pretty. This thing is so old and scruffy it's embarrassing."

"Yeah, I was thinking of replacing it with a Shop 'n Save bag."

She watched Tildie's brief flicker of hope turn to long-suffering patience.

"I could add a Winn-Dixie bag later on. For variety."

Tildie sighed. "What's wrong with a set of matching luggage?" Tildie placed the underwear carefully in the pocket of the suitcase.

"I never go anywhere, for one thing." Maggie felt a stab of regret. Luggage she didn't have suddenly symbolized the restlessness she was feeling. But where would she go?

"Well, you should. You haven't been anywhere in…I can't remember when."

"Except for visits to Aunt Belle, years. Many, many years."

"Well, this is a good start. When will you be back?" The pajamas were precisely lined up in the bottom of the carry-on.

"Tomorrow night."

"Weren't you going to pick Dad up at the airport tonight?" Tildie placed Maggie's socks in another pocket.

"He won't be home until late tomorrow morning. Can you pick him up at eleven?"

"Yeah, sure."

Maggie watched Tildie meticulously fold the silk blouse, placing it carefully in the suitcase.

Then she broached the subject. "Look, Tildie, while I'm gone, can you sort of…" This was touchy. "Take care of Pookie?"

Tildie bent over the suitcase, her long, black hair shimmering as silky strands slipped forward around her face. "What's to take care of?" Her voice was remote and taut.

25

"Well, see that he gets supper. He's at a cross-country track practice. He'll be back in an hour or so. And see if he wants to go to Doug's, maybe?"

Tildie picked up the navy slacks and hung them back in the closet–her body stiff, a familiar, closed expression on her face. She riffled through Maggie's clothes and finally pulled out a pair of bottle-green slacks made of soft crepe. Crossing to the suitcase, she held them close to the blouse and nodded to herself.

When she finally spoke, her voice was flat. "Andrew and I are going out to dinner. He's picking me up in five minutes. We won't be back 'til late." She appeared to be absorbed in lining up the creases of the slacks, folding them into the suitcase beside the blouse. Then she straightened up, pushed her glossy hair back over her shoulder and looked at Maggie.

"He's fourteen. There's enough food in the refrigerator to feed him and all his friends for a week. He knows how to use the microwave, and he's very self-sufficient. Leave him a note. He'll survive."

She moved back toward Maggie's closet then paused and turned toward her. "It's not like he hasn't ever been alone before."

"I know." Tildie was right. She struggled with over-protecting her grandson when he was hurting.

In the closet, Tildie scanned Maggie's shoe rack and emerged with a pair of woven leather, low-heeled shoes. "If you're not going to do a lot of walking, these..." She trailed off, glancing sidelong at Maggie. She lifted the lid of the suitcase and put the shoes in the outside zipper pocket. "Look, Violet said she'd be here for a while tomorrow to wax the floors. He won't be alone."

"He was supposed to go to that father and son thing tomorrow morning."

Tildie's head snapped toward Maggie, her eyes open wide. "And Dad won't be here. That's...wow, that's...well, that just plain sucks. Okay, tonight I'll come back early and give him a ride to Doug's house if he wants to go."

"That would probably be the best thing. Thanks."

Tildie looked at her watch. "Okay, well, Andrew will be here any minute."

She reached the door and turned. "A little makeup wouldn't hurt. You still have that peach tone foundation I gave you? No? Well, all you'll need to do is put in your hair dryer and toothbrush. Otherwise, you should be all set." She disappeared.

"Matilda, wait."

Tildie stuck her head back inside. A genuine smile lit her eyes as she met Maggie's. "At least throw some mascara in that suitcase, will you? And have fun in Boston. Tell Grandpa I said 'Hi' if I'm gone when he gets here." With that, Tildie made her escape.

Maggie looked at the small, framed photo on her dresser. Smiling back at her was the person who most pulled at her heartstrings–Samuel Nicholas Wiser III–otherwise known as Pookie. Maggie had been the only mother he had ever known, and she and this child had been on the same wavelength ever since he could walk and talk.

When her daughter-in-law Miki was killed in an automobile accident, Sam and Maggie invited Joel to come live with them for a while so Maggie could help with eight-year-old Tildie and the six-month-old infant, Pookie.

Joel never remarried, never moved, so Maggie played a significant role in raising the kids. When she and Sam divorced, no one questioned that Joel should move his family to Maggie's new house.

But Tildie never quite recovered from her mother's death, and her brother seemed to symbolize her loss. It had taken Maggie years to make a crack in Tildie's protective shell, but Tildie had never let Pookie into her emotional inner circle.

A car pulled into the driveway–Andrew. The kitchen screen door slammed, and Tildie was gone.

The phone rang again. She looked at her watch. Sam would be here in forty-five minutes, and she still had to shower. Let the answering machine downstairs pick it up.

Otis drained his glass. As he sat through a Friday afternoon happy hour, a fragment of his conversation with Lincoln Montgomery yesterday kept tripping through his mind like the words of a song that wouldn't go away. "...this project will move forward. Trust me."

Counting out change, he headed toward the pay phone near the bar. His digital watch showed 7:35. He'd left Maggie a message earlier that he'd call back. She should be home by now. What would he say when she answered? He was stupid to be calling her anyway, but he couldn't think of anything else to do.

He dropped the change in the pay phone slot and dialed her number, thinking he shouldn't have had that last drink. Or the one that followed.

What should he say? He didn't want to give too much away. He'd just say, "Maggie, you have to get a hold of Sam and ask him to call me. He won't return my calls. It's important–it's a matter of life or death." No, no, I can't say that. I'll just say...

Maggie's answering machine picked up again. Damn.

When it beeped, he said, "Uh, listen, Maggie, I, um, I need to talk to Sam right away. He won't want to talk to me. But, Maggie, for his own good, please. Convince him to call me right away. Please. I'm going home now, and I'll be there all night. It's a matter of...it's very, very important."

Because, Maggie...I think his life may be in danger. And mine–mine is going into the sewer.

He put the phone on the hook and leaned his head against the wall next to the pay phone so he could think.

Finally, he reached for the phone again and called a cab. If he got caught for OUI again, he'd go to jail. Suddenly, the idea of going to jail for operating under the influence struck him as funny, and he laughed as he headed for the door. If NADCO followed through, he'd be in jail for a lot longer than an OUI charge would hold him.

Boston

"Yabo," aka Ernest Yablonski, couldn't believe his luck. He had a real job. One he'd get paid for, and, if he didn't screw up, one that could take him into the big time.

He'd heard that you have to be in the right place at the right time, but this was the first time in his twenty-two years it had ever happened to him.

In fact, he was usually caught in the wrong place at the wrong time, which is why he had spent almost three years of his life, in bits and pieces, incarcerated.

He strolled down the street on this early Friday night with an automobile license plate clamped under his arm. Head down, his shoulder length blond hair swinging forward, anyone watching him would think he was looking at the sidewalk, but he was watching out of the corners of his eyes, scanning the hospital parking lot. Yabo was looking for the right car– one old enough that it didn't have electronic locks, and sorry enough that the owner wouldn't have some kind of alarm.

He wasn't going to need the wheels for long. When Jewel had singled him out from the guys hanging around the pool hall, he asked Yabo if he could pick up a car to use for the job. Yabo had said no problem.

Jewel had also asked him if he could handle a gun. Yabo had said, "Yeah, sure." Actually, he had never fired a gun, but he had flashed one once when he tried to hold up the Lebanese Deli over on 2nd Street. The fact that it wasn't loaded was the reason he had done only a year at Concord State Prison.

But the "yeah, sure" worked. The luck of it! Yabo continued to stroll, but he had stopped looking for cars. All he could think about was the entrance Jewel had made when he'd come into Dolly's pool hall a couple a weeks ago. He was a stranger, so everyone paused and looked him over from his unlaced Nikes to the do-rag on his head. He was black–which was pretty usual in the neighborhood– tall, and good looking. Even a guy could tell that.

The most impressive thing though was the way Jewel looked around like he was judging *them*; then, he strolled over to the bar as if he owned the place. Everything stopped, even Dolly quit wiping the bar, and the place was so silent you could almost hear the dust settle. Jewel leaned his ass on a bar stool and swung around so he could see the pool tables. Smiling slowly, his eyes challenged...go ahead, make my day.

Denny coughed; Big Ed cleared his throat. But nobody moved. Finally, Zak, the guy who called the shots at Dolly's, bent over his cue stick and slapped a shot in the side pocket, telling everyone to get back to business. Slowly the click of pool balls started up again.

Jewel played a few games of eight ball with some of the others. Whether he won or lost, the games were always close. Eventually, Jewel played Zak. They agreed to two out of three. There was tension in the smoke-filled room as the two men worked their way around the table. The only sounds were the click of balls, punctuated often by a ball slamming into a pocket so hard you could feel it in your chest. The games were close; Zak won the first, Jewel the second. The competition was down to the wire, and everyone could see Zak sweating it.

Jewel's turn–an easy eight ball in the corner pocket. As he leaned over the table, Jewel looked up, stared directly into Yabo's eyes and winked. Then, he missed the shot. The place broke up as Zak cleared the table. With relief, Zak's boys patted him on the back, hooting about taking down "new blood." It took Yabo a while to puzzle the whole thing out, but he finally realized Jewel had thrown the game. Conned Zak into thinking he was still the man.

But Zak wasn't the man anymore. He just hadn't caught on yet. Yabo sensed an excited air–a buzz–whenever one of the burned-out potheads spotted Jewel coming across the street; pool balls clicked louder, laughter "amped up," and the air swirled around Jewel as he slid through the door barking, "Wassup, my peoples," then clapping the nearest wall holder-upper on the shoulder. Zak still strutted and preened, but they all danced to Jewel's beat now.

Jewel came back the next three days, mostly hanging around, making cracks to the brothers–the kind that Yabo, being white, couldn't make. Like when Jewel slapped Big Earl, the biggest mountain of a black guy Yabo had ever seen, on the back.

"Big Earl, my man," Jewel asked innocently. "What's your sister doin' these days?"

Flattered, Big Earl stammered, "Ah, hell, I dunno."

Jewel licked his lips. "She doin' me tonight...right after yo' momma done." The bar broke up in howls.

Jewel never came over to talk to Yabo and his punk friends, but every once in a while, when Yabo dared throw a glance his way, he'd catch Jewel's eye. Made him feel good.

One day, Yabo had been sitting around Dolly's, conversating with his cousin about how much parole time he had left and how his parole officer was an asshole, when Jewel handed him a beer and dropped into the chair across from him.

Yabo ended up telling Jewel about the time he had done. Nine months in juvie hall when he was sixteen for stealing a 1978 Chevy Volante that was so fat in the chassis it couldn't take a corner without shifting into second...a rust bucket hardly good enough to put tires on. Yabo told Jewel he couldn't believe it when they put him away for that one. Hell, they should a paid him for cleaning up the city streets. Jewel got a laugh out of that.

Yabo had been picked up for auto theft–just joyriding–three times before, but the judge had always let him go home with his mother. And that Chevy was such a piece of shit he figured he did the owner a favor when he totaled it. Jewel laughed even harder at that, so Yabo kept talking.

He told Jewel about the two one-year stretches that he did in the county jail, but he couldn't remember exactly what they were for.

He was pretty sure, he said, one time was for stealing that white stretch limo.

He grinned, now, thinking of how Jewel had doubled over with laughter. Even to this day, Yabo was impressed with himself for stealing such a fine piece of automobile. He didn't know why more of them weren't stolen, he had told Jewel. Boosting limos was so easy. You didn't even have to hotwire them. They were often parked out in front of churches on Saturday afternoons, and sometimes the drivers just walked away to have a smoke and left the keys in the ignition! By the time Yabo had finished the story of his joyride in the white limo including turning the wrong way down a one-way street, driving on the sidewalk to avoid oncoming traffic, scattering people right and left, and ending up in a duck pond, tears were running down Jewel's face. "You cool, man," Jewel said when the laughter stopped. "You cool."

And for the first time in his life, Yabo felt cool.

Finally, carrying two bottles of beer, Jewel had steered him over to a booth so they could talk quiet-like. Yabo hoped everyone noticed that Jewel had singled him out for friendship. He noticed the black leather jacket Jewel was wearing over a black T-shirt and wondered if he should get himself one.

Jewel slid a beer in front of Yabo. "G, you one crazy motherfucker, you know that? 'Course you white boys is always the crazy bastards, y'know? Hear 'bout a high school get shot up–white boy. Mass murder–white boy. Used to be, black folk never watch the news 'cause every time somethin' went down, we was afraid it'd be a black face. Now that you white boys are the crazy fuckers, black folk can watch the news again." Jewel face split into a wide-open grin. He shook his head appreciatively. "Yeah, G, you one crazy white boy."

If anybody else had said that shit to Yabo, he'd a been eating his teeth–but with Jewel–well, saying them things was a compliment, and he felt warm, like he was with a brother. G? Why did Jewel call him G? He'd have to remember to ask him one day.

After another beer, Jewel told him he was looking for the right man to help him with a hit. Yabo choked on his beer. For a second, he didn't know if he had heard right. One look into Jewel's eyes confirmed it. His thoughts ran in a slow, tight circle. A hit. Murder. You got maybe life for that, with no time off. A hit.

He dropped his gaze, picked at the label on his beer bottle, and tried to get himself together; he was flattered, that was for sure. Jewel thought Yabo was big time, and he didn't want to give away the fact that he had never killed anyone. His heart was hammering, and his breath was short. He tried to think of what to say.

"You can handle a gun, can't you?"

Yabo nodded, still looking at his beer. "Yeah, sure."

"You doan have to be the trigger man," Jewel said softly. Yabo had looked up then and into Jewel's eyes. They were so deep and compelling; he felt a surge of excitement like he had never known before.

"I'm your man," he'd said. He knew then, he'd do anything Jewel told him to—even pull the trigger.

"You the man." Jewel grinned and shook his head appreciatively. "You one crazy-assed white boy, G, but you'll do."

You'll do. So he would. He'd do anything. Even...

Suddenly, Yabo realized he had walked right on by the parking lot. He had assured Jewel he could pick up a car before midnight—no problem. Yabo spun around and hurried back. Jewel had given him some tips. Man, if I'd a known these things before, he thought when Jewel had told him, I'd a never got caught.

The car had to be "low profile," meaning, Jewel explained, couldn't be one you would notice much—no dents, no bright colors, no white limos for sure. It should be eight, ten years old because the cops don't get too excited about old cars getting stolen. Yabo turned into the parking lot and headed to where the night workers left their cars. This was also Jewel's idea—nobody would miss the car until morning.

He reluctantly walked by a slick Mazda RX7 and a red Miata convertible. Finally, he saw the car: a humble, maroon Mercury Tracer. In thirty seconds, he was in the car and had it started. Motor sounded good. Yabo eased the car out of the lot and rolled down the road. He stopped a few blocks away, exchanged plates, and headed to where Jewel said to meet him. He turned on the radio; it even worked.

Slapping the steering wheel, he whooped for joy. He just couldn't believe his luck.

Maggie sipped her Manhattan as the waitress placed Sam's martini in front of him. Inevitably, they had ended up at Abercrombie's. Under the table, Maggie slid her bare feet around, her toes feeling for the sandals she had slipped off when they first sat down.

She gave up the search and looked around. In the ten years since they had been there, nothing had changed. The carriage lamps mounted on the walls glowed softly against the dark walnut paneling and reflected polished brass accents from around the room. On each table, a glass hurricane lamp soothed lines from tired faces and set a mellow tone for quiet conversation. Just beyond their booth, a ceiling fan turned slowly overhead. From the sound system came the muted tones of a tenor sax playing *My Way*.

The waitress approached to take their order, but Sam caught her eye and shook his head. They hadn't even looked at their menus yet. Maggie swiped a bread stick through the cheese dip and took a bite. "You want to talk about the mall thing some more? What was NADCO's argument when you met with them? Is that the name, NADCO?"

Sam nodded. "North American Development Corporation. There were two of them there from the company. Somehow, they had gotten the information I drink martinis–probably from Otis–and he, one of them was a lawyer named Beauchamp, shows up with this bottle of Bombay Sapphire Gin."

Maggie whistled. "Your favorite to soften you up."

Sam nodded. "And four martini glasses to create an amiable atmosphere in the reference room at City Hall. You should have seen Otis' face. He hates martinis. The NADCO guys tried setting the tone, I guess–joking around–but they sounded like traveling salesmen. Beauchamp could tell I wasn't buying the mall idea.

"Finally, he laid the whole thing out, talking square footage and the big sell– how 'this will be a gold mine for the city.' But I kept asking questions about just how the mall would benefit the economy, and he kept answering with cliches."

Maggie studied Sam's intense face as he stared into his drink. "I know you have no patience with that."

"Well, I accept the world runs on hyperbole, but I'm not going to agree to a goddam mall just because someone from out of state decides we should have one."

He cocked his head to one side. "Am I being unreasonable?"

He seemed sincere, asking her opinion. A new Sam?

"No, I don't think you are. The whole thing sounds like a railroad job. And I understand your reservations. Without new revenue coming in, the economic pie would just be divided into smaller pieces. The smaller stores would go out of business, and nothing would be gained in the long run. But now you are also worried about the wildlife sanctuary."

"Well, yes. More than worried. The planned location of the mall is contiguous to the sanctuary. I can't imagine that NADCO can do anything with the forest land...I think Ernest Archibald, he inherited the land from his grandfather, has it tied up as a wildlife refuge, but I'm sure as hell concerned."

Maggie nodded. "That's always been my understanding of the situation. I can imagine it would be enormously appealing to a developer, though."

"I'm going to check on it first thing Monday morning. I'll have to do a little digging. I haven't seen Ernie Archibald around for a couple of years. I heard he moved."

"It's probably nothing to be concerned about," Maggie said. "Otis probably got it wrong."

"Well, I don't know. This is why I'm concerned. You should have seen his face when I challenged him. He was scared. I don't think he'd have reacted that way if there weren't something substantive in what he was telling me about the land. He also admitted accepting a bribe."

Maggie reacted with a jolt as she remembered how nervous Otis had been at breakfast yesterday. Then she thought about the numbers Angie had pointed out. Big numbers. "A bribe? How much?"

"I don't know how much. He didn't say. I didn't ask."

Well, I know, Maggie thought. Three hundred thousand dollars. They had paid him in advance, and he hadn't delivered Sam to them. She should be disapproving, but a part of her felt sorry for Otis. He'd gotten himself between a rock–that would be Sam–and a hard place—NADCO.

Sam shook his head. "Back to the meeting, the guy had the audacity to imply that I should approve the mall because it would get me re-elected." He turned to the approaching waitress. "Could you give us a few more minutes?" She nodded and melted away.

Maggie selected another breadstick, her fourth. It was almost nine o'clock, and she hadn't eaten since she'd had a salad for lunch. Sam speared the olive in his martini and popped it into his mouth. "I was ready to leave at that point. Then the head guy said something like, 'Well, Counselor, I'm sure you'd like to think this over and talk to your law partner. NADCO has every intention of asking Wiser & McComber to handle all of the legal details for the mall.'"

A familiar, lopsided smile formed on Sam's face, and he shook his head. "It's ironic now, but at the time, I thought my head would explode. I thought something like, 'You assholes think I'm for sale for as little as that? That my integrity has such a cheap price?'" Sam finished his drink and gestured toward the waitress for another. "Turns out they were willing to bid a little higher."

Sam fished a rumpled napkin out of his pocket, laid it on the table, and smoothed it out. He pushed it toward her and smiled. "I kept the napkin so I could show you...talk about a cliche–slide the napkin across the table...and that's the amount of the bribe."

The napkin had become damp after it was written on, and the blue ink had bled a little, but the figure, $500,000, was still very clear. Maggie noticed the dollar sign with two vertical lines through it was just like Otis wrote it.

Sam took the napkin back, tore it into four pieces, and dropped it on the table.

She whistled. "That is definitely higher than I would have guessed."

Sam shrugged. "Desperate times call for desperate measures, apparently."

Maggie leaned forward. "Listen, talk about desperate..." She reached for the menu. "Let's order. Please. I'm starving."

Reading the four-page menu with its cream and wine sauces was mouthwatering, but she'd been good on her diet today, well...except for the breadsticks tonight. She had even passed up a donut at the office, so she'd probably choose a broiled haddock and a salad with light dressing.

Sam ordered broiled salmon and a salad with vinaigrette dressing. Figured. He sat there lean and trim–had never been over his ideal body weight a day in his life. And he'd always made it clear she could control her weight problem if she followed his example.

The waitress looked at Maggie. "I'll have potato skins with sour cream for an appetizer, then the Chicken and Almond Alfredo on fettuccini."

There, that would show him. Then, realizing how ridiculous this was, she decided to change her order, but the waitress was already bustling away. Oh, well. Start again on Monday. Story of her life.

She leaned forward, considering her words carefully. "Sam. Listen, I agree with you completely regarding the mall, but about NADCO's method of operation–well, I don't want to sound cynical or even unsympathetic, but maybe this is the way business is done, nowadays–maybe it's always been done that way–bribes save time, cut through political red tape. Bribery might be an unethical way of doing business to you and me, but to developers, perhaps it's an efficient way of life."

He shrugged. "But the fact remains that whatever they have planned will be harmful, not helpful, to Amesbury. And they're not going to get what they want–not as long as I'm on the city council." His voice was hard and flat.

She nodded. "I had a visit with Otis yesterday morning. He asked me not to mention it to you, but I think I should. Now that I have some background, it seems clear that he was on the edge of panic. I didn't understand, so I ignored it. Now, with what you've told me..." She felt a slice of fear in her stomach. "Sam, do you think these people are dangerous?"

While the waitress placed salads in front of them, Sam folded his napkin into his lap and considered a moment.

"No," he said finally. "They're just businessmen, incredibly sleazy, greedy businessmen, but probably not dangerous. Not dangerous in the sense I think you mean. They've got something on Otis, though. That's why he was so desperate. To him, they probably seem dangerous."

"I have an idea what they might have on him."

Sam raised an eyebrow.

"I can't tell you because of client confidentiality. But I'll tell you this. There is something someone could hold over him."

"What do you think I should do?"

"About the mall? Vote your conscience, Sam. What else?"

"No, about the land deal–the wildlife thing. Do I wait and see if the whole thing blows over when I block the mall, or do I start asking questions about the Archibald Estate Monday morning to see what's going on?"

"Wouldn't that put Otis in more hot water? If he wasn't supposed to tell you? Why not wait and see what happens?"

He grimaced. "My mother always told me that 'good things come to those who wait.' It doesn't feel like this will play out that way."

Their meal arrived, and conversation stopped for a moment as they fell into devouring their food.

A lopsided grin lit Sam's face. "It's good to be friends again."

"Yeah, it is." She paused. "You mean platonic friends, of course."

"Sure." He smiled. "You never know when you might need a platonic friend."

"What do you mean?"

"You're probably going to need this platonic friend to get your sandals out from under the table."

A soft rain was falling when they left the restaurant. As they drove in comfortable silence along Route 1, Maggie rolled down the window and held her hand out, enjoying the coolness. She watched the tourist-type businesses slide by–hotels, restaurants, miniature golf courses standing shoulder to shoulder, their signs winking and blinking their wares against the black night.

As if he'd been waiting for the right moment, Sam spoke. "Pookie and I went down to work on the sailboat a couple of weeks ago. Did you know?"

No, she hadn't known. She turned that over in her mind for a minute. This was the sort of thing Pookie would have normally told her. Moreover, he wasn't very close to his grandfather–had never, that she could remember, spontaneously sought him out. "Nice of you to ask him. I'm sure he enjoyed the visit." She sounded stiff even to her ears.

"I didn't ask him. He called me. I was as surprised as you are." Maggie sensed Sam was giving her time to process the news.

"I wondered if he had an agenda, and as it turned out, he did," he said mildly.

Maggie looked at Sam and waited.

"Seems he had some things he wanted to talk about." Sam paused as he made the turned through the rotary.

"Sam. What?"

"He wanted to talk about girls. Dating and such things. How to ask a girl out."

Maggie experienced a ripple of quickly changing emotions. First, alarm–it was too soon. Pookie was too young to date–but she realized, immediately, he wasn't. He was fourteen.

This thought was followed by a sudden wash of sympathy for Pookie, and tears stung her eyes–the poor kid with compelling life questions and no one to talk to. He certainly couldn't have asked her. She had, of course, given him the facts of life at an earlier age, but the technical information was only the bare bones of what he would be wondering about, now. His father was out of the question. The last person on earth you could talk to about these things was a parent.

She felt a wave of admiration for her grandson, who had solved his problem by calling his grandfather.

This was immediately eclipsed by a need to preserve his privacy. If Pookie wanted her to know the details, he would already have told her.

"Without violating a confidence, did the talk go all right?" she asked after a while.

"Yeah, I think so. He was shy...took a while to get around to what he wanted to ask. He, ah, likes a certain girl, and ah..."

"Sam, you shouldn't tell me."

"Well, I think it's okay just to say he's a little scared about rejection, hoping for acceptance–and wants to know a little about dating etiquette. And–"

"What?"

"He asked if we could go sailing in a week or two. So, I guess he felt comfortable with the whole thing."

An unreasonable sense of loss gripped her. Pookie was growing up. And now he needed his grandfather–not her.

Sam put his hand on her arm. "You okay?"

They turned onto Route 95. Sam sped up to slide into traffic.

She closed the window. "Yeah. I was just, ah, feeling a little like I did the first day he went to kindergarten." She smiled a little at her dismay.

"Maggie, I know it's too soon to talk about us, but–"

"You're right, it is."

"But one of the reasons I keep thinking about our getting back together–you must know I've thought about it–one of the reasons is I want to have a family life again. I want to be able to say to you, 'Remember when...' and have you know exactly what I'm talking about."

"Yes, I know, but we can do that as friends." Maggie's discomfort grew. She had become so completely satisfied with her single life. By the time their separation and subsequent divorce was final, she already knew she was ready to be independent. To live alone—well, except for Joel and the kids. She relished it. She had no interest in giving any of that up.

He pushed on as if he hadn't heard her. "I missed so much of Joel, and then Tildie and Pookie, growing up. I don't want to miss any more."

There was a long pause during which she was aware of a familiar, deep sadness in her heart. "You didn't miss some of it, Sam. You missed it all."

He fell silent at this rebuke, but she could sense the words had rankled. Maggie decided she wasn't sorry. He *had* missed it all, and she had tried to tell him, so many times.

"You know," he finally said, "if you hadn't planted yourself between Pookie and the rest of us, we might have had a chance to get to know him while he was growing up."

Pure anger gripped Maggie. Sam had been completely and totally against her taking a break in her career for five years to raise her motherless grandson. She remembered heated discussions followed by long days of silent rejection. She tried to focus on the sweep of the windshield wipers, to gain control of the anger that shook her.

She had understood Pookie's being ignored by his father; so staggered by the loss of his wife, Joel walked through life in a fog that no one, not even his daughter, seemed able to penetrate. And she had enormous sympathy for Tildie, gripped and tied in knots by the loss of her mother and what she interpreted as rejection by her father.

But for Sam there was no excuse. He had shown little interest in Pookie as an infant, a toddler, or a young child. After a while Maggie had stopped caring what he thought.

So, it was Maggie who taught Pookie to throw and catch a ball; it was Maggie who helped him build a birdhouse; it was Maggie who ran down the road holding up his bike until he was pedaling on his own.

What had made her so mad fourteen years ago was that Sam's position was a complete reversal of their earlier arguments. She had insisted on working while Sam was in law school so they could be as independent from his family as possible. When Joel was born, she continued to work for the same reason, and her job was a constant source of tension between them. Later, when they moved back to Amesbury, she enrolled at Marston B & T, and Sam was fit to be tied. He didn't want a working wife. Period.

She studied and worked, anyway.

Years later, however, when Stoney offered her a partnership, she turned it down to take care of Pookie. Sam was wild–he wanted her to take the step forward in her career, and he never softened in his position. Now, he was rewriting history– twisting it so that he could blame her for his lack of involvement.

The silence was palpable, weighing them down.

"I'm sorry. It appears I'm still the master of the cheap shot," Sam said, finally.

She nodded an acknowledgement. There was no way, she realized, they would ever work through this issue. This fight would eventually blow over, and months from now they would probably be friends again. Friends who cautiously avoided this subject.

One good thing had come out of this, though. Pookie was growing up. She had to start preparing to let him go.

Cambridge, MA

The hot water pounded Sam's neck, each pulse shouting "Idiot!" He thought he'd exorcized the "it was your fault" demon for good, and yet, at the worst possible time, it had jumped back up and bit him.

In his head, he'd run through many versions of a conversation with Maggie where he tried to tell her what he'd learned, how he planned to make up for lost time. And when the opportunity actually came, he blew it.

The progress he'd made had been a long, slow journey. Deep reflection accompanied by three martini evenings spent alone by the fire. Joel didn't call, Pookie and Tildie didn't come by to visit. The seeds of indifference he'd sown so evenly had borne painful fruit–lonely nights in his $500,000 house. At first it was easy, trying to blame Maggie.

And then, one day, Pookie's picture was in the newspaper. He'd won the seventh-grade cross country meet. That had been one of Sam's favorite sports events in high school, and he hadn't even known Pookie was running track. He cut out the picture and showed it to a couple of clients who had kids. Finally, he framed the newsprint photo and displayed it on his desk.

Then he dug up his favorite photo of Tildie, the one Maggie snapped right after one of her high school soccer games, face still sweaty, a dirt smudge on her forehead, lustrous black hair cascading down from her bun, some matted to her face–an achingly beautiful girl, so close to being a woman while still clinging to her scraped-kneed adolescence...his granddaughter. The one who always giggled at his "ho, ho, ho" when he called at Christmases after the divorce. But he wasn't there for those Christmases, and he hadn't been at the soccer game. In truth, he hadn't been to any of them.

Sam flipped off the shower, grabbed a towel, and jammed it against his eyes.

How was it possible he'd thought he didn't have the time? Now that his business was flourishing and less demanding, he had a lot of time to think, and introspection crept in, often uninvited, at the oddest quiet times.

He saw Tildie, pigtails flying behind her as she soared on a swing–but he'd never pushed her on a swing. Images of Pookie, grinning in triumph as he teetered toward him on tiptoes, arms up, as he came to him. But drool didn't go well on $1200 Italian suits. Annoyed with Maggie for allowing him to get into such a situation, he'd turned away from the toddler and left for work.

He dried himself vigorously, trying, now, to stop the familiar slide show. Pookie first called him "'Ampa," he remembered. When his grandfather didn't respond, he turned cheerfully to Maggie, and called her by the same name.

Maggie. His throat ached as he pulled on a robe, lay down on the bed with an arm across his eyes, and thought about his wife...ex-wife. The reed-thin girl who'd caught his eye when he first walked into the restaurant where she was waiting on tables. The determined young dreamer who'd defied his parents and found a job while she was pregnant, who continually propped him back up after all-night cram sessions, who'd gotten tipsy on champagne the night he'd passed his bar exam and made glorious love to him right there on the lawn. The mother who'd waited patiently by the phone for the inevitable late-night "I'm still working, Mags" call, and who left a foil wrapped plate for him in the oven. The woman who courageously struck out on her own, started a career while still taking care of Joel, the house, the bills–their life! –and made it all the way to a partnership in a respected accounting firm. Had he ever told her how proud he was of her? He didn't think so. He reached for the phone, and then he stopped.

Would she listen to him now? She'd heard more excuses, changed more plans, invented more Daddy/Grandpa-can't-be-here-today reasons for the kids, probably when she didn't even know if he wanted to be there. How long had she covered for him? Forever.

But he'd changed...okay, was in the process of changing, and he wasn't going to do any more backsliding. He wasn't going to strike out at her, ever again. He wasn't going to give up the ground he'd gained with Pookie, and he wasn't going to give up any of the ground, however small, he'd gained with Maggie this past year.

He turned off the light. Maybe he couldn't get the past back, but there was still the future.

Yabo sat at the kitchen table looking around at the little one-room dump. This wasn't where Jewel actually lived, he could tell. No plates in the cupboard, no TV. Nothing but a few clothes in the closet and a trash barrel full of pizza boxes and McDonald's bags.

He looked in awe at the Beretta in front of him on the gray Formica table. Jewel really was going to trust him with a gun. At the same time, a ball of fear punched him in the stomach, and he had trouble breathing. Guys that pulled jobs with loaded guns got sent up for a long time. He didn't want to go away for a long time–hell, he hoped he was out of there forever.

Jewel stood there with his arms folded. He no longer wore the do-rag; in place of that, his head was covered with impressive Jheri curls. Jewel said it was a disguise. Yabo looked at the gun and nodded his satisfaction.

"Looks good."

"Not getting cold feet, are you?"

Yabo looked up at Jewel. He was so...alive and solid. Like Samuel Jackson in "Pulp Fiction." Jackson was so smooth. Like Jewel. Yabo had total faith in Jewel's plan. He was the Man.

"Nah," Yabo said. "I don't get too jittery."

"True, dog. Tha's why I pick you, G. Got some pizza comin'. Then we go on a stakeout fo' while."

A worn, blue couch with skinny wooden arms and legs sat against a nearby wall. A brown gym bag stuffed full of something sat on the couch. Jewel unzipped it and pulled out a Ziplock baggie. Yabo's heart did an extra beat. Crack or some other kind of shit. If Jewel needed shit to do a job...

"Here the peas for your pea shooter." Jewel winked as he handed him the bag with silver-tipped bullets in it. "Go head an' load it."

There was a knock on the door. "Mus' be the pizza." Jewel pulled out the small wad of bills he kept in his front pocket and headed for the door.

Yabo opened the baggy and looked at the bullets. He didn't know, for sure, how to load the gun. He could figure it out if he played around with the piece for a while, but he didn't want Jewel to see him fumbling. He looked up. Jewel was talking to the pizza guy. Peeling bills off the wad.

Yabo half stood up, slid the bullets out of the bag and slipped them into his jeans pocket. He picked up the gun as he sat back down. Rubbing his thumb over the stock, he tried to look like he was studying the gun.

Jewel laid the steaming pizza box on the table, pushing the empty plastic bag aside. He nodded at the gun. "Not gonna be needing that 'til tomorrow. Tell you when. Here." Jewel indicated the pizza covered with pepperoni and onions. Yabo's mouth watered.

"Help yourself. Keep up yo strength, G." Jewel opened the fridge, pulled out a bottle of Pepsi and put it in front of Yabo.

Yabo couldn't wait–he had to know. "Jewel, why do you always call me G?"

Jewel laughed. "Gangsta, bro, short for gangsta. You one badass gangsta."

Yabo pulled a large piece of pizza loose, breaking off long strings of melted cheese. He'd load the gun later when he was in the can. Wasn't a big deal, anyway. Jewel had said he wouldn't actually be the trigger man. This was good pizza. And Jewel calling him "gangsta?" Life couldn't get any better.

Chapter 3

On Saturday morning, Charles Beauchamp pulled into the parking lot of the Hudson Valley Rowing Club at 5:50, ten minutes early. Roy LaCroix was already there sitting on the lawn, stretching his hamstrings. LaCroix appeared to be in as good a shape as he had been when the two of them were teammates on the Harvard rowing team thirty years ago.

LaCroix waved as Charles climbed out of his black Toyota Sequoia SUV. "Great day for it," LaCroix said. "Get stretched out. I'm in the mood for a good workout."

LaCroix's business philosophy was that you didn't discuss anything in the office you wouldn't put in a memo. His personal philosophy was to combine the resulting out-of-office business with vigorous exercise.

Ten minutes later, they lifted a two-man shell off the rack and carried it to the dock. As usual, LaCroix took the rear position. They rowed in unison out onto the calm Hudson River. The sun was already warm, and they rapidly worked up a good sweat.

LaCroix broke the silence by calling out a slower cadence, then addressed the business Charles knew they had come to talk about.

"In Maine..." LaCroix paused to recall the name of the town.

"Amesbury," Charles supplied, having already spent months there doing the groundwork, mostly by himself.

"Of course." LaCroix's hearty voice talked to the back of Charles' head. "That local politician never came around. And he's apparently not interested in a retirement fund."

As the shell sliced through the water, the morning air cooled Charles' sweat-drenched shirt. There were questions he didn't want to ask. Answers he didn't want to know. But it was what it was, he supposed. He finally spoke. "Yes, as we've discussed, the vote has to be unanimous." This was a fact he himself had brought to LaCroix's attention months ago when he'd headed up the exploration team.

"Exactly," said LaCroix. "It won't do a diddly damn bit of good to put any more effort into this. Wiser's not going to budge. We've known that for a while."

I've known it for a while, Charles thought, as he rowed silently. What could he say…nothing like waiting until the last minute?

LaCroix broke the silence. "It's not a matter to be concerned about. We've had the information for a while regarding Wiser's speaking at the law conference, thanks to you. Lincoln has been preparing–a quick and easy, you might say satisfactory, solution. And then in a few months, the lucky people of Amesbury will be thanking us for their sudden prosperity."

Not all of them, Charles thought. "You are determined that we should move forward with this?"

"Of course. Only good can come from this–a gift that will keep on giving for a long time to come. That big-time real estate developer can't wait to get the bit in his teeth. He thinks he's getting the best of the deal with the four hundred acres we'll sell him–all of it on the coast. He'll build multi-million-dollar homes with breath-taking views, each with its own forested buffer zone. We'll be very well compensated, but he'll also do well–eight figures at least."

He'd heard it all before. Roy was right. There were only a few easy hurdles left. Most of the work had been done in the exploration and planning phases. Charles nodded. "We'll put the utilities–water, electricity, sewerage–close to the forested land when we put in the mall."

"Exactly. And, as you'll recall, we'll develop the next four hundred acres ourselves. A top-notch hotel that will also have an ocean view and an exclusive golf course where the nineteenth hole will also have an ocean view. It will be surrounded by multimillion-dollar mansions. That we will build. The income from these developments will be ours."

"You're holding back four hundred acres?" This was new.

"Yes. When reflecting on it, I realized the land values will skyrocket once the property has been developed. And we can then decide how much to sell the final four hundred for–probably break it up into parcels. Or we could develop it ourselves. Let's put that on the back burner for now."

Charles could see the sense in what Roy was saying. He has always had excellent vision when mapping out a plan for NADCO growth.

LaCroix continued. "Regarding the latest little hurdle, nothing for you to do. Relax. Lincoln will solve the problem before Monday, I'm sure. I thought you needed to know so you aren't startled by anything you might come across in the Amesbury Times."

The only sound Charles heard besides his own breathing was the water gurgling against the boat. "You still have Montgomery on a short leash?" he finally asked.

"Yeah. He does what he's supposed to and no more. He's not too bright and not creative."

"I seem to remember he was quite creative in college. There was nothing he couldn't come up with if someone would pay for it."

He stopped short of saying, "That's how you pulled off the A's. You used the exams your frat brother Lincoln stole for you."

"Oh, he produces, all right. But he toes the line."

"I'm glad you're the one who has to deal with him," Charles said.

"Don't worry about Lincoln. We need him for the time being. He has a lot of contacts...makes him useful for tying up loose ends."

"What if...things..." Charles hesitated. "What if things go sour?" He felt increased power in LaCroix's stroke. He adjusted his to match, and the shell shot forward.

"We cut him loose–a wacko employee acting of his own volition. There's nothing to say otherwise. We, the board members, are clean. Okay, let's pick up the pace." Roy LaCroix called out a double-time cadence.

They rowed in silence for a minute before Charles spoke again, gasping a bit. "You didn't bring up the Clearwater project in the meeting." Sweat dripped down his back with each pull on the oars.

"Don't need to bother Chip with details on old business–ten years ago, before his time with us. Do we have more news on that?"

"Yesterday. The citizens' group that's claiming the landfill we did on Burleigh Drive is causing cancer–they're planning to file a class action lawsuit against NADCO, probably next month." Charles paused to catch his breath. "I'm sure they're wrong...but defending ourselves will be costly. If we're going to stop the litigation, now's the time. The group is spearheaded by...a crusading mother of five."

LaCroix didn't seem to be breathing hard at all. "They may not be wrong. We cut a lot of corners in the early days." He sounded philosophical. "There's the cost of litigation we want to avoid, certainly. But even more, we want to avoid a public relations fiasco. We've come too far. Built our reputation. The brass ring is right there–ready for us to grab. So, let's not act too fast on the Clearwater problem. Trying to stop a group at this point would be like throwing stones at a flock of pigeons. You might hit one, but the rest would get away, and a new leader would emerge. Wait until they've filed.

"Because" –LaCroix chuckled– "we've got a better chance dealing with a judge."

Amesbury, Maine
Saturday

Fourteen-year-old Samuel Nicholas Wiser III, otherwise known as Pookie, clattered down the back stairs, two-stepping a cadence that caused every second footfall to thud heavily. He did it because it annoyed his sister. He didn't need the thick smell of coffee drifting up the stairway to tell him she was in the kitchen. She'd be there because it was eight-thirty on a Saturday morning, and her schedule was as precise as Greenwich Mean Time.

He entered the kitchen and slapped his basketball down hard on the counter. Not as hard as he wanted to, but enough to make a statement.

Tildie glanced up from the newspaper and gave him the look. Then, without comment, she turned back to her reading.

What a bitch. He glanced sideways at her. Even though she was eight years older than him, all his friends went stupid over her, thinking she was some kind of beauty queen or something.

Tildie looked more like their mother than he did, and sometimes he was jealous. From photographs he had of his smiling mother, Tildie had her brown eyes and long, black hair.

Guys could be stupid about stuff like hair and eyes. But they didn't see the rigid line of her mouth and her eyes when she cut him that look that was supposed to make him drop dead.

Ever since he could remember, Tildie mostly ignored him except when she was irritated at him. He wasn't sure if he loved his sister, but sometimes he admired her, like when she won the state trophy in the karate tournament. And when she was the captain of the high school soccer team, junior and senior years. But he had long since distanced himself to keep from getting hurt.

He looked for the cereal bowl he'd left out when he'd eaten earlier, thinking he might eat another bowl after he'd dressed, but it was gone. In the dish drainer, already washed. By Tildie.

Man, he had the urge to get the bowl back out, bang it on the counter, and pour more cereal just to show her she had been a little too hasty in deciding he was irresponsible. But he had something else to accomplish quickly before he gave her another chance to take a shot at him.

He felt like they were locked in a war of who was better than who, and no matter how he tried, Tildie always seemed to win. He turned abruptly, walked past his grandmother's little office, and rounded the corner into the mud room where their jackets were hung. He opened the door to the carriage house and stepped down onto the dirt floor.

The carriage house had been converted into a two-stall garage. His father's car was in the far stall waiting his return from whatever stupid business trip he'd gone on this week. His sister's silver Camry occupied the closest stall.

Behind her car, his Cannondale bike was partially disassembled. He'd worked on the derailleur last night until he realized it was after midnight. This morning he still had to put the wheel back on and attach the brake cables before Tildie bitched him out because she couldn't move her car. He should've worked behind his father's car, but the only place he could see well enough was by the light fixture above the door that led into the house.

Hurrying, he slipped the wheel into place and sprocketed the chain, managing to pinch his finger in the process. He didn't really ask anything of his sister, not even kindness, but you'd have thought she could have at least come to one of his basketball games or cross-country meets. That's what families do. He went to all of her soccer games, sitting beside his grandmother, asking questions about the rules. He threaded the brake cable under the frame and attached it to the bar.

Of course, anyone could see that her situation wasn't the same as his. As a little kid, he'd been pretty excited about watching his big sister play in high school games. Okay, she'd probably be bored by little kids' games. Just once, though, maybe she could have come.

But who the hell cared, anyway? The thing he was really pissed at now, was something he couldn't ever forgive her for. She'd given him the nickname of Pookie–the only name he'd ever been called for as long as he could remember.

In junior high, he got a lot of laughs from classmates when new teachers called him Samuel, and he'd look around pretending he didn't know who they were talking to. When teachers ended up calling him Pookie, he could tell that his classmates knew he'd won a victory. He picked up the wrench and tightened down the nut that held the brake cable.

But now he felt different. Because...well, he just did. He hated the nickname, and last week he'd told his family he hated it, but nothing had changed. And it was all her blinking, stinking fault.

He sighed. The name could be worse, he supposed. There was one kid in his class called Pudgy. Now what was his real name? Edward. Would he like to be called Ed or Eddy? Then there was a girl who used to be called String Bean, and after a while everyone had shortened her name to Bean. He couldn't even remember what her real name was. That's the way nicknames go. Maybe he should find out, and then people could start calling her by her real name.

The door opened and Tildie stepped down into the carriage house. He tightened the last nut slowly. He waited for her clipped voice to tell him to move the bike. He'd move it when it was done. And not before.

"How much longer?" she asked softly.

He glanced up at her impassive face in surprise. "One minute. Almost done."

"I'll get your basketball. You're taking it to Doug's?" She disappeared into the house.

He opened the overhead garage doors and wheeled the finished bike outside. What the hell had gotten into her?

Cambridge, Massachusetts
Saturday

Jewel sat in the light blue 1994 Ford Crown Vic. He'd picked it up last year for $500 from a kid who'd boosted it from a towing company impound lot. He always had one or two "burner cars" stored in his garage.

He sat beside a sliver of a park across from the Roscoe Pound Administration Building, part of Harvard's Law School.

He was mildly annoyed. There was a woman with Wiser, a freaking witness. Lincoln–his NADCO contact–had said on the phone yesterday that Wiser would be alone.

Around midnight, he and Yabo had seen not one but two people get out of the black Lexus. When he saw the second person was a blond woman, he assumed that Wiser had picked up a hooker.

This morning, Wiser and the woman ate breakfast together at the hotel. She was, he saw immediately, in her fifties or sixties and not the hooker type. As the two of them passed the sugar and stirred their coffees, they seemed stiff, like they didn't have anything to say to each other. Who might she be? An old classmate, registered in her own room, attending the same conference? A new squeeze and they were getting off to a slow start?

After breakfast, the two of them headed for Harvard with Jewel tailing three cars behind and Yabo two cars behind him. The blond woman was behind the wheel of the Lexus, so she probably wasn't a colleague. Did that mean they would be together for the weekend?

The question was answered a few minutes later when the woman dropped Wiser off in front of the law school and left with his car. So they were together; she'd be back. Jewel pulled into a nearby parking spot, and Yabo found one a couple of cars behind.

Well, damn. He knew he could find a way to salvage the job–having to adjust to changing situations, creating new plans, sometimes minute by minute, was the zing in this job. The need to improvise didn't happen often, but because of the unpredictability of human nature you could never control every situation. A broken play often gave him a chance to do his best work.

So, the question wasn't *could* he salvage the job, but *should* he salvage it? Did NADCO need Wiser taken out this weekend, no matter what? Or was it more important to wait until he was alone?

He drummed his fingers on the steering wheel and tried to put himself in NADCO's shoes. He considered possible scenarios they might be facing, but he didn't have enough information. All he knew for certain was that the job had to be taken care of in Massachusetts, and it had to look like an accident–one that would get only minor press and cause little investigation. No exploding car, no assassin's bullets. Sure as hell, not a hit.

How careful did he have to be with the woman–either as a witness or as a potential corpse? He had a reputation for clean hits with no loose ends.

But what constituted a loose end here? Creating a vested, concerned witness or creating an extra dead body who could be...anybody? She could be a high-profile politico, someone for whom the police would begin a full-scale investigation. She might even work for NADCO. Maybe they had sent her along to be sure the job got done.

After several minutes of deliberation, he decided to play it safe. He and Yabo would follow Wiser, watch for an opportunity when he and the woman were separated. If that happened, they'd take him out as planned.

Jewel opened the door and eased his six-two frame out of the Crown Vic. He glanced around. In the maroon Mercury parked two cars behind him, Yabo appeared instantly alert. Jewel gave a slight shake of his head. Would Yabo stay put?

By the time Jewel got to the intersection of Mass Avenue and Waterhouse Street, he still hadn't heard the Mercury car door open and close. Yabo had gotten the message. Good.

Nonchalantly, hands in pockets, he threaded his way among the residents of Cambridge who strolled beside the Common with less urgency on Saturday morning than they did during the academic week. Still, he covered the three blocks to Harvard Square in minutes. He dropped some change in a public phone and dialed the number filed in his memory.

"The Concorde. May I help you?"

Jewel spoke in his cultured, non-accented voice. "Good morning. Could you connect me with Samuel Wiser in 623?"

"Just a moment, please." There was a slight pause. "Uh, Mr. Wiser has already checked out. Sorry, sir."

"Thank you." As he hung up the pay phone, a fresh shot of adrenaline shot through his veins...a change of plans. They must have brought their bags to the car before breakfast. He laughed out loud. They had almost given him the slip.

He bought the Boston Globe from the kiosk in the square and crossed the street to a bakery. The smell of coffee and pastry hung in the morning air. He purchased a cup of Venezuelan coffee and a raspberry turnover. The young clerk smiled shyly at him as she placed the items in a bag. He rarely missed a chance to enjoy his effect on women. He gave her his slow, deep, I'm-looking-into-your-soul smile and watched as red flushed her cheeks and her pupils dilated with confused pleasure.

She allowed their hands to touch as she took his money and gave him change. He winked as he turned and left the shop.

Retracing his steps down the brick sidewalk, he considered his options. Wiser and the woman might be stopping somewhere else tonight before returning home, but since they had checked out of the hotel, he had to assume they would be headed home today. That meant moving sooner rather than later.

As Jewel walked toward the Mercury, he could see Yabo watching him. Music, *All Star* by Smash Mouth, blasted from the car while Yabo rocked out the rhythm.

Jewel slipped into a relaxed gait...had to keep the hired help cool. He ambled up to the driver's door and placed the take-out bag on the roof. Bracing his wrists above the car door, he leaned down. Yabo was wearing the same clothes he'd had on for three days: jeans and a Bruins T-shirt. His shoulder-length, stringy blond hair was uncombed. His thin, pale face was covered with a noticeable stubble. Perfect.

"My brother, how's it goin'?" Jewel asked. Yabo's eyes looked grateful for the familiarity.

"Good, good. I'm, ah, good."

"How 'bout turn down the tunes a little. Doan wanna call 'ttention to ourselves, do we?"

"Nooo! Sorry." Yabo snapped off the radio.

"We gotta step up our schedule, G. Move on this today. You 'member what we gonna do?"

"Yeah, I been thinking 'bout it. I get it right just about every time we practice. I know I can do it. Listen, I was just wondering..."

"Wondering what, G?"

"If I do okay, you know what I mean–if I do this just like you said and don't screw up none, will I get some more jobs with you?"

"Hey, Tonto, this jus' the beginning." Jewel smiled and punched Yabo's upper arm gently. "Do the way we practiced. Remember, gotta be badass to be my partner."

Yabo's eyes narrowed, and his chin jutted out. The tough dude look. Badass.

"Listen, now. The gas station thing look like the best scene, but we hang loose. See what happen. How ever it go–watch for my signal, then you move in."

"Good thing we siphoned most of the gas out of his tank last night, huh?"

"Sharp thinking, amigo. Thass why I pick you."

Yabo grinned and relaxed into his seat.

Jewel handed the bag through the window. "Here's some breakfast. Sit tight now."

Jewel walked back to his own car and hesitated. He was too restless to be cooped up in the car, and it was getting warm. With the newspaper under his arm, he entered the tiny, wedge-shaped park and headed for the only bench. Time to cogitate.

Did Wiser plan to stay here all day? Too bad he couldn't just walk in and check the conference schedule. He thought about how he looked–baggy jeans, long t-shirt and leather jacket, his hair Jheri-curled, shaggy beard. No good. He chuckled out loud at the corner he'd gotten himself into. What he needed was a telephone booth–he needed to turn into effing Clark Kent.

He'd have to wait and see; if lunch time came and Wiser didn't show, he'd send Yabo for sandwiches. He stretched out his long legs and crossed his ankles.

As one possible scenario after another played across his mind, Jewel could feel himself begin to zone–to gather and harness his inner energies for a complete, total focus. His sensory perceptions sharpened and his mind quickened. When he was like this, he was stronger and quicker, both physically and mentally. When he was in the zone, he always found a way to solve the unsolvable–everything came together.

Earlier this year, Lincoln had sent him to San Antonio to take out a county judge who turned out to be a frail, sixty-something grandmother– Judge Judith Sakowitz. When he got there, he found her surrounded by round-the-clock court security guards, because, imagine that...her life had been threatened by somebody she had crossed during the commission of her judicial duties.

Like any of the jobs he did for NADCO, this one had to look like an accident. The security officers had represented an obstacle, and Jewel was working against a deadline.

He wondered, as he got familiar with her routine, what the hell this white-haired old lady had to do with anything. How could her piece of the puzzle be that important to NADCO? Not that it bothered him to take out a granny. He just found himself wondering, once in a while, maybe to alleviate the boredom, how piece A fit into piece B and what the whole puzzle looked like.

Two of his plans to take her out had fizzled, and he was running out of time; but he was in the zone, and he knew he could make it happen.

There he was in the heat of June in San Antonio on the Riverwalk–the Spurs had just won the NBA title. He knew from past experience they ran the barges down the river to celebrate everything from Fiesta to the crowning of the Mud King.

Judge Granny's party barge, which was filled with front office staff, was about to pull away. At the last second, he vaulted onto the deck and flashed the badge of a security guard he'd cold conked.

Over the hubbub created by the crowd, he shouted to the court cop, "Riverwalk Security. Whew, I almost missed you. I don't get many chances like this." Eye contact, delighted boyish grin. The barge cast off, and they were on their way down the winding, narrow river that channeled along under low, arched footbridges.

Jewel turned to the court cop who was giving him the eye. "Hey, could you believe it? Avery Johnson hitting the winning shot? And they said AJ couldn't stick the jumper." As he talked, Jewel had mimicked a slow-mo jump shot, arching his wrist at the top of the move. The cop laughed. "I've been saying all year..." and started rambling about his assessment of Avery Johnson. Jewel was in.

Delirium reigned among Judge Granny's passengers. Jewel raised his arms above his head and joined them in ecstatic victory hoots. The cop grinned and relaxed. Five minutes later, Jewel wandered next to the elderly judge who was leaning over the rail, bathing in the recognition her city gave her. No more than a slight lift and nudge sent her head into a stone bridge abutment as she went over the side–dead before she hit the water. Jewel, himself, sounded the alarm, screaming for help. When the barge slowed, he leaped off to help pull the boat to the side then melted into the crowd at water's edge.

A couple of months later, thumbing through the national newspaper, he got to see, for once, the whole pizza pie. He read about San Antonio's plans for a new $200 million dollar basketball arena–to be built and owned by NADCO and leased to the city. They had hit a snag though...a delayed building permit issuance to be ruled on by the court. It had been expected a judge would rule against NADCO, causing expensive delays. However, the judge had died in an accident and the newly appointed judge had ruled in favor of NADCO. Jewel had put that problem to bed.

He went back to playing the scenes in his mind, picking out, for further examination, those ideas which held promise and gave him the most room to improvise.

Maggie followed the flow of traffic with no particular destination in mind. Last night, on the way to Abercrombie's, she formed a vague plan for this morning–perhaps drive into Boston and tour the Isabella Gardner Museum or maybe do a little shopping. Now, she had no heart for either activity.

She had gotten little sleep last night, and she suspected Sam hadn't slept much either. They had been having such a good time before the argument, and she sorely regretted that the raw nerves of their discord had been exposed again. For no gain; neither of them would ever change their perception of the events in their lives.

Maggie wheeled the Lexus around another corner and found herself heading for Memorial Drive. Another turn onto a tree-lined street, and she was driving along her favorite part of Cambridge. The lazy Charles River sparkled in the morning sun, close by on her left; on her right, ivy-covered buildings stood solidly, gracefully in the shade. Ahead, she spotted a rare sight, an empty parking space, and pulled the Lexus into it.

Along the sidewalk that bordered the river, athletic, suntanned young women in shorts effortlessly maneuvered on roller blades around indifferent pedestrians. Times had changed, she thought with a smile. When she lived in Cambridge, the only young women on the sidewalks in the morning were pushing baby carriages.

When she had been a very young wife and new mother away from home and her parents for the first time, this place, with its grace and serenity, was where she had been drawn. This was where she brought her troubles, where she renewed her spirit.

Suddenly she realized there was someplace else she'd like to see. She glanced back at the river a last time as she pulled away from the curb.

In only a few minutes, she was heading down Massachusetts Avenue. Two left turns brought her into a lovely, residential area of large, elegant, single-family homes, most of them built in the late 1800s.

She turned left once more onto Maple Street, pulled next to the curb, and rolled down the window. There was the house in which she and Sam had rented a small apartment on the second floor from Mrs. Kahn–a widow who needed a little income to supplement the nest egg her late husband had left her.

Maggie had gotten her first job in Cambridge when she was four months pregnant because she needed to preserve whatever sense of self-dignity and pride she had left.

Sam's parents had been shocked and outraged when Sam told them she was pregnant. They hadn't even known he was dating her.

Born Margaret Shaughnessy into a working-class family, Maggie hadn't known she was socially unacceptable. Her father was a foreman on the railroad. He provided a comfortable living for her mother and her. Her mother, always of fragile health, had had several miscarriages before she had given birth to Maggie during her eighth month. It was the last pregnancy the Shaughnessy attempted–they had their child.

She and her family were part of a larger unit–the Catholic community. Within this close-knit, safe haven, families attended church, visited each other, and helped each other raise their children. As she grew up, her friends were children of railroad and mill workers, and people like the Wisers might as well have lived on another planet for all she knew of them.

The Wisers quickly made it apparent they wished *she* were on another planet. Without ever meeting Maggie and without telling Sam, they requested the presence of her father and mother at the Wiser home. They offered to pay for her "lying in wait at the best home for unwed mothers," after which she would give the baby up for adoption.

Her parents were disappointed in their seventeen-year-old daughter and terribly embarrassed at her "condition," but the Shaughnessys were not going to give up a grandchild. They had waited too long for a child of their own. They refused the Wisers' offer. If Maggie wanted to go away to avoid embarrassment until the baby was born, they told her later that night, she could go visit her aunt in Lewiston. But then she would return, and they'd help her raise her child.

Maggie smiled. That's what would have happened if Sir Samuel Wiser had not climbed on his white charger, when he found out what his parents had done, and insisted that he marry Maggie with or without his family's blessing. First there were threats of refusing to pay for law school, then of disinheriting him. But the elder Wisers finally capitulated to their only son once the wedding was over. Not, however, before insinuating, implying repeatedly, in front of Maggie, that she had planned the pregnancy in order to trap a wealthy husband.

The result was that Maggie wanted nothing to do with their money—wanted to distance herself as much as possible from the privileged class. If Sam needed his parents' money for tuition, it was none of her business, but she would accept nothing from his parents for their living expenses.

She had been waitressing weekends when she met Sam. Once in Cambridge, she got a job doing the only thing she knew—waiting on tables. After Joel was born, Mrs. Kahn had been overjoyed to take care of him in the evenings while Sam studied at school. Maggie found a job at a better restaurant, higher tips. She took GED classes two nights a week so she could graduate from high school and continued her job four nights making enough money, as long as they were frugal, to pay for everything they needed.

She wondered which had infuriated the elder Wisers more: thinking she wanted their money or finally realizing she would have nothing to do with it. Probably the latter, she thought with some satisfaction.

Maggie casually scanned the Lexus's instrument panel and noticed the car was almost out of gas. But Sam had filled up the car in Hampton just before they'd arrived at Abercrombie's. Could they have really used a whole tank of gas from

Hampton to Cambridge? No, certainly not. It couldn't be more than fifty miles. She'd have to call Sam's attention to it when she picked him up.

She glanced at her watch. Time to begin moving in that direction. Because parking was so impossible, she and Sam had agreed to meet in a parking lot several blocks from where she had dropped him off.

She took a meandering route toward Harvard along narrow, shady streets down which she used to walk pushing a stroller and later holding the hand of a toddler. As memories washed over her, she realized, not for the first time, she had not been nearly as devoted a mother to Joel as she was to her grandson, Pookie. She had been too young, eighteen when he was born, and too full of her own agendas to fully appreciate the gift named Joel. But when Joel's son came into her life, she was ready, at the age of forty-seven, to be a mother.

She remembered Pookie on the first day of kindergarten, walking away hand in hand with his father. She noticed his thin, little neck and how he squared his skinny shoulders and marched off, scared, but ready to deal with the world he was about to enter.

There had been other rites of passage: tying his shoes, learning to read...each of them to be celebrated but each with its own bittersweet twinge. She had failed to appreciate these accomplishments with Joel as much as she should have. And that had taught her these moments were fleeting, never to be experienced again.

Now it was a girlfriend, next, it would be a car. Then college. She swallowed past a lump in her throat and brushed away tears. Was she ready to let him go?

At noon, Jewel watched as men and women, briefcases in hand, emerged from the door he had watched Wiser enter three hours ago.

He was alert and ready now–expanded with power and vigor. Ten minutes went by. The stream of people slowed to a trickle, and he was beginning to think Wiser wasn't leaving for lunch. He glanced down the street at Yabo who was still nodding his head to a beat that Jewel couldn't hear.

He looked back at the door and saw Wiser, taller than anyone else, already walking down the sidewalk. His gut lurched–he had been inattentive for only four or five seconds. Jewel slowly got to his feet and folded the newspaper while he scanned the traffic in the street for the Lexus and the woman. Nowhere in sight. If the woman showed up, he would have to get into his car and follow them. If Wiser stayed on foot, he'd also stay on foot.

Wiser crossed the intersection and walked briskly down Waterhouse Street. So, it's going to be a mugging, he thought. Not his favorite method. Momentarily losing sight of the tall, gray-suited figure, he jogged casually to the end of the narrow park. When he reached the intersection, he spotted the man immediately, still walking down Waterhouse Street.

Crossing to the same sidewalk, Jewel reflected: a mugging lacked style and imagination. You needed only muscle and a few brains–and, to be successful at it, a good sprint. It also was not without risk, particularly in broad daylight. He'd have to be quick, very quick. The idea was to get very close which should be easy. No one, including Wiser, would be looking around to see who was behind him at noon in Cambridge.

Wiser was a little more than half a block ahead of him. He was probably heading for a restaurant, but there weren't any in the next couple of blocks, so he had plenty of time to overtake him.

Jewel reflexively touched the slender blade concealed in the sleeve of his leather jacket; he scanned ahead, watching for escape routes. His stride was long, and he walked faster. He was half a block away now–close enough to see details. Jewel noticed Wiser's suit was the latest cut, the newest fabric, tailor-made. Nice.

He continued to scan, rapidly gathering information. There was no one walking within a block of them. He rehearsed what hold he would use. Wiser had gray hair, but Jewel wasn't fooled. The man was powerfully built and walked with the grace of an athlete. He wouldn't make the mistake of underestimating him.

Jewel pictured the immediate tensing, the struggle when he grabbed him from behind with his right arm. Jewel was left-handed, something he had often used to his advantage. He would insert the knife in the back between the ribs on the left side and sever the aorta. He had a momentary twinge of regret at having to cut that suit.

Just as in a tennis serve, he visualized the follow-through. He pictured the man going limp while Jewel still held him. It would be over in seconds. But he would have to grab Wiser's wallet to make it look like a mugging. Add three seconds. Then he'd sprint off to the right on foot, cutting between buildings, getting immediate cover. He wouldn't go for his car; he'd be trapped in traffic.

He was ten feet away, now. His heart pumped; adrenalin flowed. One final glance to his right to select his escape route between two houses.

Just behind Jewel, a car horn tooted lightly three times; he glanced over his shoulder and saw the black Lexus, the woman behind the wheel. She pulled over to the curb in front of Jewel; Wiser climbed in. As they pulled away from the curb, Jewel maintained his stride for three counts, then turned and ran back down the sidewalk.

Sam buckled his seat belt. "That was good timing. Saved me two blocks."

"How did your speech go?" Maggie eased into the noontime traffic on School Street.

"It went fine. Listen, Maggie, can we have lunch and talk? I want to, ah, apologize, and you know how much easier it is if I can sip a martini at the same time."

She reached over impulsively and held Sam's hand. She had never known anyone for whom apologies were so difficult–often impossible.

"Do you suppose that Lebanese restaurant is still doing business?" she asked.

He squeezed her hand gratefully.

Jewel reached the corner, looked over his shoulder–the Lexus was signaling a left-hand turn–and sprinted toward his car, fifty feet away. He saw Yabo's startled face through the windshield of the Mercury and signaled him to follow. Jewel yanked open the door of the Crown Vic, shot into the seat, and turned the key he had left in the ignition.

Shit! He had parked the car three hours ago. Since then, others had come and gone, and some self-centered asshole had parked a Cherokee almost on Jewel's bumper. He indulged in a split-second image: the owner stood beside the red Jeep inserting his key–Jewel dropped him with one shot to the head.

He let the fantasy go–never let emotions screw up a job. He inched the Crown Vic back and forth three swings and was out of there. Heart pumping, he turned onto Waterhouse Street, but the Lexus was gone. He estimated he had lost two minutes more or less–depending on the traffic lights the Lexus had encountered. It was more than enough for him to have lost them.

At the end of the street, he turned left into the heavy noon traffic and headed toward Harvard Square. Where the hell would Wiser and the woman be going? Lunch, of course, but impossible to guess where.

The traffic light ahead was green; he glanced in the rear-view mirror. Yabo was there, one car back. Jewel allowed instinct to guide him; he turned right. There was only a slight chance he would find them, and he was already forming a backup plan.

The next light was yellow as he approached and red when he sailed through it. Jewel glanced in the rearview mirror; Yabo followed to a blare of horns.

He had first considered Yabo for the job because he had been told Ernie Yablonski could handle a car. Jewel had only to establish that Yabo had a record and a limping IQ to know he had found his man.

The traffic slowed to a crawl and then stopped, backed up between lights. Pedestrians darted across the road between the idling cars, ignoring comments from frustrated drivers. His light turned green and then red again, but no one moved; the intersection was jammed, plugged. Ridiculous. The job would've been over now if that woman hadn't stumbled into her rescue just as he was about to finish off Wiser.

A block ahead, the light turned green; the traffic slowly began to move. He glanced behind him again, almost causing him to miss the black Lexus making a right-hand turn at the front of the line. Jewel felt another rush. "Who-ee," he whooped softly. A large, satisfied grin spread across his face. Of course, this gig would come together. He hadn't really doubted it.

The Lebanese restaurant was now Italian, but other than a Mediterranean makeover, it looked much the same as it had twenty years ago–dark walls, small tables–but red, white and green Italian flags hung from the high ceiling now.

Sam didn't wait for the martini. He started talking as soon as the waiter disappeared with their drink orders.

"Look, I know I was out of line. Let me tell you what happened when I spent that afternoon with Pookie. I realized he was a person. He was mature, he was funny, he had interesting stories to tell–he made me laugh. He was a person I'd love to spend time with. Suddenly, it hit me like a ton of bricks. I had missed out on all the things that made him that way. You and Joel have done a wonderful job raising him, Maggie, and I suddenly realized I didn't contribute a thing. I missed the whole damn party..."

The waiter arrived with the martini and white wine. Sam waited until he left.

"And I can't ever get it back. It was a shock, and I was angry. I wanted it to be your fault–I really wanted it to. It's a hell of a lot harder when you're hurting, and you know it's all your own fault." He sipped his martini. "I've been struggling with this, and I know I'm not done yet, but I do know that I don't want to let any more time go by. I really want to see more of this kid."

She looked into Sam's eyes; there was pain there–something she had rarely seen.

Suddenly, he grinned lopsidedly. "This is all by way of an apology."

"I know." She smiled back. "I recognized it."

"I thought I was over the part where I wanted to blame you."

"It's okay. Really, Sam. We'll get past it. I'm happy you're getting to know your grandson." She paused, debated, then offered, "Would you like to have Thanksgiving with us? Meanwhile, call him when we get home. You can ask him yourself about spending time together. Take him sailing."

She saw his shoulders relax, his face soften, and it suddenly felt right having Sam and Pookie get to know each other.

As they left the restaurant, Maggie handed him the car key. "You mind driving now? I've had enough for today. Oh, I almost forgot. We need gas. The gauge says it's almost empty."

"Impossible," Sam said as he slid behind the wheel. "I just filled it up."

"I know. But look."

"I see. But how in hell...I thought my gas cap was jimmy proof. We're going to have to stop before we get on 95. If I remember right, there's a gas station a couple of blocks from here."

Boston suburb

Seventeen-year-old Willie Edwards counted the customer's change and nodded an acknowledgement to his "thanks." As the man left the combination gas station and convenience store, Willie saw a Lexus pull up to the pumps. Before he could even get out from behind the counter, the driver of the car, a tall white man with gray hair, emerged from the car and pulled the nozzle from its metal cradle. He was going to pump his own gas. Willie was surprised how many old guys did that. Not him. When he got a car, he was going to sit in the driver's seat, power the window down just enough to see the attendant and tell him to "fill it with Super." Then he'd sit back and listen to the stereo until it was time to slip a twenty through the window and say, "Keep the change."

A blond woman got out of the passenger side, went around the rear of the car, and headed toward the store. He took up his position again, behind the counter.

"Do you have today's Boston Globe?" the woman asked.

He pointed to the rack against the wall. He didn't talk much to the customers. Only when he had to. Especially the white customers. Especially women. When she brought the newspaper to the counter, he snuck a quick glance and found her smiling at him, looking right into his eyes. Her green eyes and freckled face were so friendly he couldn't help grinning back.

"Dollar fifty."

"Sorry, all I've got is a twenty," she said, smiling. "Want me to buy some gum?"

Willie felt his grin stretch wider. "No, ma'am. I got change for a twenty." He glanced at the Lexus outside. The man was still pumping gas. A second car pulled into the yard and headed toward customer parking beside the store. Must be coming in.

"He'll be in with a credit card when he's done," the woman said.

A third car pulled in, also heading for one of the three parking spots. It was going to be a busy afternoon.

He nodded to the woman and pulled cash from the register. He handed her two quarters and three ones. "Two and three make five." He laid a five and ten on top of the bills in her hand. "Five makes ten and ten makes twenty."

Noises from the other side of the plate glass alerted him to trouble. Shit. Sounded like a dogfight going down. Man. What should he do? His hand moved toward the telephone. Years of living in the trenches told him to not call the cops unless he had to. This felt like a 'had to' time. He started to pick up the phone.

Angry, booming male voices split the air. Looking out of the plate glass window, Maggie's stomach squeezed, and she froze to the spot. She scanned for Sam, trying to make sense out of what she heard and saw. There he was, standing beside the Lexus, staring at the shouting men.

A maroon car had pulled toward the parking spaces and stopped short. A tall, scruffy looking man who had been shouting now shoved open his door and leaped out with wrathful energy. His greasy, blond hair swung around his shoulders. His dirty clothes hung loosely on his tall frame.

A blue car, whose approach to a parking spot had been blocked by the maroon car, sat angled toward it. Behind the wheel of the blue car, a black man leaned out of his window. His face was contorted, wild with fury. The blond man ran around the back of his car, heading toward the other car, shouting incomprehensible things at the other driver. The black man turned away.

No one was shouting at Sam. He'd gotten back into the car and was looking in her direction. With relief she shook herself loose and headed for the door. They had to get out of here, fast.

As she pulled the door open, a gun appeared in the black man's hand. Oh, God, the other man also had a gun. She ran toward the Lexus.

Ernest Yablonski had warmed to his task. He jumped out of the car. "You get your fucking car out of my way. You fucking cut me off!" He reached inside the car, pulled out his gun and pointed it toward Jewel.

Still seated in his car, Jewel screamed at him waving his own handgun in the open window. "Move your car, or I'll fucking blow your brains out."

Yabo grasped the gun in both hands, straightened his arms and aimed his gun at Jewel–just as they had practiced. "Kiss your black ass goodbye," he shrieked.

Deliberately, Jewel aimed the gun and fired.

The bullet tore into the gray-haired man in the Lexus.

Yabo stared at the blood splattered on the inside of the Lexus windshield, running down, now, in little rivers. Shit! Jesus, Mary and Joseph. We killed a guy! His stomach lurched. His head reeled. What had they done? He had to get in the car and out of there before he puked. He glanced back at Jewel.

The last thing Ernest Yablonski saw was a gun aimed at his chest and Jewel's focused face behind it.

Chapter 4

"Sam!" Maggie screamed, running toward the car. She was vaguely aware of squealing tires, people running and shouting. Blood. There was blood all over the windshield. The driver's side window was gone.

This couldn't be happening.

Seconds ago, everything was fine. Sam was fine.

Arms grabbed her from behind. She pulled herself away and reached the car. Where was Sam? Then she saw. He was slumped toward the dashboard, away from the door. There was blood everywhere. She yanked open the car door and grabbed his shoulder. "Sam!"

Arms grabbed her from behind again, trying to pull her away. "No, no, no!" She struggled, trying desperately to pull away. Sam needed help. She reached for him again, but her hand came up empty as she was dragged away from the car.

"Help him. We have to help him. Somebody. Help him!"

"Missus, we're getting help." The voice was close to her ear.

"First aid, we have to help him. Let me go–"

"No, ma'am. We can't help." The arms held her tight. "They're on the way. Police and ambulance–on the way. Nothing we can do."

Nothing we can do.

This was a nightmare.

This was impossible.

"He's...he's," her voice broke in a sob. "He's not..."

"Yes, ma'am. I'm sorry. They're both dead."

Reality dawned, and she screamed uncontrollably as sirens wailed in the distance.

From the dashboard, Jewel retrieved the two shell casings that had ejected from the Glock and slid them and the gun under the gym bag on the passenger seat.

As he pulled out, startled pedestrians stared in the direction of the gas station. A kid on a bike accelerated in that direction. At the intersection, Jewel made an immediate right turn onto the main thoroughfare, a four-lane street in a commercial area. Traffic was light at two-thirty on a Saturday afternoon. The first traffic light turned red as he approached. He looked at his watch...thirty seconds had elapsed since the second shot.

"Good timing, good timing," he said to the red light. He picked up the nine-millimeter from under the gym bag and pushed the magazine release. The empty magazine fell into his hand, and he flipped it into the gym bag. He racked the slide back ejecting the "just in case round," though he had never doubted he'd only need two shots to get the job done. The unexpended round landed in the passenger seat; he scooped it up and dropped it in the bag.

He pulled the trigger on an empty chamber, pulled the slide back an eighth of an inch, and pulled down on both sides of the slide lock. Then he pushed the slide assembly forward off the frame, removed the recoil spring assembly and finally the barrel. He dropped the gun parts and frame in the gym bag. He looked at the watch. Ten more seconds had gone by.

Gotta go.

He looked forward. The red light glared at him.

And then it changed.

He resisted the impulse to step on it and drove slowly across the intersection.

He was in rhythm with the green lights now. Block after block, he scanned right and left: a church, a locksmith, a lumberyard, a real estate office, an orthodontist, a wine store, a nail parlor, for chrissake. He could hear a siren a few blocks behind him. Must be the first arrival at the gas station. He glanced at his watch.

Three minutes.

A lot had to happen in the next few minutes. But what he needed would present itself shortly. Because things always fell into place. He just had to be alert, and...and yes, there it was, a fast-food restaurant on the right, surrounded by a nearly empty parking lot. The only cars at the back of the lot were probably employees' cars. He signaled, pulled in, and drove slowly to the rear of the lot. He stopped by a tall trash container lined with a black, plastic bag. He stepped out of the car and dropped the barrel, two shell casings and the live round into the hinged door opening of the trash container. More sirens in the distance. He ambled toward a second trash container and dropped in the mainframe and spring. He got in the car and pulled up to the last trash can where he got out and dropped in the magazine and slide. Shame. Though he hardly ever used a gun, he'd been fond of this one.

He wasn't worried it would be found. The kids who emptied these trash containers never looked into the messy bags. They just knotted them closed and threw them into the dumpster.

Back in the car, he looked at his watch. Four minutes.

He drove onto the street and scanned block after block. He would have to find something soon. If anyone had gotten a description of his car or saw the plate number, there'd be a BOLO. And he was running out of territory—a few blocks from here, he recalled, was a swanky, residential area where his options and his strategy would have to change radically. Five minutes.

There, on the left. That would work. He signaled at the light and pulled across the road into the driveway beside a large, one-story building that housed several businesses. As he'd guessed, the parking area behind the building was densely packed with parked cars. He pulled into an empty spot that couldn't be seen from the street. He wiped down the key and slipped it under the seat, then wiped the steering wheel and the inside door handle. He grabbed the brown gym bag from the passenger seat and, with the wipe, snapped the door lock and stepped out of the car. He clicked the door shut knowing he had burned that bridge–he was irrevocably on foot. But cutting his connection with the car was the only course of action.

Turning toward the car, he dropped the gym bag and feigned locking the door while he wiped down the door handle.

He picked up the bag and casually strolled toward the Chinese restaurant that took up one end of the building, noting the large dumpster in back. He entered through the front door. The dim restaurant was nearly deserted. Head down, he ambled into the men's room. He peered under two gray metal doors–empty. Looked at his watch. Six-and-a-half minutes.

There was a deadbolt on the outside door; he twisted the knob. Locked. In a stall, he pried the sneakers off with his toes while he pulled his tailored leather jacket off. From the gym bag, he pulled out a plastic grocery bag and, with a pang of regret, stuffed his leather jacket into it. Sitting on the edge of the toilet, he quickly stripped off his jeans and shirt and put them in a second plastic grocery bag. Good riddance. He pulled gray sweatpants and a New England Patriots sweatshirt out of the gym bag. He yanked on the sweats and jammed his feet back into the sneakers. After digging a small pair of scissors out of the gym bag, he stuffed the full grocery bags into it. Seven and a half minutes.

With the scissors, he cut his beard close to the skin. He flushed the hair down the toilet. His fingers worked the hairline at the back of his neck until he could pinch the edges of the magnificent Jheri-curled wig. Inch by inch, he removed it from his head. He quickly cut curls off the base, then cut the base into strips, and in four batches, flushed them down the toilet. Two-and-a-half more minutes gone. Ten total.

He transferred cash, his cell phone, and his personal keys from the gym bag to the pockets of his sweatpants. The only items left in his gym bag were the clothes he had just removed. He hesitated, looking at the grocery bag with his leather jacket in it. He closed the gym bag. Ten and a half minutes.

Alert for the first sign of someone trying the door, he took another thirty seconds to trim his quarter-inch beard more evenly. He grinned at his reflection. A college-type jock out for a jog.

Satisfied, he exited the bathroom. Under the sign that said 'Order Here' he asked for a Pepsi. He glanced at his watch. Twelve minutes since the job was done—he was cutting it close.

"What's the address here?" he asked the clerk who handed him the Pepsi. The kid gave him the address. Jewel put a five on the counter and waved off the change. He walked outside the restaurant and turned right. Just another guy out for a stroll.

There was a pay phone outside a grocery store next to the restaurant. While he waited for the cab company to answer, he drained his Pepsi.

"Five minutes," the dispatcher said.

While he retraced his steps to the parking lot behind the building, he pulled the lid off his drink, and stuffed the cover and straw into the empty cup.

The dumpster he had noted on the way in was half-full of trash from the Chinese restaurant. Jewel slid the side door open and casually tossed in his Pepsi cup and, from the gym bag, the two grocery bags.

He looked at the bag that held his leather jacket.

"Nah, dog," he muttered, and pulled the leather jacket out of the dumpster. Couldn't do it. He walked over to a down-and-out guy who was lying near the Chinese restaurant's back door. Jewel held out the jacket. "For you, my brotha."

The bum nodded, as if it was the most natural thing in the world, that a stranger would slip him a five-hundred-dollar jacket. He stuffed it under his head as a pillow. "Thank you, my friend. God bless."

Jewel chuckled. Things had a funny way of working out.

He ambled to the next dumpster behind a grocery store and flipped in the empty gym bag. He continued on to the alley beside the store and turned toward the street. As he neared the mouth of the alley he leaned against the wall, half-hidden by shadows, and waited for the cab. Fifteen minutes.

A cruiser drove by slowly, two cops looking left and right. So, the law was on the ball, starting a sweep, combing the blocks around the crime scene in ever-widening circles, looking for the car. Looking for a Jheri-curled black man.

He patted his bald head.

But they wouldn't be looking for him.

Patrol Officer Daniel McDougall pulled into the combination convenience store and gas station and stepped from his cruiser, visually processing the scene. He knew only that it was a shooting. He didn't know if the shooter was still on the premises. His partner, Miranda Leighton, slipped out of the passenger side with her gun drawn. He dropped his hand to his own weapon and thumbed off the safety snap of his holster as he scanned the area.

There were two cars: a Lexus near the pumps, a maroon Mercury, in front of the store.

A small crowd, creating a loud buzz of excited conversation, milled around, looking at the body that lay near the Mercury.

"He got away!" an elderly man said. "He went that way!"

So, the shooter was not still at the scene. Officer Leighton holstered her gun and assertively made a path through the crowd. "Police," she said. "Move, move back please!"

McDougall followed her. "Move away, move away. Please, stand back."

"Over there," Leighton said. She pointed to the body that he had only glimpsed before the crowd moved. It was face up on the ground near the Mercury. The driver's side door was open. The man's shirt had a hole in the chest; blood pooled under him. A handgun lay nearby.

Avoiding the blood on the ground, Miranda Leighton squatted close to the body. She looked up at McDougall and shook her head. There's no question, her look said.

Yeah, he's dead all right alright, McDougall thought. He was still staring at the body on the ground when the elderly man cleared his throat. "I think there's another one over there. In the other car."

McDougall was vaguely aware of Officer Leighton herding witnesses back from the two vehicles. He approached the Lexus and peered inside. Part of the man's head was gone; shattered pieces of safety glass covered his body.

"Holy Mother of God," he whispered as he crossed himself. There was a sudden hush among the huddled onlookers.

"Officer McDougall!" Leighton said sharply. "Call it in! A double homicide."

Snapped out of his shock, McDougall nodded. Standing beside his cruiser he advised Dispatch of the shooting and the number of bodies. He watched for a couple of seconds as Leighton continued to urge onlookers to back out of the way.

"Do something," he told himself.

"Okay, who here saw what happened?" he asked, wondering how, in the middle of his traffic control shift, he was asking questions at a homicide. A double homicide. A few people raised their hands.

"We were across the street," a woman said. "My husband and me. We saw the whole thing."

"Yeah, we did," the husband offered. "And a woman saw it. She's inside the store. I think she was with the...with the dead guy inside the car."

"Can you wait over there out of the way for a minute?" McDougall said to the couple. "Officer Leighton will talk to you, take your names and get your information." He glanced at his partner, and she nodded.

"Anybody else? Okay, yes, thank you. Okay, you and you, and anybody else who saw what happened, we need to talk to you. Go over in front of the building, and please stay there. I'm asking you not to move around. Thank you for your cooperation. The rest of you, step back away from the cars. All the way back toward the side street. This is a crime scene."

Now new people were joining the crowd, some running from across the street to see what was going on. "Stop!" he shouted at them and held up his hand. "Move back! You really need to move back. More vehicles will be arriving."

He hoped it would be quick. He was way out of his depth. What next? Right...the crime scene had to be cordoned off. But Leighton was quickly creating a crime scene barrier with yellow tape, forcing the crowd to back up.

"Done," Miranda said to him.

She turned to the onlookers. "You see that tape I just put up? You stay on that side." She glanced at McDougall as he approached. "They come on this side," she stage-whispered, "and I'll shoot 'em myself."

McDougall looked around, wide-eyed. "Hope to hell none of them heard you. Don't want that to show up on the front page of tomorrow's paper..."

Leighton chuckled and then looked around. "Already have two people waiting to talk. You find any others, send them my way." She walked across the gas station lot where the couple waited.

McDougall gazed across the crowd. "Anyone who did not witness anything, please stand back, way back. Emergency vehicles will be arriving," he said. "If you saw something, whether you think it's important or not, talk to Officer Leighton." He nodded her way.

He caught her eye and tilted his head toward the store to let her know he was going inside to talk to the witnesses.

Sirens wailed in the distance. They couldn't get here fast enough for Danny McDougall.

Inside the convenience store, he found two eyewitnesses. A white woman and black teenager sat side by side on a bench. Tears ran down the woman's face; the boy awkwardly put his jacket around her shoulders.

"You both saw what happened?" McDougall said.

They nodded.

"I need to talk to you separately."

"There's an office right back there," the kid said.

"You work here?" McDougall asked.

"Yeah. I called the police."

'Okay, I'll talk to you first."

McDougall quickly found out the kid had had the presence of mind to get the plate number as well as the make and model of the getaway car. He jotted down the details and strode outside where Leighton was talking to the couple who had seen the shooting from across the street.

Two cruisers pulled into the lot, effectively blocking the main entrance to the convenience store and pumps. Officers jumped from their cars. McDougall strode over to a newly arrived officer and gave him the information he'd gotten from the quick-thinking kid. The officer nodded and radioed dispatch. Now a BOLO would go out. He looked around with relief, realizing that the once chaotic scene was now becoming secure. Soon the detectives and crime scene investigators would arrive. That would probably bring a whole new level of chaos. But at least it would be police chaos.

He returned to the store. The woman was rocking back and forth on the bench. "Can you come into the office?" he asked. He eased the dazed woman into a chair in front of the desk. She started rocking again. "Why did he kill Sam? I don't understand. This can't be happening. He was just alive. We were heading home. Why would anyone want to kill him?"

Though the day was warm, she was shaking. She pulled the jacket closed and held it in one fist. "I don't understand. This can't be happening!"

Her eyes, wide open, stared at something unseen. Her shaking increased. Suddenly she leaned sideways, gagged, and vomited into a wastebasket.

Shock, thought McDougall. "You alright, ma'am? What can I do for you?'

"I'm okay," the woman said. She pulled a tissue out of a box on the desk and wiped her mouth.

"You're experiencing shock. An ambulance will be here in minutes. Take slow deep breaths if you can."

The woman nodded, took a deep breath and shuddered on the exhale.

"Okay," she said. "Ready. What do you want to know?" She took another deep breath.

He was still holding his notepad. "For now, just a few things. Your name, relationship to the deceased..."

She made eye contact with him. "Sam is gone, isn't he? He's dead."

"The victim, the man in the Lexus, I'm sorry, yes. What was his relationship to you?"

"My husband," she said. "Um...ex-husband. We were on our way home."

"And home is ...?"

He wished one of the newly arrived officers would come in and relieve him. Someone who would know what they were doing. He pushed on and led her through the necessary questions, made notes, remembering to tell her she would be asked to make a full statement at the police station the next day.

She slowly shook her head. "But why? Why did some random person shoot Sam? On purpose."

"You think Mr. Wiser was the intended victim?"

"Yes, of course. He turned toward Sam and shot him. The man had been arguing, screaming at someone else, and then he turned and shot Sam."

She shuddered and pulled the jacket tighter.

McDougall looked at his watch. Ten minutes since dispatch had been called...good chance they'd find the car shortly.

In the cab, Jewel thought about the job. He hadn't seen that the woman had come out of the store until he was driving away. Now she was a goddamn witness. A goddamn witness who was still alive. But what had she seen?

Ten minutes later, the taxi left him off at a Mass Transit entrance. He walked three blocks to Logan Airport–long term parking. He slipped the key into the lock of his dark blue Ferrari F355.

The woman, he thought.

That damn woman.

Maggie stood up in the little office but didn't take a step. She felt dizzy.

"Mrs. Wiser? Are you hurt? Is that your blood?" asked an EMT, putting his hand at her elbow.

"No..." She looked down, seeing the crimson stain on her blouse for the first time. Sam's blood. "It's my husband's blood." Her knees buckled, and she went down.

When she came to, she was lying on a gurney that was being maneuvered toward an ambulance. "You're going to be okay," said the EMT. "You fainted."

Her eyes searched for the young man, the store attendant, who had pulled her away from the Lexus. And, after questioning, he'd held her hand until the EMT had taken over.

Now his soft gaze caught hers; tears ran down his face. He moved beside her as they neared the ambulance. "Missus, do you have anyone who can come get you? Family or anything?"

"Not here. No. I don't know what to do."

"They'll take you to the hospital, make sure you're okay. You call someone from there, okay?"

She nodded. She would never be okay again. Then she saw anguish in his eyes. He was only a kid–not much older than Pookie. So young to see such horror. "Thank you. Thank you for...everything. Your jacket..." She tried to sit up.

"No ma'am, I don't need it. You keep it for now."

* * *

McDougall watched the ambulance maneuver between the cruisers that blocked the main entrance. He realized Officer Leighton was standing beside him.

"Howzit goin'?" he asked.

"The four that I talked to didn't agree on anything except the color of the car, blue. And the shooter. Black."

McDougall and Leighton watched as the ambulance pulled slowly onto the side street, now the only way in and out of the area. Then, almost simultaneously, broadcast vans from two TV stations pulled up on the main street in front and tried to squeeze between the cruisers to get into the cordoned off area. Blocked by the cruisers and two officers who waved them off, the vans parked along the street. Camera men jumped out, frantically hauling equipment out of the vans. The news correspondents immediately started talking to the growing cluster of the curious and the thrill seekers.

McDougall felt way out of his element, repeatedly saying "no comment," as microphones were thrust in his face.

Then, a vehicle drove in the side street entrance, followed by the crime scene van. Detective Steve Burrows got out of his vehicle and waved to the driver of the van to park in a way that would block that entrance. Thank God, thought McDougall.

Detective Burrows yelled to one of the patrol officers, "Get them the hell out of here. Get the camera crews out of here! This is a crime scene."

Burrows turned and stopped to talk to one of the other officers, who pointed to McDougall. Burrows strode over to McDougall and Leighton.

"You two were first on the scene?" Burrows glanced between Leighton and McDougall. "What do we have?"

"Double homicide," McDougall said. "One shooter left the scene in a blue Ford Crown Vic."

"Yeah, I heard the BOLO."

"The other shooter is dead." Leighton nodded toward the body on the ground. "Another victim in the Lexus is also dead."

"Did you get any statements?"

Leighton nodded. "The witnesses I talked to say the two guys, the one over there and the one who left the scene, were shouting, arguing, and then they shot at each other."

"You got the witnesses' contact information, right?"

"Yes, sir," Leighton said, holding up her notebook.

McDougall nodded. "I talked to two witnesses. The store attendant who called it in and the ex-wife of the guy in the Lexus. She just left in an ambulance. Not injured. She fainted. She's from Maine. They're both from Maine. Funny thing is, the woman thinks her husband was the intended victim. The gas station attendant is over there," McDougall pointed. "He's the one who got the info on the getaway car."

"When the ME identifies the body, we'll know who the other dead guy is," said Burrows.

"I've seen him around," said Leighton. "I don't know his name, but he hangs out at Dolly's pool hall. I think he lives within a mile of here, give or take a block."

"Okay, good. I'm going to have Detective Warren talk to you," he said to Leighton.

To McDougall he said, "Clear the peanut gallery back a little more. There will be more vehicles arriving. Be ready to have an officer move back a cruiser to let them through."

Burrows conferred with the newly arrived Detective Warren and pointed toward Leighton.

McDougall was relieved to do something he knew how to do, crowd control, and to turn responsibility for the homicides over to the detectives. Other officers, he saw, were now protecting the perimeter of the crime scene or taking witness information.

Not sure what he should be doing, McDougall watched Detective Burrows confer with the Medical Examiner who had been squatting beside the body on the ground. The ME put a wallet into an evidence bag and handed a driver's license to Burrows.

"Good," Burrows said. "A name and an address."

McDougall's attention was drawn to a crime investigator who squatted next to the gun lying on the ground beside the dead man. She carefully picked it up with her gloved hand, released the magazine, and pulled the slide back. She started in surprise. From where he stood, McDougall could see the magazine was empty. Puzzled, the woman sniffed the barrel, looked up at Burrows and shook her head.

Startled, McDougall turned to the detective. "Detective Burrows. The gun hasn't been fired. It's not even loaded!"

Burrows glared at McDougall, motioning with a jerk of his head for McDougall to follow him inside. Burrows plunked his heavy figure down in a gray metal chair and scowled at McDougall. "What the hell were you doing out there? The press is all over the place. You don't give them anything. Nothing but our official statement. They get more than they need on their own. You want the shooter should discover everything we know on the six o'clock news? You got it?"

McDougall's face burned. He nodded.

Burrows leaned back in the chair. "Ever seen a homicide before?"

McDougall shook his head, his stomach clenching as he thought about the guy in the car. He knew his name was Sam. He had an ex-wife who still cared about him. Someone who thought he was shot on purpose.

"First time," was all he said.

Burrows nodded. "This is a good one to start with. So, rule number one: don't make it harder than it has to be. Not much mystery about what happened here."

"What do you think happened, sir?"

"Well…" Burrows ran his fingers over his thinning hair and then swept his arm toward the scene beyond the plate glass window, "given what the witnesses said, two punks got pissed off and tried to pop each other. Dollars to donuts it's a local disagreement, maybe a gang thing, maybe a grudge thing. Unfortunately for the tourist from Maine, he got in the way."

"But the other dead guy didn't have any ammo in his gun. Why would he pull a gun first if it wasn't loaded?"

"Who knows? When we get the results of the drug and alcohol tests, we'll probably find he was stoned out of his mind–he just forgot he wasn't loaded."

"One of the witnesses, the ex-wife of the guy in the Lexus, said that the other guy aimed the gun directly at her husband. Ex-husband. Swung the gun and fired right at him. She didn't even know anyone else had been killed."

"That leads us to rule number two: the ex-wife is not a reliable witness. She's emotionally involved, trying to make sense out of a senseless act, maybe a little hysterical. She passed out, didn't she? And, from what I've gathered, none of the other witnesses corroborate that part of her story. Right?"

McDougall nodded and shrugged an agreement. He stared out the window absently watching the TV crews preparing for tonight's news. The face of Margaret Wiser forced its way into his mind. She had seemed so sure. He tried to find the words that would explain how convinced he was by the woman.

Burrows spoke first. "Let's see. These people were...are from out of state. They're here for the weekend, maybe. They stop for gas, probably at a station they've never been to before, an argument ensues between two locals, and she thinks her *husband* was the target?"

"Um, Ex–"

"Listen. If he was the target, there'd have to be a motive. You'd be suggesting, *she'd* be suggesting that this was some sort of a charade–a setup to kill the husband? It's just...it's ridiculous. Did the lady say just what the motive was supposed to be?"

"No. I didn't, ah, I didn't ask her." Damn. Another stupid mistake. "Sir, you haven't talked to her yet, but she seemed so–"

"I'll talk to her when I take her statement at the station tomorrow. You told her to come down, right?"

McDougall nodded.

"Good. So anyway, this looks like a pretty straightforward case. Three cars are doing a sweep right now; we'll find the Crown Vic soon, because I can guarantee you, it's already been ditched. The computer will match the prints of some hood that some precinct is looking for–ours, if we're lucky." He paused, then flashed a grin.

"Look, McDunnough. McDougall? Okay, McDougall. I think we'll find this is open and shut...a case of two low-lifes trying to knock each other off. The world can only benefit. It's a shame about the other victim, but he had the misfortune to be in the wrong place at the wrong time." Burrows stood up and headed toward the door. Over his shoulder he said, "Rule three: Don't make a conspiracy out of this."

McDougall was embarrassed, but Burrows turned back. "Wait, here's something helpful you can do. You and your partner run down Yablonski's next of kin and break the news. Ask a few questions. Lemme know if you learn anything."

He's throwing me a bone, thought Officer Daniel McDougall, but he was glad. He would like to follow up on this.

Jewel's black-windowed Ferrari wound sedately through the sparse afternoon traffic. He assessed the day's work and decided the job had gone astonishingly well given the curve he'd been thrown. Despite the complication of the woman, he'd succeeded. Witnesses would say Wiser was an unfortunate bystander in a case of road rage–possibly racially motivated. Yabo had a record, and no one got too excited about racial shootings as long as they involved small-time players with no connections–usually it was good for one- or two-days' press. With Wiser as an unintended victim, the hoopla would last a couple more days, but with no other leads the trail ended with Yabo. The cursory investigation would close very quickly. Unless the woman presented a problem. How much had she seen from where she stood?

Jewel activated the garage door opener and the Ferrari crawled up his paved driveway and into the garage. He parked next to his brand new, Oxford blue Range Rover and deactivated his house security alarm.

He climbed the stairs to the first floor of his house, glancing at the kitchen clock as he passed by–4:00 p.m. He hadn't slept in thirty-four hours.

In the upstairs bathroom shower, he shaved all of the remaining hair from his face. As the pulsing hot water beat against his skin, he relaxed for the first time in two weeks. Finally, he allowed himself to luxuriate in the tiredness and satisfaction that came with a job well done.

The late afternoon sun slanted through the windows and skylight of his spacious home office downstairs, reflecting off the stark white walls. Tribal African artifacts, placed among Egyptian antiques, graced the walls and decorated the interior. The only other accent was an enormous jade plant that thrived sitting next to a narrow floor-to-ceiling window.

Dressed in sweat bottoms, he walked across the thick-piled, dark blue carpet in his bare feet and pressed the answering machine button.

Sixteen messages–none that needed immediate attention. He looked through the mail, addressed to Jules Chadwick, that had piled up for the last three weeks–bills and business correspondence. One letter from the Boston Museum of Art and two from out-of-state universities. Everything could wait. Time to get some sleep.

It was dark outside when he awoke from his nap. He checked his Rolex. Nine o'clock. He selected a charcoal gray Armani suit and a white shirt. After considering several selections, he chose a silk tie with subdued white and yellow flowers on a gray background. As he tied his tie in front of a full-length mirror, he smiled at his reflection. The Montel Williams look. Then he winked.

Ten minutes later and five blocks away in a neighborhood restaurant and bar, Jewel ordered prime rib, baked potato, and a salad. He ordered a $150 bottle of his favorite Cabernet Sauvignon. As usual, he would only drink half the bottle–the gift of the remaining half to the waiter and maître d' had guaranteed him red carpet treatment and the best table every time he walked in the door. He ate a leisurely dinner. He nodded to a couple of his neighbors but fended off their invitations to join them with a smile and a wave of his hand.

Just before eleven o'clock, he moved to the bar and ordered cognac. Regardless of where he was in the world after he had made a hit, he caught the news in a public place. It was the one indulgence he allowed his ego. The bartender obligingly turned the channel to a local station.

A woman holding a microphone appeared on the screen. Jewel recognized the gas station in the background.

"Earlier today, two men were shot and killed, and a third escaped, in what appears to be the second case of 'road rage' in two months. Eyewitnesses say that two cars approached this gas station–both cars arriving at the same time. According to witnesses, one vehicle cut the other off, igniting a heated argument between drivers."

Jewel stifled a smile as his script unfolded on the screen. A mugshot of Yabo appeared.

"Ernest Yablonski, a Boston resident and a three-time convicted felon, pulled a gun and aimed it at the other driver, whom witnesses describe as a bearded black man in his early thirties.

Jewel was intensely satisfied. Jules Chadwick was so far removed from the description, he might as well be in another country. Yet, here he was out in public nine hours later and only ten miles away from the scene. Yes.

"Witnesses state that the two men exchanged shots, one of which killed Yablonski. The shooter reportedly fled from the scene, uninjured, in a blue Ford Crown Victoria. Police say he is to be considered armed and dangerous. Additionally, we have an unconfirmed report that Yablonski's gun was not loaded at the time of the shooting."

No. Jewel stared at the amber liquid in his brandy snifter. Damn! This is what happens when you trust others. He'd needed Yabo's fingerprints on the gun *and* the bullets. And the dimwit hadn't loaded the gun.

Stupid whitless, honky cracker. This is what happens when you bring in an idiot.

The scene switched to the anchorman at the news studio.

"Also killed in the same incident was Samuel Wiser, a Maine resident, who appears to have been a bystander caught in the line of fire. Witness to the violent murders was Wiser's ex-wife, Margaret Wiser, also from Maine, who was traveling with him at the time. The couple were on their way home from Cambridge.

Although police are reluctant to discuss the issue, witnesses say that the argument between the two men appeared to have racial overtones. A police spokesman says they are following up on several leads.

In other local news..."

Jewel closed his eyes. Even if the woman had seen him aim at Wiser—and, okay, from her angle, she could have–the police might discount the ex-wife as a hysterical witness. But would they be more inclined to take her seriously with the complication of Yabo's empty gun? Would they become curious enough to track down Yabo's haunts and get a description of Jewel from his pool hall buddies? A description that, except for beard and hair, matched the description of the witnesses at the gas station? And the fact that the Crown Vic wouldn't have had any viable fingerprints when they found it, might lead them to Wiser, not Yabo, as the intended victim.

The instructions from Link had been standard for a NADCO job. It had to look like an unintentional death, and that was Jewel's specialty.

If the police started a serious investigation, Jewel was confident they could not track the job to him. But if they simply concluded that Wiser's death was intentional, would they find that NADCO had a motive? If so, he would have failed. He had never failed before. At anything.

He opened his eyes and took a sip from the snifter, warming his tongue and throat with smooth fire, feeling the heat spread to his belly. He had to control his thoughts, not let emotion cloud his judgment. The first question: If he fucked up, and it looked like he might have, and if NADCO was pissed, and they probably would be, would they try to put out a hit on him? Eliminate the connection between Wiser and themselves?

As inconvenient as it would be, perhaps he should lie low for a while, not follow his usual routines, take another trip. Where?

A hand clapped him on the back. "Jules! I thought that was your shiny, black billiard ball over here."

Jewel turned, offered his hand. "Hey, Porter. How're you doing?" Porter Newson was his next-door neighbor and occasional tennis partner.

"Judith thought she saw your car pull in today. Just get back?"

"Yeah. Can I buy you something?"

"What are you drinking? I'll buy *you* a drink. Courvoisier? Victor?" He signaled the bartender. "Two Courvoisiers." He turned to Jewel.

"So where are you back from this time? India, was it?"

"Egypt. Not a productive trip, though. Several of the pieces I was most interested in were frauds. Or honest mistakes. But not genuine."

"Too bad."

"Can't win 'em all, they say."

"Must be tough, financially, to make the trip and come up empty."

Jewel smiled at him. "The good ones make up for the ones that go sour."

"You must be tired. You look a little peaked and pale."

Jewel laughed at the joke. Many of his neighbors, digging into their politically correct social pockets, fawned over him and vied for the opportunity to show him off at their dinner parties. He played and enjoyed the game that gave him the opportunity to occasionally sleep with their daughters...and, more often, their wives. Porter, though, played things straight.

"Listen, before you're off globetrotting again and I can't reach you, Judith and I are having a thing on Labor Day out at the cottage–mostly family, a few friends. Can you join us? Bring a friend? Or we'll provide one."

Jewel smiled again. Judith had tried before, unsuccessfully, to matchmake.

"Thanks. Sounds great, but, unfortunately, I won't be around then."

"Leaving again? So soon?" Porter raised his eyebrows.

"Mmm. When I got home, there was a letter from a London firm I work with. They want me to authenticate some African artifacts, and they're anxious to get them into a museum." He smiled. "It's a tough life, but somebody's gotta do it."

"Yeah. You ought to try working for a living, Jules. When're you going?"

"Next couple of days. Let's do lunch before I go."

On the way home, it came to Jewel where he was going to be spending the next few days...maybe longer. He'd leave tomorrow.

Guess lunch with Porter was off.

Chapter 5

The sea was getting rougher. Maggie was at the helm; Sam was trying to reef the sails. She had never seen him struggle so–he nearly slipped off the wet deck of the boat. He yelled something, an instruction, but the wind whipped his words away. He desperately clung to the boom and pointed. He must want her to turn the boat to port. She pulled the wheel to the left and the boom he'd been holding onto struck his head; he flailed backwards into the ocean. She ran to the side and held out her hand for him to grasp. Each time she seemed to have his hand, hers came up empty as if his had melted before she could get a good grip. She screamed, "Sam, hold onto me." But he slowly slipped beneath the black water and was gone.

Maggie fought her way to consciousness, struggling to escape the nightmare. Still groggy, she felt overwhelming relief. It was only a dream. She probed this comforting reality searching for confirmation to reassure her, to wipe out the tentacles of terror still threatening to pull her under.

She looked around the unfamiliar room in confusion. She was in a motel room. Suddenly, a memory more horrifying than the nightmare descended upon her. Fighting to escape it, her mind crabbed around, groping blindly for a solution. There was none. Yesterday, Sam had been killed.

The full weight of the reality threatened to immobilize her. She jumped out of bed and headed for the bathroom. Nausea and dizziness struck, and she made it to the toilet just in time. When she finished vomiting, she wet a washcloth and washed her face. The memory of a vitally alive Sam, the Sam she had sat beside minutes before his death, filled her mind. Suddenly, she found herself sitting on the edge of the tub muffling, with a towel, great, heaving sobs.

By the time Joel and Tildie knocked on her door half an hour later, she was shaky but dry-eyed and ready. She had phoned them from the hospital yesterday, and they arrived three hours later. Joel found them rooms in a motel then insisted, over her protests, she take the sedative the emergency room physician had given her. Then Tildie sat with her until Maggie had fallen asleep.

Now, standing in the doorway, Joel's stoic face looked blanched and ashen. The fog she'd been in since yesterday afternoon had cleared, and she thought, for the first time, he's lost his father. She glanced at her granddaughter standing behind her father.

Tildie's eyes had that haunted, wounded look she had seen before, and the memory was almost Maggie's undoing. She knew, from their past experiences, Tildie would keep her own grief tucked away in a private place behind carefully constructed walls that she allowed no one to breach. Maggie frantically blinked back the tears that were threatening to spill, knowing a display of emotion at this point would shake Tildie's tenuous control.

Joel put his arms around Maggie. "Do you want breakfast first, or..."

Maggie shook her head.

He kissed the top of her head. "Okay, let's get the police station over with."

While Joel explained to the dispatcher why they were there, Maggie nervously fingered the dog-eared business card the young police officer had given her yesterday and tried to calm her butterflies. Maggie handed the card to the uniformed woman. She turned it over and read where the young police officer had written "Detective Burrows" on the back.

"That's who I'm supposed to see."

The dispatcher nodded. "He is with someone right now. I'll let him know you're here." She handed the card back and gestured toward a bench against the opposite wall. "Why don't you wait over there."

When the outside door opened ten minutes later, two young men walked in. Maggie recognized the boyish, friendly face of Officer McDougall as well as the young man who had pulled Maggie away from Sam's car and had sat with her while they waited for the police.

McDougall said, "Mrs. Wiser, this is William Edwards, from...yesterday. Willie, this is Mrs. Wiser." The young man smiled at her.

"I'm glad to meet you," she said. She stood and handed Willie the jacket he'd lent her. "Your coat. Thank you. I can't tell you how much I appreciate all your help."

Willie nodded shyly.

Maggie turned to McDougall. "I'm here to give you my statement. Um, Detective Burrows, actually."

"Yeah, I'm sure that he will be with you soon, Mrs. Wiser. I just gave Mr. Edwards here a ride in so he could make his statement also. I see your family is with you."

"Yes, this is my son, Joel, and my granddaughter, Tildie."

Joel shook McDougall's hand. The officer then grasped Tildie's.

"I'm sorry for your loss, Miss Wiser. Tildie? That's an unusual name."

A blush rose on the young man's face as he released Tildie's hand.

Tildie smiled. "It's a nickname. My real name is Matilda. My father is a Harry Belafonte fan." She nodded toward Joel.

"So am I," McDougall blurted. "A big fan." He blushed. "I mean, I like both names. Tildie. And Matilda."

Joel shuffled his feet impatiently. Willie Edwards studied the ceiling carefully while he twirled his hat in his hands. The dispatcher leaned her chin in her hand and watched the scene with amused interest.

Suddenly self-conscious, the young officer said briskly to Maggie, "Well, yes, okay, while you folks wait, I can get you a cup of coffee. Tildie? Or, actually, you can help yourselves...down that hall, first door to your right." He glanced sheepishly at the dispatcher.

Burrows came out and looked at the assembled group. McDougall made the introductions.

Burrows nodded. "Officer, why don't you take Mr. Edwards to look through mug shots while I talk to Mrs. Wiser?"

Burrows brought Maggie into a tiny, cluttered office. He led her through the events of yesterday in a businesslike, matter-of-fact way, which helped her to stay calm.

"And then he aimed at Sam and..." She faltered.

The image of Sam's car with the window blown out swam before her eyes.

Burrows rescued her from a place she didn't want to go.

"We know there were at least two shots fired from the same gun, one of which hit the other victim and the second, your ex-husband. Mr. Wiser and the other man were not very far away from each other. Is it possible that the gunman tried to hit the other man with his first shot and missed, hitting Mr. Wiser by accident?"

"No, it was very clear."

The detective nodded. "Well, yes, your account is a little different from other witnesses. But this is par for the course," he added. "Witnesses often disagree on the details."

She supposed that yes, this was true, but something crystallized solidly in her mind. "I could be mistaken, of course, but I feel so sure of what I saw. I could see the man, the man with the gun. I could see his face. When he turned the gun toward Sam, he didn't look angry anymore." She forced herself to picture the fleeting image. "His face was calm and...focused, I guess you'd say." She paused and made solid eye contact with the detective. "The other witnesses weren't seeing it from the same angle I was."

Burrows nodded, made some notes, and then looked up. "But you didn't see the other man killed?"

Maggie shook her head. "The last time I noticed the other man, he was still alive and yelling. And waving a gun."

"Could you identify the man–the man who did the shooting if you saw him again?"

She tensed as an image swarmed into her vision again. "Yes. I think so."

"Good. I think that will do it, Mrs. Wiser. I'll have your statement typed up, and you can sign it before you leave." As he closed the notebook, he seemed to have an afterthought. "Tell me, if you don't mind, Mrs. Wiser, why do you think someone would want to kill your ex-husband?"

Maggie hesitated. She had tried to work through this exact question while she was at the emergency room last night waiting for Tildie and Joel to arrive, but her drugged mind couldn't make the pieces fit. This morning, on the way to the station, she sifted through as much as she could remember of what Sam had told her. Could those events possibly be related to his death? One minute the idea seemed absurd–nightmarish imaginings–the next it was plausible.

Would her speculations sound ridiculous to this experienced policeman? But, it's probably now or never, she thought.

"Sam is a..." She took a ragged breath. "Sam was a city councilman. He opposed the building of a mall in Amesbury by a company called NADCO–"

"Nadco?" Burrows reopened the notebook.

"Yes. All capital letters."

He wrote the word in the notebook.

"There also might have been something, ah, something wrong with a land deal–the same company was involved in both. They offered Sam a large bribe, but he turned it down. Just, um...Friday. Afternoon." She was shocked at how long ago it seemed.

Burrows jotted a few more words and closed his notebook.

She didn't blame him. That was Amesbury, this was Boston. How could local events in a small city in Maine be connected to Sam's death here?

"I know it sounds pretty silly." She picked up her purse.

"I've made a note of it. You never know. Would you mind looking through a few mugshots? We could get lucky."

Burrows led her to the room where Willie had been going through mugshots. Burrows raised his eyebrows in question. McDougall shook his head slightly. They hadn't come up with anything. Willie Edwards left with Burrows, and Maggie sat down at the metal table. Joel materialized beside her with a cup of steaming coffee which she gratefully accepted; then she sent him back to stay with Tildie.

Maggie pored over page after page of photographs that all began to look alike until, after a while, the image she held in her mind began to blur. She doubted, now, she would recognize the man even if she saw him in person. She was relieved when the young officer closed the book and thanked her for her time.

He escorted Maggie back to Burrows' office. There, she read the concise, amazingly short statement. The events of Sam's death. There was only one page. She signed her name at the bottom.

McDougall accompanied her to the door. Willie Edwards sat with his elbows on his knees, again twirling his cap in his fingers.

Maggie shook hands with McDougall, caught at glance from Willie and nodded a smile.

"Thanks for your cooperation, Mrs. Wiser," said McDougall. "Are you heading for Maine today?" He turned to Joel. "I don't think the car will be released until tomorrow. Paperwork."

Maggie felt distant and weary. "Where is it?"

"The towing company will have it in their lot."

"We don't want the car," she said. "Would a junkyard buy it?"

"The towing company buys and sells some. They might be interested in yours. If you think of anything else, please call Detective Burrows. You have the card with his number?"

Maggie nodded.

"Thank you, folks. Take care." McDougall extended his hand to a pale and drawn Tildie. A blush spread up his face as she placed her hand in his. "A pleasure to meet you, Miss Wiser."

"Tildie. Thank you." Tildie smiled but the spark was gone; she was drained.

They walked into the bright sunlight. Suddenly, Maggie realized that during the whole process–the statement, the mug shots–she had held the crushing weight of grief and horror at arm's length. The emotions returned now with greater force, bonding irrevocably with raw-edged anger. Somewhere, someone out there was alive and breathing. Someone who had taken Sam from his son, from his granddaughter and from his hopes of building a relationship with his grandson. Taken Sam from everything he had loved about being alive.

Maggie, in spite of a lifetime of pacifist views, wished, in an explosion of fury, that she could be present to watch the killer die in the same manner that Sam had died. And even his death still wouldn't be enough to assuage her anger. Then she was breathless and trembling with shock and guilt. She, who had always been appalled at violence, had never suspected herself to be capable of such primitive feelings.

Lincoln Montgomery swiveled his high-back leather chair around to face the huge window in his office. As he stared out at a gray Manhattan Monday morning, the first raindrops hit the window and ran down in rivulets. He caught his reflection in the window: short black hair that he wore swept back in tight waves above thick eyebrows; the pronounced nose, reflecting his Greek heritage. He pulled gently on each gold and ruby cufflink to adjust his sleeves. He looked confident. Professional. He turned from the window.

This morning a videotape of the Boston weekend news arrived by courier. He now sat back and watched it, momentarily amused and impressed at the method Jewel had chosen for the hit. Seconds later, he bolted upright in his chair and hit the pause button. Wiser's ex-wife had been with him. Lincoln rapidly worked out the implications.

There was little doubt in Lincoln's mind that the woman knew whatever Wiser had known. There was no way they would have spent the night together without Samuel Wiser unloading what was on his mind concerning the meeting with Oxley—which must have been the reason that Wiser had included his ex-wife in his weekend plans at the last minute. And now, Lincoln mused, he had a disaster on his hands.

With the remote control he continued through the tape, fast forwarding to the segments that contained news of the shooting. Sunday's account was more of the same with a few additions: they had found the killer's car...apparently no drugs involved...police deny racial issues were involved...they confirmed that bullets for the empty gun had been found in the victim's pocket...following up leads...confident they will apprehend killer soon.

So not only did Margaret Wiser have information she shouldn't, the hit had been bungled. At nine o'clock Lincoln was supposed to wire transfer $250,000 to a prearranged account, which, after several more rapid transfers, would end up in Jewel's account in the Cayman Islands.

Now, that was off. Lincoln wouldn't make the transfer until he was able to ascertain the extent of the damage. He rubbed his chin. It was entirely possible the second half of the fee would not be paid.

Visibility outside the window was now almost zero. The rain, driven by gusting wind, pelted against the glass. Swiveling around, he placed his elbows on the glass-topped mahogany desk and carefully steepled his manicured fingers.

The first order of business was to make initial plans to eliminate the Wiser woman. But had she already told the police that Wiser might have been the target? Would they believe her? Would her immediate demise add credibility to her story? He'd have to play this close to the vest.

He pushed the intercom button. "Kathy, will you let Mr. LaCroix's secretary know that I'd like to schedule a round of golf with him?"

"Yes. When should I tell them is a good time for you, Mr. Montgomery?"

"As soon as possible. Tomorrow, if the weather clears."

Was there more to be concerned about than how much the Wiser woman knew? Jewel, Lincoln's first choice whenever he was available, never left loose ends–until now. The police were confident of an arrest. Public relations or the truth? Had Jewel been arrested since last night's eleven o'clock news?

There was no doubt who would be held responsible when LaCroix was informed of events. In his position, Lincoln thought, I'd be thinking of how to get rid of me. But Lincoln had an ace in the hole. He knew how to take care of the dirty work. He was the one with the contacts. He also kept records.

Very detailed records.

Lincoln sighed, pushed back his chair, and got to his feet. He removed a painting from the wall, exposing a large wall safe. Rapidly spinning the dial, he opened the safe, removed the emergency cash bag, and retrieved the bound, five-by-eight-inch, black notebook. He returned the cash bag to its place and put the videotape beside it before closing the safe.

For the next fifteen minutes, Lincoln made careful notes in small, precise handwriting. He reread what he had written, inserting a few commas he had missed, and was satisfied.

The last ten pages of the notebook were reserved for his resources–the names of contacts and methods of contacting them. He ran a manicured finger down the list.

He'd need a pipeline into the police station to find out what the woman had told them. He'd also need immediate surveillance on her. Arturo "Artie" Mancuso was already in Amesbury–he could get the audio equipment started today. The Wiser woman probably wasn't home yet–he'd have to check on that. If not, it would be child's play to get in and out of her house. Then Artie could assemble his crew and begin around-the-clock visual surveillance. Unless it turned out she knew absolutely nothing, he'd have to have her removed.

Lincoln returned the notebook to the safe, spun the combination lock, and hung the painting back in its place. Straightening his sleeves and his necktie, he headed out for a public phone.

"What can I getcha this morning?"

"Just coffee." It was Jewel's third cup of coffee in a third greasy spoon that morning. This one was imaginatively called Hal's Diner.

He tapped a manicured finger on the headline of the Monday morning issue of the Amesbury Times. "Local guy, huh?" he looked up at the waitress, whose name tag said Winifred.

"Ain't it a shame? I could hardly believe it when I saw the whole story on TV, when was it? Saturday night? I said to my husband, 'Come look at this. Sam Wiser was just killed. Shot!'"

She shook her head. "Can you imagine? What's the world coming to? Of course, that was in Boston. Nothing like that could ever happen around here. Nobody runs around shooting people in Amesbury. My husband's always talking about us taking the kids to Boston, you know, to a Red Sox game? I always say, 'me and the boys're staying right here in Amesbury where we don't have any of them drive-by shootings.'"

"I can certainly understand that." Jewel's voice was deep and sympathetic.

He turned back to the newspaper. "Did he have any family?"

"Oh, yeah. I think the...whaddya call it...the obituary is on this other page." She leaned over and flipped his newspaper to the second page. "I heard the funeral is going to be Wednesday. It'll be some packed–big shot like him." She leaned over again and tapped the photo of Samuel Wiser with an acrylic fingernail. "Yeah, here it is, right here. It lists the survivors. Not too many, really. Maggie, that's his ex-wife, she's a sweetie. His son. Two grandkids. And an aunt."

"Sounds like you know her...the ex-wife."

"Oh, yeah. I mean we're not friends or anything. She's Hal's bookkeeper." Winnie tilted her head toward the kitchen behind the counter. "Usually, Hal leaves the stuff at her place, but she comes in for breakfast a lot. A real sweet lady. Nice to everybody. Does a good job, too, everyone says."

She suddenly straightened up, remembering her role. "Can I get you anything else?"

"Actually, I think I'll have some breakfast after all." Jewel folded his newspaper. "That bacon smells good. How about the special?"

"How do you want the eggs?"

"Over easy and I'll have the wheat toast. And tomato juice. The largest you have."

"Coming right up."

While he waited for the heart attack special, Jewel examined once more why he had come to Maine. Would Lincoln want him to take care of the woman? If so, he'd already be on hand. He could do some investigating, be ready.

Or, on the other hand, if Lincoln dared to take out a hit on him to eliminate the connection between them, and therefore between himself and NADCO, he'd be where they would least expect. And a tête-à-tête with another professional might be amusing, especially one culminating in handing the hit man's head to Lincoln.

But, if he was honest with himself, he was here because he had a reputation to protect. In his specialization there could be absolutely no loose ends. He needed to see this through.

Of course, he wasn't going to fix something if it wasn't broken. He wouldn't take her out unless he had to, which, if he did, wouldn't be much of a challenge. She had inadvertently given him a few bad moments in Cambridge, but the old lady wasn't going to be much of a player in this story.

"You from the college, then?" Winnie asked, taking in his tan sport coat with leather elbow patches and white polo shirt. She set the juice glass and the plate piled high with sausage, bacon, and eggs in front of him.

Jewel nodded. Before he left Chelsea, he had checked Amesbury out on the internet and found it was the home of a business college and a small liberal arts college. "Sort of. I'll be consulting with the museum people at the college. Nice town you have here."

"We like it. But we call it a city." Her eyes crinkled in amusement. "Probably looks small to someone from away."

"No, not at all. Looks just the right size. Small enough to know the people who live here, not big enough to have drive-by shootings."

She smiled, looking gratified. "Exactly what I say. Can I get you anything else?"

He smiled, making brief eye contact. "No, I'm good."

"I hope you come back." She laid his check on the table upside down. On the back she'd written, "Thanx!" The dot under the exclamation point was a circle filled in with a smiley face.

He nodded. "Thank you, I will. The service was great." He'd gotten as much information as he could without raising suspicions. He would drop back in for breakfast each morning while the subject was still hot news among the locals–they'd be buzzing about it for days–and see what else would be forthcoming. He assumed it would be a few days before the Wiser woman started coming in for breakfast.

So, his target for today's surveillance did some bookkeeping in her spare time. That altered his view of her a bit. The ex-wife of a prominent attorney, and Wiser had been successful judging by his car and his suit, should be living on alimony in the style to which she had become accustomed–trips to Spain, and, since she was "sweet," volunteering one afternoon a week at the hospital. But not taking in work as a bookkeeper.

He drove back to his motel, changing into black, baggy jogging shorts and an oversized black t-shirt–something that allowed him to walk around a residential area without looking like a roving evangelist. Since he couldn't exactly blend, he'd have to look like he was connected to Marston Business and Technical College or Amesbury College.

Should be easy in "Hicksville." Winnie-the-waitress had certainly bought his story.

He had used his computer to obtain a map of Amesbury before he left home. At the motel room last night, he'd also looked up the Wiser woman's address and then confirmed it in the phone book. Now he spread the city map on the bed, quickly locating Maple Street. He packed a few items in the pockets of a navy-blue windbreaker. He was ready to go.

By noon, he'd parked his car, tied the windbreaker around his waist and walked the three blocks to Maple Street. There he got another surprise. He had really expected the woman would live in something more splendid. Her house was located in an older neighborhood where most of the lots were narrow but deep. The modest houses sat way back on the property, leaving well-trimmed green lawns and landscaping in the front.

Unlike the others in the neighborhood, her house sat close to the road, leaving, Jewel guessed, a lot of room for lawn at the rear of the property. The house was a two-story, pale yellow Victorian with dark blue shutters.

The front walkway, composed of ancient, moss-covered bricks, was nearly overgrown with knotty grass. This entrance was seldom used, telling him there must be another one to the side or rear of the building.

On the sidewalk just past the front entrance, he dropped to one knee and began retying the laces on his running shoes. He was aware of the scent of rain-soaked soil and the fragrance of some flower he couldn't identify.

Tall lilac bushes, thick with green leaves, rounded out the sides of the house, but the building still appeared narrow, rambling backward on the property–probably three times longer than wide.

To the right of the house, a long driveway led though maple trees and curved back to an old-fashioned carriage house. The carriage house, in which two modern garage doors had been installed, was attached to the house. Along the side of the house near the back, sheltered from view by thick juniper bushes and large rhododendrons, there appeared to be another entrance–probably the one used by the family. Toward the rear of the property a separate garage was located on the other side of the driveway.

He straightened up casually and tested the tightness of his laces with heel and toe raises. The neighborhood seemed to be deserted, but he always assumed there was a little old man sitting at a window petting a little old cat, watching Jewel's every move.

Jewel alternated walking and jogging as he moved around the block, getting a sense of the terrain. After the first lap, he had determined that her house lot was bordered on three sides by trees, shrubs, and wild grapevines– effectively separating it from the view of neighbors.

He started around again, turning left at the intersection of Maple Street and Waverly and left again at the intersection of Waverly and Orchard Hill. This put him on the back side of the block relative to Margaret Wiser's house. This part of the neighborhood was less built up and included a sizable, wooded area that separated two of the house lots on Orchard Hill. This piece of real estate, with a stream running through a shallow ravine, was mostly undeveloped.

He pushed his way in among a thick cover of spruce trees. The woods were noticeably cooler. Small twigs, hidden under a carpet of pine needles, cracked loudly as he stepped on them, but speed was more important than silence. He pushed aside branches at face level, and in seconds he was deep enough to be invisible from the road. Soon, the evergreens were replaced by deciduous trees that gradually thinned, allowing sunlight to filter through as he side-stepped down the small hillside. Now the twigs that snapped under his weight were hidden by old layers from past years of broad leaves that gave off the pungent, sweet odor of decay.

As he gained the top of the hill on the other side of the gully, he glanced at this watch. If the woman wasn't home from Boston yet, she would be soon. He came to the end of the wooded cover and oriented himself. The rear of the carriage house was visible as was the garage. He crouched low and ran, finding cover in the low shrubbery that separated the properties.

Getting into a mark's house was a necessary phase he called discovery. In this case, he would accomplish a couple of things. He might find out enough about her to judge whether or not she'd be taken seriously by the police or anyone else she might talk to. If she did Hal's books, she probably wasn't empty headed, but judging from her house and the location, she was not one of the powerful elites in this burg.

Also, by going through her house, her possessions, he'd likely come across some information, maybe a hobby, that would suggest how she should meet with an accident. If he subsequently decided that the accident had to happen at home, he needed to know everything about the house in advance.

As Jewel pulled himself into the niche between thick evergreens, he realized he couldn't be seen from any direction unless someone stood only a few feet away.

There was no sign of life from the house. He ticked backwards: if the funeral wasn't until Wednesday, there would be a viewing or two on Tuesday–today was Monday, and it was possible the body wasn't even back in Maine yet. Perhaps the old ex-wife had delayed returning in order to accompany the body of her former hubby home.

Fifteen minutes later, a heavy set, jowly man dressed in brown coveralls, carrying a small package and a clipboard, walked up the Wiser driveway and headed for the rear side door. The man rang the doorbell once, twice–waiting each time for a minute or so. Jewel expected him to turn and leave, but, instead, he pulled an item from his pocket and proceeded to pick the lock.

Smiling, Jewel shook his head in disbelief. The uniformed man, who must have been hired by Lincoln, had taken an unnecessary risk. While he picked the lock, he was in plain view to anyone looking out of the second story windows of the neighbor's home across the road and the building across the street. The guy was an amateur, but he had an advantage over Jewel; he was white. In this neighborhood, he'd hardly be noticed, and the uniform made him nearly invisible.

Jewel had already spotted his own method of entry–a cellar bulkhead door on the opposite side of the house that was screened from view from the street and was most likely unlocked. Even if the door was locked, it would hardly slow him down.

The coverall-clad intruder entered the house. So, Lincoln and NADCO were interested in the witness. Who else would have hired someone to break in? If they were worried about her enough to break into her house, that probably made her a loose end. So where did that leave him? He'd never had to contact Lincoln before. Lincoln had always contacted him.

Ten minutes later, the man exited by the same rear door, walked casually down the driveway and disappeared. Jewel wondered about the timing. He'd like to believe Lincoln had planned the break-in knowing the woman's ETA. Well Jewel could just piggyback on that and go on in. Or had they just risked getting caught?

He knew for sure there was no one in the house right now, and there might never be a better time to move than the present. From the zippered pocket of his windbreaker, he extracted tight fitting latex surgical gloves– the type with ribbed fingertips that allowed for greater digital precision–and pulled them on. He left the protection of the dense vegetation and crossed the yard, skimming close to the hedgerow, to the opposite side of the house from where the man had broken in. The bulkhead doors were not locked, saving him time. He couldn't believe how frequently people locked their houses up tighter than a drum but forgot about the cellar. In ten seconds, he was in.

When his eyes adjusted to the dim light that filtered through small dusty windows, he picked his way to the stairs, crossing the cellar which was littered with the miscellany of life's cast offs–broken weight bench, bicycles minus various parts, unlabeled boxes stacked in a hodgepodge jumble.

One stair was loose, and two others complained loudly under his weight. He made a mental note of the squeakers. Next time he came in, the house wouldn't be empty. He tested the door. It wasn't locked. The stairs exited into a hallway next to the kitchen which was visible to his left toward the rear of the house. While he was coming up the cellar stairs, he had noticed a companion stairway overhead which led to the second floor. At the foot of those stairs was the entrance through which the uniformed gatecrasher had entered– through which the woman would likely come when she returned home.

He glanced at this watch. He'd give himself twenty minutes to reconnoiter.

Turning left, he passed through a dining room and into a living room at the front of the house. Off the living room, a second stairway led from the front door to the second floor. He went up. The Wiser woman's bedroom was at the top of the stairs.

He paused for a second, taking in the condition of the room. A bedside table was littered with hand lotion, a partially filled out crossword puzzle, pencils, and ballpoint pens. Two open books lying face down on top of each other were in danger of falling from the table. He shook his head. He'd figured her for a neat-as-a-pin fussbudget.

Tilting his head, he glanced at the titles of the books. *Shade Gardening in the North* and *Secrets of Plant Propagation*. Jesus.

A Stuart Kaminsky novel lay open on top of another stack of books next to the bed. So the woman read more than one book at a time. And she was interested in mysteries–no doubt to fend off the mind-numbing boredom of *Shade Gardening in the North*. Not to mention bookkeeping.

A pile of discarded clothes–looked like a gray suit–lay over one arm of a chair, pantyhose over the other, shoes were scattered around the room. On a desk, a large stack of opened and unopened mail had been shoved together. A slight breeze would send the pile to the floor. A dirty coffee cup balanced precariously on a newspaper in the cluttered work area and a waste basket overflowed.

Clearly Madam Wiser wasn't compulsive. He wondered if she would have cleaned up a little if she'd known she was going to have company.

He crossed to the opposite side of the room and looked out of the huge bay window. Her room overlooked the street.

The top of her bureau was crowded with framed photos. One was a family gathering–an outdoor shot where a younger and much slimmer Mrs. Wiser grinned at the camera. Standing beside her, a preoccupied Samuel Wiser gazed just off to the side of the camera. A second adult male, who resembled Wiser as much by his facial expression as genetic likeness, stood on the other side of the woman who was holding a toddler. In front of Wiser, a girl, maybe ten years old, squinted into the camera. The girl had a slightly Asian look, as did the boy.

Later photos were mostly of the children, showing a progression of growth. The girl, her hair in long braids, looked fiercely determined as she kicked the ball during a soccer game. Another of her in a karate gi holding a trophy almost as tall as she was. The boy, about eight, was captured in an oversized baseball uniform, bat cocked over his shoulder, ready to swing. The next frame showed the same kid, at twelve or so, going in for a layup under a playground hoop.

Jewel scanned the other photos. In the most recent one, the pigtailed girl had become a beautiful young woman. He noted her full, slightly tilted eyes and sensuous mouth. She was wearing a cap and gown. Her shiny, jet hair lifted in the wind. Standing on each side of her was Proud Dad, this time smiling at the camera, a grinning Sam Wiser and a gangly brother. There was no Margaret Wiser. Probably had taken the photo.

These people were Wiser's "survived by's" in the obituary. From a pocket, he pulled out his small Nikon 35Ti and took pictures of each photo. He would commit their faces to memory.

A full bathroom adjoined her room. A second door in the bathroom led to the hallway at the top of the stairs. Back in the bathroom, he went through her medicine cabinet. All of the contents, including a pink razor, looked like they were owned by a woman. He moved first-aid items and half-empty containers of cosmetics, looking for prescription bottles. Only thing he found was a glucosamine bottle. Figured.

His first hit, back in his college days, had involved prescription drugs. His research had turned up the fact that the mark's wife had a prescription that, if it interacted with the one the mark was taking, would kill him. It was fundamental stuff–putting some of her pulverized medication into his capsule and waiting. The autopsy results showed that the unfortunate man had been a victim of confusion–had accidentally taken one of his wife's pills. It happened.

If the Wiser woman had any prescriptions, she had them with her. Nothing he could use here. He checked the bedroom closet and bureau drawers. No sign of male occupancy or a frequent male visitor. If Wiser and his ex-wife had been keeping company, he probably hadn't been sleeping here.

Back in the bedroom, he popped the earpiece off her bedside phone and found a bug. There it was–proof that Lincoln and NADCO were more than a little concerned about Margaret Wiser. That was enough for him.

He left the bug in place. He took photos of the room from three angles. He might not have to enter this house to eliminate the woman, but if he did, he needed to have the house and all its contents committed to memory.

Down the hall he found a second bedroom which was probably the room of the kid in the photographs. Beside the narrow bed, was a nightstand with three books piled one on another: *Sorcerer's Stone, Chamber of Secrets* and the newest in the series, *Prisoner of Azkaban.* A Harry Potter fan. Made sense. There was a display of sports cards, baseball and basketball, on the wall, a computer on a small study desk, a basketball in a corner. Did the kid live here or was the room used for visits to Grandma's? Two pairs of very worn basketball sneakers were lined up beside the bed. He picked up the tired pairs and looked at the soles. One pair was ravaged and worn; the soles of the second pair were in perfect condition. The kid had a special pair reserved only for playing on a wooden court. He lived here.

The next room down the hallway could belong to the woman's son. He went through the bureau and bedside drawers checking for a gun, but there was none—nothing more to discover here.

A huge fourth bedroom, probably 20 by 20, captured him for a moment. It was located over the carriage house, he guessed. Three large skylights enhanced the cathedral ceiling. Double windows on each of three exterior walls admitted light that reflected off stark white walls. The dominant color in the room was a dark gray rug, similar to the one in his office. Unlike the other "cozy" rooms in the house—over decorated, over furnished—this was a room one could breathe in.

He snapped back to the task at hand. This room was normally occupied by a young female—judging by the floral bedspread and the selection of CDs that were neatly piled on a table next to a stereo. She had to be the beautiful young woman in the photos.

Her telephone on the nightstand had also been bugged. He noticed wrinkles in the lavender and blue bedspread where Mr. UPS had sat. A square-based lamp was turned at an angle on the nightstand. In this immaculate, neat-as-a-pin room, the occupant never would have left it that way. He smoothed the bedspread and straightened the lamp. He hoped the guy didn't try to make a living at this stuff.

Now he knew. The whole family lived here. Which raised an interesting question. Where were they right now? He looked at his watch. Ten minutes left.

Downstairs, he continued the exploration, taking photos to record details he didn't have time to observe now. As he scouted, he swiftly put chair legs back into the depressions in the carpet, straightened lamp shades that the buffoon had likely moved. Fucking fool! Where had Lincoln found him?

He found bugs in the living room, hall, and kitchen telephones–the kind that would pick up voices in the room as well as both sides of a phone conversation.

At the back of the house, off the kitchen, he found a home office that must be where the Wiser woman did her bookkeeping for Hal's Diner. On her desk was a worn but expensive leather briefcase. Maybe this Granny meant business. Inside were four bulging file folders. So she had more than one client; he corrected his view of her again. Tucked into a small pocket were business cards that read Stonefield and Wiser. Margaret Wiser, CPA. Well, well, a professional–not exactly what he'd expected. Perhaps the police had taken her seriously. Was this why NADCO was nervous? Was Mr. Brown Coveralls the new hitman? Were the bugs planted to find out what the woman knew, or were they there to gather enough information on her so they could plan another hit that would look like an accident?

There was nothing more in her briefcase except a notepad, listing things to do. The last entry was underlined twice: talk to Ben about Angie– raise? Her handwriting was brisk and angular–not like the Winnie-at-the- diner's loopy hand with circles for dots over the i's. Other items were business notes–things to check on specific accounts. His respect for Ms. Margaret Wiser, CPA, was rising. A little.

He was examining the contents of each desk drawer when he heard the crunch of tires on the gravel driveway. He bent at the waist and ran through the kitchen. He had to cross the hallway to reach the cellar door–the same hallway where the outside door was located. He could hear car doors slamming, voices approaching the house.

He reached the cellar door and yanked it open. He heard the key turning in the lock. He slipped soundlessly inside the cellarway as the outside door clicked open. He heard the creaks as someone climbed the stairs over his head. He waited until the other voices, a male and a female, moved to different parts of the house before he slowly descended the stairs, avoiding the seventh and fifth creaking steps and the broken second-from-the-bottom stair.

In the cellar, he found a comfortable place behind a cubicle piled with debris. From here he could study the whole area including the nearby furnace. If someone came into the basement, he could drop behind the debris and be completely out of view. He'd wait until dark for an exit. He considered, for a moment, the possibility of going back upstairs that night, taking the Wiser woman out–be done with it, go home. But, without more preparation, there was no way to make the hit look like an accident.

Or to know if NADCO wanted him to.

Or if he wanted to, out of a sense of personal pride...to clear up any loose ends.

Just in case.

Officer McDougall drummed his pencil on the patrol officers' desk. Tuesday morning–three days after the shooting and not much had changed. Did he want to stick his neck out and talk to Burrows or not? Burrows was probably pissed at him because, just as he had feared, the fact that the deceased's gun was not loaded was on the Sunday evening news. Rookie mistake. He didn't want to make another.

But the case that probably wasn't even a case was bugging him. Oh, what the hell. He was early and had a little time before his shift started. He should probably get behind the wheel of his cruiser and forget the whole thing, but the little nagging details didn't add up. He pushed himself away from the desk. He knew his feet were going to carry him to Burrows' office.

Sergeant Burrows sat at his desk in the tiny office, a stack of files at his elbow, one open in front of him. McDougall stood in the doorway, reluctant to interrupt. The silence stretched; he thought Burrows knew he was there. Was Burrows hoping he'd go away? Stubbornly McDougall held his ground and cleared his throat.

Startled, Burrows said, "Yeah?" He dragged his eyes from the file folder to Daniel McDougall's face and nodded.

"Could I talk to you a minute?" McDougall asked.

The detective sighed in resignation, closed the file folder and slid it to the side. "Sit down. I wasn't doing anything important, anyway," he said as he stared at the file.

McDougall grabbed the back of a wooden chair, pulled it farther from the desk, and sat down. "I'd...I'd just like to talk to you about the Wiser case."

Burrows looked genuinely blank.

"The shooting. Saturday."

"Oh, yeah. Sorry. What do you want to talk about?"

"Well, have we gotten anywhere with it?"

Burrows shook his head. Folding his arms across his belly, he leaned back in his swivel chair. "Funny thing, though. Got the report back from forensics yesterday on the Crown Vic, the killer's car. Prints all over the car except for the steering wheel, the shift lever, the driver side door handles inside and out. The prints were overlapping and badly smudged so no match there. Then they ran the VIN and got a fast match." Burrows raised his eyebrows; an amused, I-gotcha-look played across his tired face. McDougall waited.

"Seems they belong to a retired cop in upstate New York."

McDougall sat bolt upright in surprise.

Burrows waved his hand. "Naw, nothing to get excited about. It was a mothballed cruiser. The guy bought it for his son in college. Apparently, the son didn't think the cop car image was cool. Left the Crown Vic in long-term parking at school. Kid didn't even know the date it was towed away except that it was over a year ago. Then it was stolen from impound and never recovered. 'Til now."

"But no prints on the wheel, the handles...so he wiped it down."

"It would appear," Burrows said dryly. "I'd say he had some street smarts."

"What about the other car?"

"Stolen the night before from a hospital employee parking lot. Plates changed."

"Both cars stolen? Isn't that suspicious?"

"Not in the case of Ya... Yakow..." Burrows tipped forward and fished through the stack of file folders.

"Yablonski," McDougall offered.

Burrows looked up, raising a questioning eyebrow.

"I passed the word on to his brother...next of kin like you told me," McDougall explained. "The name sort of stuck in my mind. And, ah, well, as you pointed out, it's my first. Homicide."

Burrows smiled. "Right." Lacing his fingers behind his head, he leaned back again. "You get anything from Yablonski's family?"

"Yeah, the brother says Yablonski didn't like guns, didn't own a gun, didn't have money for one. I asked a cop in the neighborhood, and he said Yablonski wasn't known to carry."

Burrows sighed and lowered his chair to the floor. "Look, ki...McDougall. Danny, is it? Look, Danny. Just because you had questions about this case, I took some extra time looking over Yablonski's record. Among other things, like auto theft he's done time for, he was convicted of robbery–held up a Mom and Pop–with a .38 Smith and Wesson. He got a light sentence because..." Burrows paused, "the gun didn't have any bullets in it."

McDougall felt deflated. Another rookie mistake: he'd been taken in by Yablonski's brother.

Burrows smiled. "You still don't look convinced."

McDougall flushed again. "I should be. It's just...it's nothing, I guess. The woman was so sure of what she saw."

Burrows nodded. "Yes, she was sure. She, ah, said her ex was involved in some local political dealings, bribery..." He tipped forward and picked up a coffee cup. "Crud."

"Well, yeah, probably–"

"Crud in my cup. This one's been sitting here a couple a days, I guess. Stuff floating in it. Maybe mold." He reached for another cup, peered into it and took an experimental swig before draining the cup.

"Listen, Danny. She seems smart–but she's grasping for answers. Grasping at straws, you know? And what're the odds? What're the odds that a shooting between two hoods in Boston has anything to do with some politics in Middle of Nowhere, Maine. What is the possibility that the victim was offered and turned down a bribe on Friday and then got offed on Saturday?

"Right now, it doesn't even look good for picking up the shooter. If we did pick up a suspect, without fingerprints on the car, we'd need a corroborated positive ID, and we'd still have trouble convicting. We can't even tie him to a weapon because we don't have one."

McDougall nodded, feeling silly.

Burrows put the coffee cup down. "I understand you got your wind up about some things that didn't add up. That's good. It makes you a good cop. But believe me, this case is going nowhere. Okay, I'll tell you what. If you want to nose around a little on the street, keep your ears open, go ahead. If you come up with some information–well, we'll take another look at it then. We still might not have a case, but we'll look at it. Best I can do. Okay?" He folded his hands in front of him on the desk, but his eyes glanced sideways toward the closed file folder.

McDougall nodded. Burrows had real detective work to do. There was nothing more to talk about.

"Thank you, Detective Burrows."

"No problem, Danny." Burrows' mind was already someplace else.

He'd been given a bone to stop his whining, McDougall thought, as he walked down the hall. But Burrows was probably right. There was just no case.

It was a step up, though, he decided as he headed for his cruiser, to be called "Danny" instead of "kid."

* * *

Wednesday morning Lincoln whomped his black umbrella open and descended the steps from the commuter plane onto wet tarmac at the Portland Jetport. He hated flying in this weather. Nothing but gray outside the rain-streaked window for an hour. New York weather had begun to clear yesterday afternoon, but he seemed to have moved right back into it as he flew northeast. He pulled the collar of his L.L. Bean jacket up with his left hand and then shoved the hand into his pocket.

He'd been unable to arrange a meeting with Roy. His boss knew only that the job was done–not that there were complications.

Yesterday morning, he didn't have a copy of the woman's official statement, only second-hand station scuttlebutt. One of the cops was asking routine follow-up questions, but no one seemed excited about the shooting. There didn't seem to be any real investigation going on. But later in the day, a copy of her statement was in his hands. The Wiser woman said she thought Jewel had aimed at her husband. She mentioned, as a possible motive, his dealings with NADCO. He'd been offered a bribe.

There it was in black and white: a connection between NADCO and the death of Wiser.

His first instinct was to call LaCroix, immediately followed by self-preservation. LaCroix would see this as Lincoln's mistake.

He thought for a moment. What LaCroix didn't know wouldn't hurt him.

Wouldn't hurt any of them.

This piece of information, the connection between a bribe and NADCO, now in the hands of the police, would remain buried. He folded the paper and put it in his safe.

He'd lain awake all night trying to decide what to do regarding the Wiser woman. He believed the more time that elapsed the more danger she presented. Wednesday morning he'd awakened, after four hours of sleep, with the answer.

LaCroix depended on Lincoln, as he had since their college days, to solve problems and take care of "annoying details." LaCroix didn't say how.

Just get the job done.

Which is why he was in Maine.

Arturo "Artie" Mancuso stood just inside the terminal entrance. He was a stocky man with sagging jowls, deep bags under his eyes, and bushy eyebrows. He met Lincoln's eyes briefly and nodded a greeting. "Morning, Mr. Montgomery. Flight okay?" Years of smoking three packs a day had rendered his voice a wheezing rasp.

Lincoln closed his umbrella. "I only have two hours until my return flight. Let's talk in the car."

Mancuso led the way out of the terminal into the drizzle. Lincoln snapped his umbrella open again and followed.

Lincoln noticed the man walked with energy and power that belied his soft paunchiness. He was intelligent and had street smarts.

It was going to take street smarts to get them out of this mess.

Lincoln had already been working part time for his frat brother, Roy LaCroix, when Vinni Mancuso from the old neighborhood gang contacted him and asked if he could find work for his older brother, Arturo. Artie had just got out of the pen after a ten-year stretch for armed robbery and aggravated assault. Lincoln could and did accommodate him.

When Roy created a full-time position for Lincoln fifteen years ago, Arturo Mancuso was part of the deal. Lincoln never regretted the alliance.

Mancuso led the way to a black Cadillac DeVille, unlocking the doors with a remote as they approached.

Mancuso opened the back door. As Lincoln slid in, he could see that the open ashtray in the front had been emptied of butts, but it hadn't been washed, and the car smelled of stale cigarette smoke. In spite of the rain, Lincoln lowered the window two inches.

Mancuso looked sheepish. "Sorry, Boss. Didn't have time to get it detailed. You want maybe we should rent a car?"

"No, Artie. Don't have time. Let's go, drive around. I'd like to be back here in an hour so I can check in. Just close that damn ashtray."

They drove down the ramp and entered the southbound lane of Interstate 95. Mancuso pulled into traffic without looking back.

Lincoln looked over his shoulder to check the lane. "Everything go okay with the woman's house?"

"Yeah, piece a cake when no one's home. You never know, though. Three other people live there besides the woman. You accounted for two, the son and granddaughter. Don't know where the other one was at the time. Looks like a kid." Mancuso patted his suit coat pocket for his cigarettes, then remembered and put his hand back on the wheel.

"You get the devices in place?"

"Loaded the house with them. We got the audio guy listening."

"I contacted someone by the name of Lee. Henry Lee. You ever hear of him?"

Mancuso shook his head. "You talking a hired gun, Boss? No, I never heard of him."

"I tried a couple of others." Lincoln said. "The ones I reached weren't available on such short notice. This guy was recommended third hand. Best we can do. I met and briefed him last night."

Mancuso glanced in the rear-view mirror. "And?"

He put on his blinker and pulled into the passing lane.

"He seemed like someone who wouldn't hesitate knocking off his mother for a ten spot."

"What you're looking for, isn't it?" Mancuso asked.

Lincoln smiled. "Guess I was hoping he'd look smarter."

"It's not how he looks that's important. Am I supposed to have contact with him?"

"I'd like to think you won't see him. If he's good..."

Jewel was that good, Lincoln thought. Still hoping he could rely on Jewel, he'd called the temporary number Jewel gave him, but he wasn't surprised when there was no answer. He couldn't see Jewel sitting around waiting for the phone to ring after the job was done. But the deal was, had always been, Jewel got the second half of his fee on completion of a clean hit. No use ruminating about it now, but Lincoln was sure Jewel could have taken the woman out, right from under Mancuso's nose.

"But he might not be that good," Lincoln said. "Since you're watching her, you'll probably see him. And I gave him your number in case he has any questions."

"Okay." Mancuso reached for his cigarettes again, stopped himself, and put on the blinker. "Okay if we get off here and head back north? Get you back in time?"

Lincoln nodded. "Those Camels burning a hole in your pocket?"

"Nah. I'm down to two packs a day. Give or take a pack," Mancuso said and chuckled.

Lincoln looked at the passing scenery. Trees and more trees. "Why does anyone choose to live here?"

Mancuso shrugged. "It's a place. You get used to it."

That's the difference between you and me, Lincoln mused. I'd never get used to it.

"So what's the deal?" asked Mancuso. "If he contacts me, I put him in touch with you?"

Lincoln had been thinking about this ever since he'd met Henry Lee. The assassin knew the job had to be an "accident." Yet if there were any problems, questions...

"There's no good way he can talk to me directly, Artie. I can't sit in front of a goddamn public phone all day in case he needs his dick held."

Lincoln thought for a moment. "I'm giving you some discretionary power. Think on your feet. Field the ones you think you should. Anything else, you call me. Don't give this guy any way to get a hold of me personally."

"Sure thing, Boss. What's he look like?"

"Stocky, balding, maybe forty-five. Has glasses thick as the bottom of a Coke bottle."

"What the hell? Now anyone thinks he can be a hit man."

"That has me worried, but he isn't going to be using a gun anyway."

Mancuso put on his blinker for Exit 7A near the airport.

"That wraps it up. Just watch her," Lincoln said. "Until there's nothing left to watch.

Chapter 6

Tildie slipped her hand into Joel's and gripped his fingers so hard it hurt. He brushed the top of her head with a kiss.

His eyes rested on the flower-covered casket that, incredibly, unbelievably, held his father's body. Now that his father was gone, it was stunningly clear that, even as an often-absentee parent, he had been the largest presence in Joel's life. He had seemed indestructible.

His mother had told him last night that, just before his father's death, he had expressed remorse at what he'd missed with Joel and the grandchildren. Had expressed a desire to reconnect with them.

For several minutes Joel had been consumed with anger. First at his father for having waited so long to come to this realization, then at whoever had killed him–sealing off forever any chance for Joel to work on a relationship with his father, for any chance for his father to develop relationships with his grandchildren.

Now, Joel lifted his eyes from the casket and scanned the cemetery, pausing for a moment on a black man kneeling in prayer at a grave far away...his gaze moving on to other mourners placing flowers on the graves of their loved ones.

Joel realized then he had always held out hope he and his father would someday be close. But the opportunity had arrived and then been snatched away before he even knew it existed. The irony was crushing.

There had seemed to be so much time left. He looked at Pookie standing beside him. How much time was anyone guaranteed?

He put his arm across Pookie's shoulders and felt him relax. On his other side, Tildie continued to grip his hand. She pressed her lips together trying in vain to keep her chin from quivering. He could feel her body tremble in an effort to keep from crying. He squeezed her hand and she leaned against him.

* * *

Jewel knelt in front of a headstone in Holy Cross Cemetery, a distance from the mourners at the Samuel Wiser burial festivities–his victim about to be interred. This was the first time in his career this had happened, and it amused him. The job was over, and he should be out of here; nevertheless, here he was on surveillance. He had selected a headstone that would allow him to view, from a distance, the funeral party without appearing to. He immediately identified the family members of the Wiser household. The woman. The damn woman, Margaret Wiser, known as Maggie to Winnifred the waitress and probably everyone else in town; the tall man, Joel, he remembered the name from the obituary, must be her son. On either side of him were Wiser's two grandchildren, the boy who read Harry Potter and the young woman who, probably on her own, had created a bedroom that rivaled his professionally decorated one.

The man who had bugged the Wiser house was not here, but what he found interesting was the presence of a balding, stocky man wearing glasses, who lurked thirty yards away with his thick arms folded over his chest, staring directly at the funeral party. If the police had attended this event, they'd have had this guy in their sights before the casket was lowered.

Jewel put his finger to his lips, touched the gravestone, stood up and headed for his car. He was fairly certain the man worked for NADCO. Their new hit man? Fifteen minutes later, Jewel tailed at a distance, a light blue 1995 Caprice with New York plates, to a motel. As he thought …not a local.

Later that afternoon in his own motel, Jewel thought about it. He knew, because NADCO had searched and bugged the Wiser woman's house, she was definitely of interest to them. The presence of this other outsider confirmed his suspicions. Were they going to eliminate her? Would it be an accident? Would this guy get Jewel's other half of the fee? Well, that would get under his skin. He didn't need the money. It was the principle of the thing. Was that what was keeping him here? He should just check out and go back to Boston.

Maggie sat in her kitchen, an untouched glass of wine at her elbow. The funeral was over; the gathering of friends and family had left. Violet, the family's housekeeper for fifteen years, washed dishes while Tildie dried. The two of them discussed Tildie's senior college classes she had just started. Joel poured himself another cup of coffee. Leaning against the window frame, he gazed, seemingly lost in thought, at the back yard.

Seated across from Pookie at the kitchen table, Maggie watched the late afternoon sunlight create rainbow fragments across her grandson's dark, glossy hair. His head was bent over his task–spreading peanut butter on apple slices. Suddenly, she was in the past, sitting at a child's table watching two-year-old Pookie help her with his morning snack, laboriously spreading peanut butter on apple slices, licking the excess off his fingers, handing her every other slice.

Now, without a word, fourteen-year-old Pookie slid the plate of neatly arranged apple slices slowly across the table to her. Tears pricked her eyelids; she blinked, trying to keep them from spilling over. She nodded her thanks and took a slice.

Violet turned from the sink and dried her hands briskly on her hips. Her red hair, streaked with silver, was pulled back in a careless bun; as usual, random sprigs had escaped and sprung out like petals peeling back from a bud. She exhaled upward, blowing her bangs off her eyebrows, and folded her arms in front of her. "All right everyone, listen up." From years of training, four pairs of eyes gave their total attention.

"There's no more I can do today, and I got play rehearsal tonight. You got enough food in the fridge to supply Benedict Arnold's army. I'll be back tomorrow aforenoon. You all see to it your grandmother gets rest. Hit her with a two-by-four if you have to. Joel, you going to be around for the next while? Or you got some more gallivanting to do?"

"I'm not going anywhere. I canceled my San Francisco trip this morning. I have enough work at the office to keep me busy for a while."

Tildie and Pookie's heads snapped toward their father. Pookie's jaw dropped. Violet nodded with satisfaction. "Good. The cellar needs to be cleaned out. You got so much stuff down there, I can't even get to the toolbox anymore. I need to fix them cellar stairs next week. Pookie?" She raised her eyebrows in question.

Pookie nodded enthusiastically. "Yeah, I'll help. I want to clear a space to work on my motorcycle."

And visit with your father, Maggie thought. She smiled at Violet. The gentle bullying they were so accustomed to was a comfort, a structure they could rely on.

"Good enough," said Violet. As she walked past Maggie, she momentarily rested a hand on her shoulder. Then she was gone.

"What are we going to do with that woman?" Joel asked.

"The question is, what would we do without her?" Maggie replied.

Joel topped off his cup of coffee and started to leave the kitchen. "I'm going to listen to the messages."

"No!" Tildie whirled toward her father, her eyes open with alarm. "No. Please don't. I...already did. I started to. Grandpa...Grandpa's voice... I just couldn't believe..." She fiercely brushed a tear from her cheek.

Maggie closed her eyes for a second. Sam said he had been calling all afternoon. Her heart went out to her granddaughter. Tildie's eyes were frequently puffy and red, but Maggie had not seen her cry.

Since Tildie was eight years old when they came to live with Maggie, she had been fiercely private, furious when anyone got too close and threatened to undo her self-control.

Maggie stifled a sigh. Tildie had lost her mother, two sets of great-grandparents and now her grandfather. How much control could one person muster?

"I'll just get rid of it." Joel's voice was husky.

"No!" Maggie and Tildie spoke simultaneously.

"Let's just put the tape away for a while, Joel," Maggie said as she stood up and moved toward the hallway. "We...I might want to hear it...sometime. I'll put it in the drawer and put a new tape in."

In the hall, she remembered Tildie had sat there only a few days ago, chatting with Andrew, telling Maggie that Sam had called. Maggie was gripped with a longing to go back to that moment in time and change something to make the outcome different. To do what? Not go with Sam? Would her absence have made any difference? Would Sam still have been at the conference instead of the gas station if she hadn't been with him? Or would he have been killed that weekend one way or another?

She picked up the phone. She had to talk to somebody about the questions that kept circling in her mind, the questions that wouldn't let her sleep.

Her neighbors, Wade and Jessie Maxwell, had been here this afternoon, but there had been no appropriate time to talk to them. They were sensible, no-nonsense people. If they thought she was crazy wondering if Sam's death was connected to his meeting with Otis, then she'd stop thinking about it.

Jessie answered on the first ring.

"Are you busy tonight after supper?" Maggie asked.

"No. Well, I'm baking for our Florida trip, Wade's outside buttoning up the place. Would you like to come over? You can help with the baking. We'd love to have you."

"That would be wonderful. I'll be there. Seven okay?"

Now that she had the appointment, Maggie felt foolish. She was just imagining things. Crazy things.

She ticked her concerns off on the fingers of one hand. Otis' bribe and fear, Sam turning down a bribe, the empty gas tank, the gunman aiming at Sam. Putting them together, it sounded scary. But dealt with one at a time by her levelheaded neighbors would be a totally different experience.

She was just overwrought causing her to be over imaginative, and in a few hours, the Maxwells would tell her so.

Thursday morning, Lincoln and Royal left the clubhouse a little after six a.m. Lincoln was anxious to tell Roy he had everything under control. Five days had passed since the Wiser job, and this was their first chance to talk in private.

The air was pleasantly cool, and the dew sparkled on the close-cropped grass. As they played and finished the first hole, he filled Roy in on the problems that had occurred over the weekend. He did not mention the Wiser woman's statement to the police regarding a NADCO connection to Samual Wiser.

Roy had just eagled the second hole as Lincoln got to the part of his narrative where he'd contacted an "eliminator."

"That's not our next step, Lincoln. Surely you know that."

Lincoln had not yet said he'd briefed the assassin on Tuesday and turned him loose. Had not said he himself had flown to Maine on Tuesday to brief Mancuso.

Royal's hundred-dollar haircut kept his salt and pepper hair perfectly in place while he scooped his ball from the hole. Lincoln stared at the top of Roy's head, stunned at the words he'd just uttered.

As Roy straightened up, Lincoln glanced down the fairway to cover his reaction. Struggling to keep his composure, he focused on his own ball sitting four feet from the hole. With a show of patience, Roy waited as Lincoln made two practice passes before gliding the putter against the ball. It rolled straight toward the hole and stopped an inch short. Lincoln let out a frustrated stream of air through his teeth.

Roy walked to the third tee and gazed down the fairway.

Lincoln snatched up his ball, muttering as he joined Roy.

Roy selected an eight-iron for a one-hundred-and-sixty-yard shot. He rested the club behind the ball, then wound it back over his shoulder and released a perfect PGA tour swing, holding the follow-through for effect.

Roy shaded his eyes as the ball soared and landed on the green, rolling to a stop some eighteen inches from the pin. Nodding in satisfaction, he turned toward Lincoln and smiled.

In spite of his best effort, Lincoln's emotions must have shown on his face, for Roy's smile disappeared and his eyes hardened for a mere second before he pulled down, like a shade, an expression of gentle sympathy.

"Lincoln, Lincoln, Lincoln. Since when has removing someone been our default setting? Hasn't such action always been our solution of last resort? We may have to consider something of that order later on, but not at this juncture."

Feeling his jaw tense, Lincoln put a crushing grip on the ball in his hand. Slipping a tee between his fingers and against the ball, he bent to push the tee into the turf and stood up. He was speechless. What could he say that wouldn't give away his thoughts?

He'd gotten where he was today by riding Roy's coattails, which was more than irksome because Lincoln had the brains. Without him Roy wouldn't be where he was today. Not even close.

Lincoln graduated second in a high school class of nine hundred. He scored 1500 on his SATs. Harvard was his parents' only choice. They could afford Ivy League.

He knew before he arrived on campus that life would be better if he were in a popular fraternity. But he wasn't naive; he didn't have the looks, the social skills to ensure his acceptance. In a couple of days, he zeroed in on sophomore Royal LaCroix as his ticket in. Roy was a tall, gifted athlete and handsome enough to be the subject of intense interest to the popular girls on campus.

Always a good planner, Lincoln managed to be in the right place to offer Roy a ride in his Miata. During the ride back to the university, Lincoln offered Roy a fifth of whiskey, letting him know he could supply more.

From that beginning, their symbiotic relationship developed. Getting Lincoln into the fraternity was a lead pipe cinch. Roy passed along to the frat brothers everything Lincoln procured for them: liquor, drugs, the answers to any multiple-choice exams they wanted. This secured Roy's position in the fraternity as top man on the totem pole. In exchange, Roy allowed Lincoln to tag along as a sidekick, to share in the bountiful social life.

It always went without saying, however, if anything went wrong and they were caught, Lincoln would be the fall guy. Probably still would be, Lincoln groused to himself as he snap-hooked his iron into a greenside bunker.

"Hey, don't take this so hard, Lincoln. You did the right thing when you took care of the original problem. But we don't want to be too hasty on this one. Two 'accidents' so close together?" He shook his head. "Uh uh. Not a good idea."

They walked to Lincoln's ball, where it was buried deep in the sand. "You need to get out here more often, Lincoln. Your swing is okay, but the results don't match the effort."

It didn't sound like Roy was talking only about golf. Finally, when he could trust his voice, Lincoln asked, "So what are our plans regarding this woman?"

"Well, first we see what she knows and, more importantly, who believes her. There are many checkpoints along the way. For instance, even if there were an investigation, I'm assuming you have a way to keep tabs on it?"

Lincoln nodded.

"An investigation would probably produce no results if your man is as good as he has always seemed to be. But even if it did, there are over-worked, underpaid law enforcement people who would appreciate an unexpected contribution to their own personal retirement fund. Then, further along the judicial system..."

Lincoln flopped his bunker shot onto the green. The ball stopped quickly, still far from the hole. "You're still away," Roy said, nodding for Lincoln to putt. "I'm sure you get the point. We have more than one tool in our arsenal."

He put his hand on Lincoln's shoulder. "We need to use the appropriate ones at the appropriate times. Not every nail requires a sledgehammer. At some point, if a situation with the woman does develop into a problem that has no other solution, you can move on solving it your way. But not yet." He dropped his hand from Lincoln's shoulder. "Never apply more force than necessary to do the job. Something I'd like for you to keep in mind."

Lincoln's mind raced. How fast could he wind this up, phone Mancuso, call off the assassin?

Lincoln's par putt spun out of the hole.

Roy dropped his birdie putt.

As they walked to the fourth hole, Lincoln had a vision of the Wiser woman, her foot frantically pumping brakes that had "failed," driving off some Maine cliff into the Atlantic Ocean.

He should be so lucky.

Lincoln noticed that Roy had stopped walking. He turned to see Roy with a bemused look on his face.

"Listen, Lincoln. I think you should get an office in Amesbury. You can keep your finger on the pulse. Enjoy autumn foliage, Indian summer. Matter of fact, why don't you oversee the whole operation for a while? On-site manager. Stick around for the winter. Get in some skiing."

Lincoln was speechless. It wasn't "clean out your desk," but it was a demotion.

"You're probably thinking three holes are enough for today," continued Roy. "Things to tend to, I imagine. Quickly."

Had he guessed how far Lincoln had already gone with the plan to eliminate the woman? It sounded like it. Lincoln had to get the hell out of here.

Get Mancuso on the phone.

And put a lid on this mess.

Minutes later, he was on a pay phone. Mancuso answered immediately.

"That guy I sent up?"

"Henry Lee?"

"Yes. Find him and call it off. Understand?"

"Yeah, I got it. But I haven't even seen him yet. Waiting for him to make contact."

"Okay, then for now your job is guarding the goods. Protect the goods in question at all cost."

Mancuso was silent.

"Artie, we can't fail. I could go down on this one. And if I go down, you go with me."

Chapter 7

Seven-thirty Thursday morning Maggie bent over, grasped the handle, and yanked upward. The overhead garage door rattled reliably through its track–the sound so ordinary and familiar, she drew solace from it.

She had stayed up until one o'clock last night talking with her neighbors, Jessie and Wade Maxwell. For hours they had turned her concerns upside down and sideways. To her surprise, they had not dismissed her questions about Sam's death. She'd found this both comforting and alarming. Truly, she'd wanted to be talked out of her fears.

Instead, they had fed them.

After a night of fitful and too little sleep, she'd awakened early and jumped from her bed to escape the dream remnants that lingered. Every night, in dreams, she relived variations on the theme of Sam's death, sometimes awakening long enough to believe it was only a dream, just to plunge into despair and horror when she realized it wasn't.

This morning, she had to do something normal, something that would convince her that some part of life remained unchanged. As she passed Pookie's room and paused, she could hear his soft snoring. They often biked together, but she couldn't bear to interrupt his peaceful sleep–to awaken him any earlier than necessary to another day of sadness.

Wanting to be out of town, away from traffic, she lifted the bike carrier from the wall. The Old School Road that wandered through fields and occasional dairy farms would be perfect.

Pookie awoke from a deep sleep. He lay in bed trying to figure out what had awakened him. The garage door, he decided. He rolled out of bed, scuffed to the second story window, and pulled the curtain aside.

His grandmother backed her ten-year-old, tan Buick out of the garage. He looked at his watch. Seven thirty-five. She must be leaving for work early. Then, with a jolt, everything came back to him. Life, as usual, had ceased to exist, and she wouldn't be going to work today, not for the rest of the week.

Below, in the driveway, his grandmother lifted the bike carrier and hooked it to the rear of the car. Pookie grabbed his jeans from the floor and, hopping on one foot, yanked them on. He snatched his shirt from the chair and scooped up his boat shoes by the door. On the way down the stairs, he pulled his shirt over his head then paused at the bottom to drop his shoes on the floor and jam his feet in.

Her bike already on the rack, she snugged down the straps and tugged on the bike to be sure it was firmly fastened. He hesitated at the screen door. Maybe she wanted to be alone. She caught sight of him as she moved toward the driver side car door. Her smile dispelled his doubts.

He pushed open the screen door. "You, ah, got room on that rack for one more bike?"

"Sure. I was wishing you could come with me, but I didn't want to wake you up."

In companionable silence, they undid and refastened the straps to include his bike and backed out of the driveway.

Maggie parked on the wide verge of the Old School Road and waited while Pookie unloaded their bikes. As they pedaled side by side, Pookie rode in his usual place, closest to traffic. For most of his fourteen years, his grandmother had ridden in this position to protect him. Last year, he had taken over this role, and without saying anything, she had let him.

Now, as they rode past cornfields, their long shadows riding beside them in the early morning sunshine, a light breeze touched him, releasing, for a moment, the heavy emotions that had descended on him when he had been told of his grandfather's death. He hadn't known his grandfather well, but he had really liked him. Yet he knew the loss suffered by his father, his sister, and especially his grandmother was so much greater than his. Of those three, his grandmother was the person he felt a need to be close to.

In the early morning stillness, there was a sudden din as a flock of crows, disturbed by something unseen, rose out of the cornfield, cawing their alarm to each other. When he saw his grandmother's mouth widen into a smile as she watched the black birds flap and fly around before settling once more into the field for their breakfast, some tense thing that had been coiled inside him relaxed.

Pookie scanned for traffic and noticed, in his mirror, a vehicle approaching from behind.

"Car," he said.

As the outside rider, he had the responsibility to give the warning that would cause his grandmother to pedal ahead; he would fall in behind her until the vehicle passed. The light blue Caprice passed them slowly, the driver turning to look at them. Probably a biker, Pookie thought. Bikers seemed to be more cautious and considerate when passing. He shifted gears and pedaled until he was once more aligned with his grandmother.

The cornfield gave way to a hay field which dropped away from the shoulder, leaving a stony embankment to their right. Near a small stream, a maple tree displayed a few early red leaves. His grandmother pointed to it, and he nodded his appreciation.

He was directing her attention to a squirrel scampering up a tree trunk when a flash in his peripheral vision pulled his gaze back to the road. From beyond the crest of the hill ahead of them, a light blue car appeared to rise out of the pavement: first the roof, then windshield, the grille, and finally the whole car. It was the same car that had passed them a couple of minutes ago. That was strange.

"Look!" his grandmother said, laughing. In front of Pookie, two chipmunks, their cheek pouches full of nuts, dashed across the road and up a nearby maple tree.

As Pookie's gaze returned to the road ahead, he realized that the car was crossing to their side of the road and accelerating rapidly. He glanced at his grandmother, but she was looking over her shoulder at the chipmunks.

When he snapped around again, the car was yards away and coming directly at them. Instinctively, Pookie turned his wheel to the right, toward his grandmother and leaned hard against her. He was vaguely aware of her pitching over the embankment as the car hit his front wheel.

In what felt like slow motion, so slow he had time to think, this is how I'm going to die, he slammed against the side of the car, and flew off his bike into the air.

Maggie caught the flash of a vehicle out of the corner of her eye a split second before she was catapulted off her bike. As she crashed to the ground on her back and slid down the hill, she watched in terror as Pookie flew over the embankment.

In the same moment, his bike spewed out from under the rear wheels of the car, flipped into the air and clattered to the ground.

Pookie tumbled down the rocky embankment and landed hard beside her. Her heart was in her throat. His ashen face appeared dazed, but he was conscious.

She scrambled onto her knees and put a restraining hand on his shoulder. "Don't move! Are you okay? Are you hurt? What happened?"

"That jerk tried to kill us!" He took a deep breath and winced in pain. "I think I broke something."

She reached for his pulse as he went limp.

Jewel decided to have one last breakfast at Hal's Diner and then he'd head out. Nothing more to keep him here. But before his coffee was poured, he heard scraps of conversation that included the Wiser woman's name. By the end of his meal, he knew that the moron had tried and failed to ice the woman. A hit and run. A grandson, presumably the owner of the sneakers in the Wiser house, had been taken to the ER. Now Jewel was irritated. He himself put a great deal of planning and thought into his jobs, and this buffoon had bungled a simple hit and run! And gotten the wrong victim. He bet that would complicate things for NADCO.

He dropped a tip on the table and headed out. Contemptuous of the incompetent bonehead who'd replaced him, Jewel knew he wasn't quite ready to leave.

At the office, Lincoln paced, willing his phone to ring. Every time he glanced at his watch, only a few minutes had passed. Mentally, he kicked himself for his impetuous decision that had led to this, then raged inside at Royal Fucking LaCroix.

Whatever happened, it was not going to be good. Even if Mancuso stopped Henry Lee, Lincoln would still be exiled to spend the winter in Purgatory, Maine. He was clear on that.

If Mancuso failed and the woman eliminated, Lincoln would make a break from here; there was cash in his safe and his passport was ready. He'd have to make two stops to pick up the rest of his accumulated cash retirement fund on the way to the airport. It'd be a one-way flight. To anywhere but here.

An hour and a half later the cell phone rang. He pushed the button. "Yes?"

"Station four," Mancuso's voice rumbled through the earpiece. Then he hung up.

Lincoln left the office and ten minutes later dialed the phone number to a public booth that Mancuso had designated as station four, one of eight they used for secure phone calls.

"Yeah?" Mancuso answered.

"Well?"

"You might have a complication. Maybe not."

"Artie, for God's sake, what the hell happened?"

"I'm gonna tell you. She went for a bike ride with the kid this morning. They loaded the bikes on her car and drove out to a country road–no houses, no cars–and off-loaded the bikes. My guy went to where they started, but figured, hey, you can't tail someone on a bicycle on a country road without being made, so he went back to pick 'em up when they got back into town. Thing is...they didn't come back."

"What the–"

"Whoa. They came back. In a fucking ambulance."

"And?" Lincoln had the phone jammed against his ear. His other hand pressed against his temple on the other side.

"And I figured if they was in the ambulance, I'd know where to pick 'em up later. Then I drove up the road to see if I could figure out what happened. What I found was the bikes–one of them mangled. Run over."

"But she wasn't dead."

"Wasn't even her. It was the boy. And he ain't dead, neither."

"Christ." This was a colossal screw up. Lincoln conceded Roy's point, now. If the woman had been wiped out by a convincing accident, it would have stretched belief in coincidence as far as it could be stretched. But if the boy had been taken out, then a third accident to take care of the woman would be inconceivable.

"It was Lee," Mancuso said. Lincoln could tell Mancuso had lit up a cigarette. He heard the rattling exhale.

"But he found me an hour later," Mancuso continued. "I called him off. Told him to stick around and lay low until I got back to him."

Lincoln exhaled. He didn't realize he'd been holding his breath. "Good."

"Ah..."

"Ah what, Artie?"

"He's, ah...I guess you'd say weird. He weren't none too happy when I told him to hold off. I guess he wants to collect and leave."

"Tell him to stick around until you hear from me. He's got the down payment. We might still need him. We'll have to see how this plays out."

"Yeah, well, I'll tell him."

"Okay, any suspicions raised about the accident?"

"Boy's got a broken arm. Granny went with the police back to the scene but looks like they're treating it as an accidental hit-and-run."

Lincoln wouldn't have to tell Roy about this. He was damp with relief.

"This is ass-backwards now, Artie, but do whatever you have to do to keep that Wiser woman alive."

Ten o'clock Thursday night in pitch-black without a flashlight, Maggie slipped out of her back door and headed across the grass, still damp from the brief but torrential downpour an hour ago. The tall, thickly-tangled hedgerow created an effective barrier around her entire backyard–except for the one small, nearly invisible footpath Pookie had created when he was six.

She had been transplanting hostas one morning while Pookie, with his glove on one hand, repeatedly tossed a baseball into the air. She'd glanced up, and he had disappeared in the space of a minute. She screamed his name; he answered her immediately–from the other side of the hedgerow. It had taken her several minutes before she could find the opening that Pookie had slipped through when he'd heard sounds of sawing in the backyard beyond his. That's how she got to know the Maxwells.

Through the years, the path had widened slightly, but if you didn't know it was there, you wouldn't find it. She slipped through it now, pushing aside familiar branches, and came out into the Maxwells' backyard.

Wade Maxwell, who celebrated his seventy-sixth birthday in July, was almost a generation older than Maggie. His wife Jessie split the difference; she was sixty-seven. Despite the age differences between Maggie and the Maxwells, they had been friends ever since Pookie discovered their backyard.

As Maggie entered, she saw Jessie at her kitchen counter wrapping sandwiches and placing them in a cooler. Her tall, angular figure was softened by the fine, silvery white hair piled gracefully on top of her head and fastened in a bun. Short wisps of hair escaped the hair pins and fell damply against the back of her neck.

Maggie looked at the piles of wrapped food on the counter. The Maxwells carried along a three-day supply in their Airstream trailer so they could avoid eating at greasy spoons while on the road, Jessie always said.

"Looks like you're almost ready to leave," Maggie observed. "I should have thought to bring over some of the leftovers in our refrigerator and freezer. I can't believe how much people brought. Violet does most of our cooking so it's not like we were going to go hungry."

"Folks feel better when they can do something," said Jessie. "Death makes 'em feel helpless. Baking and fussing, well, they feel like they're helping."

Maggie pulled out a chair from the kitchen table and sat down.

"How's Pookie?" Jessie asked.

"In bed. Asleep. They gave him a shot to ease his pain, and then they put the cast on. I'm not sure if the shot has completely worn off yet. And something like this tires you out even if you're a kid."

Jessie wiped her hands on a kitchen towel and joined Maggie at the table. "How serious is it?"

"It's just a fracture, and there wasn't much swelling. He'll only have to wear the cast for three weeks, they said."

"Shame about the bike. Probably can't be fixed? He loved that bike."

"Yeah, he did," Maggie said. "And no, it can't be fixed. On the upside, Joel has promised they'll go shopping for a replacement next week. Pookie is excited about that."

Wade carried a huge suitcase and two duffle bags into the kitchen and put them near the back door. Across the table from Maggie, he turned a chair around and straddled it. His narrow, handsome, weathered-tanned face was a wonder to her. She had never seen anyone with so many wrinkles, and they all seemed to form a map composed solely of deep smile lines that ended at his small, elegant chin. His handsome face was dominated by the most splendid mustache she had ever seen. It made him look like Sam Elliot. Maggie could tell he'd been a good-looking man in his youth, but age had added character to his face. At seventy-six, he was so arrestingly interesting to look at that people had trouble taking their eyes off him. But the most riveting thing about Wade was the shrewd intelligence that sparkled in his blue eyes, especially when he grinned.

He pulled a pipe from the sooty pocket of his green work pants and tapped it in the ashtray in front of him. Unburned tobacco and ashes fell from the pipe. "Boy's okay?"

The question was not as casual as Wade tried to make it. He was enormously fond of Pookie. The two of them had formed a mutual attachment that first summer as Pookie followed Wade around, learning how to use a hammer and a saw.

"He's going to be okay. It'll be healed before basketball season begins. Matter of fact, they just put a soft cast on it–said he could start cross-country in a couple of weeks. He's mad, though. He's convinced it was a deliberate hit and run."

Wade and Jessie exchanged looks.

"You reported it to the police?" Wade asked.

"Yes, of course. Well, the emergency room physician asked me to. Two policemen came to the hospital and talked to Pookie. Then I went out to show them where it happened. Not that it was helpful. There wasn't anything to see except the bikes. I heard one of them say to the other that it was probably some teenager who has the car hidden in his father's garage, wondering how he's going to explain the dents."

Wade scraped the bowl of his pipe with a tool he carried in his shirt pocket. "Been thinking about what you told us last night. I nosed around a little today. The Archibald property has a mortgage on it."

"Really?" Maggie was startled. "It was my understanding when Thomas Archibald left the property to his grandson, it was supposed to become a wildlife refuge. At that time, it was free and clear of encumbrances. I'm sure of that. He was a client."

"Well, don't know how, but does look like the property is moving toward foreclosure. Take a while, though. Won't happen right away."

He tapped the pipe in the ashtray again. "So Oxley could be right." He pulled a tobacco pouch from his pants pocket, unfolded it, and tapped the contents toward the open edge of the packet.

He glanced at her. "I been 'supposing' all day. Just suppose, Maggie, for the sake of an argument, everything Oxley said was true."

His clear blue eyes held hers for a moment. Then he gave his attention to tapping the pouch, shaking tobacco into the bowl of his pipe. He tamped it down, moving the stem from side to side and filled it again. Maggie watched, fascinated. He was the only person she knew for whom lighting a pipe was an art form.

"Suppose..." He looked at her again. "Suppose this company, NADCO, is it? If this company was planning a mall *and* a high-end development, seems like it could mean big money for the developers. Multi-millions, I would say." He clamped the pipe stem in his teeth and pulled a match book out of his shirt pocket. "Got to be. They offered Sam, alone, a half million-dollar bribe. You go spreading bribes like that around here and there and you can burn a hole in your profits pretty quickly.

"Anyway, let's say, for now, that things happened the way you think they did–this guy killed Sam on purpose. It happened right after Sam refused to take a bribe Friday afternoon. Overnight, a tank full of gas..." He pulled a match from the matchbook, put the head between the cover and striking strip and pulled. He touched the flame to the tobacco and drew on the stem. The flame bent to the tobacco as he dragged air through the pipe. "A tank full of gas came up empty. So you have to stop for gas. They get their business taken care of away from home where nobody's going to give a hoot who Samuel Wiser is."

Wade tapped his teeth with the stem of the pipe and squinted, a faraway look in his eyes. "We could be all wet on this. But I'm inclined to think we're not. And if we're not..." He shook his head. "If we're not, we've got an immediate problem." He lit another match, touched it to the tobacco and puffed on his pipe. The sweet aroma of apple tobacco filled the air.

"What problem?"

"You."

"What about me?"

"You're a witness."

"Well, I'm sure the police don't see it that way. And they haven't caught the guy yet, anyway. I called them yesterday morning."

"The guy, who, if we're right, can be referred to as the 'hit man,' probably isn't important anymore. His job's done. Whoever hired him is who would be interested in you."

Jessie patted Maggie's hand. "Wade hardly slept last night, thinking about this. We're worried about you."

A sliver of fear sliced through Maggie's stomach. "What are you saying? You think *my* life is in danger?"

Wade nodded. "Yours...and Pookie's, it would seem."

Maggie's stomach lurched. "So you think Pookie is right? It was a hit and run?"

"Don't want to go sounding over-dramatic, but this is something to give serious thought to. Those kids depend on you. And you've still got a lot of livin' to do, yourself." Wade's face cracked into his customary grin, showing perfect teeth. "You've got to catch up to me."

"Or at least me," Jessie said.

Wade leaned over and kissed her forehead. "I haven't even caught up to you yet."

"It's true," Jessie said. "But you're not done."

Maggie weighed Wade's words. She would have thought she'd be relieved if Wade and Jessie had simply reassured her she wasn't crazy. But now they were painting a picture larger than her fears. She hadn't imagined that was possible. "Should I talk to the police again?"

Wade glanced at Jessie, shrugged, and then spoke. "Lemme ask you a couple of questions. When they took your statement at the station, it was a detective?"

"Yes."

"And you told him about the attempt to bribe Sam? What did he say?"

"He didn't really say anything. Like an afterthought, he made a few quick notes in his notebook, the name of NADCO, but the look on his face was like he was trying to be patient. Like he thought I was being silly, but he wanted to be polite."

Wade nodded; his eyes narrowed.

"Let me tell you right now, I believe they are not going to investigate this–the NADCO connection. Looking at it from their point of view, I can see why. But I think very likely there is something to all this."

Maggie wanted Wade to be wrong–wanted herself to be mistaken. "I can't believe all this. I mean I know what I saw, but I can't believe that puts me in danger. I'm not sure I could even recognize the man if he were standing in front of me."

"It's not important what you think you can do," Wade said. 'What *they* think you can do, that's what's important. Listen. Will you do something for me?"

"What?"

"Walk home through the backyard. Don't go inside, don't talk to your family. Just get in your car and drive a few blocks downtown and back. Stay where there's plenty of streetlights and traffic. If you have the chance, try a quick turn without signaling. I'll be around watching. Give me a five-minute lead, okay? Just want to see if anyone follows you. Won't tell us anything if no one is tailing you. Will tell us a lot, though, if they are."

"Wade." Jessie traced the pattern on her tablecloth with her index finger. "Is this necessary? We don't want to make Maggie a sitting duck."

"I don't believe she'll be in any immediate danger. If our theory is right, NADCO went to some lengths to keep Sam's death from looking like a hit. It would be even more critical for Maggie's death to look like an accident. They need time to set up an accident. Another accident."

Maggie's nerves were on end. They were discussing her possible demise. The vision of Sam's coffin poised above the grave flicked across her mind.

The sight of Pookie's crumpled bike replaced it. Followed by a surge of anger.

She didn't need to protect only herself.

She had to protect her family.

"Okay, I'll do it," she firmly said. "I've got a spare key in the garage."

Twenty minutes later Maggie was back in Jessie's kitchen helping her wrap the ginger snaps they had made last night. They made small talk about the trip to Florida, wanting to postpone any real discussion until Wade came back.

Five minutes later, he came through the door. The look on his face chilled her to the bone.

"Jessie, honey, is there any coffee left in that pot?" Wade pulled three mugs from a rack near the stove.

"No. Let me make a fresh pot."

Wade said, "Tea good for you?" He raised his eyebrows in question at Maggie. She nodded.

"Jessie, don't bother with the coffee. I don't want you fussing around over the stove. I need you here." He pulled a chair back for her, ran the tap water, and put three mugs in the microwave.

He looked at Maggie as he sat down. "You were followed. I wish to Christ I was wrong on this. Right now, he's back where he can see your house again, parked up the road apiece."

He glanced at Jessie; in a long second, something passed between them. Maggie sank into a chair across from Wade. The microwave dinged. Wade got up, dropped teabags into each cup and brought them to the table. "Let's talk. Is there any place you could go? We're pulling out tonight. We can deliver you anywhere. Didn't you tell us about Sam's aunt you visited a few years ago? Somewhere in the Carolinas? North Carolina, wasn't it?"

Maggor nodded, but half an hour later, she was still saying, "no."

"Wade, I can't. I can't leave Stoney without notice. It would take weeks to interview and hire someone to replace me and a month to train someone to take over my accounts. A month at best."

Jessie took the empty cups to the sink and came back. "I know Benjamin Stonefield. He'll cope. He'll get some accounting student in and pay them minimum wage. That's the way he started you."

"And I can't leave the kids. Especially now, with Pookie in a cast."

"Listen, Maggie," Wade said. "I know how close you are to the kids. But if you're in the crosshairs, then everyone in your household's in danger. You've already seen what could happen to Pookie. Ruthless people don't care if a kid is fourteen if he gets in their way. Suppose someone decided to ram a semi into your car and Pookie or Tildie was in the passenger seat. What if they decided to torch your house with an electrical fire? Rig your furnace to produce carbon monoxide?"

Fear crawled through Maggie's body, cramping her stomach, numbing her fingertips.

Jessie cleared her throat. "Maggie, even if nothing happened to them, do you want to put them through grieving for you? Haven't they lost enough?"

Again, Maggie saw Sam's coffin–imagining Joel, Tildie, and Pookie standing by her coffin before it was lowered into the ground and then returning to the house without her.

Forever.

She started to speak, had to clear her throat and begin again. "Do you agree with all this, Jessie?"

"I'm afraid I do. Listen, if Wade's wrong you haven't lost much. But if he's right, well, the consequences of you letting yourself be a target are unacceptable as far as I'm concerned."

"I have to think about it. Talk to Joel...talk to Stoney and see what they say."

Wade shook his head. "Can't do that, Maggie."

"What are you suggesting? Leave *without* talking to them?"

"Yep. Going on the assumption that I'm right, your house, your telephone are already bugged. They'll be listening, trying to get a sense of your schedule, trying, maybe, to find out what you know."

The idea of someone violating the privacy of her home was so offensive, she was at a loss for words.

"You don't want to tip anybody off," Jessie said. "You need to disappear without a trace. Just a few weeks, maybe, then see what happens."

"But I have to tell them. Tell Joel, tell the kids. They'll think I've been kidnapped."

"You can take care of that. Go home, don't say anything–just normal conversation. When they've gone to bed, pack a bag, only a few things. Leave them notes that you have to get away for a little while. They'll understand with the stress you've been under. Say they'll hear from you soon. We'll work out a plan where you can keep in touch."

"But you can't mean I'm in danger right now, tonight. Let me talk to Joel away from the house. I'll do it tomorrow."

Wade shook his head. "Sam turned down the bribe on Friday. Saturday afternoon he was dead."

Jessie put her hand on Maggie's again. "It's thinking of your family needing you that's holding you up. But they have Joel."

"This afternoon he said he canceled his next trip. He's planning on being around for a while."

"Good. And they've got Violet. Good God, Maggie, with that woman around, they don't even really need you." Jessie smiled.

Maggie nodded weakly. "Yeah. I guess."

Wade scraped back the chair and stood up. "I've got a few more things to take care of before we leave. Why don't you two look over the atlas and find out how we get to North Carolina on the way to Florida. That aunt of Sam's. Do you have her address?"

"Not memorized. It's in my address book on the computer."

Heading for the back door, Wade glanced over his shoulder. "Don't look it up on the computer," he said with a firmness that convinced her.

"If you can find Beaufort, North Carolina, I can find her house," Maggie replied. "She'd be in the phone book. I could call her when we get close."

Wade's tall, slender frame paused in the doorway. Suddenly he broke into one of his dazzling, multi-wrinkled smiles. "You're looking a little peaked. Let's go take a vacation."

He started out of the door then turned.

"Please, Maggie. Do it like we discussed. No cheating. Our lives may depend on it, too."

The thought caught Maggie by surprise, nearly taking her breath away. It implied someone would try to kill her, and the Maxwells, as well, while they were driving away. "Then I can't put you both in danger."

The door firmly clicked shut behind Wade.

Jessie shook her head gently and caught Maggie's eye. "We're going to be okay." She patted Maggie's hand in an uncharacteristic gesture. "Do you know what Wade did during the war?"

Maggie couldn't remember Wade ever having mentioned the war. "No, what?"

Jessie chuckled. "We'll have to tell you about it someday."

Except for a small light over the kitchen stove, the house was dark when she finally arrived home; everyone had gone to bed. The microwave clock showed it was ten minutes after midnight. She turned out the light, found her way through the dark house, and climbed the stairs to her bedroom.

Most of the wall across the room from the door was taken up by a deep, bay window made up of four separate, tall windows.

Leaving the light off, she crossed the room, pulled aside the lace curtain that hung from the angled window and peered through an open mini-blind. At the intersection of Maple and Waverly, the dark car that Wade said followed her was parked just out of the glare of the streetlight.

Panic gripped her. Her hand shook as she twisted the wands of the four blinds that lined the windows. Her nerves jumped at a nighttime creak of the house. Sitting at the desk in her bedroom, she snapped on the green-shaded, brass desk lamp, and pulled out several sheets of stationery. In the dim light, she wrote notes to each member of the family saying she needed a rest and would be in touch soon. She asked for their understanding.

Then, as she sealed the last envelope, she realized, in a moment of crystal clarity, the whole thing–the conspiracy theory, the need to run–was ridiculous. The car parked up the street simply belonged to an overnight visitor of the Poulin family whose house was near the corner. Pookie had been hit by a careless teenager. She would wake in the morning, and in the light of day, see how silly this all was. In relief, she threw the notes into her wastebasket. It was one o'clock in the morning and time for bed. She snapped off the lamp.

Headlights of a passing car swept slowly across her window blinds and fear seized her again. She lifted a single blind and peeked out of a corner of the window. Her heart hammered as a light-colored sedan, maybe blue, passed under a streetlight and continued on. Was it the blue car that had hit Pookie?

She glanced in the other direction and noted the dark car was still at the intersection. As she was about to release the blind, a tiny red spark glowed brightly from inside the car and then dimmed. Someone was inside the car, smoking.

Ears alert for the sound of a returning car, she snapped on the lamp again and pulled the notes from the wastebasket. Then she added one for Stoney apologizing for leaving with no notice and giving him a list of priorities for her clients.

The small weekend suitcase she had used for her trip with Sam stood, still unpacked, in a corner of the room. She couldn't bring herself to touch it yet. Her large suitcase was stored in the attic. If she tried to retrieve it, she would wake everyone. She rummaged through the top shelf of her closet and produced a tattered brown gym bag that she had used when she and Stoney used to play racquetball.

By the faint light of the desk lamp, she threw only what would fit into the small bag–three changes of jeans and shirts, sweats to use as pajamas, and five changes of underwear, socks. One pair of sneakers. That would hold her for a few days. She yanked the zipper shut.

If she stayed away any longer than that, she'd buy more clothes. She went back to her bureau and dragged out another change of clothing and pulled it on over the clothes she was wearing.

In the bathroom, she grabbed a spare toothbrush, a hairbrush, shampoo, and a few articles of makeup, but there was no way to fit them into the bulging gym bag. She looked around frantically, grabbed a pillow from her bed, peeled off the case, and stuffed the toiletries inside.

Sitting on the side of her bed, she checked her wallet. Four of the five twenty-dollar bills that she had withdrawn from the ATM in anticipation of shopping in Boston were still there as well as the change she'd gotten from the gas station and an "emergency" fifty that she always carried. It was plenty.

She paused, held her breath, and listened carefully to the sounds of the house. Nothing unusual, she decided. She expelled her breath. She had one more letter to write. Sitting at the desk once again, she wrote a letter to Violet asking her to deliver Stoney's note to him, asking her to make sure Joel took Pookie to the doctor for a checkup, and finally, apologizing for leaving her with so much responsibility.

As she sealed the envelope and wrote Violet's name on it, she felt a searing anger at Sam. If he hadn't been so goddam stubborn and gotten himself killed, she wouldn't be leaving her family right now. Life would be as it was a week ago. Then she was swallowed up in remorse and guilt. Sam, whose crime had simply been integrity, was irretrievably gone. She was still alive.

At the door, she took a last, swift look around, then crossed the room and picked up a gold-framed photo of Joel, Tildie, Pookie, and Sam taken at Tildie's high school graduation. She slipped the picture into the pillowcase, slung her pocketbook over her shoulder, and picked up the letters. She paused at the top of the stairs and listened. Nothing. She tiptoed down the stairs, put the letters on the hall table, and headed down the hall toward the kitchen.

A few feet from the back door, she stopped and retraced her steps through the dark house to the front hall. She fumbled in the drawer of the telephone table until her fingers touched the message tape with Sam's voice on it. She dropped it into her pocketbook and headed back.

As she came down the hall into the kitchen, she heard a furtive noise at the back door—a tiny scraping sound. Then a tap and more scraping. She stood paralyzed, fear shooting through her limbs from some central core. The blinds, closed over the door's window, were slightly illuminated by the yard light next door. For a second there was no sound save the blood pounding in her head. Then a shadow crossed the lower half of the window followed by more quiet scratching on the glass.

Her first instinct was to run from the danger. But the intruder would be in the house before she could even get upstairs to warn the others.

The others.

She couldn't let this menace near her family. Not taking her eyes off the moving shadow, she silently lowered her bags to the floor, pulled open the knife drawer, and extracted the carving knife. She looked at the weapon and realized it was no good. The intruder would never let her get that close without overpowering her.

The shadow grew larger as if someone were straightening up. She grabbed the large cast iron frying pan off the counter and stepped behind the door. If he came in, she would hit him from behind.

She raised the frying pay to shoulder level. The shadow moved down, disappeared, then moved up again. More tapping on the glass. Silence. Then a scratching sound on metal.

Through her fog of fear, it dawned on her that the sounds weren't threatening; they had an almost random quality. She tried to sense, to feel, the threat on the other side of the door. Though the sounds continued, she realized if someone were actually trying to get in, they would probably have succeeded by now.

Resting the pan on her shoulder, she reached out, grabbed the pull strings on the blind and yanked it open. Staring through the window at her were two small black eyes. Startled, the raccoon ducked down, leaped off the top of the trash can and ambled out of sight into the black night.

Weak with relief, Maggie sagged against the wall, laughing at herself. This had happened a couple of years ago, only then it had been a skunk that had come to rummage in their trash. And if she hadn't been so spooked, so nerved up tonight, she would have remembered that.

She replaced the pan on the counter and picked up her bags. She opened the back door a crack and listened once more. No sound other than cricket chirps disturbed the damp night air. She scanned the yard before edging outside. Through wisps of ground fog, she crossed the yard and slipped through the hedgerow.

Wade and Jessie pulled out of the yard at three a.m., hauling the trailer with Maggie in it behind them. Instead of turning right and heading for the Interstate as she had expected, the Dodge Ram extended cab pickup turned left and wound away from the residential area. Maggie watched from the darkened interior of the Airstream as bits and pieces of familiar terrain slipped by the window.

When they reached a sparsely populated country road, Wade doused his headlights and drove by the ambient light of the half-moon that was just above the horizon. The road, dotted with dairy and chicken farms, twisted and turned in gentle curves. After the road had risen and fallen in a series of small hills, he turned abruptly into a small, wooded lane and parked.

Maggie's nerves were on edge. Isolated in the Airstream, she had no way of knowing if Wade and Jessie had seen something or if he was just being cautious. Five minutes passed before Wade backed out. He must have been convinced they were not being followed, since he now headed for the Interstate. This taste of intrigue increased Maggie's tension. Once on the Interstate, it was easy to imagine a car coming up beside and spraying their trailer with gun fire. For a while, she flinched whenever a car passed them.

After an hour, she lay down and dozed off, every once in a while jerking awake in alarm. As the first traces of light announced the dawn, a sense of unreality engulfed her. What was Margaret Wiser doing bumping along in a trailer, rapidly separating herself from family and friends? They didn't even know she was gone yet.

She noticed the fine thread of a spider web trailing from the top of the window just above her head. "Well, little guy," she said to the small spider swinging from the silver thread. "We're both headed away from home. At least I had something to say about it." Rummaging around in the cupboards, she found what she wanted and then sat down waiting for the spider to ground itself.

Chapter 8

Maggie was roused from a fitful sleep an hour later when they pulled into a rest stop on the Massachusetts Turnpike. Seconds after the pickup came to a halt, Jessie opened the trailer door and sunshine spilled into the trailer. "Time for a break, and then you'll probably want to join us in the truck. I'm going to drive for a while. Come sit in front and ride shotgun."

A stab of fear sliced through Maggie until Jessie burst out laughing. "I'm sorry, Maggie. Poor choice of words. Oh, Lord, you should have seen your face. How about, 'Come sit in front and be my co-pilot?' Wade can sit in the back seat."

Maggie grinned "Well, you did give me a start. You imagine all kinds of things when you're back here. Including shotguns under the front seat."

Shaky from the burst of adrenaline and stiff from lying in one position too long, Maggie gingerly tested her knees and then reached back to pick up something from the arm of the couch.

"I have something for you," she said.

She descended the trailer steps and handed an upside-down glass to Jessie. "This little guy is a stowaway."

Jessie reached out to take the glass that was closed off with an old postcard. "What…?"

"It's a spider. I thought we should release him here."

Jessie squinted at Maggie. "I'm curious. Why didn't you just kill him? Squeamish?"

"No," Maggie laughed. "It's just that I never kill spiders. They have their place in the world. Every living thing has its place in the world. I always carry them outside. I taught the kids to do the same. Nobody kills things in our house."

"I see," said Jessie, taking the glass holding cell from Maggie's hands. "Come on." She walked to the edge of the parking lot.

Jessie bent down and carefully released the spider. "There you go. A change of living quarters. Maybe for the better. It's probably warmer here than in Maine. And you can thank her for that," she said, nodding toward Maggie. Jessie placed the glass and postcard inside the door of the trailer and closed it. Maggie felt a tiny bit of tension leave her midsection and nodded with relief. At least she had saved something.

Inside the building, at the end of a hall was a bank of public telephones. An enormous impulse, like a physical urge, hit her. She wanted to phone home. It's what you did if you were in trouble. You turned to your family. You at least phoned to say you were okay.

Jessie glanced back at her and shook her head. Maggie forced her feet to move past her link with home.

At eight, they stopped somewhere in Connecticut and Maggie offered to drive. It felt good to get behind the wheel. Jessie rode in the back seat, and Wade sat in the front dividing his attention between his side view mirror and passing cars. Finally, he relaxed enough to doze.

Ten-thirty, Friday morning Lincoln Montgomery stepped into a booth at Kennedy International Airport. He'd gotten a phone call on his office phone forty-five minutes ago. Arturo Mancuso needed to talk to him. Mancuso answered before the end of the first ring. "Yeah."

"What is it?" If the news was bad, Lincoln didn't want to chitchat.

On the other end of the line Mancuso took a drag and exhaled. "She's gone."

Lincoln's heart slammed in his chest. "He took her out?"

"No, I don't mean that kind of gone. She flew the coop. Without a trace."

Lincoln groped for the meaning in Mancuso's words. "You think she got spooked and ran?"

"Can't say why, but she's gone. Looks like sometime last night. From her house."

"You were supposed to be watching her around the clock."

"Yeah, we were."

"Bullshit."

"I'm telling you."

"You couldn't have been watching, or she wouldn't be missing. You stopped to eat; you took a leak."

"No." Mancuso's gravelly voice rumbled with dead certainty. "No, sir. We're not amateurs. We watch in four-hour shifts. My guys bring food and drink with them. And a piss bottle. We don't miss anything. But last night I was on all night. Nothing got by me. I'd stake my job on it."

We both might stake our jobs on it, Lincoln thought. "You've been doing an audio surveillance?"

131

"That's what tipped us. This morning her family was beefing about how she lit out without saying goodbye."

"But you don't think it was our friend eager to get the job done?"

"I don't think so. She went into her house and didn't come out. And we don't have a body."

"I want to be on site, but I can't get there until Monday."

"Yes, sir," Mancuso rasped.

Lincoln thought for a moment. "Bring me a copy of the surveillance tape. Meet me this afternoon at the bar in Queens. Four o'clock. Can you make it?"

"Yeah, I can catch a flight out of Portland in a couple of hours."

Lincoln hung up and sat staring at the push button numbers of the pay phone. Three possibilities occurred to him. Jewel had managed to take her out, even if she wasn't part of the contract. Or Henry Lee had abducted her and taken her out, but that would constitute an egregious violation of the contract–having her missing then turning up dead. No way to call that an accident.

The other possibility caused Lincoln's heartbeat to race. What if the cops had decided she had to be protected? But why? As far as he could tell from his source in the police station there was no investigation. Could it be the Feds? Was NADCO already in their line of sight? Did they wave off the local police?

The fucking Feds?

Wouldn't that just be the cherry on top of this colossal friggin' mess?

Just before the Tappan Zee Bridge in New York, Wade woke up and looked around.

"You want me to take over now before you get to the bridge? Traffic will be heavy once we get across the bridge–from here to...well, it's hectic until we get past D.C."

Maggie shook her head. "If you don't mind, I'd like to drive a little longer. I've never driven through New York and New Jersey before..." She turned toward Wade and smiled broadly. "And I wasn't hauling a trailer at the time." Jessie guffawed. Wade shook his head, and, she suspected, rolled his eyes.

When they approached the middle of the bridge, traffic came to a standstill. The truck was hot inside, so Maggie rolled the driver's side window down and was rewarded by a cool breeze off the Hudson River.

"Maggie? You okay?" Wade studied the river on his side trying to make his question sound casual.

She turned to look at Wade and then realized the traffic had begun rolling. She let the clutch out and moved slowly forward in first gear. "Just lost in thought."

"Maggie, there's a lot I have to tell you about how to stay hidden. No use being this careful now and having them pinpoint you in North Carolina in a couple of days."

Maggie nodded. "Go ahead."

"Can't use your credit cards."

"What?"

From the back seat, Jessie patted Maggie's shoulder. "If they're any good they can track you by your purchases. If they can't, they can intercept a copy of your credit card bill. Take them a bit longer, but they'll still find you. Most people don't realize when they use their plastic money, they leave a trail so wide, it's like a herd of elephants going through jungle undergrowth."

"Well, then I'll just call my bank and have them transfer money to a bank in North Carolina. Assuming, of course, that Sam's aunt can take me in for a few days."

Wade shook his head. "Tell me, do you check on your bank account by computer? Or telephone?"

"Telephone."

"You have a code number?"

"Of course."

"You have it written down?"

Her mouth clamped shut. Guiltily, she thought of the personal identification number taped to the front of her office telephone.

"I can get Stoney to wire funds from our business account."

She could tell in her peripheral vision that Wade was looking at her. She took her eyes from the road and glanced at him. His raised eyebrow told her to be serious.

"But how could that be traced?"

"Anything that leaves an electronic trail is traceable. Everyone knows you're a partner at Stonefield and Wiser. Wouldn't be too hard to access either the business account or any personal account Ben has."

"There must be a way."

"Not for now, there isn't," Jessie said. "Wait a bit until the heat is off. When they come up empty, they'll check again, but as days or weeks go by, they'll check less frequently. Eventually, they'll stop. Likely, anyhow."

Maggie pushed her hair behind her left ear then massaged her temple. Weeks. "How will we know when that happens? I can't–I won't–stay away for very long."

"Because," replied Wade, "we'll find ways to see if they're still looking for you. Easy as catching a politician in a lie. Drop some bait here and there and see when they stop snapping at it."

"Like what kind of bait?"

"I'm thinking we, Jessie and I, we pick up a bunch of postcards in Florida, get them to you. You write them out…saying, 'having a great time. See you soon…' and we mail them from various cities and towns in Florida. We'll see if they come looking."

"And if they do?"

Wade laughed and glanced sideways at her. "Then we do some planning. Call it stage two."

"We could go to the police."

"We'll see. Not likely, though."

Maggie turned and glanced at Wade. His mustache broadened as he broke into a wide grin. Maggie had never seen his face so animated. He was enjoying himself!

He said, "You'll have to stay out of sight for a while."

"Well, yes," she said. "That's why we're headed to Beaufort." She put on her left blinker and slid into the passing lane.

"No, I mean really out of sight. You can't peek your nose outside in daylight–maybe not at night, either. I can tell better when I see the layout of the place."

Maggie stifled the urge to giggle. This cloak and dagger stuff was just too much. How in the world would anyone possibly find her in North Carolina if they hadn't followed the Airstream, and if she hadn't left an electronic trail, as Wade called it? Assuming someone was trying to. Frowning, she signaled to switch back to the right lane and tried to puzzle it out herself.

He finally broke the silence. "Give up?"

She smiled, knowing he was getting a kick out of reading her face. She nodded.

"Didn't you say your Aunt Belle's address is in your computer address book?"

"Yes...and probably in my Christmas card address book in the hall drawer." Suddenly, a knot formed in her stomach. "You're saying they'll search my house." But the answer to her own question dawned on her before she finished the statement. If someone was after her, of course they'd search her house. In fact, now that she thought of it, if her telephone was bugged, they would have already entered her home. She hadn't thought through the implications of that when Wade first mentioned it, but now, thinking someone had invaded her house chilled her to her depths.

A wild need to protect her home from intruders gripped her. She had retreated and left her home unguarded, open to violation by strangers. She pictured Joel's room, Pookie's room, Tildie's room, and her own room. She was gripped with belly-tightening anger.

She finally realized Wade had been speaking.

"...and if they really know their stuff, no one will notice anything's been touched. You've been gone for" – he looked at his watch and calculated– "nine hours. Likely, they're only just figuring out you're gone. They'd have to watch your house for a while, catch a time when everyone's gone. If they've got electronic surveillance already going, it's easier for them to pinpoint when it would be safe to go in. Families talk about where they're going, when they'll be back. They may search today because they'll figure everyone will be home over the weekend. Monday at the latest."

"And then what?"

"I figure by the time they put together a list, prioritize it, and divide it up, we'll be in Beaufort and have you out of sight."

"So, assuming all this is true, they'll go to Aunt Belle's?"

"No doubt," said Jessie. "They'll try the most obvious possibilities first. Likely have several operatives looking for you if they're good. And they probably are."

Wade nodded in agreement. "Hand me one of those nutritious raspberry turnovers, Jessie darling? Maggie? Oh, no, you're probably on a diet," he teased.

Maggie was stunned. How could he eat at a time like this? Her stomach was in knots. Maggie shook her head at the turnover Jessie tried to hand her.

Jessie asked, "Who will be on that list, Maggie?"

"Uh, I don't have much family left. A great aunt. Lives in Lewiston. A couple of cousins. How would NADCO know who is the most obvious?"

"Anybody located close by, for starters. Is there any way to separate friends from family in your book?"

She shook her head. "No."

"Okay, my guess is they'll start with the closest addresses, and they'll also be very interested in anyone whose last name is Wiser. Or Shaughnessy."

"How would they know my maiden name?"

"If they did a dossier on Sam when this whole thing started, they've already got it. Depends on how big an operation they have and how thorough they are. You got married in Amesbury?"

She nodded.

Wade took a huge bite out of the turnover and chewed in obvious enjoyment. With a forefinger he brushed particles of pastry from the underside of his mustache. After he swallowed he said, "Records are easy to get."

"Aunt Belle's name is Wiser," Maggie said.

"Uh huh. You told me."

"Well, then why're we going there?"

"That's why we're driving straight through. Get you settled before anyone shows up. One of us should sleep now. Jessie, can you navigate while I nod off here? Wake me up when you're tired, Maggie."

She nodded. A wiggle of fear squirmed around her stomach. If she were, indeed, being hunted, her pursuers would not drive from Maine. They would fly. She pressed the accelerator, urging the truck and Airstream to do the same.

The overpowering smell of stale beer almost gagged Lincoln as he walked into the gloomy, nearly empty dive bar. At four o'clock, the early drunks had long since staggered away, and it was too early yet for the Friday happy hour crowd. Mancuso was sitting in the vinyl-covered booth, a half-empty glass of beer in front of him.

As he sat down, Mancuso gestured toward the bowl of large pretzels on the table between them. "Help yourself."

The idea was revolting to Lincoln. An ashtray in front of Mancuso held three ground out Camels; smoke curled from a fourth cigarette which Mancuso held between his thumb and forefinger, the embers dangerously close to his fingers.

Lincoln waved off the approaching waitress. "Has Henry Lee been in touch with you since we talked? Can we eliminate the possibility he took care of her?"

Mancuso tilted his head to the side and closed one eye as he dragged on the cigarette. He nodded as he stubbed the butt out in the ashtray.

"He wanted to know if we knew where she was. He lost her, too."

How could the woman give two professionals the slip? "Give me a rundown of the last twenty-four hours."

"Yesterday morning she went for a bike ride with the kid like I told you. You know about the accident, and then she and the kid went home from the hospital at noon."

Mancuso pulled a small, dog-eared spiral notebook out of his inside breast pocket.

"My man on watch said a dozen or so people came and went yesterday afternoon–some to see the kid, sign his cast. One woman to see the Wiser woman. Said she couldn't come to the funeral so she was stopping by. Condolences. Anyway, I came on at eight and stayed all night. Figured I had to watch for dumbass Lee, make sure he didn't try anything. And I, ah, I'm thinking she disappeared during my watch."

He shook a Camel from his pack, held it between his teeth while he fished out a gold lighter and snapped it open. The air was still, but Mancuso cupped the weed protectively as if there were a breeze. He glanced briefly at Lincoln and lit the Camel. In that fraction of a second, Lincoln realized Mancuso was worried he had screwed up.

"Something made you suspicious?" Lincoln prodded.

"No, not then." Mancuso exhaled the smoke his lungs had been embracing. I didn't think anything was wrong until the audio guy got a hold of me at" –he flipped a couple of pages in the notebook– "eight twelve this morning. He said I should come listen to the tape."

Mancuso put the notebook back in his pocket. With the end of his cigarette, he pushed the remains of the last cigarette into the bottom of the tray. The movement gave the old butt new life. "I've listened to it twice since then."

"And what of significance is on the tape?"

"Not much. Friends calling, yakety yak. The last time her voice was heard in the house was last night after supper when she called a friend name of Jessie and asked if she could come visit. An hour later she did. Or she started to. Got in the car at ten forty-two and left. Then it looked like she changed her mind because five blocks later she circled around and went back home. I followed her the whole way."

Mancuso gestured with a sweep of his hand causing ashes to flutter off the end of his cigarette. His voice sounded unconvinced. He leaned his forearms on the table, cupping his hands in front of him. Smoke curled from the cigarette held between two nicotine-stained fingers. His head sank between his shoulders. There was something more on Artie Mancuso's mind.

"What, Artie?" Lincoln tried to keep the edginess out of his voice. If Mancuso had a theory, he wanted to hear it.

Mancuso crushed the fragment of paper and tobacco in the ashtray. "After I called you this morning, I listened to the tape again and did some thinking about it. See, when she got in her car and pulled out of the driveway–she drives an old tan Buick–I never thought nothing about it. I followed her downtown, she turned around and came back. Like I said, I figured she changed her mind about wanting company. I didn't know we were watching for a skip, or I would of had a second man on to follow her, and I would of stayed at the house."

"What are you getting at?"

"Boss, is there any reason someone would of been helping her disappear?"

The implications of that thought turned Lincoln cold. His voice was distant and wooden. "Maybe. Probably not. But maybe. Go on."

"I'm thinking maybe a decoy–someone her height, build–like the woman who went to visit yesterday–goes into the house and doesn't come out. So, I'm thinking, after dark, the decoy leaves in the Buick and gets me to follow her for a few blocks while someone picks the Wiser woman up and takes her away. Or she walks away. She doesn't drive. The car came back. It's still there."

"But her family would have to be accomplices. They'd know." Lincoln thought about that. If the family hadn't discussed her impending departure on tape, it would mean they had been briefed not to talk about it to each other. By whom? The Feds?

"No, no. Not necessarily," Mancuso said. "If she or someone else arranged this, they probably wouldn't tip the family. And I don't think they know anything. Didn't sound like they were faking it on the tape this morning. They sounded pissed."

Lincoln stared, unseeing, at a point beyond Mancuso's head. For a wild moment, he considered going directly to the airport, taking the packed bag he stowed in a locker there and the one briefcase full of cash, and disappearing.

Mancuso cleared his throat. "I'm not saying it happened that way. Just could of. This morning, after I listened to the tape the second time, I checked the Greyhound schedule. Last bus out was 9:00 p.m. Only one taxi in town—they didn't pick anybody up at her address.

"Then I stopped by her business; they hadn't seen her. Said they didn't expect her for a day or two. Seems a member of her family had just died." He raised one eyebrow and chuckled through a wheeze. "Poor bastard."

"The local airport?"

"Yeah, it's dinky—what you'd expect in a jerkwater town, but small private planes go in and out all the time, so I checked it out. If she left that way, no one filed a flight plan. No one remembers her."

"How'd you get that information?"

"Flashed a fake PI license with a fifty underneath it. They never look at the license. It's the fifty that gets their attention. I wanted to cover any base I could in the time I had."

Lincoln nodded, satisfied. "So, you think it happened that way... someone helped her, and she left around ten forty last night?"

"Her voice wasn't heard again on the tape after she left and came back."

"Any other possible explanations?"

"Coulda walked away, but she woulda had to go through woods and across house lots if she went in any direction except the road."

"Could someone have entered the house from the wooded section, subdued and removed her?"

"And given her time to write notes for the family first?"

Lincoln conceded the point. "Did you bring a copy of the tape?"

Mancuso pulled a plastic-cased cassette from his inside breast pocket and laid it on the table. "The guys did a quick edit so you can hear her talking. Then comes the bad part. You don't hear nothin'."

Lincoln stared at the tape, deep in thought, for a minute before he spoke.

"I'll be in Amesbury Monday. I'll call you Sunday night, let you know when to pick me up at the Portland Airport. I'll need an office. I'll bring Kathy with me, so I won't need a secretary."

He watched Mancuso forming questions he didn't ask. Lincoln certainly was not going to fill Mancuso in on his exile. "Assuming the Wiser woman doesn't turn up by Monday morning, we'll need a couple more men for out of state field work."

Mancuso nodded. "We'll do an all-out search."

"If you can't get into the house before tomorrow, start with her office," Lincoln said. "Tap the phones while you're there. Compile a list of relatives and friends and tap their phones, too. I'll bring in the equipment for computer searches and a tech to run it. He'll need an office. We'll turn every stone, and we'll have her in a week or less. She's an old lady. How hard can it be?"

He picked up the cassette tape and slipped it into his jacket pocket. "Keep me posted."

With a nod to Mancuso, Lincoln slid out of the booth, left the bar, and walked three blocks to the parking garage.

What he hadn't said was that if the Wiser woman had been placed into a witness protection program by the Feds or the Marshals, it meant NADCO was already in their sights. It would take a lot longer than Mancuso predicted. They'd have to wait until she surfaced, and that wouldn't happen until indictments took place. They could still take her out then. No matter what she may have been told before her ex-husband was killed, no witness, no case. But he didn't have to think along those lines. Yet. He could continue to walk the fine line and put his energy into containing and correcting the situation. And bringing his notes up to date.

Every word he wrote in his journal had a spin on it that incriminated the partners, especially Roy LaCroix, and cast himself in the role of a gopher simply carrying out orders. With the diary and a willingness to testify against Roy, Lincoln wouldn't do a minute of time behind bars. It would almost be worth it to squeal to the Feds just to watch Roy go down in flames. Even a country club prison wouldn't have a golf course.

It wouldn't come to that, though. If Lincoln had enough warning something was coming down, he'd just split. He'd prepared his escape route a few years ago–enough cash located in lockers in the city to give him a running start. He had offshore bank accounts that would allow him to disappear in comfort for a while. But not for as long as he wanted. Not yet. He would stick around and see how long he could make this gig last.

Meanwhile, there was no denying he'd have to inform LaCroix of the woman's disappearance.

Jewel settled at what was becoming his favorite table. He was here often enough, he was beginning to be ignored by the locals. His location was far enough away from the regulars that he wasn't obvious but close enough to the usual crowd to hear all the bad jokes and local scuttlebutt. Hal's was becoming a strategic location. But today it was Winnifred who gave him the news as she poured his coffee.

"Hal has already started your breakfast," she said. "Oh, did you hear the latest? Remember we were talking about the guy who was killed? Sam Wiser?"

Jewel nodded, careful not to change his expression.

"Well, his wife Maggie disappeared this morning. I mean she left without telling her family. Her housekeeper's mother, Effie, she does catering, well, this morning she came in to deliver the homemade pastries we serve here and said Maggie had up and left without telling a soul. Imagine! I guess Sam's death was harder on her than anyone thought. Maybe she had to get away."

Jewel nodded slowly. "Well, I'm sure she'll be back soon. Didn't you say her family lives with her? She's probably taking a few days to herself."

"Yeah, I guess. But, funny though. Her grandson was just injured in a hit and run. I mean, not bad, they say. Only a broken arm. But still, disappearing? It doesn't seem like Maggie to me."

Well, to me, it seems like Maggie's dead, he thought. The hit man finally did the job. Party over. It would be worth it though to stick around another day. See how he had accomplished it. Professional curiosity.

After breakfast he drove by the hitman's hotel and was startled to see his blue Caprice still there. He should be long gone. What the hell? He pulled into the parking lot and slowly rolled by the car. There was a dent in the front fender on the driver's side. As he figured, the hit and run vehicle.

After lunch, the car was still parked at the motel, but in a different spot. Not like the hitman had abandoned it, but like he'd used it to go to pick up food.

The woman was gone. The assassin was here. Jewel rubbed his chin in thought. What am I missing?

Wanting to get another look at the Wiser woman's property, he used the route he'd taken when he first examined her house and arrived at the hedgerow that separated her property from the neighbors behind her. As he was about to step into the muddy diagonal path, he saw them. Woman-sized footprints, three of them, leading from her property to the neighbors'. When had it last rained? Yes, last night around nine–a quick but hard downpour. So, between nine o'clock last night and this morning, the woman had walked this way. And had not returned. Jewel eradicated the prints with his shoe. No use helping anyone else.

He drove past the backyard neighbors' house and there, on a post beside the road, was a rural delivery mailbox. Stenciled on the side were the names Jessie and Wade Maxwell. He had driven by there once before and was sure there had been a white Ram 3500 pickup and an Airstream trailer parked beside it in the driveway. Today, the driveway was empty. Neighbors gone. Wiser woman gone. Too easy, he thought.

Okay then. He was staying. See how it played out with NADCO and their second-rate hitman. NADCO, who had the balls to screw him out of the remainder of his fee.

Well, screw them.

He'd go when he was ready.

And he wasn't nearly ready.

An hour later, he knocked on a neighbor's door, the only other house on Orchard Hill Road. He had a bouquet of yellow flowers in his hand. When a woman answered the door looking with delight at the daffodils and tulips, he asked, "I'm looking for..." He glanced at a card in his hand. "Jessie Maxwell."

"Oh, yes. Aren't they so pretty. Well, Jessie lives across the road and down a bit." She gestured. "That way. But, that's too bad about the flowers because they left for Florida today. Well, actually, they would have left last night. They like to do the first leg at night so they can get through New York without so much traffic. My goodness, I wonder who they are from?"

"Um, it just says, 'Thank you for all your help. Irene.' Do they usually go for a long time? Not that it matters, I guess. The flowers won't last long anyway."

"Oh, yes. They go away for the winter. Every year. They love it. Me? I wouldn't want to spend so much time in the muggy weather. Would you?"

"No. I'm with you. I like the winters here. Well, thank you for the information. Hey, listen, why don't you take the flowers? No need for them to go to waste."

Jewel smiled as he walked back to his car. Women and flowers. A sure thing.

Back at the motel, he wrote the Maxwell's Amesbury address on an envelope and printed "address correction requested " at the top. In two or three weeks, the post office would return it to him with their vacation address. If need be, he could take care of her in Florida though he'd prefer Amesbury, Maine, where he could get maximum effect when he nailed her...right in NADCO's face.

After all, the Wiser woman was his loose end.

But not for long. This gig was almost up.

Chapter 9

Maggie, Wade, and Jessie reached Beaufort at ten o'clock Friday night. In an historic, residential neighborhood, Maggie found the white house with a four-pillared front porch more easily than she had imagined. Wade drove by it, circled through town, and drove by it again. There was only one car in the yard, and it had North Carolina plates. Maggie insisted on phoning Belle Wiser first to keep from startling Sam's eighty-three-year-old aunt, so they drove into town again.

Wade nodded. "We got enough lead, but still try to get a sense, when you talk to her, is anything wrong–give her a chance to volunteer if anyone has contacted her asking about you."

Belle Wiser picked up on the second ring. "Well, Margaret! Bless you honey. What are you doin' in North Carolina?" she asked once Maggie told her she was in town. "You just git right on over here."

Five minutes later, Aunt Belle hugged her warmly. Sam's aunt had aged somewhat in the five years since Maggie and the children had visited, but her slender five-foot-two frame stood as erect as ever. Her wrinkles had deepened and multiplied, but her pale blue eyes hadn't changed, forming merry crescents when she smiled.

Aunt Belle held Maggie at arm's length. "I'm sorry, Margaret, I couldn't make it to Sam's funeral. My spirit was willin', but I just wasn't up to it. I'm so sorry, honey. What an awful thing." She looked at Wade and Jessie and cocked a shrewd eyebrow. "But y'all are not here to talk about that. Somethin's afoot."

"These are friends of mine. Jessie and Wade Maxwell. They brought me here because, well, I need to ask a really big favor of you." Feeling even more unsure of herself now that she stood in front of Sam's aunt, she blurted, "If you want to say no, it's okay. It won't be a problem. There're other solutions." What they were Maggie didn't know yet.

Belle smiled. "Come, come. Let's go into the kitchen. Have y'all eaten? I have homemade rye bread and some corned beef. Sit down, sit down. I wasn't goin' to get any supper for myself, just a cup of tea and toast, but now I realize I'm hungry. Matter of fact, I have a strawberry rhubarb pie in the freezer. The rhubarb is from the patch in my backyard. A friend lives behind me. He gave me the strawberries. Y'all like rhubarb pie? I've been lookin' for an excuse to thaw it out. Cain't be a better one than this."

Maggie watched Aunt Belle bustle around pulling food from the refrigerator and cupboards. Typical Belle Wiser, extending warm, southern hospitality to her and these unannounced strangers.

"Aunt Belle, what do you say we just put everything on the table, and we all dig in and make our own sandwiches?"

"Good idea. Why don't y'all do that, and I'll zap the pie in the microwave."

Corned beef was not on her diet, but, for the first time in days, Maggie discovered she was hungry. Ravenously hungry. Out-of-control hungry. They piled corned beef, cheese, pickles, and onions on rye bread and slathered horseradish mustard on top. Maggie felt her saliva kicking in almost before she could get the sandwich to her mouth.

"Okay," Belle said after she'd chewed her first bite, "what's this big favor I can say no to that's not all that important and hardly even justifies y'all coming all the way from Maine to Beaufort to ask it?" Her blue eyes sparkled as she spoke.

Maggie did most of the talking. Wade and Jessie jumped in only when they thought she'd left out a pertinent piece of information. Around mouthfuls of food, Maggie told Aunt Belle the events of the past seven days.

Aunt Belle patted Maggie's hand. "How awful for you. Well, then, you need a place to stay." It sounded like a declaration–a *fait accompli*.

Wade nodded. "May not be for long. But she'll be underfoot. Can't leave the house for a while."

Belle folded her wrinkled hands on the table in front of her. Her eyebrows pulled together, and she looked thoughtful. "Now let me see. Be here alone or have Margaret for company. Hmm." She shook her head, frowning. "That's a tough one."

Jessie smiled. "Yeah, I'd have to think that decision over once or twice, myself."

"She's got bad habits," Wade warned.

Belle tilted her head and met Maggie's eyes, making tsk-tsk noises with her tongue.

"Messy and a bad cook. But I can reform," Maggie said.

"Bad habits would be a welcome challenge. I'll be glad for the company."

Maggie almost sagged with relief, and she suddenly realized she was exhausted. Now she had a place to rest, she had to resist the impulse to get her clothes from the trailer immediately.

"I always liked you, Margaret Wiser." Belle's face crinkled into mischief. "No matter what Sam's folks said about you."

Maggie laughed out loud. She could imagine what Sam's parents had said about her–probably until the day they died.

"Thank you, Aunt Belle. I think I'm going to like it here."

Wade cleared his throat. "Thing is, Mrs. Wiser–"

"Belle, if you please."

Wade nodded. "Thank you. Thing is, Belle, it'd be better if she weren't actually in this house for a week or so. Need to give the bad guys time to scope you out, search your house, tap the phone. When the coast is clear, she can come back."

Maggie watched Aunt Belle's face for signs of alarm, but she just nodded. In fact, she actually looked pleased. Did she understand "scope you out" and "tap the phone"? Maggie was about to clarify when Belle glanced sideways at her and gave her a thumbs up. No clarification needed.

"But," Wade said and cupped his chin, deep in thought, "the thing is, I don't want her in a motel. They'll likely check all motels, inns, and B&Bs around here."

Belle pushed herself away from the table. "Okay. I know what we do. I'll have to call a neighbor." She looked questioningly at Wade. He shrugged, but he looked doubtful.

"He's a good friend. You can trust him. He's the one brought me the strawberries."

Wade shrugged and nodded.

Belle picked up a wall phone and dialed.

"Sandy? Good, you're home. Listen, dear, you had supper? Yes? Well, then why don't you come over for some strawberry-rhubarb pie? Yes, ice cream would be good. Do you have any? Well, vanilla, don't you think? Wonderful. Sandy, I have some people here I want you to meet. They have a problem, and you have the solution."

A few minutes later Belle answered a knock at the door. Sandy McAllister was a robust-looking man, stocky in build. He appeared to be in his mid-fifties. His sandy-colored, wavy hair brushed the tops of his ears. A thick lock, laced with silver threads, dipped across his forehead. He occasionally brushed it back with his fingers. His squarish face, though it couldn't be described as handsome, was very pleasant to look at, Maggie thought.

After introductions, Sandy filled an old-fashioned glass percolator with water and coffee and put it on the stove. He took mugs from a cabinet and brought them to the table. Maggie tried not to show her surprise at how familiar he was with Aunt Belle's kitchen, how he made himself at home.

Belle cut the warm, fragrant pie while Sandy scooped the ice cream onto each plate. Jessie and Belle moved their chairs further apart so he could pull a chair up to the table. Sandy listened thoughtfully to their story–this time told mostly by Wade, who seemed to sense Maggie's exhaustion. Sandy glanced at Maggie from time to time as if to confirm the details.

The smell of perked coffee filled the kitchen. As Wade finished the story, Sandy brought the coffee pot to the table and poured for everyone. From his own cup of steaming black coffee, he took a cautious sip then sat down.

Finally, he looked at Belle. "Are you thinking what I'm thinking?"

"*Saline Solution,*" she said.

Sandy nodded thoughtfully.

Maggie was puzzled, and she could see Wade was equally mystified.

Sandy turned toward them. "Yes. I think that would be perfect. I have a boat tied up at a dock only a few blocks from here. We can stock her with food, fill the water tanks..."

Wade's blue eyes twinkled. "Now that's what I call a perfect *solution*. What kind of boat?"

"Columbia sloop. Forty-five footer."

Wade whistled. "Should be comfortable."

"She is. And as long as Maggie stays below, no one would guess she was there."

"I'm a little concerned about taking Maggie there directly. I don't believe anyone would have gotten here this soon, but I don't want you to be followed to the boat and then go off and leave her alone."

"That's easily solved. My backyard connects to Belle's. There's a wooden fence that separates our properties, but I installed a gate in it to shorten the route to Belle's home cooking."

He looked at Maggie. "Much luggage? No? Then we go through the fence, into my garage, get in my car–you can duck down–and we'll drive down to the boat." He gave Maggie a conspiratorial grin.

Wade looked at Belle. "Like to watch your house for a few days. Stay out of sight. See if anyone shows up. Okay with you?"

"Mr. Maxwell. Wade." Belle paused. "I'm very sorry for Margaret's troubles, and I feel real terrible about Sam bein' gone, but I haven't had so much fun in years. 'Course it's all right."

In spite of her fatigue, Maggie took a shower, dried her hair, and changed into clean clothes before leaving.

When she came back into the kitchen where the four of them were still visiting, she saw her gym bag and bulging pillowcase sitting by the back door. Belle handed her a plastic grocery bag with a few extra tank tops and T-shirts and a couple of books.

Sandy was holding the door open. Maggie turned to wave goodbye to Wade, Jessie, and Belle, assailed by pangs of separation anxiety. The familiar people she was leaving behind were her security and her connection to her life. She was walking away with a total stranger.

And into God only knew what.

The dock was deserted, not a car in sight in the parking area. They walked to the boat without speaking. As they stepped on the deck, Sandy put a hand on Maggie's elbow in case she lost her balance, but the movement of the boat didn't faze her.

Once they were below, he turned on the lights, showed her around, and explained how to use the head. He told her he'd lock the main hatch from the outside and showed her how to lock the forward one from the inside. That way, if she did need to get out, she could. She seemed comfortable with his suggestion that he turn off the lights as he left so as to not draw attention to the boat. He left her with a small flashlight and a promise to bring her some food in the morning.

Interesting evening, Sandy thought as he walked toward the car. Far cry from falling asleep watching the Home and Garden Network.

Was there any real danger to Margaret Wiser? He wasn't sure. Both Maggie and Wade were convincing, and he knew from his own life's work that the movers and shakers of society were capable of skullduggery–even murder. But in this case? Hard to say.

Even Maggie was a reluctant believer at best, that much he could tell.

Interesting woman, too. Fatigued, sad, and frightened, yet her sense of humor was evident. When Wade or Belle said something that tickled her, laughter bubbled to the surface, and her startling green eyes sparkled momentarily, pushing the fears aside. And she never focused on herself. Many people in her circumstance would have been impressed with their own pathos. Dramatizing it, even. Not her. Straight forward, as far as he could tell.

When he'd turned on the light in his garage before they'd left, he waited with pride while she inspected the MG Midget painted an eye-catching British racing green. She had nodded and said, "Thanks for showing me your Matchbox collection. But where's your car? Oh, wait," she'd added, noting his bike hanging on the wall. "Too bad your bicycle wasn't built for two."

Then she grinned mischievously and made eye contact, which passed through him like a bolt of electricity that nearly blew out the soles of his shoes.

Now he slid into the little car and pulled out of the parking lot, chuckling. If he'd been finding his life a little too predictable lately, this sure stirred things up. No, he was not interested in any relationship with Maggie Wiser. Not by a long shot. He'd already taken two disastrous detours into romance since his wife died, and he'd finally concluded he would rather be celibate than put his arm into that buzz saw again.

Still, the next few days could be fun playing support personnel in Wade's conspiracy theory.

Better than vegetating in front of the TV. Even if it was the *Home and Garden* network.

Jewel settled the last of his clothes into his leather Globe-Trotter suitcase and snapped it shut. He had been living at this budget motel since he'd arrived, but now he had an efficiency apartment in Amesbury.

The first thing he had done when he signed the lease was mail the envelope requesting an address correction for the Maxwells. He should be getting it back soon with their address in Florida. Finding the woman would be a piece of cake after that.

He turned his attention to his second piece of luggage, a rich tan Ghurka Cavalier leather duffle bag. Still locked in the false bottom of the duffle was a small assortment of weapons, his tools in trade. A rifle, a knife, and a few other items that he seldom had to resort to. But he wanted them accessible. He filled the other part of the duffle with small items and toiletries.

Jewel had been busy keeping track of the bungling assassin who had rented an apartment under the name of Henry Lee. In this economically depressed town, it was easy to find his own rental less than a block away on the other side of the street.

But Jewel had other business to attend to in the next few days. He needed a garage to house a second car he would keep out of sight–a Nissan 300 ZX, specially modified and fitted for his needs. It was registered in Massachusetts under a false name. He'd have to take a train to his home and drive it back to Amesbury. A lot of trouble to go to when he didn't know if he'd need it; he didn't know if the situation would play out in Florida or Maine, but he'd rather be overprepared. He'd already found a garage a block away to house the automobile. Once it was in Maine, it would be under lock and key and would not come out unless the need presented itself. He picked up both cases. He was out of this dump.

Glancing toward the hotel desk clerk, Jewel set his suitcases down and pulled the room key from his pocket. The Ice Queen was on duty. Stringy brown hair drooped around her pinched face. In contrast with her chalky white skin, her thin nose was perpetually red. Her mouth tightened into a disapproving line. She pulled her cardigan together at the neck and sniffed as Jewel approached the desk.

"Checking out?" Her lips moved stiffly. "Sir," she added reluctantly.

Jewel nodded. He placed his gold card on the desk just far enough away from her so that she had to reach into his space to pick it up. While she processed his credit card and pushed the slip toward him to sign, he amused himself with the image of her looking up from a pillow, with that disapproving, censuring expression, while her husband screwed her.

She caught his smile and pulled her bony, thin frame straighter. "Was everything satisfactory? Sir?" Her tone was brittle.

If anyone ever tried to put his hand up this woman's skirt, he would get frostbitten, Jewel decided. He felt his smile widen as he returned his credit card to his wallet.

"Everything was superb, Ms. Sandorff. I'm sure this is one of the finest hotels in Maine. And I'm especially fortunate to have timed my departure with your schedule." He caught her off guard; he made eye contact the second her watery, pale eyes flicked toward his. "It would have been my loss had I not been able to say goodbye." He allowed his voice to drop, subtly. He watched the confusion register in her eyes.

"Oh. My. Oh, well. Yes. Well, we're sorry to see you leave, Mr. Chadwick."

He caught and held her eyes for another fragment of a second then quickly lowered his. "Your hospitality has made my stay in Amesbury most pleasant."

"Well, yes. Um, yes, we try." With her right hand, she fingered her wedding band for a moment then took a deep breath and smiled primly. "Well, yes...well, Mr. Chadwick, have a pleasant trip. Are you going back to Massachusetts?"

"No, as a matter of fact, I've found an apartment. I've been asked to consult with the director of the museum at Amesbury College, and I'll be delivering a few guest lectures."

"Ooh, really. Well, Mr. Chadwick. Isn't that fortunate for the students. Antiques, did you say? You're an antique dealer?" She pulled a tissue from her sweater sleeve and vigorously pushed her nose from side to side.

Jewel sought her eyes one more time, held them for an extra, meaningful second, and then smiled slowly, intimately. "You have an excellent memory, Ms. Sandorff. Just...excellent."

He noticed a tiny, quick, intake of breath. Then a blush spread from her neck to the roots of her limp hair. She blinked rapidly, and her breath came in little puffs. She opened her mouth as if to speak, but nothing came out. Jewel found it very easy now to hold her gaze. Her eyes were locked on to his.

With a slight nod and elegant smile, he said, *"Ciao."* Turning, he picked up his bags and left. He chuckled all the way to the car. Her thin, bloodless face came to him as he placed his bags into the back of his Range Rover. He wondered if she had any kids. He hoped not.

Some people should not be allowed to procreate.

Saturday morning, Lincoln got out of the cab at East 72nd Street and Fifth Avenue and entered Central Park. Of course, Roy would have picked a location that required walking. When he had told Lincoln where they would meet–Bethesda Terrace–Lincoln had never heard of it. He asked Kathy, his secretary, if she knew of it. She did, and an hour later, provided him with a map of Central Park.

At eight in the morning, it was mostly dog owners strolling along the paths with an occasional down and outer lying on a bench after a hard night, Lincoln guessed.

He stopped in his tracks when he saw the scope of the Terrace. How did he not know of its existence? Not that he would have been a visitor, but he felt in a one-down position with LaCroix. Hell, even with Kathy.

He stood at an upper level of some sort of ornate stone edifice. He could go down two flights of broad stone stairs, through the arches, into a building that appeared to be a highly decorated walkway to the broad circular pavilion that had a huge fountain basin, in the center of which was a giant statue of an angel. Or he could just descend one of the exterior staircases that bordered each side of the edifice. Then he spotted Roy sitting on the edge of the fountain basin waving to him. Enough equivocating. He went down the wide outside staircase, two flights.

When he got to the huge, round, brick-paved pavilion, he saw that Roy was feeding birds from a small brown bag, reaching in and scattering seeds as the pigeons bobbed around, pecking at the bird food.

Royal LaCroix rose as Lincoln approached and put out his hand for a handshake.

"Lincoln, Lincoln. What a fine day! The sky—not a cloud. Seventy degrees, perfect." He folded the empty paper bag and put it in his suit coat pocket. "Let's take a walk."

He headed for the stone stairs, and they climbed to the top level.

"How long since you've been here?" Roy asked.

"It's been a while." Lincoln wasn't going to admit he'd never been here.

Roy nodded sympathetically. "Hard to find time to get away, isn't it? As I'm sure you're aware, a little later this morning there'll be nannies chasing running children, pulling them away from the fountain. A street musician will set up to play his guitar, there will be food carts, and tourists and New Yorkers alike will be posing for and taking photos. Then there is nature." Roy swept an arm across to indicate the green foliage on both sides of the path. "These majestic elms. They've been here a long time, over a hundred years. Ahh, nothing like nature, eight hundred acres of it, in the middle of New York City, right, Lincoln?"

"Right." At least it's not a golf course, he thought.

"A few years ago, NADCO donated three mil toward the Park Conservancy, particularly the Bethesda Plaza. Every year, Mary and I attend the benefit that takes place right back there in the Plaza. Quite an affair. The proceeds go to restore and maintain Central Park."

Roy took off his suit jacket and flung it over his shoulder, holding it by two fingers. "So, what is it that you needed this emergency meeting for?"

Although he'd been rehearsing for this meeting, coming up with various openings, Lincoln now felt stuck for words.

"I'm assuming it's about the project in Maine."

"The woman's gone," Lincoln blurted.

Roy stopped short. He motioned toward a bench, and they sat. He turned toward Lincoln with a raised eyebrow and waited.

"I don't know how it happened. No, she wasn't eliminated. She disappeared from her house in the middle of the night. We had around-the-clock surveillance. We found out because, in the morning, her family bitched about her being gone and only leaving them notes. No in-person goodbyes."

"And you're sure your guy didn't get excited and overreach?"

"No, he doesn't know where she is."

"Ahhh. Lincoln, Lincoln, Lincoln. Unfortunate. This changes everything. Everything. She wouldn't disappear–leave her job, run from her family–for no reason. She knows something. She probably knows everything."

Roy laid his jacket across his lap, crossed his legs, and leaned back with his fingers laced behind his head. He looked up at the towering trees in thought. Then he sat up, nodded, and stood.

"Okay, Lincoln. Handle it your way. Find her. Take care of her. Preferably away from Amesbury. This needs to be handled quickly and with finesse. You can take care of this, can't you Lincoln?"

Lincoln nodded. He cast about trying to find the words that would confidently reassure Royal, but he couldn't think of any.

Looking preoccupied, Roy stood up and took a deep breath. He slung his jacket over his shoulder again. "It's a beautiful day. I'm going to walk for a while. Have a good day, Lincoln."

Half an hour later, Mancuso took a phone call from Lincoln.

Mancuso cleared his throat because his voice was gravelly even in the morning. "You're saying what, Boss?"

"I'm saying, 'It's on again.'"

"As in…back to plan A? Ah, elimination? Just want to be clear."

"Yes. Preferably out of state, but if it's local, make it look like an accident, for chrissakes, not some goddamn hit and run. You can get a hold of him?"

"No problem. I'll go find him now." In truth, Mancuso had no idea where Henry Lee was, but he'd track him down.

Lincoln continued. "An accident, the sooner, the better. We're clear on this?"

"Yes, Boss. Crystal clear. Ah, how do we find her?"

But the line went dead. Sure thing, boss, he thought. We'll wrap this up in the next hour.

Jewel strolled languidly into the cool air in one of the two Amesbury bars. He'd been keeping track of the vehicle that had hit the Wiser kid and followed it, but nothing happened. Until this afternoon. He'd followed the Caprice here and decided he needed to work on his pool skills. He almost laughed when he saw Henry Lee lower himself into a booth across from Mr. UPS. Well, here was confirmation, if he needed it, that this was a NADCO deal.

The heavyset man who'd broken into the Wiser home and done such a bad job of bugging it, waved the waitress away. They didn't intend to stay long, then.

Jewel walked over to the pool table and picked up a cue stick and a piece of chalk. He chalked the end of this stick and watched the pair from the corner of his eye. He figured the "UPS man" was in charge. The man took a breath and leaned toward Lee. At that moment, Jewel accidentally dropped the chalk and leaned down to pick it up.

"...and take care of her."

"So, it's on again? Will somebody make up their minds?"

Jewel felt around the floor, picked up the chalk, and turned his attention toward the pool table.

He heard only fragments. "...out of state–or look like an..."

Accident. So there it was. NADCO was afraid of the woman. And it had been an on, and then off, and then on again, situation. That now made sense with what he knew. The bungled hit and run, for instance, where the hitman did not leave town. At least now he knew for certain what their goal was.

Okay, Jewel thought. Game on.

On Wednesday morning, Maggie awoke to the drubbing sound of an approaching motorboat. She raised up on one elbow and looked out of the open porthole at the busy harbor. Every morning at the same time for the five days she'd been on the boat, the same skiff motored by, the owner at the wheel, a passenger sitting in the rear. They always glanced toward the finger docks where Sandy's boat was tied up, but they didn't appear to take any more interest in his boat than any of the others. Made her wonder, though.

She glanced at her watch. Eight o'clock. She swung her feet to the carpeted floor. In twenty minutes–she could set her watch by it–Sandy McAllister would arrive with groceries, a newspaper, and a daily report relayed from Wade.

She pulled on shorts created from a pair of jeans she had cut off at mid-thigh. When she packed in Maine, it hadn't occurred to her it would be warmer in North Carolina. She rummaged in her bag for a shirt or top, but she was out of clean clothes. Reluctantly, she pulled out the red tank top Aunt Belle had lent her and tugged it over her head. It was small for Maggie's broader, five-six frame and too short, fitting her like a waist-length camisole.

Barefooted, she padded across the pale blue carpet and looked in the plastic vanity mirror. Her hair stuck out in every direction. Tucking her head under the faucet, she gasped as cold water poured over her head. There was a shower on the boat, but the water supply was limited, and they'd have to run the motor to heat the water, so she'd decided to restrict hygiene to sponge baths. Heating water on the propane stove in the evening had become a welcomed luxury.

Now she combed her blond hair and pushed it into place, then, feeling foolish, she applied color to her lips from a lipstick that was down to a nub. It wasn't that she wanted Sandy to think of her as attractive. It was...she searched her feelings. It was that she just didn't want to appear *unattractive*. Yesterday, she had looked through the interior of the boat relentlessly until she found a can of acetone to remove her chipped fingernail polish.

When did it stop, she wondered sheepishly, when you no longer cared how you were viewed by the opposite sex? "I think you should have outgrown that by now, Margaret Wiser," she said aloud, frowning at her reflection.

In the salon, she caught her breath. The sun, reflecting off glittering waves, threw slivers of light shimmering on the ceiling and walls. This was the first day the sun had shone since she had taken up residence on the boat.

She hand-pumped water into the bottom of an old aluminum percolator. Measuring coffee into the basket, she savored the pungent smell of the ground coffee. The propane gas stove popped on; she adjusted the blue flame before setting the pot on the burner.

Then she pushed back the overhead hatch cover, no longer locked from the outside, to let the sun stream into the galley. In the blue sky overhead, screeching seagulls wheeled and dipped around the harbor looking for breakfast. The longing to dash up the five steps that would take her out on deck where she could indulge herself in the sights and sounds of the picturesque harbor was almost irresistible. In the past days, she had merely glimpsed this world through twelve-inch portholes. Leaning back against the ice box, she gazed up at the few puffy white clouds that barely moved and felt the sun on her face. The only thing that kept her from bolting was her responsibility to the people who were spending their time keeping her out of sight: Jessie, Wade, Aunt Belle, and Sandy.

"Not much longer," she said aloud. She had come to the conclusion that Wade, God love him, had created the exaggerated precautions out of a need to recreate some youthful glory days. The dark-of-night fears that had led her to the Maxwells had made it easy for her to be convinced that she was in danger. She was still jumpy, sure, but that was because here she was, hiding on a boat in a harbor almost a thousand miles from home. No one had shown up at Belle's.

Because no one was looking for her.

She felt silly about having gone along with the convoluted plan. On the other hand, she was getting a much-needed vacation. Since she had arrived in North Carolina, the multiple images, like still slides of Sam's death, projected on her brain, came less frequently. And if she still had nightmares about it, she didn't remember much about them when she woke up.

Yesterday, she had decided that when Wade was satisfied no one was looking for her, she would call her family, let them know where she was, then spend another week with Belle, visiting, shopping. She was itching to get at the appealing shops she knew, from previous visits, were along the harbor. Then she would use her credit card and catch a plane home.

The smell of coffee brought her back to the present. She glanced at her watch. Sandy would be arriving in a few minutes. She poured a cup of coffee, stirred in creamer and sugar, and then looked once again through the bookshelf hoping to find something to read. She had finished the second of the two mysteries that Belle had given her, and the idea of spending the day without reading material to occupy her mind was distressing.

The boat's one-shelf library housed, in addition to the framed photo of her family she'd brought from home, two technical books on sailing, three books on celestial navigation–one of these was a book of tables, row after row of numbers– one Scott Turow novel that she had already read, two text books, and several worn magazines on sailing, scuba diving, and flying in small aircraft.

Sandy was a scuba diver, she knew, because she'd discovered tanks and other paraphernalia when she was looking for the acetone. But was he also a pilot or simply a wanna-be dreamer?

She pulled one of the thick textbooks from the shelf and carried it to the dinette. She opened to the title page and had almost turned to the next one when she looked back, startled.

At that moment, she heard a familiar sound. Sandy was coming down the dock whistling a tune. She listened, trying to make out the song. Yesterday it had been *"I've Been Working on the Railroad."* The day before, *"When the Saints Go Marching In."*

As he approached the boat, she made it out and chuckled. The boat heaved with his weight as he stepped on deck. He rapped lightly on the cabin top.

"Okay to come below?" he asked in a hushed voice.

"Come on down. You caught me home."

He appeared in the opening and then looked at her face. "What?"

She realized she must still be grinning. "You're the first person I've ever heard who actually whistled Dixie."

Holding on to the grab rail, he descended the five stairs. "Well, Ma'am, it's part of my Southern heritage."

"I thought you said you were from New Hampshire."

"That's right, Miss Maggie. Southern New Hampshire."

He unloaded a grocery bag. "I brought you a couple of extra newspapers."

Maggie raised her eyebrows. He usually brought *the Carteret County News-Times.*

"I noticed you do the crossword puzzles, so I also picked up *The Island Packet, The Daily News* out of Jacksonville and *The News and Observer* from Raleigh. And here's a weekly, produced right here in Beaufort called *The Venture*– it's got a crossword puzzle. And…"

With a flourish, he pulled out two paperback books from the bag. "Two more mystery books! Don't know how good they are. But," he said, looking at her with amusement, "beggars can't be choosers. And I figure the plots have got to be better than the sun-sight tables."

He glanced at the book on the table. "Or the textbooks." He took a mug out of the cupboard, poured himself a cup of coffee, and leaned back against the ice box. "I have some good news for you. Or bad news. Depending on how you see it." He made momentary eye contact as if to assess how she would take the news.

She nodded and waited.

"Belle had a visitor this week."

Maggie felt her insides jump. "Tell me about it."

"Wade's game plan was to have Belle leave her house every day at two in the afternoon and come back at four. Monday, two people, a man and a woman, started watching her house. They rode by on bikes, skated by on roller blades, followed Belle a couple of times. They were a bit obvious, and Wade thinks they might have been from a local detective outfit."

"Monday! This is Wednesday. Why didn't you tell me yesterday?"

"Wade said not to worry you."

Maggie was put out, and it must have shown on her face.

He smiled. "I voted for telling you at the time, but Wade seems to hold the majority vote. He's quite a character, you know that?"

Still smiling, Sandy shook his head. "He's been right out in plain sight all day, every day on Belle's street. Sometimes he walks by with a cane, sometimes he limps carrying a bundle of groceries. Sometimes he shuffles with his head down. Yesterday he showed up with hedge clippers and a wheelbarrow and made an offer the owners of the house across the street couldn't refuse. He spent the day trimming their landscaping.

"His theory," Sandy continued, "is that elderly people are invisible to anyone but other elderly folks. Frankly, I didn't believe him, but he's proving me wrong. Someone should do a study on that. If I were teaching full-time, I'd try to interest a student."

The thought of the commanding and imposing, six-foot-one-inch Wade trying to be invisible made Maggie smile. But blend–that he could.

Once she saw him try on a cowboy hat and become the Marlboro man. Looked like he'd been born and bred in Montana. Another time a Greek fisherman's cap and navy pea coat turned him into a distinguished and striking sea captain.

"So, anyway," Sandy continued, "yesterday, the same two people stayed close by, doing their best to look like strolling tourists. My guess is, if Wade hadn't been watching, no one would have taken any particular notice of them.

"I guess they were satisfied that Belle's schedule was the same every day because half an hour later they came in a car with magnetic signs on the doors. Thompson Realty. They drove right into the driveway. The woman stayed in the car, as a lookout, I would guess, while the man went inside."

Maggie pictured Belle's carefully preserved, two-hundred-year-old historic house with its pedigree plaque fastened to the front, located in an area where neighbors would notice if a realtor's car was parked in the driveway. Belle must have gotten a dozen calls last night from friends wondering if she'd decided, God forbid, to sell the house. It was also a neighborhood where a suspicious character snooping around would precipitate a call to the police.

"How did he get in?" she asked.

"Belle usually leaves the door unlocked." Sandy grinned. "I'm sure the guy was prepared to pick the lock if he had to, but Belle was happy to accommodate him."

"And then?"

"He was inside for ten minutes or less. Long enough to make a quick search, determine that the only person living there was one elderly lady."

"He searched her house."

Sandy nodded, watching her through narrowed eyes.

It was true then. The knowledge hit her anew like a physical blow.

"Until now, you haven't really believed anyone was trying to find you, have you?"

"No, most of the time I haven't. How did you know?"

"I guessed as much when we were sitting in Belle's kitchen. I watched your face as Wade gave us the background. If I hadn't guessed you had doubts then, I'd have known from the look on your face just now."

She was suddenly swept away with fury at this turn her life–her family's life–had taken since Sam's death. How dare they, whoever they were, intrude on her like this. Change her life like this! She picked up the heavy textbook and slammed it back to the table. Not satisfied, she looked around for something to throw, then caught a glimpse of Sandy. He looked at her calmly, still assessing, but there was compassion behind his eyes.

"Talk to me," he said gently.

"The bastards searched...my...house! They must have or they wouldn't have known to look for me here." She started to pick up the book again. He swiftly put his hand on the cover to stop her.

"And they probably killed your ex-husband. To put things in perspective."

Tears sprang to her eyes, and a sob caught in her throat. Suddenly, the grief she had held back while they made the arrangements to bring Sam's body home, while she attended the funeral, while she had made her flight to

North Carolina, engulfed her. She was wracked by gut-twisting sobs she couldn't control.

Eventually, she became aware of a pile of wadded up tissues in front of her. She looked up. Sandy sat across the dinette table from her, a Kleenex box in front of him, a tissue ready to hand her. He did not look overly concerned and for this she was grateful. It allowed her to recover with some dignity.

She took the offered tissue and blew her nose.

"Been holding back, huh?" he asked.

"Uh huh. With everything that has been going on…"

"Very natural."

She looked at him again. "What did you say you teach?"

"I'm in the sociology department."

"Does sociology deal with grief?"

He smiled. "Only in the broadest and most superficial way."

"Did you believe Wade when he told you about all this?"

He looked down at his hands, folded now in front of him. A wave of shiny hair fell across his forehead. "I wondered. I was sure Wade and Jessie believed what they were saying. It was certainly possible. True or not, I knew no harm would be done if I helped out. Until I had more information.

"I did some checking, yesterday. On NADCO. They are a low-profile company with only three stockholders holding the majority of shares. They have developed business parks, malls, and housing developments across the country. The operation could fit with Wade's view of the company. I'll do a little more research in the next couple of days."

He grinned cheerfully, and she felt unexpectedly better.

"Listen, Maggie, I think your blood-serum level of shrimp omelet Creole is dangerously low. Let me fix some breakfast."

She suddenly remembered something and opened the textbook again. "Are you him? I mean, is this you?" She pointed to the name on the title page. Sandford McAllister.

"Mmm. Yep, 'fraid it is. Dry as dust. I don't recommend it unless you can't sleep. Or need something to throw." He grinned and cracked an egg into a bowl.

"I thought your nickname was because of the color of your hair. *White Collar Crime*. Is this sociology?"

"It's a branch of sociology. And I don't particularly want to talk shop right now, if you don't mind."

He cracked another egg and glanced sideways at her. "I'd like to hear about your family. Wade says you have two grandchildren. That must be them in the photo. Not being fortunate to have any myself, I'd like to hear about them. I understand you had a big hand in raising them. What are their ages?"

Jewel's furnished efficiency so close to Henry Lee's apartment had made it easy to bug Lee's phone, listen to conversations between him and Mancuso whom Jewel had first thought of as Mr. UPS. They didn't know where the missing Wiser woman had gone, but they hoped to find her in the next few days.

Just three days earlier, the pair had apparently gotten the go-ahead to eliminate the woman. But now it appeared they didn't know where she was. Well, let them do the legwork. When the time came for Lee to make his move, Jewel would preempt him. With pleasure. But how long would it take for this bumbling pair to find her?

He might have to make another trip to Chelsea for more clothing; this job could take a while longer.

Meanwhile, he had an excellent cover. Before leaving Chelsea the second time, he'd called Amesbury College and using his own credentials, he'd expressed an interest in the antiquities section of their museum. That inquiry led to an invitation to deliver guest lectures.

Guest lecturer at a college? Why not? It'd give him ample reason to stick around this little burg to see how it all played out. Not to mention a bevy of willing young coeds to pass idle time with. Could be worse, he figured. Could be an all-male school.

He figured Lincoln would have ordered Henry Lee to make her demise look like an accident. Instead, when the time came, Jewel would make it look like a fucking bloodbath. Henry Lee could kiss his final payment goodbye. He chuckled at the irony...the symmetry.

He'd never before used his real identity when making a hit.

But what the hell?

First time for everything.

BOOK TWO

"That which does not kill us, makes us stronger."

Friedrich Nietzsche

Chapter 10

August 26, Thursday. Maggie had been following a calendar she found on the boat, making teeny, tiny notes in the itty-bitty squares. Like a miniature diary, she thought. Today was six days since she had moved into the boat. She felt like a caged animal. No room to move, no room to exercise. What she wouldn't give for a bicycle so she could ride off the dock and through town to explore this lovely harbor. Or walk. Even better. She really, really needed to walk.

When Sandy arrived with groceries she was primed. "Look, enough is enough. I have cabin fever. Okay," she snapped, "*boat* fever. I'm serious. I'm going crazy. *And,* football season is almost ready to start. I haven't missed a football Sunday in...forever."

Sandy seemed at a loss for words.

"Okay, okay, wait, just let me get this stuff settled," he finally said, nestling the grocery bags into the corner on the counter.

"So, yeah, well let's start with what seems to be the most important. Football season has been delayed a week because of Y2K."

Maggie could feel her eyebrows raise in shock. "What? Why? That doesn't make any sense!"

"Well, you know how cautious everyone is right now. People are getting jittery, and–"

"The NFL? Is *jittery*?"

"Yeah, they don't want to hold the opening round of playoffs on January first, and they don't want teams traveling that day. You know. In case there are transportation issues due to...wait, you like football?"

"You betcha. But listen, I think Y2K is silly. By now, everything important on computers has been fixed."

Sandy nodded. "I know, I tend to agree, but panic reigns. People are canceling vacation plans, building up cash reserves, stockpiling food.

"Anyway, so, back to what *I* consider the more important issue, you're going stir crazy. It's been four days since Belle's house was searched. I know, from conversations with him, Wade is not quite ready to trust that they've given up on checking Belle's. I'll talk to him, see what he thinks about springing you in time for the NFL season. Patriots must be your team, right?"

She nodded. "Yours? The Panthers, of course."

"I like the Pats. I grew up in New Hampshire. I still root for them as long as they don't play the Panthers. Anyway, back to Wade. Maybe I'll have an answer for you by tomorrow. Meanwhile, let's see if I can get a pass for you to walk at midnight. With a strong, burly escort."

"Oh, that would be wonderful. Do you know someone strong and burly?"

"At your service," Sandy said. "I thought you'd never ask."

On Friday, Sandy reported to Maggie. "Wade said no to a Maggie-walk-about even with an escort at midnight. But he said it'll be okay to move to Belle's in a few more days if there is no further action there."

"It'll take me some time to get packed," she said. She scooped up her clothes, a few pieces of makeup, and the framed photo, tossed them into the duffle bag, and threw the books she'd been reading on top of everything.

"Done," she said. "Thanks for your patience."

"Okay, I can see you are a bit reluctant. Which is probably good. Belle is, right now, refreshing your room, hanging the sheets out to dry, and, in general, having a ball getting ready for you. Besides, Wade said, it has to be under cover of darkness, like around one or two in the morning."

"Well, that's good," said Maggie. "I have to do some deep cleaning here before I leave."

"Yeah, sure. No, I don't think so," said Sandy, folding his arms and chuckling. "This garbage scow has never been so clean, thanks to you. I was thinking of handing you some sandpaper, a brush, and a bucket of varnish."

"Now you mention it! Where was this idea when I desperately needed something to do? I'm pretty good at brightwork."

Sandy shook his head. "You continue to amaze me."

On the second Sunday in September, Sandy settled himself on the sofa in Belle's den. Belle and Maggie were already in front of the TV.

"Warren of football. Four letters." Belle poised her ballpoint pen over the crossword puzzle.

"Moon," Sandy said.

"Sapp," Maggie said.

"Sapp, it is," Belle said. "I already have the 'p'."

"Hah! I'm good. I'm good. Who da woman?" Maggie swayed in triumph.

Sandy shook his head in mock disbelief. "You da woman."

And she was. Damn, if she didn't know her football. The beer commercial ended, and Maggie leaned forward to focus on the large screen in Belle's den. Less than four minutes remained, and the Jets were ahead, 28-27. Even worse, they had the ball and were driving.

"Doesn't look good," Sandy muttered.

Then Maggie leapt to her feet. "Interception!" she crowed. "We still have a chance!"

"Sure," Sandy said. "Bledsoe will throw a bomb and the Pats will win."

"Too early," Maggie said. She squinted at the screen. "Three and a half minutes to go. Gotta burn some clock. Don't want to give the ball back to the Jets."

A short pass to Terry Glenn and two runs by Terry Allen moved the ball to the Jets' thirty-yard line.

As the referees stopped the clock for the two-minute warning, Maggie slumped into her chair, seemingly exhausted.

"You okay?" Sandy asked.

"Depends on whether or not we score," she said. "I'll let you know."

Time crawled as Maggie returned to the edge of her chair with one fist clenched. Sandy admired her ability to push aside worries for the moment and become completely engrossed in something. He wondered idly if she were that way with sex.

Shocked that he'd allowed this thought to enter his mind, he sat bolt upright and focused on the game. He'd been pushing such thoughts away since that first morning he had showed up at the boat with groceries. She was barefoot. He found himself staring at her small feet with pink-painted toenails and thinking he'd never thought of feet as sexy before. The moment seemed so overwhelmingly intimate he'd been lost in it.

On third down Drew Bledsoe completed a pass to Troy Brown that moved the ball to the Jets' seventeen-yard line.

"Tick, tick, tick," Maggie said. "Keep running, clock."

When the Patriots lost two yards on the next running play, Maggie groaned. "Go the other way!"

The Patriots obliged. While the clock continued to run, Bledsoe completed another pass to Terry Glenn. Two runs by Terry Allen, then a Bledsoe kneel-down, followed by a timeout, stopped the clock at seven seconds.

"Gotta make it gotta make it gotta make it," Maggie urged as Adam Vinatieri jogged onto the field.

When he split the uprights with the kick for the 30-28 win Maggie threw her arms up in a touchdown signal then jumped out of the chair and did a victory dance. "Never a doubt," she said.

"Not a one," Sandy said. On football Sundays, for as long as Belle and Sandy had been friends—maybe four years now—Belle cooked an early dinner, Sandy brought halftime dessert, and they watched football from one o'clock on through the evening. Belle was a Southern lady who'd cut her sorority teeth on college football, and she loved the game. He didn't like to watch alone, sports bars turned him off, and his best friend Eddy Ingles wasn't into football. Belle liked football even though she usually dozed off in her recliner through a quarter, sometime during the afternoon. Highest quality sleep you could get was in front of a football game, so he occasionally missed a few plays himself.

Until today. Now that Maggie was part of the mix, there were two reasons he wouldn't take cat naps. He was having a good time talking football with her during timeouts and commercials. And he was afraid he'd snore or sleep with his mouth open. She looked quite different from when she'd arrived three weeks ago. The smallest change was the weight loss—ten pounds, she'd said. He had supposed the strain had caused the drop, but Maggie credited it to the fact that, on the boat, she didn't have access to donuts.

"And don't bring me any!" she'd instructed.

But the biggest difference was her hair, now very short except on top where it was a mop of curls that tumbled across her forehead. The old style, he seemed to recall, had the top hair pulled back away from her forehead. And now it was a strawberry red instead of blond. Belle's idea—Belle having been a hairdresser before she married. When Maggie wore sunglasses, the change was a pretty effective disguise. It took him a while to get used to the new look, but now, as he watched the curls bob, he decided he liked her hair better short—though blond or red, he didn't care—both seemed to set off her green eyes.

Which were sparkling right now. She turned to Belle. "Pookie and Joel will be happy. They had tickets at the Meadowlands."

"They travel to New York for a Patriots game?"

"Sure. Joel often isn't in Maine for Patriots' home games, so he tries to catch the ones that are close. Ish. I hope they went to the game. The trip home is always more fun if you win."

"I'm sure they did. People realize that life goes on. Sam has been gone for over a month now, and your last postcard said you were fine."

"How did you get interested in football?" Sandy asked Maggie.

"When Joel started playing, let's see, he was eleven, I think. He wanted me to be able to understand when I came to his games. So, with some of his allowance he bought one of those little Dell Pocket Books. It explained football to women. Condescending, yes, but I was less offended than I would be now. And I got more than enough out of the little book to follow the game. Then Joel wanted us to go to high school games even though he wasn't playing any longer because of a knee injury. So he'd sit beside me and patiently explain things like the on-side kick. Anyway, I got to like the game.

"Funny, though, Sam never did. Turned out to be a mother and son activity." She grinned that wide open smile that told you she was amused. "Talk about your warped family. Hey, the next game is the Panthers at the Saints," she said. "Could be a good game."

"And I suppose you'll root for the Saints?"

She cocked her head thoughtfully. "Whew, a really tough one. But since you brought the strawberry compote, I think I'm inclined to like the Panthers."

Sandy chewed on it for a moment. Fun lady. What was the harm in enjoying her company once a week? It's not like they'd be dating. She had begun peopling his dreams occasionally, but that in itself wasn't alarming. Sometimes he dreamt about whatever waitress served his lunch that day.

As he'd told his friend and department chairman, Eddy Ingles, and his wife Donna, Maggie was a pleasant acquaintance, nothing more. He'd learned his lesson–twice–and had no intention of ever becoming involved with anyone again. His friends knew his history.

They didn't argue.

* * *

171

Jewel looked out of the rain-streaked airplane window and watched the land grow closer as the Boeing 757 began its descent toward Jacksonville Airport. Having left from Boston at 7:45 a.m., they had flown mostly over the Atlantic, but now, after a three-hour flight, they were descending, and he could see the v-shaped airport surrounded by a lot of green. Agriculture? Maybe the Okefenokee Wildlife Refuge? He didn't know. It didn't matter. He knew where he was going. And it wasn't to the Okefenokee.

By the time the passengers had retrieved their carry-ons and filed toward the front of the plane, it was eleven a.m. Surprisingly, they deplaned on the tarmac. Jewel ducked his head and stepped outside into the rain. The blanket of humidity was like breathing pea soup.

A rental car, a mid-sized, black Ford was ready for him. He drove to the Hampton Inn where he had a reservation. Once in his room, he changed into Bermuda shorts and a black t-shirt with the word Audubon stenciled in white across the back. He also had a black ball cap with the same name on the front. He packed a small backpack with a few items and was on the road in fifteen minutes.

It had stopped raining by the time he arrived at the Orange Grove RV Park. He passed the main entrance, and a mile up the road he found what he was looking for–Nature Conservancy Park. He pulled into the lot and parked near a sign that said Trailhead.

Pulling a backpack from the passenger seat, he slung it over one shoulder and entered the forest. Ignoring the trail, he made his way through the forest of cypress, live oak and fringe trees. Junipers and laurel bushes made it difficult to walk but also created decent cover. When he got to the sandy car road of the RV park, he took binoculars from his backpack and put the strap around his neck. He walked up one driveway and down another, past a variety of RVs, as he looked for the Airstream and white Dodge truck. He occasionally lifted the binoculars to his eyes and looked upward toward the treetops. It probably wasn't necessary because the heat and humidity had everyone tucked inside; he could hear the whine of ACs coming from every trailer.

In the park he found two Airstreams, one of which had a red Ford F-250 parked beside it. The other, the thirty-footer, he was sure he had seen in the Maxwells' driveway, had no vehicle in the parking space.

As he started a second circuit, it began to rain again, but the drizzle did nothing to break the humidity. The Airstream might be occupied...perhaps the Maxwells had gone shopping, maybe a day trip, and the woman might be inside. But this was not the time to check it out. He retraced the route back to his car. From the backpack, he pulled out a two-liter bottle of water and drank the whole thing.

Now that he knew the lay of the land, he'd come back at the optimum time– 4 a.m. when nobody, but nobody, would be up to observe. Back in his room after a cool shower, he lay on his bed thinking of the possibilities. The idea that the woman might be in the RV, unprotected by the Maxwells, gave him an energy surge. By this time tomorrow, he could be back in Maine with the job over and feeling the satisfaction of finally tying up this loose end. The best possible outcome was that Henry Lee would have had to take the credit. The job had to be done, though, even if he didn't have the pleasure of pinning it on Lee. Jewel set his alarm. It might be done tomorrow. He felt his face split into a grin. He was feeling good.

At three a.m., his alarm woke him. Ten minutes later, he stepped out of his room and hit a wall of 90% humidity. The car's AC helped during the twenty-minute ride, but once he was on foot, the humidity was noticeable.

There was still no vehicle parked at the Airstream. The lock on the door was easily breached. He quietly, oh, so quietly, opened the door and listened. No sound except for the AC. In fact, it felt as if the trailer was unoccupied. He was disappointed. Very. He stepped lightly into the dining area. It had not been made up into a bed. After a minute of sensing the surroundings, he was certain no one was there.

One thing he was sure of: the Maxwells were not coming back soon. The refrigerator was clear of any food that could spoil: no leftovers, no produce, no milk or cream. Just ketchup, mayo, miscellaneous things that would keep. The kitchen garbage bin was empty as was the bathroom trash. And, most importantly, there was no third person occupying this space. No extra clothes, toiletries, toothbrush…nothing. The Wiser woman did not live here. The Maxwells did, however. In a drawer, he found mail addressed to them.

Well, then. Interesting. They dropped her off somewhere between Maine and Florida. Could be anywhere. Back to Amesbury then–look for and wait for more clues. He was satisfied that he was way ahead of NADCO and Henry Lee.

On a mid-week night around nine o'clock, Belle and Maggie heard a knock on the kitchen door.

"I'll get it," said Belle. It was her little joke every time someone came to the house. Maggie was not allowed to answer the door and, in fact, when the doorbell rang or someone knocked, she always slipped across the hall into Belle's little den that had been her husband's office.

No one ever called this late at night. Who might it be? Maggie wondered. She left the door open a crack so she could listen in.

"Oh, well, hello. Um, Evelyn," Belle said.

And then a very familiar voice said, "Sorry to bother you so late, Belle. I just wanted to return your cake plate."

There was a few seconds pause and Belle, sounding like she was reading cue cards, said, "Oh, yes, of course. Why don't you come in?"

Maggie stepped out of the office and peeked into the kitchen. And yes, there was Jessie, her abundant silver hair swept back and up, holding up a piece of paper that said, ASK ME TO STAY FOR COFFEE.

"Oh, my, yes, can you stay for coffee?" Aunt Belle asked.

Jessie's blue eyes sparkled when she looked up at Maggie and smiled. She put a precautionary finger to her lips.

"That would be great," said Jessie. She held up another piece of paper that said, MAKE SMALL TALK.

Maggie watched from the doorway in amazement as Jessie began to search the kitchen–for a bug, she decided.

Belle struggled to think of something to say as Jessie felt and looked under the table, behind the frames that held Belle's embroidered bird pictures.

Jesse nodded at Belle to keep going. "Well, ah, yes, how've you been...ah, Evelyn?" she asked.

"Not too bad since my double hip-replacement surgery."

Jessie removed electrical outlet covers with a tiny screwdriver and examined behind the outlets. She waved to Belle to keep going.

"Well, yes, I heard about that," Belle said. "It must have...um...must have been an ordeal."

Jessie stood on a chair and opened up the smoke detector. "Yes, but they say when I have the double-knee replacement surgery, it'll be a whole lot worse." She winked at Belle.

"Oh, you poor thing!" Belle said. Maggie could see she was starting to get into her role. "If you are needin' anythin' when you have your knees done, you just ask me. I can bring a hot dish every day."

Jessie pulled the fridge away from the wall and looked behind it.

"I sure will. Nice to be able to depend on friends to help. So how have you been, Belle?"

"Oh…good, good. You know…good."

Jessie pulled the stove away from the wall. "Glad to hear it. Good to have our health as we get on in years."

"Yes, yes, that's for sure. So, once your knees are done, you should be in pretty good shape, right?"

Jessie climbed back on the chair and took down the globe that covered Belle's ceiling light.

"Yup. Except they say as soon as I recover, they need to do my gallbladder. Then, it'll be clear sailing after that."

Jessie stepped down and motioned Maggie into the kitchen and closed the door.

"There are no bugs in here. Probably not anywhere, but I had to check before we could talk. But first, let's have some coffee or tea, and I'll tell you why I'm here."

At the kitchen table where they had all gathered only a little over five weeks ago, Jessie explained.

"Sorry about the cloak and dagger stuff. We did some surveillance every week or ten days, give or take, and no one seems to be watching your house, but I had to make sure."

"You what?" Maggie leaned toward Jessie. "You've been here and gone, back and forth, and you didn't tell us? And! That's too much driving for you and Wade!"

"To tell you the truth, Wade has more energy than ever. And he always wanted to be a long-haul driver, anyway." She grinned at Belle.

"Look, Maggie, Wade and I have been talking, and we figure you must be going stir crazy. We're worried you might start taking risks eventually."

Maggie nodded, thinking this was not the time to tell Jessie that Sandy, Belle, and she had taken a few midnight walks already.

"So, what do you say about some training that would allow you to go out?"

"Well, how nice!" said Belle, beaming at Maggie. "That way you could go for walks. If you were wanting to, that is."

Maggie did her best to look innocent while she focused on Jessie. "Sounds good. What did you have in mind?"

"I'll teach you how to get around, both by vehicle and walking. Then, and now don't freak out, a little gun training–"

"No way on the gun thing because–"

"And then some self-defense training."

"Okay! I like that one. Then I can defend myself and not have to do any bodily harm."

"Sure. That's a way to think about it. Why don't we get started early tomorrow? Say–"

"Not too early. I don't get up until–"

"Before first light. Let's say–"

"Eight o'clock."

"We start at six o'clock."

Maggie blinked. "That's before sunrise."

Jessie smiled. "As I said. Before first light. Okay, let's compromise and say six-thirty. We'll be ready at sunrise. I'll pick you up. Dress appropriately."

It was still dark when Jessie handed Maggie a water bottle as she got in the car. "Be sure to stay hydrated. Self-defense starts with physical fitness so we're going to run a little today. Start off easy. Maybe just a mile the first day." Jessie pulled away from the curb.

"Run?" Maggie asked in astonishment. "As in, run like those nuts I see jogging past my house? Those college kids are just, you know …well…health nuts."

"As in, run like the wind. You did bring sneakers, right? Good. You can't run in those sandals you're wearing. You can't do anything in sandals except sashay into a restaurant."

Maggie was silent while Jessie drove along quiet streets. In a few minutes, they pulled into a parking lot where there were only two other cars. A sign said Nature Trail.

"Don't worry, we'll start easy," Jessie said.

"But, I don't run. Maybe I've never told you this. I bike. I've never run." Maggie slipped off her sandals and pulled on a sock.

"In a few minutes, you won't be able to say that again."

As soon as Maggie had the laces tied on her second sneaker, Jessie started jogging down the tree-lined trail. Twenty minutes later, after two stops to catch her breath and hold her aching side, Maggie caught up with her. At the car.

"It'll get better," Jessie said. "We'll increase the time every day, and pretty soon it will be easy." She pulled two granola bars out of her backpack and handed one to Maggie. "Here. After a bite of breakfast, you'll learn to shoot."

"Shoot? A gun? Today? Now?"

"Yeah. Just as a precaution," said Jessie. "We know you won't likely ever need it, but we'd rest easier if you knew how to use one. Think of it as an appreciation gift to us."

They pulled into a back road and drove deep into the woods. A concrete building came into view, and they parked.

Jessie opened her car door. "I know this is totally against something you feel strongly about. But consider this. If Joel, Pookie, or Tildie were in danger, wouldn't you want to be able to protect them?"

Yes, she thought. Yet every fiber of her being resisted the idea. With weak knees, wobbly legs, and a queasy stomach, she followed Jessie inside.

Jessie placed a tan case on a shelf in front of them and opened it. Inside, cushioned by plastic foam, were two pistols. Maggie's tension escalated.

"I want you to hold each of these and see which is the most comfortable." Jessie held out a pistol.

Maggie willed herself to extend her hand for the weapon.

Jessie shook her head and rolled her eyes. "It's not going to bite you. Hold it like this."

The gun was much lighter than it looked, and it fit her hand as if it were made for a woman.

"In this revolver, a Smith and Wesson .38, the frame is made of aluminum alloy, and the cylinder is titanium, so it's really light. Now try this one."

"It's heavier. And a little bigger."

"It's a semi-automatic—a Walther PPK." Jessie chuckled. "James Bond's favorite gun."

Maggie handed it back. The image of Sean Connery holding a gun made it seem more lethal.

"No, try it," Jessie said. "This one, because it's heavier, has less recoil, so don't reject it yet. Here, let me have it." Taking the gun back from her, Jessie demonstrated a two-handed, straight-armed position. "Your left hand wraps around your right for support. Try it again."

Maggie took the gun and tried it.

"No, your left thumb has to come down on the side. Leave it back there, at the back of the grip, and the slide will come back. See this thing on top of the gun? It slides back. It'll slice your left thumb. Look, keep the right one down on the side and the left thumb on top and parallel. That's right, you got it. No, don't put your finger into the trigger guard until you're ready to fire. Good. Now plant your feet solidly like this. You're right-handed, so your right foot will go back a little so you're balanced."

Maggie adjusted her stance. "You said recoil. What's recoil?"

"The weapon will kick back a little each time you fire. Doesn't hurt and you don't even really notice after you get used to it. But the less recoil, the more accurate you're apt to be on the next shot."

"What next shot? Jessie, I won't be shooting at all after today."

Jessie nodded slowly. "Once upon a time I said that. Anyway, up to you which gun. Try them both again."

The smaller gun fit Maggie's hand better but was so light it almost seemed like a toy. Better to have one that felt like a real weapon to keep her aware of its potential danger. "Okay, that one."

"PPK it is. Wade will be proud of you. It's his favorite. First, let's talk about safety. Number one, treat every gun as if it's loaded. Almost goes without saying–never point the weapon, loaded or unloaded, at anything you are not going to shoot at. Always point it in a safe direction, down, away from your body."

"And anyone else's. Got it."

"But let me expand on this. Picture in your mind a laser beam coming from the end of the barrel. You don't want the laser beam to pass over anything. Thinking of it this way will prevent you from pointing it unawares at someone far away or crossing over some of your own body parts–foot, hand."

"Oh, I see. That's a good idea."

"This gun has a magazine to hold the cartridges." From the gun case Jessie picked up a rectangular metal container Maggie recognized from movies.

"Some people call it a clip, but the correct term is magazine. This magazine is empty–no bullets, yet. Goes in the grip like this." Jessie slid the magazine into the bottom of the gun handle.

Maggie laughed. "Jessie, you're supposed to be baking cookies. Not looking like someone from the FBI Files. How did you learn to do this?"

"Well, way back, when I was a kid, my dad taught me how to shoot a .22 rifle. That's a gun with a long barrel. We used to target shoot, mostly. But...you don't want to hear this."

"It's okay. You can tell me."

"Well, we used to shoot garden pests–critters that ate our corn. By the time I was fifteen, I could shoot the eye out of a crow at thirty yards. At least that's what my dad told the boys."

Maggie tried to push the visual image out of her mind. Suddenly, she felt a need to appear tough. Not let Jessie think she was a wimp. "You never told me about that." Maggie reached for the gun and held it in two hands, arms straight. "But these guns aren't for shooting garden pests. How'd you get to know about them?"

"Originally Wade taught me when he was in the OSS. The gun was a snub-nosed Smith and Wesson .38 Special." Jessie's voice held a note of affection.

Maggie planted her feet apart, the right a little bit back. "OSS. Wasn't that some kind of spy thingy? During the war?"

"Don't lock your elbows. Leave them slightly bent to help absorb the recoil. Good. Espionage sorts of things, dear. Forerunner of the CIA."

Maggie couldn't keep her eyes from opening wide and her head from turning toward Jessie.

"First, we're going to try a dry fire. No cartridges in the magazine. See this, here? It's the safety. You can keep it on when the gun is loaded. Or not. There's a good reason for not."

"Seriously?"

"Uh huh. With the safety on it's one more thing to remember to do in a high stress situation."

"But couldn't it go off accidentally?"

"No. Not unless your finger accidentally pulls the trigger. If you carry a weapon with the safety off and follow good safety procedures, it's not going to unintentionally discharge. Wade and I always carry with the safety off. Used to, anyway."

"With the gun loaded?" She couldn't believe her ears. Wade and Jessie were her sweet and gentle, elderly, garden-tending, jam-making neighbors, surrogate grandparents to Pookie.

"Of course, with the gun loaded. Otherwise, what's the point? Now–"

"There's no bullets in this gun, right?"

"Not yet. Actually, we call it ammo. But you can call them bullets. Now you need to look at the sights. See this little post at the front of the barrel? Okay, now look at the back of the gun, here. There's a corresponding notch here between two rectangles. When you sight down the barrel, you make the front sight–the post– appear to fit into the notch. Your eyes can't focus on all distances at once, so the front sight should be the clearest, the rear sight next, and the target will be a little blurry."

"Okay, I can see what you mean."

"Now look ahead, and put your finger in the trigger guard, right here. Good. Find your target and squeeze the trigger slowly. And I mean slowly, for now. Don't think pull. Think gentle squeeze. If you pull, you're likely to move your whole hand."

"Like pushing the shutter button on a camera. Move only the finger."

"Exactly."

The paper target had a milk bottle shape on it with a small Q printed in the middle. She lined the sights up with the Q and pulled the trigger. Snap. It wasn't the least bit scary. Kind of fun, actually.

"Let me try again." She lined up the sights again and squeezed. "Well, this isn't bad. This shooting stuff."

"Now we'll load the gun. I'll do it for now." Jessie opened a full box of brass-colored cartridges. She put the safety on, pushed a button, and withdrew the magazine from the gun. She pulled the slide back and looked into the gun.

"You just visually check to be sure there is nothing in the chamber."

Jessie laid the gun down and picked up the magazine, pushing the cartridges in one by one.

"Check to be sure the safety is still on." She slid the magazine into the gun and rapped it firmly with the heel of her hand. She pulled the slide back and let it snap into position. "Okay, that puts a round into the chamber. That means one cartridge is seated and ready to fire. If we wanted to, we could top it off–put another cartridge in the magazine to replace the one that's in the chamber. That'd give you seven rounds. But we always say, 'if you can't get them with six, the seventh one won't help much.'"

Maggie could feel herself hyperventilating. She took a deep breath and let it out slowly.

"Okay, before we go any further…" Jessie picked up ear protectors that looked like headphones. "We need to wear these."

Maggie slipped hers on and looked to Jessie for approval.

"Well, Ms. Wiser, time to go to work," Jessie said, her voice muffled.

Pointing the barrel away, she handed the gun to Maggie.

"With your thumb, push the safety forward to disengage it. Okay, the gun is ready to fire. Let's start with a target twenty feet away. I'll move it into range." Jessie pushed a button next to her, activating a motor. The target moved toward them on a cable.

"Keep your finger outside the trigger guard until you're ready. Let me emphasize this. Don't ever put your finger inside the trigger guard until you've made the decision to shoot and your weapon is aimed at the target."

"Sounds like a good safety tip."

"The most important one. Yeah, that's good, but move your left thumb out of the way. The first time the slide comes back across your thumb and removes some skin, you won't forget again."

"Lot to remember. And I tend to learn the hard way."

"Don't we all? Try to stop your hands from shaking, Maggie. Relax. Fire whenever you're ready."

Think just your finger. She held her breath and slowly squeezed the trigger. The sound slammed against her chest. She felt the kick in her shoulders and through her limbs.

Her heart pounded with exhilaration. "Whoa. I didn't know it would be so loud."

"Only the first few rounds. You start to habituate to it. Won't notice it so much after another few rounds."

"Did I hit the target?"

"Nope, you didn't even aim at it. You just pulled the trigger."

"Oh, God. I told you I couldn't do this. I'm a disaster with a gun."

"No, you're a beginner. This time, when you fire, it will take a lighter, shorter trigger pull because the hammer is already cocked. Automatically. Try again. Take a breath. Relax. Then aim. No, move your thumb out of the way. Good."

She sighted down the barrel trying to steady her trembling hands. When the sight was on the Q, she squeezed. The noise wasn't so unnerving this time.

"Did I get it?"

"You're on the page but you missed the target. Not by much, though. See, it's to the right. Try again."

Maggie aimed, shot, and looked. The black dot was an inch from the Q.

"Much better. Try again."

Maggie fired three more times, the little black dots clustered within two inches of each other, though a little left of the Q. She'd been trying to compensate for the shot that had gone to the right, she realized.

"Pretty good. Your gun's empty. Let's reload and go again."

She handed the newly loaded gun to Maggie. "Let's make it a little more difficult. Let's try thirty feet. I'll change the target." Jessie pushed the button to bring the target to them.

Maggie watched as Jessie stapled a new target in place and sent it back out. A life-sized, black and white photograph of a ferocious man with Sylvester Stallone biceps filled the target. He was dressed in an undershirt which exposed the top of his hairy chest. He was pointing a huge gun at her. Everything in her view felt like it shifted sideways. The edges of her circle of vision rimmed with black. She put out a hand and steadied herself against the wall.

"Honey, are you all right? I didn't know this would be so hard for you. Do you want to stop?"

"It's a human being. I can't shoot at a human being. Well, I know it's just paper but—"

"He's a menacing human being. He's got a gun pointed at you. It's you or him. What are you going to do?"

"All right. All right. Move over, Annie Oakley. I may never shoot again, but at least I'm going to get it right this time. I plug him full of holes, okay?"

With resolve, she looked at the paper thug, aimed at a place in the middle of his chest and pulled the trigger. She looked at the target. Dead center. Okay. She shot five more rounds and looked again. The holes were clustered tighter this time.

"Hey, Ms. Maggie. Good shootin' there."

"Thanks." Maggie felt inordinately pleased. "Do you want to shoot? I could use a break." She handed Jessie the gun and shook the tension out of her arms.

Silver-haired, school-marm-looking Jessie reloaded and aimed at the target. Maggie watched as the first round hit the man in the middle of the forehead. Jessie rapidly fired five more rounds, each hole so close to the previous one, the target gunman had only one ragged hole in his forehead.

Jessie pretended to blow smoke from the end of the barrel.

Maggie whistled. "Jeesh. Good shooting, Sheriff."

"Well, this is pretty close range for me."

"How far can you shoot accurately?" Maggie asked.

"Depends on what you mean by accurately. Context is important. Today you could cover my grouping with a silver dollar, wouldn't you say?"

Maggie nodded. "Yes. To me it looked like one hole."

"Well, I was showing off, of course." Jessie winked, breathed on her nails and polished them on her shirt. "But when Wade and I were shooting competitively...."

"Competitively! Wait. I never knew. Why don't I know?"

"It's not the kind of thing that comes up in neighborly conversation. And that's probably best. We like to keep a low profile in Amesbury. Part of the reason we moved there. Creates a more relaxed retirement. But since you asked, when I practice regularly, I can hit a head shot, a tight cluster like you just saw, with my Glock at twenty yards–so three times farther than what we just did. At forty yards, I'm shooting center mass." Jessie turned toward Maggie.

Maggie couldn't stifle a small gasp.

"You know what I mean by center mass, then?"

Maggie nodded. "Yes, I'm sure I do," she said grimly.

"More room for error, shall we say. At that distance, my goal is a six-inch grouping. Nothing to earn a ticker tape parade for, but I do okay competitively.

"One thing to keep in mind, though. When I'm shooting, I'm shooting at a paper target. That isn't moving. And it isn't shooting back."

"Right." She was constantly making huge adjustments to her view of Jessie.

"We've been at this long enough. You've done well. Very well. I can't wait to tell Wade. We'll be back tomorrow. Your shooting's fine, but you should get a little more familiar with the gun and learn to reload by yourself."

"I wouldn't mind doing this again. Kind of fun." Maggie laughed. "But, Jessie, I don't have to know how to reload. What do you think? I'd fire six rounds, reload and start firing again?" Maggie shook her head, laughing and handed back the gun. She pulled off the ear protectors and ran her fingers through her hair.

"This will be your gun, Maggie. Take it with you. It's yours. For now, anyway." Jessie handed the gun back to her. "I have a case for it in the car."

"Oh, no. No, you don't. I won't keep a gun. Jessie, you might as well know. I could never kill anybody. I mean anybody. Not even that guy up there." She nodded toward the target.

"I actually think you could, in self-defense. But, if you don't think so, then let me paint you this picture once more. Suppose Tildie or Pookie were in danger."

"Okay, okay. Well, maybe I could shoot in order to save someone, but I couldn't kill them. I'd have to wound them or something."

"First of all, if anything happened that you had to use this, you almost certainly wouldn't be shooting at someone as far away as the target. More likely it would be closer up, and you wouldn't have time to get particular about where you aim. But if your reluctance means the difference between pulling the trigger or not pulling the trigger, aim for the midsection. Maybe they won't die."

"Jessie, did you ever–"

"Some other time, Maggie," she said with uncustomary bluntness. "Let's pack up. I'll keep the gun for now. You start self-defense training in an hour. Let's grab a quick lunch."

"Self-defense. So maybe I could defend myself without a gun? Without killing someone?"

"So that you could stop an attacker for a second or two while you get away. This is assuming you don't have your weapon handy.

"But," Jessie said as they walked away, "*always* have your weapon handy."

"How long do you think you'll be here?" Maggie asked Jessie at lunch.

"You mean how long will this torture last?"

Maggie laughed out loud because that was exactly what she was thinking.

"Let's see how it goes. At least two weeks. I'd like a little longer."

"Two weeks! What do I need to know that will take two weeks?"

"Maggie, when I did this kind of training, it was six months. With you, we'll try to cram it into a couple of weeks."

"I bet it includes running every day, doesn't it?"

"Oh, sure, that's the easy part. We're going to learn some counter-surveillance. It's an essential method of determining–"

"If I'm being followed by a deli *counter*, right?" Maggie smirked at her own joke.

"Cute, Maggie. No, to see if you're being followed by someone who wants to put two hollow points into you."

"Okay, well, giving it some careful thought, I'd like to avoid that if possible."

"Wise choice. You are probably aware of surveillance as in what the police or the FBI does. But it works both ways. In your case, surveillance would be when you are being watched and followed–for sure with no honorable intentions. Counter-surveillance is when you are watching out for that and trying to counter it. That's what you're going to be learning."

"Oh. My. Oh, is that really necessary? It sounds so cloak and dagger."

"Let's lighten it up. Think of it as a challenge, a game. You can change your look, wear disguises. Have some fun with it. But get good at it. Your life could depend on it. No pressure."

At the self-defense class, Maggie was relieved that the other five women didn't look any more in shape or athletic than she did. Two were older than she was.

"This is not a martial arts class," the instructor said, "though you will learn some basic martial arts moves. Your goal will never be to stay and fight off an attacker, but to divert his attention with pain so you can get away. But first, let's stretch a little."

The next day, Maggie found herself looking forward to returning to the firing range. As a hobby, target practicing wouldn't be bad. The combination of sound and power could possibly relieve frustrations. She remembered all that Jessie had taught her, and she learned to reload. An hour later, when they were done, Maggie slipped the unloaded gun and a box of ammunition into her backpack. It would be rude to not accept the gun after what Jessie was going through so she could protect herself.

Accepting the gun felt like a contract, though.

Taking time off for only one football game on Sunday, Maggie spent the next four days doing the most strenuous physical activities of her life. Jessie showed her how to stretch before and after the run and added five minutes to the run each day. Despite sore muscles, Maggie had to admit it was easier by the fifth day. She no longer had to stop to gasp for breath twice before they were done. And she was feeling, what? Empowered? Yes, that was it. Kind of on top of her game. Whatever that was.

"I feel sheepish telling you this, since I was a wimp about running," Maggie said as she sat along a dock's edge with Jessie, dangling her toes in the water as she cooled down from a jog. "But I kind of like it. I might keep it up."

"You better keep it up," said Jessie. "And today we're adding strength training. I have you booked at a gym."

"Strength training?"

"Weights. We'll see what you can bench press."

"You're kidding."

"No. We'll start you off light."

By the end of the week, Maggie actually looked forward to the gym and, surprise of surprises, to jogging. But on Saturday, when Jessie picked her up, she drove in a different direction.

"We're going to the firing range again. Today, we're going to work on disassembling a Glock and give you a little more target practice. The first thing you do is—"

"Wait, aren't we going running?" Maggie said, surprised by her disappointment.

"Oh, we'll run. Don't you worry. But we can do that at any time of day. For shooting, I had to make an appointment."

When they got to the firing range, Jessie said, "So, as I said, we're going to learn how to disassemble a Glock. My Glock, as a matter of fact."

She opened the case, took it out, and handed it to Maggie.

Maggie pulled her hand away, clasping her hands behind her back. "Now really! Why the hell do I need to learn how to disassemble a gun?"

"Well, if you're really in a pinch, you could always throw the pieces at someone."

Maggie laughed. "Yes, that does sound more like me."

"No, the idea is to become more comfortable with a weapon. You want it to be an impediment to someone else, not to yourself. And anyway, all we're talking about here is the magazine, the frame, the barrel, the slide, and the spring. That's it."

"Sounds simple."

"After you do it a hundred times, yes. Then we'll work on–"

"Give me the damn gun."

An error message appeared on Pookie's screen. He had to reboot. While the computer crackled and whirred, he looked over the hard copy of his report due first thing in the morning. He checked the calendar. Tomorrow was October 12. He'd been working on it for a week. It was his best effort and worth an A, he hoped. All he needed to do was print the bibliography, and he was done.

The error message came up again. Damn! He rebooted again with the same results. Well, geez, he had to have the bibliography. Without it the report wasn't worth shit.

His father, the computer genius, was away "winding up" one of his out of state accounts. This was the first time he'd left home since...since everything had changed.

When the fourth attempt produced the same results, he dumped his wastebasket on the floor looking for his handwritten notes. Not there. Violet must have emptied it. Yesterday was trash collection day. Well, dammit anyway. He knew better than to get rid of the notes before everything was done. Except the report had been done–just the bibliography to print. Oh, man. Ten items in the bibliography. He couldn't think of a way of retrieving the information.

Then he heard Tildie coming down the hall. She was pretty good with a computer. But even though she'd been a little nicer to him lately, he still couldn't imagine asking her for a favor. Ever. She'd level him, make him feel like an idiot. An F on the paper wouldn't be as bad as that. He'd still pass the class.

She tapped on his door.

"Yeah?"

She opened the door. "I was wondering what you were doing tomorrow night. Dad won't be back yet, and I thought if you wanted to go to Doug's, I could give you a ride."

"I got an away-meet the next morning." He sighed. She never remembered there was a cross country meet every Saturday morning.

At least she looked embarrassed. "Oh, yeah, sorry, I forgot."

"Why do you want me to go to Doug's?" He knew she wasn't looking around for something nice to do. And if she really wanted to do something, she could fix his damn computer.

She looked uncomfortable. "I have a date."

"And so?"

"We thought we'd stay in and cook dinner. For two."

The thought of Andrew cooking anything made Pookie want to laugh. The big guy would probably starve if not for the women in his life. "So you want some privacy. Is it pop the question night?"

Tildie's eyes widened in disbelief.

He didn't even believe it himself. "Sorry. I can probably stay at Doug's house, go to the meet with him. I can take my track stuff to school in the morning. I'll call Doug and see if it's okay with his mom."

She stared down at her feet and then out of his window. "I...would...really be, uh, grateful."

Boy, you could tell that was hard for her.

But maybe the "grateful" could pay off. "Listen, I'm having trouble with my computer. Would you–?"

"Sure. Move over. What's going on with it?"

Tildie pushed her hair behind her ears and pulled the corner chair up to the computer. Lying on the desk in a neat pile was Pookie's report. She read the words on the front cover.

The Separation of Government Powers
By S. Nicholas Wiser

Her insides jumped. S. Nicholas. Not Pookie. Not even Samuel.

"What did you say was wrong?" she asked him.

"I keep getting this error message when I try to print. Let me show you." He leaned across and typed.

Suddenly, she was in the past. Her mother was holding the new baby against her shoulder, patting his back and crooning. Tildie hated him. She didn't want a baby in her house. Then he spit up sour smelling stuff all over her mother's arm. After her mother cleaned the gunky stuff off the baby's face and her own arm, she laid him in the cradle and went to get clean clothes for him. Tildie looked into the cradle and said to him, "Pukey baby. Yucky, pukey baby." She said it softly though, because she had long since been told puke was not an acceptable word. Polite people said "throw up" or possibly "vomit." She tested the word once more with satisfaction. "Puke. Disgusting. Gross. Pukey."

She'd suddenly noticed her mother almost beside her. Tildie adored her mother. Afraid she might have been overheard, afraid she would receive a disapproving raise of an eyebrow, she changed the word to "Pookie."

"I call him Pookie, Mommy. Because he's so cute." Her mother smiled and nodded, picked up the baby and cooed at him. For days afterwards, maybe weeks–she couldn't remember now–she called him Pookie, and no one stopped her. She was beginning to enjoy the trick she was getting away with when she realized other people were calling him Pookie. She felt an overwhelming stab of victory–she had gotten the adults to play her game, and they didn't even realize it–followed by crushing guilt. And she was frightened to have that much power and responsibility.

"Do you know how to fix it?" Pookie looked at her, puzzled.

She pulled herself back to the present and started troubleshooting, her fingers flying over the keys.

"That's a different error message than I got," Pookie said.

"Yeah, I think I know what it is. Maybe I can get around this."

If her mother had lived longer than six months after the baby was born, Tildie would have told her the truth because the burden of guilt was becoming heavy. Her mother would have laughed, hugged her, and fixed the whole thing. But her mother hadn't lived.

So he remained Pookie.

And her guilt never left.

At the time, she thought her mother had left them because Tildie had been bad. And the baddest thing she knew she'd done was give the baby his awful name. She blamed the baby more than ever. If he'd never been born, she'd never have been bad, and her mother never would have left them.

"Hey! I think you've got it."

Tildie nodded, letting her hair slip forward to cover the tears that rimmed her eyes.

Eventually, as she was able to understand her mother's death, she realized the truth, but it was years before the guilt over her brother's name decreased at all. Eventually she divorced herself from the whole damn problem by calling him "Twerp."

Which was miles better than Pookie.

"Okay, is this the file you want printed?"

"That's it."

She saw him cross his fingers.

The printer made its bowing and scraping noises, and a sheet of paper moved into place.

"Yes!" Pookie hissed.

She suddenly felt something that might be remorse. Not daring to look at her younger brother–now taller than herself–sitting beside her, she nodded. "Let me know if you have any more problems."

She pushed back her chair. Now he wanted a name change. In fact, he'd said something a while back, but nobody had taken him seriously–she hadn't, anyway. She guessed he was due, but she was certainly not going to tell him how the name came about.

She sighed. The name was so firmly attached to him that when he scored points in his junior varsity game, even the newspaper called him Pookie Wiser. How could he change his name now? Guilt settled in its familiar resting place as she got up to leave.

"Thanks," he said to her retreating back. The word sounded heartfelt.

She turned around. "Pick you up from Doug's Saturday night?"

He nodded as he added the printed page to the end of his report.

She wanted to add something and almost left the room before she realized what it was. "You got a home meet next week?"

"Yeah."

"I'll be there."

His head came up in astonishment, but she slipped out and closed the door before she was forced to meet his eyes.

It wasn't much.

But it was something.

"What does Sandy think about your training?" Jessie asked while she tightened her shoelaces. Today, instead of running, they were going for a "vigorous" walk while Jessie instructed her.

"I don't know," Maggie said as they started off down the path. "I haven't seen him. He didn't come watch football with us Sunday. Or last Sunday. Belle says that's very unusual. 'Unheard of,'" she said.

"Hmmm. Well, Wade has come up with a plan that will have to include him. Maybe they will talk this week. We've got Sandy's phone number. Anyway, today, we're going to begin the counter-surveillance we talked about.

"If you're being tailed, in the beginning, it will probably be with the goal of the tail getting information. They, let's say *he,* for the time being, let's assume it would be one guy–he wants to know where you normally go, what your routine is, what your favorite stops are. He's gathering information so he can make a plan. If that plan is to wipe you out, he wants to know...where is the best place, the best time, the best circumstance, where he can get away with it and not be detected."

"But how would anyone know where I live?"

"For training, assume your cover is broken, and you've been discovered. That's the premise of all this work."

"Okay, got it. Hey, you know what? I can walk and talk without getting out of breath!"

"Let's see how you're doing in an hour. Moving on, if you're in a vehicle and being followed by a vehicle, he won't randomly come across you. He'll already know where you live and will be waiting someplace where he won't be noticed. He can pick you up as you go by. Therefore, the best time to start watching for vehicle surveillance is when you first start out. Here's my point. It will be the same thing if you're on foot. Vigilance at the beginning of any outing has to be there when you walk out of the door."

"This scares me a little."

"I hope it scares you a lot, so you take this seriously."

"Scared a lot. Got it."

"If someone started following you in your neighborhood, you would likely notice, so he would have to stay more out-of-the-way and farther behind. He might try to blend in with the neighborhood, like maybe somebody raking leaves. When Wade does surveillance, a lot of people who are not home get their yards groomed.

"Once you are in a more crowded area, he can get closer and blend with other pedestrians. He can also use the buildings and parked automobiles to avoid being detected by you. But the same goes for you. You can also use your surroundings to spot surveillance or to duck out and disappear."

"Disappear?"

"Appear to disappear."

"So, you're going to teach me strategies? I feel like I'm in a spy movie."

Jessie nodded. "But the reality is much harder than a thirty-second clip in a movie scene. It's important that whoever is following you, doesn't realize that you've spotted him. This is critically important. That leaves him in gathering information mode. If he thinks you've spotted him, it may push him into acting sooner rather than later. Therefore, *never* give an indication if you think you're being followed. Never turn around and look.

"There are ways for you to figure out if you're being followed, and I'll talk about them. Once you think you are being followed, you can lead the surveillance guy into restaurants, stores, malls, supermarkets, public locations. Some public locations may have stairways or elevators, escalators. Often there are one or more other exits from the building.

"Let's say you suspect you are being followed. You can stop to look in a store window. With peripheral vision, see if he also stops. Then go into the shop, step away from the window but where you can still see outside. Does he stop and look like he's browsing the window? Does he glance toward the door but keep on going?

"Right away, I'm suggesting that as soon as we're done with your training, you become familiar with most of the stores in this area."

"Oh, I already am, kind of. Aunt Belle and I used to go shopping whenever we visited."

"Good. So, think your way through where you'll go once inside. Find out if there's another street exit. You have to be on your game, always observing, understanding, and retaining much more information, many more details, than you, or anybody, does in your daily life. You have to think consciously about it all the time.

"Attention is the most critical aspect of surveillance detection, because, without attention, perception and retention are impossible."

Maggie chuckled. "You sound like an instructor in this counter-espionage stuff."

Jessie smiled almost imperceptibly without looking at Maggie.

"Oh? Ooooh! You?"

"Not for a few years. Maybe I miss it. Maybe Wade does, too. Okay, focus. Listen, when you take a photograph, do you look at the entire frame? See everything that will be in the photo? Adjust to make it what you want it to be?"

"Yes, of course."

"Then you're halfway there. Except while you're walking around, the frame changes second by second so you can't ever stop noticing and remembering the details. When we get back to the car, we'll drive downtown. We'll souvenir shop, and I'll point out ways that you can lead your tail down a rabbit hole, how you can slip away. Okay, let's run the rest of this trail." And Jessie took off like the wind. Maggie managed to catch up with her as they both got back to the car.

"Your sprint at the end is getting impressive," Jessie said. "You could probably give Pookie a *run* for his money." Jessie chuckled as she got behind the wheel.

Maggie slid into the car. "Ha ha. Cute. But, really, maybe when I get back, we can run sometimes instead of bike. That sure would surprise him."

"Surprise everybody, I would guess," Jessie said, smiling. She started the car and backed up.

"Now, be still my beating heart, because I believe you just said we'd go shopping."

"Yes, but the purpose of this is not to acquire stuff, but to acquire more knowledge. Strategies. But, what we're going to do next will be the fun part. You will learn how to change your appearance. While on the move. Start with basics, sunglasses, a hat."

They didn't buy much, and Maggie was exhausted after two hours of fake shopping and trying to remember everything Jessie told her.

"Okay, let's head back to the car," Jessie said.

"Let's get an ice cream first," Maggie suggested and, grabbing Jessie's arm, steered her into the General Store, a shop they had visited just an hour ago. They sat on a bench out front, licking their cones in the afternoon sun.

"Well, this afternoon certainly has been informative," Maggie said.

"Well, I'm not really done. I have one more thing to say for today. On foot at night is a different ballgame because darkness provides cover for your tail, but then again, he can't see you as easily, so he has to follow more closely. Limit your nighttime exposure to absolutely *zero*. That's all I will say about that. Zero! That should not be too hard."

As they drove the few short blocks to Belle's, Jessie used the time to wind up her discussion.

"Something to remember as you and Belle make your plans for your graduation day. Yes, I'm sure Belle will want to be involved."

"Wait! Graduation day?"

"Informally, sure. Wade and I will challenge you to do a walkabout and see how often you give us the slip. Won't be easy, as he and I will not be together. But, easy isn't the objective."

"Oh, wow. A test, you mean. Well, okay, sure. I can get Aunt Belle to help?"

"I think you'll need all the help you can get. So...I'm running out of time. Listen up! A surveillance guy relies a lot on things like height, weight, dress, and mannerisms. Mannerisms are the most easily overlooked aspect of changing appearance. He will be watching for things like bearing, pace of motion, posture, and form for recognition because they are unique to you and will stay the same. If you don't make a conscious effort to alter them, he can observe these from a distance. Okay, end of lecture. Here we are."

"Okay, sure. I can hardly wait to tell Aunt Belle. And I will pass the test."

"I like your confidence. See you tomorrow."

During supper that night, Maggie told Belle about Jessie's plans for the future—a counter-surveillance test on Thursday.

"Well, that sounds like great fun," said Aunt Belle.

"Which part?"

"All of it. 'Specially the part where you disguise yourself, change your appearance, if you have to, while you're out and about. I think I can help you with that. If you don't mind an old lady buttin' in."

"I will take any and all help. You can run for me, if you want."

"Seriously, Maggie, Arthur and I used to belong to a drama club over in Morehead City. We put on all kinds of plays, and I was also the keeper of the props and costumes. I have trunk loads of stuff. I can't wait. This just keeps getting better and better."

Wade had stressed 0900.The counter-surveillance test would begin at 0900.

Therefore, Maggie decided she would slip from Aunt Belle's back door a few minutes before 8 a.m. One time she'd heard someone say, "If you ain't cheating, you ain't trying." But she didn't see it as cheating, anyway. She saw it as winning creatively. But winning was not the point of this exercise. Survival was. So it seemed.

While Wade or Jessie could slip up behind her and say "gotcha," an assassin could just as easily slip up behind her and, what? For the first time in weeks, the memory of Sam's bloody head flooded her mind. She took in a sharp breath. She could not think of this as a game.

"Good luck," Aunt Belle whispered behind her as Maggie went out the back door, a backpack slung over her shoulder.

Maggie pushed open the gate in the small fence separating Belle and Sandy's back yards. The left side of Sandy's yard was lined with red chokecherry and dogwood bushes; on the right were mountain laurel and rhododendron. She crept along the left side, the dogwood brushing against her legs. When she reached Sandy's garage, she quietly entered the side door.

Just as she hoped, the red Raleigh still hung on the wall. She had noticed the bike when Sandy spirited her away to hide on the boat.

Better to beg for forgiveness than ask for permission, she thought as she strained to lift the bike from the wall hooks. It was so much heavier than her own Cannondale. She adjusted the seat to what seemed right. Lifting the rear wheel off the ground, she spun the pedal and squeezed the right-hand brake. The wheel stopped short.

Well, okay then, she thought. All systems go.

She glanced at her apparel: holey, grungy jeans Aunt Belle had found at the thrift store, and a worn, baggy gray sweatshirt. She imagined it added twenty pounds to her appearance.

Like you looked not so long ago, she mused. She jammed a Panthers ball cap on her head and donned the tattered backpack. Good enough for a start.

She steered the bike out the side door and around to the driveway. Putting her left foot on the pedal, she let the bike roll down the sloped driveway, swung her right foot back and over the saddle, and turned onto the street.

It was exhilarating as the breeze brushed her face while she rode.

But not for long. Tend to business, she thought as she approached the end of the block. She leaned left and the bike tracked around the corner, heading to the intersection at the end of Belle's block.

Halfway down the block, there was Jessie, ambling slowly along, looking like a grandmother pushing a stroller. Someone you'd hardly notice, Maggie thought.

Is that how it could happen? Someone who seemed innocent could get close to you. Someone who could end your life.

Maggie slowly stood up to pedal, picking up speed as she minutely lowered her chin so the cap would better shield her face. Just another woman on an early morning bike ride.

As Maggie approached her, Jessie bent down and tended to an imaginary baby. Maggie slowly pedaled by.

No need to look back. She couldn't look back. Jessie said never look back. And, since Wade wasn't in sight, trouble would still be in front of her.

Abandoning her original plan to bike directly downtown, Maggie turned left, then left again at the next side street. When she did, she couldn't resist; she dared a quick glance Jessie's way.

Head tilted toward the imaginary baby, Jessie pushed the stroller down the street.

I might as well go back to the plan, Maggie thought. She turned right.

And there he was, maybe twenty yards in front of her. Wade.

He limped along, leaning heavily on a cane, gazing at the flowers that lined the sidewalk.

Her spirits immediately sank. He had her.

It's not over until it's over, flashed through her mind. Don't give up.

Without flinching, she coasted down Turner Street.

Once past him, she pulled in a ragged breath. Get it together, woman.

Focus. Don't treat it like a game, where a "gotcha" could be laughed off.

Treat it like your life is at stake. Because, despite her resistance to the idea, maybe it was.

Passing by a parking lot on her right, she swerved across the street and coasted onto Middle Lane, then up a narrow path behind a corner coffee shop. She braked, slowed the bike, and dismounted. She leaned it against a dumpster and entered the coffee shop's back door.

"What'll you have?" asked the young man behind the counter as she approached.

Maggie scanned the list of coffees. "Just a hot coffee, medium," she absentmindedly said.

"Dark roast?"

She nodded. She didn't really care about the coffee. What she cared about was…where was Wade?

She edged toward the front window. There he was, limping along on the other side of the street.

Wade stopped as a dog and its owner approached. He bent down to pat the dog and chatted amiably with the dog's owner, a mid-fifties gent with a long, gray braid hanging down his back. From time to time, Wade glanced at the plate glass window of the storefront next to them.

He's using it as a mirror to see what's on the other side of the street, Maggie thought. Exactly where I am.

She eased away from the window. Pulled in a long, slow breath. Relax. Don't get rattled.

She returned to the counter, paid for the coffee and waved away the change.

"My bike's in the back alley," she said to the attendant, "but I want to do some shopping. Can I leave it there for a couple of hours?"

"Well, um, sure. Yeah."

"I don't have a chain and lock."

"Oh, don't worry," the young man said, chuckling. "Nothing bad ever happens here."

Maggie entered the bathroom at the rear of the coffee shop, locked the door, and poured the coffee down the drain. She peeled off her jeans and sweatshirt and grabbed a navy blue, calf-length skirt from her backpack and slipped it on. She then donned a loose-fitting light blue top. Nothing to see here, she thought. Just a tourist.

She put her jeans and sneakers in the backpack and slipped her feet into sandals. A shoulder length blond wig and narrow cat's-eye sunglasses completed the look.

She unlocked the door and put her hand on the doorknob. She would be trapped if Wade had come into the coffee shop. But she couldn't stay in the bathroom forever. She slipped her backpack over one shoulder and took a deep breath.

Next time, don't paint yourself into a corner, she thought. Or the jig could be up.

She pushed the door open. Glanced around.

No Wade. No Jessie.

No immediate threat.

She pivoted, took three steps, and was out the back door. She moved the Raleigh out of sight behind the dumpster and turned down Middle Lane. She immediately felt exposed.

Breathe. She paused for a moment and remembered Jessie's words: "Never give an indication if you think you are being followed."

I'm a tourist. So walk like a tourist.

Whatever that's like, she mused, stifling a chuckle.

Maggie opted for a slow, leisurely stroll, trying to let her hips sway as she walked down the lane behind the stores that faced onto Front Street. Then, she entered a gift shop from its rear entrance.

Only a few customers and no Jessie or Wade. She strolled around, then picked up and put back various souvenirs, trying to look like she hadn't a care in the world.

Finally, she bought a pair of oversized sunglasses and tucked them into the backpack. Reassuring herself it was okay, she left the shop and stepped out onto Front Street.

There, across the street, was Wade. Again. With Jessie this time, who'd ditched the stroller.

Maggie turned and walked slowly to the next shop and paused, looking at the items in the window. In the reflection of the plate glass, she watched them as they chatted, glancing around the nearly vacant street.

Looking for me, Maggie thought. Well, I'll give them something to look at.

Slowly, casually, Maggie moved past the next two shops. At the last store on the block, she stopped and dared glance at the window, hoping the reflection would show them.

Jessie and Wade had parted and were moving in opposite directions.

Maggie glanced casually toward the bay. Between the stores across the street, she could see the early morning sun on the water. She crossed Craven Street to the next block.

Passing an office, a restaurant, and a two-story house incongruously squeezed between the commercial shops, she spotted what she was looking for: the General Store where she and Jessie had bought ice cream cones only a few days before.

She entered the store. No ice cream today.

She examined the gift items and bought a navy-blue tote bag with a ship's wheel imprinted in white on it and a black pirate's hat.

She turned toward the rear entrance and entered the bathroom. She stepped out of the skirt, pulled off the top, and stuffed them into her backpack. From the pack, she pulled out a blue t-shirt provided by Belle that said STAFF on the back. She slipped it over her head, then donned a pair of knee-length khaki shorts. She pulled off the blond wig and replaced it with a braided, brown one. She pulled the plaits in front of her shoulders and placed the pirate hat on her head.

"You look pretty silly for a woman of sixty," she said to her reflection in the mirror. She stuffed the clothing and wig into the backpack, then the backpack went into the tote. She swapped the sandals for boat shoes. Ready.

She opened the bathroom door, took one step out and glanced toward the front of the shop. Jessie walked in.

Carelessness kills, Jessie had told her many times in the past couple of weeks.

Now I know what carelessness feels like, Maggie thought as she did a slow about-face and exited by the back door.

Had Jessie spotted her? Would she also leave by the back door?

Can I get to another store before Jessie sees me? Maggie wondered.

Probably not.

Just outside of the store, there was an attached laundromat to the left. Maggie ducked in. As she did, she realized it was a bad move. There was no other exit. Painted myself into another corner, she thought.

Think, don't panic, Jessie had taught her.

But she'd panicked instead.

Now it was time to think her way out of this.

At the end of a line of washing machines, there was a small space to duck into. Someone had left a half-filled basket of laundry there; Maggie pulled it away from the wall and sank down behind it, pulling her knees to her chest and the tote on top of her knees. She pulled some clothes from the basket and draped them over her head and shoulders.

Nothing to see here, just a pile of dirty laundry.

She pulled the laundry basket toward her, hiding her legs. It wasn't much, but it was something.

The door opened.

She fought to slow her breathing. It had to be Jessie. Maggie could hear her move slowly and quietly between the washers and the folding table.

Maggie imagined a killer with a gun. He would creep slowly around, looking in every nook and cranny. Eventually he'd stop in front of her. He'd slide the clothes off her head. Shake his head at her feeble attempt to hide.

And finish her. Again, the memory of Sam. Blood on the windshield. Two hard hammers of her heart.

She willed herself smaller. She willed herself invisible. She willed herself alive.

The footsteps stopped.

The laundromat fell silent. Deathly silent. Artificially silent. She listened for breathing. Nothing.

Maggie waited.

Then, six quick steps. The door opened, and a few seconds later it clicked closed.

Don't be fooled, Maggie told herself. If Jessie can wait, or if a killer can wait, so can you.

Ten slow minutes dragged by. Then ten minutes more. Just in case.

Finally, she moved the clothes, pushed the basket away, and stood, trying to stretch her cramped legs.

She peered through the laundromat's nearest window. The back alley was empty.

Maggie piled the laundry back into the basket, picked up her tote, left the laundromat, and slowly strolled along the gravel and dirt alley behind the stores. When she reached Queen Street, she turned right and headed to Front Street. Back to the plan.

She crossed Front Street and walked to the dock and cruise boat area. The ocean was only yards away, and beyond the bay, she could see the barrier islands that protected it.

She heard the ticking of a cane. Without moving her head, she glanced right.

There was Wade, slowly coming down the sidewalk on her side of the street. He hadn't seen her yet. He was surreptitiously scanning the shops on the other side of the street.

Maggie ducked under a barrier that kept pedestrians off the dock. She wasn't a pedestrian now; she was an employee. She dropped the tote beside a bench and walked a few yards down the dock that extended into the bay. She squatted down, fussing with the line that tied off a tour boat that was designed to look like a pirate ship. Not twenty-five feet away, Wade approached the ticket booth for Island Express Ferry.

She turned her back to him as she stood up and walked down the dock, where a private boat was tied. The captain pulled up a bucket of sea water and sloshed it along the deck.

"Going out or coming in?" Maggie asked.

"Coming in," he said. "Clean up time. Then I'm going out to anchor."

They chatted for a minute or two. When she looked again, Wade had disappeared.

"Enjoy your stay," she said to the captain, waving as she headed back toward Front Street. She retrieved the tote and scanned the way in front of her as she walked. Neither of the Maxwells were in sight. Maggie nonchalantly pulled off the pirate's hat and wig and stuffed them into the tote.

For the first time today, she was almost without a disguise, but her hair was now very short and shockingly red thanks to Aunt Belle's ministrations last night. The breeze blew across her sweaty hair, and she ran a hand through it to make it spike. From the tote, she put on the oversized sunglasses. She crossed Front Street again and headed back to the coffee shop, not dodging into stores, barely looking in the windows, walking with purpose. As if she lived here.

She wasn't home yet. Not by a long shot.

But for the first time in months, she finally felt free.

"Never saw hide nor hair of you," Wade said as he sipped an iced tea.

Maggie shifted her glance from him to Jessie and back. "You saw me numerous times," she said. "You just didn't *see* me." From the backpack she pulled out the jeans and sweatshirt, the skirt, blouse, and blond wig, then the brown wig and the pirate hat.

"I'll be jiggered," Wade said, and Jessie cackled beside him.

"Well, it wasn't really fair," Maggie said as they rehashed the morning. "I knew who to look for. If this were real, I wouldn't know if a stranger was stalking me."

"It's a start," said Jessie. "Years ago, for us, it was real. Today, it became more real for you."

"Given what you saw today, am I free to move about the country, or, well, the town, anyway, if I'm careful?"

Wade nodded. "Nothing is certain. No guarantees. But…as long as you stay extremely aware and cautious, I think you'll be okay."

"And continue to run every day," Jessie added with a chuckle.

"Excellent. I know where I'm running to first," Maggie said.

"Shoppin' for clothes that fit?" asked Aunt Belle.

Maggie smiled. "Hmm. That too. Yes, I think I should own a dress."

Chapter 11

On a warm Saturday afternoon in the middle of October, Sandy grimaced and then opened the sail locker on the port side. No use putting off the odious job any longer. The leak around the stuffing box was getting worse. He'd delayed already because it was the job he hated the most.

Picking up the stuffing box wrench, he leaned forward, lowering his head, then shoulders, then the whole upper half of his body into the locker. As usual, he couldn't quite reach, so he rested his back against the hull and elevated his feet so that he was almost upside down.

He stretched forward and angled the wrench onto the large nut. The wrench slipped off. He tried again, wiggling further into the locker to get a good purchase. As bad as this job was, the worst part of his life was that he'd decided two weeks ago, right after the third game, not to watch football anymore at Belle's. With Maggie.

As early in the week as Tuesday, he'd found himself looking forward to the next Sunday. The realization slowed him down like a cold shower. How foolish could he get, thinking he could hang out with an attractive, intelligent woman and not start to, well, want to see her more? Fool, damn old fool. That's what he was. No more Sunday visits to Belle's.

He got a good grasp on the stuffing box and turned the wrench. There was so little room he could barely move the tool an inch at a time. To make sure he followed through on his resolve, he'd invited a couple of guys from his department to come watch football. Beer, chips and salsa supplied. They'd also ordered some buffalo wings and pizza. He wasn't too fond of beer, but he would have felt silly sitting there with a Manhattan or martini. And he hadn't known what buffalo wings were, but he'd found out they weren't bad. He turned the wrench again, scissoring his legs to stay in position.

Click. The sound of a camera shutter and a giggle. No, it couldn't be. Maggie was an amateur photographer, and she always had Belle's 35mm within arm's reach. But she hadn't been out of Belle's house during the day since she'd left the boat and moved in with her. What was she doing here?

"Bottoms up?" He could hear the laughter in her voice.

Well, damn. If she had to show up, it would have to be when his butt was waving in the wind.

"It *is* you," she said. "I'd recognize you anywhere." She took obvious delight in his undignified position.

"Uh, be right out." How perfectly annoying. Didn't she believe in phoning? What was she doing here anyway? He didn't remember handing her an open invitation.

"Take your time." Click. "Listen, if anyone had told me you weren't dedicated to your boat, I'd have to say they'd given me a bum steer." Click.

"You're not taking pictures, are you?" Dumb question.

"No. The camera is. Just a few shots...for posterior. I mean posterity." This time she giggled out loud.

He couldn't help but smile. "Listen, he–or she–who laughs at the expense of others will get her comeuppance."

"Confucius say?"

"No, Golden Dragon fortune cookie say."

"All right, I think I'm under control. So, when are you come-upping from down there?"

He made the final turn and was rewarded by seeing the trickle of sea water stop. Then he began the difficult ascent which meant, damn it all, waggling his lower half back and forth as he pushed himself up and out with his arms.

She guffawed. "Well, that tukus a few minutes to get face to face." Her eyes sparkled, and her face was lit with good humor.

He feigned reaching for her. "No, no," she said and laughed. "Really, I'm under control now." She wiped tears from her eyes with the back of her hand. "Don't know what got into me. Inspired by the view, I guess."

He ignored that. "So, to what do I owe the honor of–"

"This unwarranted, inconsiderate, and unannounced visit?" Her smile was mischievous and not at all apologetic. In fact, she seemed to be humming with a little more excitement than usual. And something was different with how she looked. What was it?

"Jessie and Wade have been here for over two weeks. They wanted to train me so it would be safe for me to get out and about. Jessie's been pushing me into shape. I can run now, I'm stronger by a little, I can do some impressive self-defense moves."

She raised her forearm and did a karate chop. "Hi-yah! Well, I got that part from a movie. We didn't actually do that. And probably the best part is I can spot someone tailing me and give 'em the slip. So, the first thing I did was to go shopping. What do you think?"

She turned around to model an emerald green and black flowered, calf-length dress that seemed to drift around her form. It was the first dress he'd seen her in, dependent as she was on the clothes she'd brought with her from Maine.

"Nice. Well, that's all good news for you."

She nodded and grinned that excited, wide-open smile where her eyes appeared to engage you at some depth you weren't prepared for.

"Jessie is heading back to Florida tomorrow. She was wondering, Aunt Belle was wondering, and well, I was also wondering if you could stop by Belle's tomorrow." She smiled and raised an eyebrow waiting for his answer.

"No. Sorry. Previous commitment." He had his own life. He wasn't going to get sucked in.

She nodded acceptance. If she was wallowing in disappointment, he couldn't see it.

"Okay. No problem." With a brief wave of her hand, she walked away, down the dock toward the boardwalk. A pang, a sudden sense of loss, cut through him like a knife.

"Wait, Maggie."

She turned and her skirt swirled slightly around her legs. "Hmm?"

"Hey, do you want to go sailing sometime? It could be a little chilly—"

"Bracing, you might even say."

He nodded.

She met his eyes and said, "Sure. That'd be fun."

And there was that look again. The one that knocked his socks off.

Damn it to hell. Stupid, stupid, stupid. Why hadn't he left well enough alone?

Maggie sipped her coffee. "We're going sailing this weekend."

"You look happy about that, dear." Aunt Belle pushed back her teacup, brushed toast crumbs from the marble tabletop into her hand and dropped them into her empty cup.

Maggie and Belle were just finishing breakfast at the Soda Fountain. "I'd like to get out. I've felt like I've been in prison. I really love your company, but..." Maggie nodded to the waitress who approached with a coffee pot and refilled her cup.

"But you'd been a shut-in for what was it, two months, afore Jessie showed up? It's a wonder you're still sane."

Maggie thought about the last five days since Jessie left that she was able to leave the house and wander around this historic, lovely little town by the seaside.

"Yes, I can say without a shadow of a doubt, it sure feels good to be able to go out. Even going out for a cup of coffee and the newspaper is an adventure in living."

Belle glanced at Maggie, her eyes concerned. "You being careful? Doing all that stuff Jessie talked about?"

"Yup. I was nervous the first day she was gone, but now it's...it's actually kind of fun. After I go in someplace, I look out a window and watch the people who are walking or lounging nearby. I'm supposed to be memorizing faces. Before I leave, I watch again to see if anyone is still in sight who was there when I went in. If a place has two entrances, I go in the front and leave by another exit. And things like that." She smiled, thinking she might tire of all the fuss eventually, but now it had an element of fun.

"Just be careful, dear." Belle brushed the table again though it was now completely clean. "And I'm glad you and Sandy are friends. He gives you someone else to talk to besides me. Good for him too, I'm sure."

"Mmm. Yeah, he doesn't talk much about himself, but he sure does listen to me. He remembers the tiniest, insignificant details I tell him. Later, I'll be talking about something else, and he'll remember a related detail that I mentioned a couple of weeks earlier. That's never happened to me before. Sometimes it's disconcerting."

"Well, of course. Maggie, dear, the man's in love." Aunt Belle's voice sounded certain. "I'm not sure he knows it yet." Her eyes held Maggie's.

Maggie was alarmed. "Oh, no, I hope that isn't true. I can't think of anything that would point in that direction. I mean, we just talk."

"I take it you don't feel that way? In love?" Aunt Belle shook her head sadly. "I was afraid you didn't."

"Well, no, I mean–in *love*? No. I mean he's a very nice man–"

"You could do worse than Sandy McAllister."

"Aunt Belle!"

"Oh dear, what did I say that has you so aghast?"

Maggie put her hand on Aunt Belle's. "Well, you're assuming I want to...*do*. And I don't. And actually, I couldn't find anyone better than Sandy. He's a very nice man, but I don't want anyone to be…" Maggie scrunched her nose, "you know...in love with me."

She rested her chin on her hand. "I'm just marking time. Until I can get home and get my family back. And the idea of romance makes me claustrophobic. You don't know what freedom my single life gives me..." She saw the look on Belle's face.

"Oh, I'm sorry. I know you'd prefer not to be alone. Your life was much happier before Uncle Arthur died. I would feel the same, I'm sure. But that isn't my life right now."

"You said you'd been getting bored…"

"I might have been before all this happened, but I was thinking, then, in terms of a new hobby, maybe some travel."

Aunt Belle laughed. "Be careful, dear, what you wish for," she said, crinkling into her merry smile.

Maggie chuckled. "Yeah, I know. This isn't exactly the kind of travel I was thinking of. You know, Aunt Belle, in the back of my mind I was even playing with the idea of changing jobs, but not once did I ever think of finding a man to relieve my boredom. And you wouldn't seriously suggest I begin a relationship with Sandy to...relieve boredom?"

"No, I guess that doesn't sound like a good idea."

"Because I will be going home. He lives here, I live there."

"But he could move–"

"I wouldn't want him to."

"We don't always get what we want, Margaret. Sometimes we have to take it when it comes, because it might not come again."

"Please don't get me wrong. Sandy is wonderful. Those first ten days, he was the only person I talked to, and we talked about everything. What kind of music we like, what books we've read, how we feel about social issues. They were the most stimulating conversations I've had in...I can't remember when."

"Well, yes, now that you've spelled it all out, I can see the negatives," Aunt Belle said dryly.

Maggie smiled. "And I haven't even finished. He makes me laugh. He gets my jokes. And there's something else I sense in him that tells me there is a lot of...goodness, I guess you'd call it. Someone you can rely on. Someone who would always do the right thing. So, I do really appreciate him."

Belle nodded vigorously. "Okay, then–"

"But we're passing ships, you know? I have a family. And a life. He has a life. And neither of us should change that just because..." Maggie trailed off, not knowing how to finish.

Belle nodded again. "Because some interferin' old lady thinks you should."

Maggie smiled. "Will you feel better if I tell you I haven't seen anything that would indicate he feels any differently than I do? We're just temporary friends."

"Well, that sounds sensible enough," Aunt Belle said. She sighed. "I just want Sandy to be happy. He deserves happiness, what with all he's been through."

Maggie felt a stir of curiosity. "He says almost nothing about his life. What has he been through? I feel like a snoop, asking."

"I didn't know him when his wife died, but he talked about her a lot when we first became friends. I think, from the way he talked, they had really wanted children, but he lost her to MS. Long and debilitating."

"I'm sorry to hear that."

"He didn't see anyone for quite a while after she died, I gather. But since I've known him, he's had two relationships. Both of them went kaput for one reason or another. Just a few months ago, he said he'd decided not to date anymore. 'Too much hassle,' he said."

"See there? He and I are on the same page, then. I'm not even going to worry."

"You still going sailing?"

"Sure. I don't think going sailing will do any harm. Be fun."

"I think so too, dear. Just...be careful."

Not to hurt him, she meant. Maggie nodded.

Aunt Belle patted Maggie's hand. "Now let's go shoppin'. I want to buy you a warmer outfit for sailin'. Besides, you need some smaller clothes."

"No, you've already done too much for me."

"You said you were keeping records of what you owe me, right?"

Maggie nodded.

"Then don't worry. Gives me pleasure to help out. I have enough money to keep me until I'm a hundred and two. And then some. Let's go shopping on Front Street. I haven't done that for a long while."

"Okay, let's do it." She scanned the parking lot across the street. No new cars since they had gone in to eat. While Belle paid the bill, Maggie walked around to the side door. The only strollers were a couple of tourists consulting maps. They pointed down the street and wandered away.

She felt a lift in spirits. She and Sandy were just friends, and she was going shopping. What more could she ask for?

* * *

Arturo Mancuso prodded the log into the fireplace, trying to get a good flame going, but the slow-burning wood just sputtered and smoked–sap running down the sides, sizzling as it dripped onto the kindling. This sure as hell wasn't going to take the freaking chill out of the late October air.

He'd combed the area around the cabin for small twigs and branches for half an hour trying to come up with enough to start the fire. Then he'd wadded up an old newspaper, tucked it around the kindling, and touched a match to it. There had been one big burst of flame as the fire consumed the branches he'd broken into small pieces, but the logs just sat there, barely ignited.

Lincoln Montgomery would be pissed off when he arrived in–Arturo consulted his watch–ten minutes and found the log cabin colder on the inside than the forty-degree air outdoors. But what the hell did he expect? Like Montgomery, Arturo Mancuso was from the city. He'd never built a fire in his life.

Well, except for the time he'd poured kerosene on that warehouse.

But somehow it'd become his duty to warm up the cabin because the boss didn't like the cold. Hated the cold, hated Maine. The weather was only going to get worse, though. How was he going to like it when the temperature was twenty fucking below zero?

There was no more kindling and no more newspapers. In the kitchen there were two bags of groceries. He unpacked the bags so he could use the paper to try to relight the fire. Like he was some damn Boy Scout. Working with Montgomery was getting on his nerves.

Before this gig, Arturo had been able to run his own show, direct his own men. Now, Montgomery, who had no experience in field work, was calling every shot. Arturo had become a gopher.

Guess he shouldn't complain though. When he'd gotten out of the slammer ten years ago, his younger brother told him to look up his old pal Montgomery. Maybe he'd give him a job. Now, his brother was in the pen, and Arturo was making very good money.

He lowered himself to a kneeling position in front of the fireplace, favoring his bad knee, and pushed the brown paper bag under the log. He watched it catch fire. Somehow, he didn't think that was going to do it.

Last month when they were up here to scare the shit out of the Oxley guy, he'd used up a stack of wood that had probably been sitting around for two, three years. He thought maybe the wood was too old to be any good, but he had no problems starting a fire with that. Since then, he'd been forced to buy a trunk load of wood from a farmer. He must have sold him crap because this stuff wouldn't burn for shit.

In the kitchen he prepared a pot of coffee on the propane stove he'd bought in September. He was proud of having found this place out in the middle of the woods.

When he was coming off his watch during those three days before the woman disappeared, he came down the County Road a couple of times to get familiar with the area. One night he'd caught sight of the headlights of a car that had backed into the woods. He'd grinned thinking some guy was getting some.

The next morning, he scanned around and saw it was actually a small dirt road. Then, after Montgomery arrived in Amesbury to take over the operation, Arturo had time on his hands. He decided he'd like to see how far the road, thick with brush and weeds, went. He was surprised as hell when he'd found the deserted cabin that appeared to be a bunkhouse that would sleep six. He'd scouted the area surrounding the cabin and had found an outhouse and a well, but without electricity, there was no water pump.

He was sure Lincoln would think the unoccupied cabin was of no value, but the boss surprised him. The first thing they did was to bring that Oxley guy out here. Arturo chuckled. That guy was scared shitless–thought he was going to get bumped off, was Arturo's guess. If they had, Arturo was already thinking they'd hide the body in the well.

The coffee was done, and he was unpacking the deli stuff when Lincoln's car pulled up. His jaw tightened. If he, Arturo Mancuso, was running the show, he'd a stopped at Dunkin' Donuts for coffee and a bag of assorted. In fact, if he'd been running the show, they'd be meeting in Lincoln's warm, comfortable apartment, sitting in leather chairs, sipping bourbon.

Voices followed the slamming of car doors. Arturo looked out of the grimy kitchen window and saw that Henry Lee was with Lincoln. Maybe they'd get an update.

Lincoln, dressed as usual in a tailored suit, white shirt, and tie, looked around in general disapproval at the living room. "Jesus, it's cold in here." The place was furnished with odds and ends of used furniture, mostly chairs and little tables that Arturo had picked up at yard sales and brought out in the trunk of his car. When he put the braided rug in the middle of the room, he thought the place didn't look half bad.

Lee poked at the smoking log. "The wood is wet."

"The hell it is." Arturo joined him in front of the massive stone fireplace. "It was dry when I put it in there, and it's dry now."

"No, I mean it's green wood. Probably cut only a month ago. Needs to sit a year to dry out enough to burn. Whoever sold it to you saw you coming. You might get this to smolder all day, but it won't put out any heat."

Lincoln gave Arturo a scathing look, but Arturo had seen a flicker in his eyes that said Lincoln hadn't known about green wood either.

Montgomery took a handkerchief from his pocket and dusted off the old rocker before sitting down. Arturo went back to the kitchen to pour the coffee. Maybe he should get a goddamn apron and a hair net. He brought in the tray loaded with plastic containers of deli stuff, put it down on the coffee table, and took a padded folding chair facing Lincoln. Lee continued to stand in front of the fireplace, pushing on a log with a poker. Lincoln studied the hit man while he sipped his coffee from a thick diner mug.

The silence bothered Arturo. "So, what's new, Boss?" He helped himself to a pickled hard-boiled egg he'd picked up at a Mom and Pop store.

Lincoln winced as Arturo bit the egg in half. "What the hell is that?"

Arturo smiled broadly then polished off the egg and fished his cigarettes out of his shirt pocket. He was not going to let Lincoln's no smoking rule stand here. He had found and furnished this place. His turf.

Lincoln continued to look at Lee, but he spoke to Arturo. "You know this place would be Roy LaCroix's dream. No phones, no electricity, a mile and a half out in the middle of nowhere. 'Course he'd insist on a hike in the woods first." He looked impatiently at Lee standing with his back to them. "Want to join us and give us the latest?" There was a touch of irritation in his voice.

Lee leaned the poker against the fireplace and took a chair next to Arturo. "Well, sure. If you want to hear more of the same. Okay."

He placed his elbows on the arms of the chair and folded his hands across his stomach. "Been some postcards. Go where the postcards was sent from and show her picture around. Nothing. Zip. Zilch. No one seen her." He leaned slightly toward Lincoln. "If she used a credit card, I'd maybe have a shot at it."

"And at her." Arturo laughed at his joke and wheezed as he dragged on the cigarette to get it started. Neither Montgomery nor Lee laughed. No sense of humor, either of them.

Lee shook his head. "She ain't using them. No checks, no nothing."

"No phone calls?" Lincoln asked.

Lee shook his head and headed for the kitchen. They heard cupboard doors banging.

"Artie," Lincoln said. "We need to put on more tails. LaCroix is thinking of using the boy as bait, so get a guy who can pin down his schedule, tail him as much as possible."

"I know a youngster, maybe twenty, looks like a kid, could do some bike riding without being noticed."

Lincoln nodded thoughtfully. "LaCroix's right. We have to cover him better than we have been."

Lee returned carrying an old, half-empty bag and a glass thing that Arturo had seen on one of the shelves by the back door. An old-fashioned lamp, he thought.

Lee shoved the bag into the fireplace behind the smoldering logs. "Charcoal," he said. Then he twisted the lamp until it came apart in the middle. "Kerosene." He looked pointedly at Arturo, then dumped a little onto the log. Flames roared up the chimney and licked out into the room.

Lee quickly stepped back. "That'll do it, but crack the door for oxygen. Charcoal," he said to Lincoln, "burns up oxygen."

Arturo opened the front door a couple of inches and looked at Lee, who nodded.

"Mr. Montgomery," Lee said. "Since I got the go-ahead to off her, I been looking really hard...all over Florida. In the stinking heat. Be nice if I found her in Maine."

"Find her somewhere else that's not Maine–and make her disappear. For good."

"I'm good at making people disappear. Forever." Lee said. Then he smiled.

Just like, Arturo imagined, a shark smiled. Before it tore you to pieces.

Lincoln leaned forward. "Either make it look like a bona fide accident or do something to make it impossible to identify her. But if you do find her here, got to absolutely look like a logical accident."

Lee smiled again. "Here's hoping I find her somewhere else. I'm also good at 'making identification impossible.'"

Maggie turned the sailboat's wheel slightly, aiming at the buoy ahead. She glanced up. The luff of the taut mainsail fluttered. Holding the helm with one hand, she leaned sideways, grasped the winch handle, and cranked the sail in tighter. She was rewarded by a barely discernible increase in the boat's speed. She sighed in satisfaction, then felt her face split into a grin. She could hardly believe she was doing this.

She peered into the dark interior of the boat. "Ah, I have to come about, soon."

"Mmm. Yeah. Go ahead." Sandy sounded preoccupied.

"I, ah, I *said* I have to come about. We're getting close to the buoy."

Sandy appeared, put one hand on either side of the companionway opening, and looked up at her. His eyes twinkled in that amused way of his that tickled something inside her. "Uh-huh. Go ahead. You've done it several times today with me beside you. Someday you're going to solo. This is good practice."

Maggie gasped. "Un-uh. No way. Not solo."

Sandy cocked an eyebrow. "We'll see. Meanwhile, come about, Captain. I'm still working on lunch. Just don't ruin the soufflé."

"*Soufflé?*" Soufflé on a *boat*?

"Just kidding. I'm actually working on a Hollandaise sauce. Be gentle." He disappeared into the galley.

Okay, she could do this. And if she didn't act soon, they would run over the buoy, which would likely ruin their whole day.

Not to mention the Hollandaise.

She pulled the handle out of the port winch and wiggled it into the top of the starboard winch. She released the jib sheet on the port side and turned the wheel to the right. As the boom crossed over her head to midpoint, she turned the wheel further, quickly wound the starboard side sheet around the winch, and cranked it tight. The jib and the mainsail filled with a crisp whomp.

She tipped her head back and looked at the sail. She laughed in jubilation.

Sandy appeared in the companionway, stirring the sauce in a pan. "You might not be sailing-challenged after all." He disappeared into the darkness again.

"This is the triumph of my sailing experience," she shouted to him. When he reappeared, smiling, she continued. "When Sam and I used to sail, I was the passenger–actually, both Joel and I were–and Sam was the captain. When we tried to help, we never did get it quite right."

"Must have been tough on Joel."

"Yeah. He wanted so much to learn. When he was twelve, he asked for books on sailing for his birthday. That's how he learned to sail. He wanted to get his father's approval. I can still see Joel behind the helm, squinting toward the horizon, his jaw thrust out, looking so serious and so exactly like his father."

"Sounds like an element of fun might have been left out. Did he get his father's approval?"

"If he did everything exactly right. No pressure, you know?"

"Does he still sail?"

"Nope."

"Why?"

"I guess he didn't do it right often enough."

Sandy nodded solemnly. "Lunch is almost ready. Here, you can start with the mushroom salad. Let me take the helm while you eat."

Maggie sat cross-legged on the cockpit cushion feeling gloriously indulged as she ate the savory mushrooms. She had never been acquainted with a man who cooked. She found it an appealing quality.

She looked at Sandy holding the wheel and noticed his strong hands covered with gold, sun-bleached hair. His faded blue shirt sleeves were rolled above his elbows exposing skin that had been toughened and tanned by many years of around-the-calendar sun. Worn jeans and salt-stained boat shoes completed his boating garb.

Why, she wondered, was his attire so much more appealing than Sam's pressed khakis and blue blazer? Because Sandy wasn't attempting to meet a standard set by others, she answered herself. She said as much to him.

He laughed. "Boy, are you easy to fool. You shouldn't give me credit for wearing grungies–my motives might be reverse snobbery. And that's just as bad as the straightforward kind." He smiled down at her. "Or...I could just be a slob."

She liked his self-effacing humor and sensed, not for the first time, an inner strength in him that was compelling. She experienced a sudden rush of affection for him that startled her.

He stepped away from the helm. "I have to finish assembling lunch. Can you take over for a few minutes?"

She took the wheel while he disappeared below.

His voice drifted up. "You said you wanted to talk to me about something."

He caught her by surprise, and she was stuck for words. Asking him had seemed so easy–and so necessary–when she was at home in the shower.

What was she supposed to say? Are you in love with me? How silly. How could this intelligent, funny, self-possessed man possibly be in love with her? In

213

fact, how could this wise, common-sense man fall in love with anyone so quickly? If she uttered the question, which sounded so presumptuous, he would look at her with that amused glimmer in his eyes. He'd struggle not to laugh at her. He'd be thinking how egotistical she was. He'd say, "Why would you think that?"

And on the one in a billion chances that Belle was right, what would Maggie say? "Oh, well, I just want you to know I don't feel the same way."

"Maggie?"

"I, ahh, I was wondering if...I mean what are your feelings about..."

He appeared in the companionway again, holding a plate.

"Quick. This is hot. Wait, let me get a potholder." He turned back into the galley. "You were wondering about what?"

She spoke to the doorway. "Um, I was wondering, um, I was wondering what I can do to thank Aunt Belle for everything she is doing for me. She pays for all the food, insists on doing all the cooking. Well, of course that's probably self-preservation. Have I ever mentioned I'm a terrible cook?" Stop. Babbling. Just stop.

"Once or a dozen times." He gave her a quick smile through the doorway and put her plate on the cockpit seat. "Why do you think I'm making the meal?"

"Oh."

"Actually, I just like to show off. I still can't balance my checkbook." He came out of the companionway with his own plate. His eyes crinkled with laughter the way they did when he was teasing her. "I'm just one of the fortunate ones, I guess." He huffed on his fingernails and polished them on his shirt. "Anyway, I can tell you how to thank Belle in one word. Canasta."

"Canasta? I thought it was Bridge."

"Yeah, because that's what her buddies play. But she would love to play Canasta. I play with her once in a while when she talks me into it, but I never was enamored with card games. Gave them up when my cousin broke a bone in my hand playing slap jack when I was four. I decided to take up something less violent." He paused. "Chainsaw juggling."

Maggie laughed. Oh, what the hell, she thought. She'd not seen a thing suggesting that Sandford McAllister was being anything more than kind and friendly. Like his relationship with Belle but many degrees less.

She wasn't going to make a complete fool of herself by asking if he had any intentions–honorable or otherwise.

"Okay, I'll brush up on my Canasta. Hey, do you want to hear some of Jessie's thoughts on how I'm to thwart my pursuers? And, Wade and Jessie worked out an idea for how I can communicate with my family. It would include a big part for you. Interested?"

"Sure as shootin', Miss Maggie. Shoot."

Pookie was winding up his last practice lap when he noticed that the guy in gray sweats was still watching him. He had thought the man was someone's father, but now there were only three other trackies left at practice, and the guy didn't seem to be watching them.

As he finished the lap, he kept jogging toward the school and the safety of the locker room. Not that he was scared but just to play it safe. No telling what kind of ax-murdering weirdo the guy might be.

While he showered and changed, he thought about Ellen. Her birthday was on Saturday. He yearned to give her a present, something really awesome, something that would make her face light up, but he sensed it wouldn't be too cool.

During the summer, his grandfather had given him some advice about trying to figure out if a girl wanted you to pay attention to her before you went off the deep end and made a fool of yourself. The advice made a lot of sense, and for the next two weeks, he was impatient for school to start so he could try it out.

Then, a week after school started, with his grandfather's death and his grandmother's leaving, life was so screwed up he didn't think about Ellen for a while. But she was in two of his classes, and lately he didn't think about much else except her.

He was following his grandfather's advice, and, so far, he thought he might be passing the test. When he had asked Ellen if she were going to go out for the basketball team this year, she talked to him for the whole two minutes between class periods. They were late for math, and they exchanged guilty smiles before going into the classroom. The next day, he stopped by her locker and asked her what she thought of the new history teacher. She had talked to him right up until the class bell rang.

Pookie smiled. That had been a very good day. As he finished dressing, Coach Rutherford banged four locker doors shut as he walked toward him. "Pook. Looking better out there today."

"Yeah, thanks."

"You going to be okay for the meet in Brunswick, son?"

Was Coach thinking about the arm Pookie had broken six weeks ago or his family troubles?

Pookie had no intention of being an object of sympathy or pity. "Yeah, no problem. I've been lifting weights at physical therapy. I want to start time trials tomorrow."

He left the gym still searching for the answer of what to do for Ellen's birthday. As he was going through the main entrance door, an idea came to him. An idea so dazzling, he stopped for a moment to think it through. Would it work? It was worth a try, with nothing to lose if he failed.

At that moment, he noticed the same guy in gray sweats who had been down by the track. He now sat in a car parked halfway down the block across the street from the school. Pookie couldn't tell if the guy was actually watching him or just looking in the general direction of the school. He felt stupidly paranoid as he backed into the school. Especially when his bike was in the rack in front of the school. Still, no harm in leaving by the cafeteria door and exiting on a different street. It wasn't too far to walk home.

As he walked in the gathering dusk, he worked out the details of what to do for Ellen's birthday. Tonight, he'd call Chuck, Doug, and Russell, his three best friends, and see if they wanted to go to the movies this weekend. He was pretty sure they'd say okay. Then he'd call Megan Witham and tell her a bunch of them were going to the cinema and did she think it would be a good idea to ask Ellen and a few of her friends to go along as a celebration of Ellen's birthday. He'd say how about in the afternoon so it would be clear this wasn't a dating thing. They could all hang out at Shakee's Ice Cream Shoppe afterward. Megan, or even Ellen, might say no, and he'd be disappointed, but at least he wouldn't be embarrassed.

Swinging his gym bag, he started to whistle the theme to *Gilligan's Island*. He had just come to his corner when, from behind a tree, a figure stepped out in front of him. In the measure of a heartbeat, he realized it was the same man who had been watching him. He swung his gym bag up, and with both arms, shoved it with all his strength into the man's middle. The guy was caught off balance and staggered backwards. Pookie turned and ran as fast as he had ever run any sprint in his life.

Now he was scared. He cut through the Johnson's yard, hurdled their fence, cut across the Poulin's backyard, and then, because the gully kept him from going any further, he sprinted out toward the street that ran parallel to his own. No cars or people in sight. He ran to the end of the block, turned left and kept running until he came to his own street. He crouched behind shrubs and peered down Maple Street toward his house. He considered not turning onto Maple but, instead, entering the woods and working his way through until he came to his own backyard. He knew the woods well, but it was almost dark now, and there was no one in sight anywhere near his house.

His father's car was in the driveway. Legs pumping, he tore from the corner to his yard; he couldn't wait to get safely inside. His dad would call the police. Then maybe they'd go see if they could find his gym bag. He wished now he'd paid more attention to the kind of car the guy was driving.

But at least he was home. For now, he was safe.

Tildie picked up her car keys, swung her red leather backpack onto her shoulder, and headed for the door. "Come on, Twerp. I'm giving you a ride to school today."

Pookie was momentarily rooted to the floor in surprise. Tildie never offered to drive him to school.

"Well," she said, halfway out of the door, "are you coming? I don't want to be late for class." She was out of the door. Pookie felt more relief than he was comfortable with. His bike was still at school, and he hadn't been looking forward to walking alone this morning, but he didn't want to admit to himself that he was afraid.

Pookie thought about the incident as they rode the short distance in silence. His father had called the police last night and a patrolman came to talk to them. He took down all the information Pookie could remember and said they'd be looking for the guy but didn't hold out much hope that they would find him.

Pookie glanced across at Tildie as she pulled up in front of the school. She seemed to be lost in her own thoughts. As Pookie started to get out, she grabbed his sleeve. "What time is practice over?"

Again, he was more relieved than he would like to admit. "I can be done at five."

"I'll be here. Don't be late. I have a date at six."

He nodded and closed the car door. Just before it slammed shut, he heard her say, "Bye, Twerp." He glanced back, and she smiled and waved at him before pulling away.

Astonished, he watched her car until it disappeared from sight. What the heck? She'd helped him with the computer, came to a meet last week, and now she was smiling and waving at him. Boy, you never knew what was going to happen next.

Well, whatever was going on with Tildie, he knew he'd be happy to put his bike in the trunk and ride home with her tonight.

He entered the school with a light heart. Last night on the phone Megan Witham had asked who would be going to the movies on Saturday afternoon. He grinned now, thinking of the conversation. He didn't know if it was Doug or Russell that Megan liked, but it must be one of them. After he gave her their names, she gushed about what a great idea it was and said she'd call Ellen and a couple of the other girls. He suggested they all chip in and pay Ellen's way as a birthday present, and Megan agreed.

He was already planning the next step. If this Saturday went well, he'd keep thinking of group things they could do. Then he'd have a better way of figuring out if she would actually go out with him–just the two of them.

The next morning, Pookie told Tildie thanks, but he wouldn't need a ride after school today. Track practice got over early on Friday afternoon, and he planned to look for a card for Ellen at Mr. Paperback. Something funny. If he gave it to her while they were all hanging around in the group, and the card was hilarious, no one would guess how he felt about her.

He took almost an hour before he was satisfied with the card he picked. He whistled tunelessly on the way home. He hadn't seen the weirdo since the night he had run from him, but he was still a little jumpy. He was glad to reach home.

He'd left his bike leaning against the carriage house, so he put it away and then headed for the back door. Suddenly, he was yanked backwards as a hand clamped hard across his mouth.

He thought of every self-defense trick he'd ever heard of and stomped as hard as he could on the top of his assailant's foot, but the blow glanced off. He twisted in the man's grasp to get leverage, swung his heel back with all his strength, and connected with the man's shin. The man yelped and staggered, and they both crashed to the ground. Pookie rolled out of the man's grasp and leapt to his feet. He almost reached the back door when the man said, "Wait!" Whispering hoarsely, he repeated, "wait."

Pookie looked back. The man rolled on the ground holding his shin. Pookie grabbed the doorknob and turned. In another second he'd be in the house, locking the door behind him.

"Your grandmother sent me."

Shock immobilized Pookie for a second. He hesitated, keeping his hand on the doorknob.

"Please listen," the man whispered.

"Stay right there. Don't move. You get up, I'm inside calling the police."

The man nodded. "I have to talk to you, but I can't whisper the whole thing. Can we meet where I can talk to you alone?"

"You gotta be kidding." Pookie turned the doorknob and jerked open the door.

"Wait! Let me think." The man sat up.

Pookie started into the house. The man lay back down on the ground. "Please. There must be a way. Maggie's depending on me to talk to you."

Pookie's heart was still pounding, and he was breathing hard. "Who are you, anyway?"

"I can't tell you until I find a way to talk to you, and I have to talk to you before you go in your house or use your phone."

The man squinted thoughtfully, then continued in a hoarse whisper. "Okay, how about this. I will walk back through Wade Maxwell's yard and then come out on Elm Street. I'll walk to the end of the block. Then you'll be able to see me from your front yard. I'll start walking downtown. You can follow on foot or on your bike, a block behind me. I'll go to the phone booth by the drugstore and get the phone number. Then I'll go to my car. It's down by the Citgo station. You go to the phone booth, and I'll phone you from my cellular phone."

Pookie looked the man over. He didn't exactly look like the scum-bag type.

He watched the back of the limping man–careful to keep a block between them. His heart still beat hard and his breathing was still ragged. At this time of day, when the shadows were long, everyone was inside preparing and eating supper. He felt isolated and uneasy.

The downtown area had the same empty, deserted look. They continued their tandem stroll past the library, past the post office, past the bakery.

When the man glanced over his shoulder at Pookie before entering the phone booth, Pookie's tension eased, and he almost groaned. This was supposed to be a secret meeting. What an amateur. In a few seconds, the man left the booth, glanced back again at Pookie waiting at the end of the block, and crossed the road. Pookie approached the phone booth and stopped within an arm's length of the telephone.

A block down the road, the man got behind the wheel of the same car Pookie had seen him in that first day. A second later, the phone rang.

"You don't know much about this stuff, do you?" Pookie asked.

"No, I guess not. How can you tell?"

"I don't think a cell phone is totally safe."

"Apparently, neither is meeting you in your grandmother's yard."

Pookie stifled a chuckle. "Tell me something so I know you're telling me the truth."

"Your grandmother–"

"Is she in danger?"

"Not right now."

"Tell me something so I know you know her."

There was a long silence. Already edgy, Pookie figured he'd tripped the guy up. Hang up and run for home, he thought. But the guy had a car. He was on foot.

The man cleared his throat. "When you were four years old, you wanted to go fishing. She helped you dig worms, but she didn't want to touch them, so you picked them up and put them in a can. She took you to the river, but you baited the hooks. You caught an eel. When you pulled it on shore and saw what it was, you were frightened and dropped the pole. The eel flopped back into the water and swam away with your pole.

"When you were five, you realized no one had remembered her birthday so you baked her a cake from a cake mix. You made her stay out of the kitchen, but you had to ask her what some of the words were in the directions. When it was done, you put candles on the top, but the cake was still warm, and the candles doubled over as they melted. You were disappointed, but she was so touched she cried. She had to explain to you about how people also cry when they are very happy.

"When you were six, you wanted to play baseball. She bought you a bat, a ball, and a glove. She pitched the ball to you every day after school–"

Pookie hung up the phone. Hot tears streamed down his cheeks. He hadn't allowed himself to think about how much he missed his grandmother until now. His body heaved with a sob. Leaning his forehead against the wall of the phone booth, he fought for control, but he was losing. Another sob wrenched his chest.

"Did I pass the test, or do I have to take a truth serum?" The calm voice was close by. The man handed him a tissue. "My name is Sandy, by the way."

Pookie turned abruptly away to hide his tears.

"Son, can we talk in the car? We can't be doing this out here. And I'm hungry. How about a drive-thru? Is there any place close by where we won't be noticed?"

They sat in the car while Pookie wolfed down a super-sized burger and fries. Then they drove the twelve miles to Brunswick while Sandy filled him in on the details of his grandfather's death and his grandmother's sudden vacation.

"Your grandmother didn't want to involve you or put this kind of responsibility on your shoulders, but Wade thought you could handle it. And, I have to say, my own experience with you would suggest that he's right." Sandy smiled.

"And they wouldn't suspect a kid," Pookie said around a mouthful of hamburger.

"Well, don't underestimate them. You're probably being watched some of the time, which is what made contacting you so hard, but I think you're right. They're less likely to think you would play any role in this. Are you comfortable with keeping this to yourself? It's ninety-nine percent certain they're bugging your house."

Pookie nodded. "That's not tough. We don't talk much at home, anyway. Now that Grandma's not here. I never noticed it much before, but I think, mostly, we all talked to her but not much with each other."

Suddenly embarrassed to have given this intimate detail of their family life to a stranger, he crumbled up his burger wrapper and stuffed it into his French fry box. Something about this guy though–you just found yourself talking like you already knew him.

"As I said," Sandy continued, "Maggie wants to be able to get news from home. If all she wanted to do was to let you know she's okay, she could continue to write letters, mail them to Wade, and he could postmark them from different places in Florida. That's how she sent you the postcards. But she wants to hear from you."

Pookie sipped the last of his chocolate shake and nodded. "That'd be good." He tried for a casual, off-hand tone. He wasn't going to tread on shaky emotional ground again.

"This will serve a dual purpose. It will also lay a trail for the bad guys to follow so Wade can see if they are still actively looking for her. Maggie and Wade worked out the idea. Once it looks like the heat is off, she'll come home, but with a lot of precautions."

"Well, that sounds good. Very good. So, how will this work?"

Sandy pulled his briefcase from the back seat, snapped the latches, and pulled out a manila folder. Inside was a single sheet of paper with two typed columns of addresses, all in Florida.

"Okay, this is a little complicated. Not to do. Just to explain. What you're going to do is prepare a real letter and a phony letter. First, you are going to mail the phony letter. Just a sheet of blank paper if you want–no one's ever going to read it. Seal it, address it to the first address on the list, then leave it lying on your desk for a day or two. Then mail it. See, the first address is Tampa Bay. At the same time, mail your real letter to Maggie– which you should not write at home or ever bring home–"

"Because?"

"Because Wade is guessing your house is searched on a regular basis."

"I knew it!"

"How?"

"Little things. Like Tildie accusing me of going into her room when she's not home. Why would I ever want to do that? Like stuff moved in my desk. And no one, not even Violet, ever goes in my desk."

"Ah ha."

"Oh, yeah, and once my computer was on when I got home, and I never leave it on."

"Maggie isn't going to be happy about this." Sandy looked at Pookie, his eyebrows raised in a question. "But you're not unhappy, are you?"

"Hell...heck, no. I think it's fun." Then he felt a little sheepish. "Twice I set a trap. I closed a hair in the door jamb of my room, but it was still there when I got home."

"Trying a little James Bond?"

"Yeah, I guess. Then I shouldn't use my computer to write the letters, huh?"

"Right! For sure. Let's see, where were we?"

"I mail the phony letter after I leave it where they can see the address, and then mail it where I can be seen doing it. And the real letter that I write at school, I mail secretly. To the second address." He looked at the list. "Clearwater."

He looked at the man and wondered what was so complicated. Not like rocket science.

"Can you mail it without being observed?"

"Yeah, sure."

"I mean you shouldn't even be seen hanging around a corner drop-off."

"I got it." Pookie tried not to sound annoyed.

"Okay, now hopefully the bad guys will take the bait and go to the first address–Tampa Bay where Wade will be watching–for two reasons. One, so he can see if they're still looking for her and two, so he can identify whoever it is. See if they have more than one pursuer."

"Makes sense."

"Then while the pursuer hangs around the post office waiting for Maggie to pick up the letter, Wade can move on to where the real letter has been mailed."

"Clearwater," said Pookie. "Right. Seems simple."

"Well, okay but then, in Clearwater, when he's picking up your real letter, he'll mail Maggie's latest letters and cards to you and your family."

"So, the letters will have a Clearwater postmark."

"Exactly. And then–"

"Then Clearwater becomes the place where my next phony letter goes. I leave the envelope lying around, showing the Clearwater postmark. They think she's staying there because she mailed a letter from there, and I seal the deal by mailing my phony letter to her at the same post office a few days later."

Pookie was rewarded by an approving look from Sandy.

"Then. Then..." he looked down at the list. "My real letter goes to the next address on the list–Lakeland."

Sandy nodded encouragement.

"And when Wade picks it up, he mails one from Grandma that will get postmarked Lakeland."

Sandy nodded with a wide grin.

"And it starts all over again with the next address."

"By God, I think he's got it."

Pookie thought about it for a minute. "Lot of work for Wade and Jessie."

"They're like you. Can't wait to get started. Think it's fun. I suspect they'll have more fun this winter than kids at a carnival."

"You see them?"

"No. Wade and Jessie came up with this plan and laid it out to your grandmother a little over a week ago. Maggie was going nuts not knowing how your arm was. Things like that."

"Arm's fine. How is Grandma?"

He watched as a smile spread across Sandy's face. "She's wonderful." He paused and then seemed to remember Pookie was there. "She misses all of you and worries about you, but she's safe and doing well. She'll tell you as much as she can in her letters without giving away her location, I'm sure."

Pookie knew, then, that Sandy liked his grandmother. Maybe a lot. The knowledge made him uncomfortable. She belonged to them, not some stranger from away.

"I'm going to get you home now," Sandy said, "before someone sees us together and asks questions you can't answer. One more thing though."

Pookie looked at him and waited.

"I understand you have a track meet in the morning."

Pookie nodded.

"I'd like to hang around and watch for a while. You're in the relay, right?"

"Yeah, and I'm in the hundred."

"I'd like to be able to tell Maggie something more about this visit than you knocked me down, I knocked you down."

"Don't forget the kick in the shins. Sure. My Dad is coming to watch. For once. So, I probably won't be able to talk to you."

"No, we shouldn't talk again. Until this is over."

Pookie took a deep breath so his voice would be steady. "When do you think this will be over?"

"A few months, anyway. No way to know for sure. Is there anything you want me to tell her when I go back?"

A sudden urge to tell his grandmother that he was in love with Ellen almost engulfed him. That astonished him. He didn't believe he'd have confided in her if she were home. Maybe because she was so far away, it seemed safe. In any case, he wouldn't do it like this. He wasn't going to say something that stupid to this guy no matter how nice he was.

"Tell her I–tell her we miss her. And stay safe."

Chapter 12

Jewel looked over the tournament schedule tacked to the bulletin board among orange construction paper jack-o-lanterns advertising a week-gone-by Halloween party for the children of members.

From behind his desk, the club manager spotted him. "Hey, Mr. Chadwick, nice to see you. Here for a workout?"

"Jules. Call me Jules. I thought I'd get in some racquetball. Maybe get in shape for the tournament. Looking for a practice partner."

"Let's see who we've got coming in today." He ran his finger down the page. "Ben Stonefield. He's reserved court D. Sometimes he comes in looking for a partner. An old guy, but pretty sharp. Every year he takes the trophy in his age bracket. Not bad as a doubles partner, either." The manager looked Jewel over. "My guess is he could give you a good game."

"Sounds good. Okay if I warm up in D until he comes in?"

"Sure. I'll tell him when he comes through, you're looking for a partner."

Jewel whacked the ball against the front wall at an angle trying to give himself a good warm up, work up a sweat, get rid of a few frustrations.

It had been weeks since he had located Wade Maxwell and his wife in Jacksonville, but the trail ended there. He decided to establish himself in Amesbury and get as close to the woman's friends and family as possible.

That's why he'd rigged this meeting with the Wiser woman's partner.

The door swung open beside him.

"Jules Chadwick? Ben Stonefield. Friends call me Stoney. If you don't mind going easy on an old guy, let's play some racquetball."

Jewel smiled. "I've heard a lot of good things about you, sir. It'd be a privilege."

Ben cracked a knowing smile. "Don't give me that horseshit. You know you can beat the pants off me any day of the week. Okay, let's get started. Your serve. And the name is Stoney."

Jewel laughed appreciatively. Ben Stonefield was going to be easy to get close to. And after that, there was Pookie Wiser.

* * *

Pookie left the locker room and headed for the gym. Basketball practice was over, and this was the quickest way to the front door if he didn't have to go by his locker to pick up books first.

Sometimes Ellen walked through here on her way out, so before practice he packed the books he needed for homework. When her schedule matched his, they talked on the way out.

Today, though, she wouldn't be here. She'd already left for her away game. Before he even got to the gym, he could hear someone, probably one of the guys, taking shots. Whoosh, floor thud, dribble, dribble, pause…whoosh.

He was surprised to see it was Mr. Chadwick, the volunteer assistant coach. Pookie watched him make a couple of shots from the top of the key. Then he dribbled right, spun into the lane, and hit a floater.

Pookie wondered how many Mr. Chadwick would make before missing one. He sat down on the first bleacher, put his bag down, and watched. Twenty-three. Twenty-three shots before a three-point attempt clanged off the back of the rim.

Mr. Chadwick shook his head, chased down the rebound, and returned to the three-point line.

Nothing but net.

After a dozen more, the ball caromed off the rim toward where Pookie was sitting.

Mr. Chadwick retrieved the ball and then dribbled it over toward Pookie.

"Hi, Pook. I didn't see you there."

"You are really good." Pookie felt himself redden. What a stupid thing to say. "I mean of course you are. You played for UCLA."

"I played a little. I transferred in my junior year and sat on the bench for most of the season. Then one of the seniors had an unfortunate accident the next summer that sidelined him for the season, and that gave me a chance. I was a starter. It was a good year."

"Did you ever want to go pro?"

"No. I always knew I didn't have the height. Some of your tallest NBA players top out at seven feet. Hakeem Olajuwon, seven feet, Shaquille O'Neal, seven-one. Even the guys you might think of as short–Jordan, he's six-six. Pipen, six-eight, and you know Mutombu is seven-two.

"Yeah, he's a beast," Pookie said laughing. "How tall are you?"

"Only six- three. Good enough for college ball. Besides, by then I had found something else I was very good at."

Pookie nodded. "I might not even play ball in college. We'll see."

"For high school, though, you're pretty awesome. Listen, if you want to hang out after practice on some days, we can shoot around. Maybe I can give you some tips."

"Oh, man, that would be great. Really great. Well, I have to get going. I've got a lot of homework."

Lincoln rubbed his gloved hands together. "If the family hadn't been getting postcards and letters, I'd have thought she was dead." If his hands weren't buried in fur-lined gloves, he'd have blown on them. It was the middle of November, and a light frost was visible on the ground. He sat on the empty bleachers bordering a high school football field.

Roy paced the ground in front of Lincoln. "So what's changed?"

"The kid wrote to her. He mailed a letter to the last General Delivery address. I figured he was grasping at straws hoping that by telepathy she'd know to come into that particular post office and pick it up."

"But now?"

"He just got a reply. Sounded like she responded to the contents of his letter to her."

"So, she must have been hanging around waiting for his letter to arrive. That's a breakthrough, Link! You're checking this out, of course."

"Even as we speak, our man is on the road. Or in the air to be exact. I don't think it'll be much longer. He can travel faster than the post office can deliver a letter."

"You know the parameters once he finds her," Roy said.

"Without a doubt." Lincoln paused. "There will be no mistake this time. You can count on it."

"I am. This turns out well, we'll see you back in New York."

Lincoln glanced around at the barren, frosty nothingness of Maine. Because if it didn't turn out well...

* * *

Joel selected the key he'd put on his ring the day they picked up his father's belongings at the morgue. He turned the key and opened the door to the house he'd grown up in–the house he'd been an infrequent guest in for the past ten years.

He stood in the foyer, noticing the cold. Of course. The heat would have been off during the August heatwave three months ago when he had come in only to get a suit for his father's funeral.

Something more than the cold made him stand still for a moment. He realized it was the profound emptiness–as if the house had accepted that its owner wouldn't be returning and had sealed itself off.

In the living room, he walked over to the stereo and pushed the eject button. The tray slid out still loaded with the CDs his father had last listened to. Four Verdi operas and one Wagner. He caught himself thinking, as he had several times in the past weeks, that he had to do something to restore things to normal. So his dad could listen to his favorite music again. Pushing the useless thought away, he gazed out of the large bay window, remembering that's where they always had the Christmas tree. And that Christmas time had been a really big deal for his father. The biggest event of the year.

Abruptly, he left the living room. He was here for a reason. His father's law partner, Tom McComber, had been pestering him for weeks to take care of business. Joel had been paying his dad's bills out of his own pocket for the past couple of months and would prefer to continue rather than go through this chore.

He knew he wasn't ready to remove any of his father's belongings, but Tom said he had to find the original of his father's will. He entered the dark paneled study and was struck again by the withdrawn feeling of the room. He crossed the floor and opened the drapes. The sunlight dispelled a bit of the gloom.

He knew where his father had kept the safe combination. He assumed the will would be in there and it was, along with his passport, the deed to the house, and his divorce decree.

Though he didn't have much interest in the contents of the will, curiosity made him sit down and skim the document. Five minutes later he sat staring at the paper, astonished. He read it again. No mistake. He reached for the phone and dialed his father's business number and asked for Tom.

"I found an original, but I don't know if it's the latest. When was the one signed that you have a copy of?"

"Twenty years ago."

"Same here. No wonder you wanted me to look."

"You think there's a more recent one?"

"No. I wouldn't think so. This one was in the safe with a few other legal documents, like the deed to the house."

"How're you feeling about the will?"

"I don't know yet. I'll drop it off this afternoon."

"Okay. Thanks for helping."

He hung up and stared out of the window. How did he feel? He didn't need his father's money. Most of the money left to him by his paternal grandparents was still intact. He made more money than he spent. So what was the problem? Had he been thinking that his father's esteem for him—whatever that might have been—would somehow be articulated in the will? He realized now that in the back of his mind, that's exactly what he'd been hoping. His chuckle caught in his throat. That well was dry.

How astonished his mother would be to learn she was the sole beneficiary of her ex-husband's will with discretion to share the estate in any way she thought appropriate.

He glanced at the date again. The will was signed when Joel was nineteen, a month after he announced that Miki was pregnant, and he was going to marry her. His father was furious. It was over a year before Miki won him over.

His father could hold a grudge—but for twenty years? He never even changed the will to include Tildie and Pookie. Maybe he had simply been content to leave the responsibility of managing things to Maggie, as he always had—even to the disbursement of his assets, even after they were divorced. Even after his death.

Knowing his mother, she wouldn't want anything to do with his father's estate.

He was ready to leave when he noticed two scrapbooks on his father's otherwise clear desk. Idly he opened one. The pages were filled with newspaper clippings of events that Tildie and Pookie had been part of. In fact, it appeared as if every time their names had been mentioned in the Amesbury Times, he'd clipped and saved the article. The last one was from spring of this year—Pookie with a trophy for the regional track meet.

He guessed it would be okay to take the albums with him, show the kids. As he picked them up, the bottom one dropped to the floor and fell open.

It was about himself. His father's record of Joel's childhood. Report cards, awards, some of the childishly scrawled notes he'd left his father, newspaper clippings telling the result of his baseball games, football, track...even for being on the Honor Roll. There was the newspaper photo of him and classmates decorating for the junior prom, him in the lead in the senior class play. Even after college, the clippings continued with the announcement of Joel's business opening.

Despite himself, an anguished cry tore from his throat. Grateful no one was here to see him, he sat at his father's desk trying to get himself under control. He could ask for no greater proof that his father cared. And was proud of him.

If his father had left everything to him, it wouldn't have ever expressed as clearly as the album did, the love and esteem his father had had for him. The words that he'd longed to hear were no longer necessary.

He wiped his eyes. Scooping up the albums, he decided he'd share them with the kids and then continue to fill them—take over where his father had left off.

Maggie sat with her back to the windows of her favorite restaurant so she could scan the other tables and watch new arrivals. Glancing over her shoulder, she noticed the sun creating a glittering, rippled path to this restaurant on the waterfront. A seagull dipped and glided along the channel just inches above the water.

Sandy interrupted her reverie. "How's the research coming?" He took a bite of his seafood omelet that was a brunch special for Sunday morning.

She gave a so-so waggle of her hand. "Pretty good, I guess."

Last week, Sandy lent her a computer, and Belle subscribed to the internet. Sandy spent three consecutive evenings showing Maggie how to access it.

"Still slow and cumbersome. I'd thought somehow the information highway would be smooth and straight. Instead, it seems like a maze. All these circuitous and meandering paths—and there's no map."

"You aren't the only critic. Guy in my department said it's as if the books in a library dropped off the shelves and all the pages fell out. You just pick up random pages and hope to find what you're looking for."

Maggie laughed and nodded. "Exactly."

"Have you tried different search engines?"

"Yeah, but they only provide signposts—usually something like two thousand four hundred of them—and most of them point to dead ends."

"You'll like it once you figure out how to reduce your number of hits."

"I did find that NADCO publishes its monthly employee newsletter online. I'm reading them, cover to cover–so to speak–and going back through the years."

"Anything interesting pop up?"

"Great company. Employees get profit-sharing bonuses. Must keep them happy."

"And productive."

"Un huh. The CEO's name is Royal LaCroix, Roy informally. He gave money for a Little League Field and provides a gym–complete with trainers–for his employees. And he started a daycare for employees. There's even a photo of him actually kissing a baby when the center opened five years ago. The man's a saint, if we're to believe what the Internet tells us. I'm inclined to."

"Don't rush to judgment so quickly. White collar criminals often clothe themselves in righteousness. In fact, that's a profile. And that's how they view themselves–honorable, upright, virtuous, often church-going, God-fearing citizens."

"Wow, really? I don't understand."

"Well, they often see themselves as extraordinarily clever, elite, and entitled. Entitled to more than they have. Entitled to what others have. They take because they are the deserving rich."

"But murder?"

"If the stakes are high enough or the person is sure enough of the righteousness of his cause."

"Okay, I'll keep digging away at NADCO."

"Listen, I wanted to talk to you about something. Every year, Belle goes to her grandniece's house in Raleigh for Thanksgiving."

"Bill, Sharon and the twins. Yeah, she talks about them a lot."

He nodded. "But this year she said no. She didn't want to leave you alone, and she probably shouldn't bring you since you're not officially here."

"Oh, no. I'll be fine here. I'll talk to her."

"I don't think you can budge her unless she knows you have your own plans. And so I was wondering..." He looked self-conscious and a little shy.

Maggie waited.

"If you would like to spend the holiday together. Nothing like a traditional Thanksgiving. Just a casual dinner somewhere. Then Belle can go off and enjoy her family without feeling guilty."

A warm glow slowly built inside her. "Sure, I'd like to. But can you get reservations this late? Thanksgiving is..." She counted on her fingers: Monday, Tuesday, Wednesday, Thursday. "Four days away."

"Don't need reservations where I have in mind. But we'll have to fly. Are you game? I'd like to surprise you."

"Yeah, I'd love to. But can you get airline tickets so close to Thanksgiving?"

"How about if we fly in a private plane? With me as the pilot?"

She couldn't stop the small gasp that escaped. "Wow."

A crooked, reckless grin danced across Sandy's face. "I'll take that as a yes. You must be worried about what your family will be doing for Thanksgiving."

"Not worried, no. I got a letter from Pookie yesterday, via Wade. Effie and George–Violet's parents–are coming to dinner."

"Violet's your housekeeper."

"I think of her more as a family manager. And her mom, Effie, is an incredible cook. She's done fancy catering for years. They'll have a wonderful meal. It's just that..."

She paused. How could she explain what she was really feeling? "I guess Thanksgiving first became special because it was one of the two holidays when I could count on Sam being there. The other being Christmas. Christmas was Sam's big day. But Thanksgiving became my day. Probably starting from the time Sam's parents finally condescended to spend the holiday with us, maybe eight years after we were married. I was thrilled. I planned and cooked for days."

"I thought you didn't cook."

"I don't, so I combed cooking magazines a month in advance and practiced. I made detailed lists including a time schedule that started three days before. It must have worked because each Thanksgiving I got rave reviews."

Maggie shook her head. "In fact, based on Thanksgiving Day, my mother-in-law came to the misguided conclusion I was a gourmet cook. She'd say to me, 'I don't know why you have your housekeeper do all of the cooking, Margaret. You are an excellent cook.' Sam and I would steal secret glances and try not to laugh." Maggie chuckled at the memory. "Listen, are you going to tell me where we're going for Thanksgiving?"

"Nope. It's a surprise. Trust me?"

Maggie grinned. "Hmm. Guess I'll have to."

* * *

232

On Thursday morning, at the Michael J. Smith Airfield in Beaufort, Maggie was strapped in, shoulder to shoulder, beside Sandy in an idling twin-engine Cessna, which sat beside the runway at the smallest airport Maggie had ever seen. "I didn't realize it would be so loud," she said.

Sandy put headphones on and handed her a pair. "Here, put these on. It'll deaden the sound, and we'll be able to talk."

She slipped the bulky headphones over her ears. The sound muffled down to an easily bearable hum.

"Better?" His voice, coming through the headphones and directly into her ear, was so intimate it jolted her.

Maggie nodded. She was startled by another voice. "This is Piper 1177 Tango turning to final on five seven."

Sandy nudged her and pointed down the runway. "Friend of mine. He also has a boat."

Maggie watched the small, low-wing airplane approach the runway, dropping closer to the tarmac each second. She didn't realize she'd been holding her breath until the plane touched the runway, taxied safely by them, and turned off the runway.

"This is Piper 1177 Tango, clear of runway five seven."

Sandy spoke. "Piper 1177 Tango, a little hot, but nice landing, Dave."

"It's really smooth up there today. Have a good trip."

Sandy grasped two levers between them and pushed them forward. The Cessna moved slowly forward toward the runway. "Beaufort Unicom, this is Cessna 3825 Zulu entering runway five seven for takeoff."

Maggie's stomach tightened. She'd never been in a small plane. Was it too late to change her mind?

She felt a burst of power, and suddenly they were hurtling down the runway, straddling the white line that ran down the center of the tarmac which was zipping rapidly under them. Weren't they supposed to be on the right side of the line? She looked ahead and saw that they were nearing the end of the runway, lined with trees.

Sandy pulled back on the wheel, and the Cessna lifted off the tarmac. The ground fell away. She was, at the same time, electrified with fear and fascinated with the view of the small harbor, as the plane continued to climb.

"Cessna 3825 Zulu turning left from takeoff," Sandy said.

The left wing of the airplane dipped, and she had an excellent view of the ground. There was the causeway bridge, the chemical plant, the inner harbor, Emerald Isle.

"Cessna 3825 Zulu leaving pattern."

The open ocean stretched in front of them. A thrill of fear shot through Maggie's limbs. She was hyperventilating. She tried to control her breathing.

"I thought you said you liked flying," Sandy said into her ear. He turned and looked at her carefully. "You said you felt like you left your problems below when you flew."

"I guess I meant a big passenger plane."

"Oh." He continued to look at her, concern on his face.

"Can you keep your eyes on...?"

He raised his eyebrows, looking amused, waiting for her to continue.

"...the air," she finished lamely.

"Happy to oblige, Miss Maggie." He turned forward, adjusting some lever on the instrument panel.

She jumped when she felt a jolt and simultaneously heard a clunk.

"That was the landing gear retracting."

She suddenly remembered a WWII movie where they couldn't get the wheels to come back down for the landing.

Sandy reached behind her and pulled out a small, insulated bag.

"Some refreshments. Want a soda or water?"

"No, thank you."

"Could you get me one? Maybe ease off on the white knuckles?"

Maggie realized her right hand was braced hard against the instrument panel. She tried to relax back into the seat. She fumbled with the zipper on the bag.

"Look, we can go back," Sandy said. "No use keeping you up here if you're uncomfortable. A lot of people are uncomfortable in a small plane. Why don't we turn back? We can cook up our own dinner at my house."

She could tell he really meant it–he was willing to change plans, to let her make the decision that made her most comfortable.

She found herself saying, "No, I'll be okay." Besides, she was determined that he didn't think of her as a wimp. "I'll get used to it."

She was rewarded by his cautious smile.

"But we're going to be in the air for about three hours. Over water. This would be the time to turn back."

"Over water the whole time? Florida?"

"Bermuda."

"Oh, Bermuda. *Bermuda?*"

He nodded and glanced sideways at her.

"But I don't have a passport."

"Don't need one for Bermuda."

"Oh." She looked down at the water. Water that stretched ahead as far as she could see.

"Let's turn back," he said. He turned the wheel and moved his foot on a pedal. The plane started a slight bank to the left.

"No. No. I'll do it. But I have to ask. What would happen if–"

"We have flotation devices and a life raft on board. And we have two engines."

"I thought your plane was a single engine."

"It is. This is Eddie's. My friend's plane. For this sort of flight, I thought I'd like two engines. Besides, my plane is too close to needing its annual inspection. What say we turn around?" They were still in a slight bank.

Stubbornness took over. "No. I can do it. I like flying. Can't you tell?" She smiled at him. "I'll be okay. Three hours, huh?"

He glanced at his watch. "Two and three quarters, now, give or take half an hour. Depending on headwind. Hey. It will help the time go by if you take the wheel. Let me just get her straightened out again."

She shrunk from the duplicate wheel in front of her as if it were about to bite her. "Are you crazy? I don't know how to fly."

"No, believe me, this will be so easy. I won't take my hands off my wheel. Just put your hands on your wheel and your feet on the rudder pedal. Yes, exactly right. Feel what's happening? Just stay with it until you can predict what will happen. Good."

Half an hour later, with his instructions, she was controlling the plane, holding it at level flight.

"You seem to be pretty comfortable with this. Why don't I take a nap? No, no, just kidding. But why don't we get you taking flying lessons?" Sandy said.

She was about to say, "I won't be here long enough." In the past few weeks, he'd made references to things that required long-range plans. She reminded him she had a life elsewhere that she would be returning to. He nodded but looked hurt. She felt guilty, and then she would be annoyed at him for making her feel guilty.

Today she didn't want dissension. She let the remark pass and focused on the fun of commanding the power she felt coming from the engines. This wasn't a half bad way to spend Thanksgiving.

* * *

"I can't believe I'm here," Maggie said.

They were dining on the second-floor balcony of a restaurant in St. George, Bermuda. Exotic deep pink and scarlet flowers spilled from planters along the balcony rail, the air infused with their scent. From where they sat, they could see the bay. Nearby an enormous cruise ship had docked, and passengers streamed down the gangway.

The waitress with a charming British accent brought their bill.

Sandy squeezed Maggie's pinkie gently. "Want to try another adventure?"

"You mean besides flying back?"

"Uh huh."

"Will both feet be on the ground?"

"Sort of."

"As long as it isn't hang-gliding or bungy jumping, I'm probably willing."

Sandy snapped his fingers in disappointment. Maggie felt her jaw drop in disbelief.

"Just kidding," he said.

"So, what do you think?" Sandy asked. He watched her carefully. He wasn't going to push if she had any reservations. He already felt guilty that they had a few more hours of flight ahead. Though she had seemed to enjoy flying after a while. Was she putting on a good front, or did she really feel that way? How could you tell?

Maggie looked suspiciously at the red motor scooter. "I don't know if I can even drive one of these things."

"Just like riding a bike, but easier."

"But I'm wearing a dress."

It was a full-skirted dress, smooth over her hips but flaring and swinging around her legs. The top of the dress looked like some sort of halter that tied on each shoulder. Fetching.

She stepped closer to the scooter. "Where's the brake?"

"The brake's right here. Look, can we buy something for you to wear if that's not going to work."

"No. Let me see if I can manage this." She swung her leg over the scooter as she pushed her loosely flowing red skirt between her legs and sat on the seat. A couple of inches of bare leg showed above her knee. It was even more alluring than the leg that showed when she wore shorts. "There, how's that?" she said, looking into his eyes.

"It's..." He cleared his throat. "It's fine. I think it'll work."

"Okay, how do you start this thing? I'm going to practice right here before we go out on the road."

"Then we have to remember to drive on the wrong side of the road."

"Oh, no. That's right! I mean *left*." She smiled, but she'd been visibly tense when he drove the rental car on the left side from the airport to St. George.

"You go first," she said. "I'll follow. Do you think I qualify for the I'm-game-for-anything award of the month?"

She grinned at him, her eyes sparkling, and her red-gold hair, which only five weeks ago was spiky short and red, now ruffled softly in the breeze.

"Of the year," he replied. The familiar feeling of tenderness washed over him.

She laughed. "Okay, let's get this show on the road. The left side of the road."

An hour later, they sat on a blanket on a grass-and-sand covered bluff high above the ocean. She sat cross legged, her skirt draped decorously across her knees.

"Go on. You were talking about Sam," he prompted.

She nodded, thoughtfully. "For a while I thought Sam was heroic when he disobeyed his parents and married me. But as years went by, I realized he had taken only a small, calculated risk. He knew his parents; he was an only child. They weren't really going to cut him out in the long run."

"So you and Sam ran away to get married."

"Not exactly. In fact, not at all. I had to have my parents' permission, so they gave us a small wedding in our living room. His folks didn't come."

"You had to have your parents' permission? Why?"

"Well, I was underaged. Seventeen."

"You were *seventeen* when you got married?"

"Don't look so shocked. It was rarer in those days than it is now, but it happened." Maggie reclined back on her elbows and cocked a speculative eyebrow at him.

"I was just thinking how difficult that must have been. Did you...how did you handle it? Missing the best year of your high school years?"

"I didn't think about it. I mean I didn't think, 'Oh, tonight's the senior prom, and I'm not going.' Once I knew what my life was going to be, I guess I just threw myself into it."

She gazed at the horizon. "As you know, when you're seventeen, you're working hard on your identity. Well, Sam's parents had stomped all over mine when they accused me of trapping a rich husband. I hadn't even known he was rich. I was so horrified that anyone would think that of me, I burned with shame at first, and then I was just plain angry. I was going to prove to the world the Wisers were wrong. And that sort of became the map for my life. I was so motivated not to touch a penny of their money. They could help Sam in college, but I supported us until he was out of law school."

He could hear the energy in her voice. "And so your self-sufficiency and pride became your identity."

She turned on her side, toward him, leaning now on one elbow, supporting her head with her hand. She looked so appealing; he couldn't think what to say for a moment. He lay back, mirroring her position, two feet of space separating them.

"I don't want to say anything bad about Sam, but..."

"You leave that to me, right?" She smiled playfully at him. "But...?"

"Well, how can you justify Sam–a twenty-two-year-old college student–seducing a seventeen-year-old high school kid?"

"He's blameless there." She traced a pattern on the blanket with her finger and smiled thoughtfully. "When we went for a marriage license, I showed the city clerk my brand spanking new driver's license, and she said I was underage. I'd have to have parental permission."

Her smile deepened at the memory. "Sam was incredulous. He really had no idea. When we sorted it out later, we figured out what happened. I was working at Whitcomb's Restaurant when Sam came in with a friend. Sam asked about 'the blond' waitress, and the friend told him she was a student at Amesbury College. She, being Carol Whitcomb, daughter of the owners, who was just that–a college student–and who happened to be a blond that week."

Maggie smiled and looked toward the horizon as she reviewed the past. "When I talked about working to earn money for school clothes, Sam had asked if I went to Amesbury. I said 'yes' thinking he meant Amesbury High School. He meant Amesbury College."

She pulled her thoughts back to the present and lay back on the blanket. "It seems like another life. Look, the clouds are incredible—higher and puffier than I've ever seen them."

He wasn't ready to let her change the subject. "So, at seventeen, you suddenly left home—"

"And worked at surviving." She stretched, reaching for a blade of grass, breaking it loose, putting the end in her mouth. She shrugged. "I mean I had to move forward. This was now my life. There was no use thinking of what else might have been."

A personality trait that was the secret of her success in adjusting to her current circumstances, he guessed.

"But what was your life like then? You were just a kid." He scanned her face, trying to picture what she'd looked like at seventeen. A knock-out, he decided, noting her full lips and liquid green eyes. And the wide, smiling mouth that he was always trying to provoke into laughter with feeble one-liners. But he suddenly got what made her looks so arresting. Her face was decorated with a sheen of pale freckles scattered across smooth, fine-pored skin.

"I guess I looked older than I was, and we agreed we wouldn't tell anyone my age. It was assumed I was at least nineteen or twenty. For a while I just kept my mouth shut because I knew if I spoke, I would sound incredibly stupid and naive to all of these sophisticated college students. I listened a lot, and after a while, I began to offer opinions—though, of course, my opinions in those days exactly conformed to Sam's. Anyway, I was accepted by his...our friends, and no one ever asked me my age. Hey, let's talk about something else. Like, shouldn't we better be going soon? We aren't going to be flying in the dark are we? I guess that wouldn't be a problem for you?"

She rolled toward him slightly and playfully brushed his nose with her index finger. He impulsively grabbed her finger and pressed it to his lips. He heard her intake of breath. He released her hand and looked into her eyes.

She met his eyes. He didn't breathe as they came slowly, so slowly, together in a kiss that consumed him. When they separated, they made brief eye contact, moved together, then kissed again, longer. Much longer.

He reached over and tentatively untied one of the strings that held up her dress. He held his breath; would she suddenly object? He started forming an apology in his head when she reached up and untied the bow on her other shoulder.

There was no planning or awkwardness to their love making. It moved and flowed without thought, so naturally and fully, he was completely lost in the moment.

Afterward, she turned on her side again, supporting her head with her hand. "I think that was entirely and completely inevitable. I didn't realize it, though. Before. Before this." She smiled at him, her eyes engaging him playfully.

He didn't want to take his eyes off her face. "So you don't regret it yet?"

"Not unless you're not going to respect me in the morning."

"Oh, I'll respect you. So much, I'll even brag about you in the locker room."

She laughed, then said, "But seriously, this was...I mean, it's been...I haven't ever ...maybe never...well, you know."

"Yeah, I feel the same way." They laughed.

He pointed behind her toward the west. "I so hate to interrupt this, but those clouds are moving in fast, and they look like rain."

Grinning, she watched him pull his shirt on before she languidly rolled over, looked at the bank of black clouds still out over the water, and gasped. "Oh my. That looks bad." She sat up, hastily slipped her dress over her head and tied one shoulder string.

A second later, lightning slashed from black clouds that hadn't yet blotted out the sun. While she slipped into her shoes, he fumbled with the strings of the bow on her other shoulder. "I'm better at untying than tying," he said.

"I imagine most guys are."

She crammed the blanket into the backpack while he watched the sky. "I forgot. Fast-moving squalls come through almost every afternoon this time of year. They're brief, but they dump a lot of water in a hurry. Let's go. There's that hotel that we passed a way back. Maybe we can make it before it lets loose."

They were a hundred yards away from the hotel when the deluge hit. They slowed the motor scooters to avoid skidding in the water that ran like a river across the road. By the time they reached the entrance, they were thoroughly soaked and chilled. He studiously tried to avert his eyes when he noticed Maggie's nipples through the thin fabric of her red halter-top dress. The high school feeling that you were about to get slapped for being inappropriate never left you, he guessed.

Once inside, she said, "Look, there's a shop. Now I'll take you up on your offer to buy something in the way of clothes."

She picked out white, calf-length pants and a purple shirt that said Bermuda Ski Team on the back because the humor tickled her. She helped him pick out tan Bermuda shorts and a white polo shirt with Bermuda stitched over the pocket.

"I think we'll be able to pass as tourists when we get into these things," Maggie said.

"I say, old stick, I can't say as I've ever worn Bermuda shorts before. Do you think I'll pass as a Brit?" he asked in his best Queen's English.

"Only to an American. Who's never watched BBC. Now what do we do?" she asked. "We have to change somewhere."

He met her eyes again. She smiled wickedly and fluttered her eyelids rapidly in a caricature of flirtation.

"Uh, well we could, ah..."

"Exactly what I was thinking," she said. "You just said it more eloquently. Will they mind that we don't have luggage?"

A shadow of concern passed over her face. "We don't have to stay overnight if you don't want. A room here is probably exorbitant. We can change in the restrooms. They must have restrooms right around here, somewhere." She seemed flustered.

"A room," he said. "One exorbitant room, coming up. Do we call Aunt Belle and tell her we won't be home tonight?"

Wet hair was pasted against her forehead. Her eyes danced. Grinning, she nodded her head vigorously. "You betcha."

"Or tomorrow night?"

Her grin widened. "It'll probably take that long to get into dry clothes."

Chapter 13

Feeling as though she were waking from a dream, Tildie Wiser stared into the mirror in horror. What had she done?

Jody put the scissors down. "It's chic. A pixie is what you wanted, right? Makes you look very mature."

Was mature what she had in mind when she made the appointment to have her hair cut? Had she gone too far?

On the counter in front of the mirror were two fifteen-inch-long glossy tresses tied with red ribbons. One for her grandmother and one for herself. More black hair lay on the floor around her.

"It'll always grow back," Jody said. She removed the cape from around Tildie's shoulders and shook it out.

Tildie turned her head to look at the short-cropped sides, then combed her fingers through the longer hair on top that fell across her forehead. "It's so...I feel so...it's so...short."

"Well, you said–"

"I know. I just didn't think I'd feel so...exposed." Or scared; had her hair been part of who she was? Part of her identity? She got up, brushed off her slacks, and handed Jody the keepsake locks of hair.

Jody slid the hair into an envelope and handed it to her. "I think you're going to like your hair this way. Now you can wear earrings. Hoops would look good on you. And I can pierce your ears when you come in for a trim in a few weeks."

Tildie recoiled. She had no hair, and now Jody wanted to put holes in her ears. But it wasn't Jody's fault. Tildie had recklessly put herself on the slippery slope of out-of-control behavior.

"Trim. Huh. I'll need to come in more often than every three months, won't I?"

"Yeah, if you want to keep that style. Why don't you live with it for two or three weeks and then make a decision?"

"No, I've made the decision. I'm sticking with it. Let's make an appointment for when you think I'll need it. Any Wednesday or Friday morning."

"Let's see, this is December third. Let's make it almost three weeks–December twenty-second, a Wednesday morning. Be set for Christmas. Okay?"

Tildie nodded without speaking. She didn't want to think about Christmas. They had gotten through Thanksgiving, but Christmas...

She pulled her checkbook from her carefully organized pocketbook and wrote out the check in precise handwriting. "Sorry I was late today. I don't know what happened. I guess I just spaced."

"Yeah, I was surprised. I don't ever remember you being late before. I can usually adjust my clock by when you arrive."

Jody handed her a card for the next appointment. Tildie marked it in the appointment book she carried with her, then filed the card among the others in her wallet, in order by date.

She wound the white, handknit scarf that had been a birthday gift from Violet around her neck. She slipped into her maxi-length burgundy coat and buttoned every button. She started to put on the matching cloche hat, then realized it wouldn't go with her new haircut. She folded the hat carefully in thirds and tucked it into her leather handbag along with the wallet and appointment book. Last, she pulled on the matching burgundy leather gloves.

Banks, stores, and restaurants stood shoulder-to-shoulder, funneling the sub-freezing wind down the street. It had snowed four inches yesterday then tapered off into freezing rain leaving the sidewalks slippery. Tildie pulled her coat tighter around her neck. She stood, transfixed, gazing into the plate glass window. A minute passed before she realized she was staring at a display of pink and blue baby clothes.

She turned abruptly, lowering her newly shorn head into the wind, and warily trudged down the icy sidewalk, angry that she had betrayed herself again.

As a child, her fantasies about what she would become when she grew up had changed every year, but they had never, ever included being a mother. She didn't even like babies–never had a babysitting job.

In fact, as her friends had married and begun to have children, she felt embarrassed for them. They had given up their dreams and settled for less. Settled for nothing. The whole idea of having a baby was so foreign to her, she dodged her old friends when she could, crossing the street to avoid having to gush over their infants.

Three days ago, she'd driven to Portland, bought a test kit, and confirmed her fears. She was pregnant. By her calculations, eleven weeks pregnant.

The raw, harsh wind stung her face and brought tears to her eyes. She retrieved her car key from its pocket in her handbag and inserted it into the lock.

But the key wouldn't turn. Dammit to hell. The lock was frozen. What else could go wrong?

Resting her handbag on the fender, she removed her hat from the bag, located the lock de-icer, and replaced the hat. She yanked the top off the de-icer, catching the edge of the atomizer tip. The tip flew off and disappeared into the snowbank.

Overwhelmed by this final evidence of her loss of control, she kicked the front tire. A growl began deep inside her and erupted as a scream of frustration. She never wanted to be a mother. Never, never, never. She planted her left foot, pulled her right foot back, and, with more force, kicked at the tire again.

Before her boot connected, her left foot slipped on the ice. In midair, she thought–I don't even fall on ski slopes. She hit the frozen pavement hard on her rear end. The jarring impact drained her anger, and she was suddenly aware of the ridiculousness of her behavior and how funny she must have looked going down.

She crossed her arms on her bent knees and laughed as the wind yanked at her hair. She laughed until her laughter turned into sobs and tears ran down her face. Minutes later, she became aware of the cold ground. Wiping her cheeks and nose with her scarf, she pushed herself to her feet and pulled the key out of the frozen lock. Taking a giant step over the snowbank, she walked around the car to the passenger side and inserted the key. It turned.

Once in the car, the sudden cessation of wind gave the impression of warmth. She threaded her way over the stick shift, under the steering wheel, and settled herself in the driver's seat.

She rested her head on the steering wheel. She couldn't remember the last time she had really lost control. Thinking of her pratfall, she laughed again. Finally, she drew a ragged breath and felt cleansed.

A memory from last summer popped into her mind. As she left a department store with sunscreen and beach towels, she collided with Shawna who had been the goalie on Tildie's high school soccer team.

While the two of them cast about for small talk, Tildie noticed the newborn infant in the bottom of the shopping cart that Shawna was pushing. They exchanged brief news of mutual friends and promised to get together sometime for lunch. Then, as Tildie started to turn away, Shawna absentmindedly shoved her shopping cart, with the sleeping infant still in the bottom, into the nest of other carts. Unharmed, the infant slept on. Tildie didn't know which of them was more horrified: herself or Shawna, when she noticed the look on Tildie's face and realized what she had done.

Now, Tildie laughed. "That's the kind of mother I would be," she said out loud.

She started the car and put it in gear. Then she noticed her handbag still outside on the fender. She didn't let it annoy her. It was time to take control again. From the inside of the car, she was able to open the driver's side door. She got out of the car, retrieved the bag, and placed it with care on the seat beside her.

She looked at her watch. There, now she was totally off schedule; she was going to be late for yet another appointment–the third this week. She had also been late for two classes and missed one entirely. What was happening to her?

Matilda Margaret Wiser had never tolerated self-pity in herself or in others. She wasn't going to start now. Her grandfather used to tell her she had the Wiser stiff upper lip. She had a crushing problem to deal with, but she was not going to come unglued.

That thought was barely completed when she remembered she'd left her hair locks at Jody's shop, and without warning, the emotional seesaw she had been on for the past month tipped the other way. Tears poured down her face, and she was gripped with a powerful, urgent longing to talk to her grandmother.

Pookie pressed Control P on the computer, then crossed the lab to wait by the printer. The only people in the computer classroom at four o'clock besides Pookie and his friend Doug were the lab teacher and one other student who was taking a makeup test.

He watched as the single-spaced, full-page letter inched its way out. Back at the desk he wrote, Miss you. Love, Pookie at the bottom. He folded it in thirds, slipped it into an envelope and sealed it.

He opened his science lab book to page 100 and removed the list of addresses. He wrote Margaret Wiser, General Delivery, Live Oaks, FL, then put the envelope aside.

Next, he tore a sheet of paper from a spiral notebook and scribbled a note in pencil. Dec. 7 … Hi, Grandma, Things are going great. I played twenty minutes in the basketball game Tuesday night. I scored six points. This Saturday, I am going Christmas shopping. I hope everything is going well for you. We are all fine. Love, Pookie

He put this dummy letter in an envelope and addressed it to his grandmother at General Delivery, Dunedin, Florida. He put the list back in the book and nodded to Doug that he was ready to leave. The book with the list in it would go back into his locker. In the empty hallway, Pookie handed the real letter addressed to Live Oaks to Doug. "Don't forget."

Doug slipped the letter in his gym bag. "Yeah, like I'm going to forget."

"Okay, just don't forget."

Pookie had lain awake for two nights agonizing over the decision. Should he tell his grandmother what he knew? Should he burden her? What could she do about the situation from wherever she was? What could anyone do about it? In the end, though, he knew he made the decision based on his own weakness. He justified it by telling himself she would want to know.

With the real letter on the way in Doug's gym bag, he felt a burden lift from his shoulders.

At home, he checked his desk drawer. The latest letter from his grandmother–the envelope that carried the postmark from Dunedin, Florida–had been moved two inches. After Sandy's visit, Pookie had been more careful at rigging his room, and he got a small thrill when he found evidence a couple of times a week that his room had been searched.

The next morning, he looked cautiously right and left–don't ham it up, he thought, just be convincing–then he put the dummy letter in the mailbox. If the searcher didn't follow that trail, he'd have to be an idiot.

He felt another twinge of guilt thinking about unloading on his grandmother, but some things had to be handled by adults, and he, right now, was thankful he was not one.

From his seat at the picnic table in the city park in Dunedin, Florida, Wade followed Jessie's window-shopping movements across the street. She was a presence. She walked with a suppleness that was surprising for her age, and there was a handsome dignity about her. Her fine, shiny white hair, swept loosely up into a bun on top of her head, was escaping a little around her face. A familiar rush of tenderness for his wife of thirty-five years swept through him.

It was December tenth, and they had been playing tourists for a day-and-a-half in the fair town of Dunedin. The shimmering Gulf of Mexico, with anchored boats swaying in the breeze, dominated the scenery to his right. Palm tree fronds caressed and whispered overhead, and the scent of the profusion of blossoms infused the air. Wade's eyelids grew heavy in the warmth of the day and the tranquil setting.

Suddenly, he spotted the thickset, balding man with rimless glasses he had nicknamed Mr. Magoo. Wade nodded to Jessie, but she'd already seen him and was on the move. She stepped off the curb, then stopped and fumbled around in her huge straw satchel with the big flowers embroidered on the front.

Looking preoccupied and harried, she moved toward the post office, still rummaging in her bag. The man Wade had seen on two previous occasions arrived just behind her at the door. Finally, flushed and triumphant, Jessie produced two postcards from her bag. Mr. Magoo reached around her to open the door for her.

Wade strolled across the park and entered the store where Jessie had been window shopping. He examined carved wooden dolphins until, two minutes later, she joined him.

"He's showing Maggie's photograph and asking for her by name," Jessie said. "Flashed a badge this time. Your plan's still working."

Wade smiled. He and Maggie had designed it well. "Should be able to snap his photograph this time." He put his hand on the door. "Let me leave first. I'll go get the camera and telephoto lens. We can send a copy on to Maggie."

She put a lightly restraining hand on his arm. "I'd like to take the photo. Close up. It'll be clearer."

He hesitated.

Her eyes narrowed. "Do you think, Wade Maxwell, that you should have most of the fun?"

"Okay." He chuckled. "Go do it."

Back at the picnic table, in the shade of the palm trees, she undid her tan wrap-around skirt, revealing turquoise Lycra biking shorts. Under her white, short-sleeved blouse she wore a flowered, turquoise and black Lycra tank top. She unbuttoned her blouse and tied the bottom edge in a knot at her waist. From her voluminous satchel, she pulled a hot-pink fanny pack, which she fastened around her waist with the pack positioned across her stomach. Yellow-framed, cats-eye sunglasses and a white baseball cap with a yellow see-through visor completed her outfit.

Wade laughed out loud. "You're a snowbird!"

She lifted her nose in reproach. "Snowbirds have a right to live, too."

She pulled a disposable camera from her fanny pack and headed across the park. Hands in his pockets, Wade rambled slowly behind. He loved to watch Jessie work. She meandered slowly down the street keeping an eye on Mr. Magoo as he went in and out of shops and restaurants. Deciding the time was right, she intercepted him as he came out of a gift shop.

"Oh, oh, excuse me, sir?" Jessie waved the camera in front of the startled man. "Would you please take my picture? It's for my son back in Minnesota. Here, in front of the flowers?" He hesitated in his stride for a fraction of a second. "Oh, thank you. It'll only take a second. People can be so nice, don't you think? You run into them every day. In fact, I think people are much nicer than they used to be," Jessie rattled on. "I'll stand right here so these beautiful flowers will be in the picture." She started to hand him the camera and pulled it back. "You look right into this hole, and"–she held it to her face–"look through it like this, and push this button."

The camera clicked. The man stiffened.

"Oh, no! I think that was my last shot! Oh, dear. And I wanted to develop it today. Oh, I'm such a dummy." The man started to turn away.

Wade was close enough now to hear her advance the film. "Oh, look, wait, I still have one more. Oh, please." She touched his arm and slipped the camera into his hand. "It's so kind of you. I really appreciate this." She stepped in front of a cascade of pink flowers and smiled. The man quickly put the camera to his eye. Jessie's face was bathed in a yellow glow from her sun visor as the shutter opened and closed. Magoo tried to hand the camera back to her, but she fumbled with the zipper on her fanny pack.

"These things always jamb. Thank you so much, Mr...? I'm Beth. Actually, Elizabeth. Elizabeth Conroy, just visiting my daughter for a month. It's my first visit to Florida. Do you live here or are you just visiting?" She held out her hand to shake his, and he placed the camera in it.

Grunting, he turned and walked rapidly toward his car. Wade passed by a piqued Jessie who stared in mock disbelief at the rudeness of the man who had taken her photograph. She winked at Wade. He continued up the street, the muscles of his face struggling in an unsuccessful effort to keep a smile off his face.

They met at a prearranged intersection in a residential area three blocks away, where the sidewalks were paved with bricks and the landscaping was thick with exotic flowers. Jessie climbed into the pickup. "Let's go get this developed."

Wade could feel his grin stretch from ear to ear. "Are you having fun yet?"

She smiled contentedly as she settled back against the seat and removed her hat, adjusted her hair. "Yes. I'm sure we've got a viable fingerprint or two. Too bad we can't run them. Anyway, I'm walking proof of your theory. That's the fourth time that man has seen me, but he doesn't really see me. I wonder if I can get away with a close encounter one more time? Remember, years ago, when we would have liked to be so invisible?"

"Yup. Would have come in handy."

"Then we got old, and it became infuriating to be so easily disregarded."

He nodded. "Especially women. Even more than men, they're not really seen...just part of the scenery. But you know, I keep thinking how handy that could be."

"Could be...? What are you thinking?"

"Let's talk about it while we're on the road."

"Where to next?" Jessie asked.

"Next week, Live Oaks. A letter from Pookie will be there by then. I've been thinking. I seem to recall you look good in a nurse's uniform. Why don't we rent a wheelchair, and you can push me around? Maybe with an oxygen tank. There's a scenario people avoid looking at."

She pulled back onto the quiet street. "I'd love to push you around, Wade Maxwell." She smiled at him. "But I meant, where to now? There's a bicycle rental shop a few blocks from here. I was going to suggest a couple of miles of the Pinellas Trail? I seem to be dressed for it. But if you're tired...?"

Wade groaned. "Jessie, honey, you're going to run an old man ragged."

"You should have thought of that when you married a far, far younger woman. Maybe we can rent a bicycle with a sidecar for you." She threw a wicked sidelong glance at him.

He laughed out loud. "Jessie Maxwell, you're a hard woman."

"I didn't realize we were going to be replacing the vacuum pump today," Sandy said.

"We're almost done. You probably hadn't planned on spending half the day here, though. Probably had plans with the pretty lady." Alden grinned. He was a close friend as well as an FAA IA–Inspector of Aircraft. They worked side by side whenever Sandy made his own repairs on his Cessna 180, not only because he was a friend and the best mechanic around, but also because any work done on a certified aircraft had to be checked and signed off by an IA.

"I've got nothing better to do. Hand me that seven-sixteenth socket, will you?" Sandy asked.

"Make you a deal," Alden said.

"Depends. What is it?"

"You've been whistling the same tune all morning. How about a break?"

"Oh, sorry. What tune?

"*When Irish Eyes are Smiling*," Alden said. He handed the socket to Sandy. "I know you're Irish and she's Irish, but right now *My Bonnie Lies Over the Ocean* would be a welcome change."

Sandy cranked hard on the socket wrench. The tool slipped, and he grazed his knuckles as the wrench clattered to the cement floor.

"I'll get it." Alden reached under the plane, grabbed the wrench, and stood up. "Hey, you're bleeding," he said. "Let me get a Band-Aid. Hey, whoa, that's really bleeding." He turned to go for the first aid box.

"No!" Sandy pushed his stinging knuckles against his work pants to wipe the blood off and looked. Blood immediately gathered and ran down his hand. "Here, give me that rag."

Well, that was disturbing, Sandy thought. He'd been making an effort to eliminate Margaret Wiser from his thoughts. Wrapping the dirty rag around his hand, he grinned and said, in his best Monty Python accent, "Don't worry. It's only a flesh wound."

Alden shook his head. "Here, move over. Let me finish that."

"Yeah, that'd be good. Thanks."

Alden checked the torque on the bolts holding the vacuum pump.

Sandy leaned against the plane. Uninvited, Maggie's face kept forming in his conscious mind. It wasn't only the dark-lashed green eyes. She had a wide, incredibly open smile that...well, when she looked into your eyes, you felt it in your stomach. If that was her strategy, it wasn't going to work. End of story. He watched Alden thread the stainless-steel wire through the head of the first bolt.

"I'm going to need the safety tie pliers," Alden said.

Green eyes. Freckles. Halter tops. Damn her anyway.

"Hey, you with me or not?" Alden asked. "Hand me the pliers, McAllister."

Sandy handed the pliers to him. Actually, the humor and joy that erupted at times through Maggie's sadness and frustration were probably what left him momentarily breathless and in awe.

Alden twisted the safety wire on the last bolt. "Okay, that'll do it. We can put the cowling back on." He stepped away from the engine, rubbing his palms on the side of his coveralls. "Let me get someone to give me a hand. You're useless today."

"No, I can do it." Sandy tossed the bloody rag in a trash barrel and rushed over to the piece of metal that would close over the engine. He'd worked on this job all morning. He wasn't going to miss putting the cowling back on. They lifted together and walked toward the plane.

"What's the matter with you, Sandy? You got it backwards. Go around on that side."

"Just testing." Sandy grinned at him. "You passed."

"Yeah, sure. You're doing your absent-minded professor thing, again."

"Wait, I'm a professor? Nice."

"Very funny," Alden said.

They lifted and slid the metal cover in place. "Hey, Sandy. You got three rivets missing! How close to your annual inspection are you anyway?"

"Oh, yeah. I saw that. I forgot."

Incredulous, Alden put his hands on his hips and stared at him. "You *forgot*?"

Well, if that wasn't proof enough he had to forget about Maggie, what was? "It's December twelfth. That means I still have a month to go," he said in self-defense. "Let's take care of it now, though."

Alden nodded. "I'll get the rivet kit. Want a cup of coffee?"

Sandy leaned against the strut on the plane. "No, I'm okay."

"You must have Maggie on your mind," Alden said. He extended a backing block toward Sandy. "Can't say as I blame you, but we're almost done. Give me a hand?"

Sandy grabbed the backing block and leaned back to give Alden room to move the rivet gun into position.

He didn't want to hurt Maggie. He never should have had sex with her. Once that happened, the relationship was all downhill. They could have remained friends and still had fun together, but that wasn't going to happen now. He'd have to tell her. Get it over with soon so he could get on with his own life. And she with hers.

Alden straightened up. "Okay, that'll do it. I think you're done."

Sandy nodded. "Yup. My thoughts exactly."

* * *

Maggie aligned the handles of her fork, knife and spoon with the edges of the placemat while she listened to Sandy. She felt like she had just received a punch in the stomach.

She hadn't realized just how important this relationship was to her until now.

She had been the reluctant one–carefully keeping an emotional distance. But gradually, over her better judgment, he'd won her confidence, then her affection, and then...? How far had she come in letting down the barriers, allowing herself to become vulnerable in spite of the impossibility of it all?

She took a breath and looked around the restaurant where they were having dinner. Only half an hour before, she and Sandy had sat in his car, watching people go in, scanning the area for parked cars that might have someone lurking in them. When they finally entered the restaurant, she picked a table away from the windows that looked out on the bay. While the waitress brought menus, water, placemats, and utensils, she looked casually around the dining space, taking note of the other diners. They were all in groups of four or more and all appearing to know each other. Lively conversation reached her from all directions. She relaxed. She wondered how long it would be, when she got back to ordinary life, before she would stop scanning, stop being cautious, stop being suspicious.

And then Sandy had lowered the boom. "Sorry," he said and reached to cover her hand with his.

She pulled her hand back. "So, let me get this straight. We are not going to be seeing each other anymore because, like me, you don't want a long-term relationship."

He nodded.

"And so you're nipping this in the bud."

"Well, that's not exactly the way I would put it, but yes. The sooner we end this, the better off we'll both be."

The waitress stopped at their table with a pad and pencil in her hands. "What can I get you folks?"

"We'll need a minute," Maggie said without looking at her.

She forced herself to sit quietly and wait until the waitress was out of earshot, getting her emotions under control. "So, you want us to stop seeing each other *now*. And I have nothing to say about it...no discussion."

"Maggie, I never intended for this relationship to go as far as it did. I know I've been clear that I wasn't looking for a long-term relationship."

"That's why I let down my guard. Because neither was–neither am I."

"Well then, I don't see a problem," he said.

"You know this could have ended in a natural way when it was time for me to leave with Wade and Jessie. It feels like a slap that you made up your mind unilaterally and didn't allow us to arrive at this decision together."

And God knows she had looked forward to spending more time with him until the inevitable moment when they said goodbye.

He nodded and fussed with the utensils again.

She moved back from the table and stood up. "Well, I won't waste another minute of your time."

"Wait, Maggie. I am still going to go with you tomorrow."

After a phone call from Jessie yesterday, they had been planning on driving to Atlanta, Georgia for a short meeting. Wade said he'd explain when she got there.

"Oh, that would be lovely. And just so much fun. No. I don't think so."

"You can't go alone. I was going to rent a car so we'd be comfortable. I'm willing to go that far with you. You need someone. To be sure no one is following us."

"Goodbye, Sandy." She softened for a moment. "It really has been fun. For me anyway." She felt a searing pain ripping through her body as she walked among the tables of happy patrons and left the restaurant.

She remembered there was a gas station a couple of blocks away and walked in that general direction. She asked to use the phone and called Aunt Belle to come get her. She was in Morehead City–too far to walk to Beaufort at night. In heels. And there was no way she was going to ride home with him. How humiliating that would be.

"Oh dear, how awful," said Aunt Belle. "I don't want to make any excuses for him, but I know he's just protectin' himself from his own feelin's."

Maggie nodded. What about her feelings?

"Okay, it won't help right now to hash this over, will it?" Belle said. "We have to figure out how to get you to Atlanta tomorrow so you can meet with Jessie and Wade. You're sure you should still go?"

"Yes. There's no way to tell them I won't be there. They'll think something has happened to me."

"Well, I am surprised to find myself saying this, but wouldn't this be a good time to have one of those new cellular phones?"

"Yes, I guess. Wade has said he would get one for me. After tonight, I guess it would not be a bad idea. I'd have to shop for a bigger pocketbook to carry it, though." She smiled. "That would be fun."

They brainstormed over coffee and came up with a plan. Belle couldn't spare her car for an overnight trip because she was taking a friend for out-patient surgery the next day. But they could drive to a bus station and Maggie would continue on to Atlanta by Greyhound. Charlotte, North Carolina, was decided on because Belle happened to have a Greyhound schedule for Charlotte in Arthur's desk. If they could reach Charlotte by 4:00 a.m., Maggie could catch the bus to Atlanta at 4:25 a.m. and arrive by 10:20 a.m. That would give her time to get a taxi and meet the Maxwells at noon.

"That does sound like it will work. I'll be happy to be part of this," Aunt Belle said.

"I don't think I have the energy to look for an alternative solution. And it feels good to be doing some problem solving on my own. Well, with your help," she said and gave Belle a hug. "Flex my independence muscle."

They drove away from Belle's at 10:45 p.m., Maggie feeling fairly safe under cover of darkness. Still, they watched the road behind them for cars that might be trailing them. After midnight, there were long stretches when no one at all was behind them. She was confident no one was following well before they arrived at the Greyhound station in Charlotte.

When they arrived, Aunt Belle used the restroom, kissed Maggie goodbye, and headed right back out again. Now, Maggie leaned against a vending machine, preferring to stand after the five-hour drive. She watched the handful of people mill around and listened to their conversation.

She was quite sure no one had followed them or knew she was here. For practice, though, she assessed each waiting traveler–a mother with a toddler beside her and an infant on her lap; a very young man saying goodbye to his even younger wife, telling her he'd send for her as soon as he got his first week's pay; a teenager in a military uniform saying goodbye to his crying mother and stiff-upper-lipped father. After she had examined the other half dozen passengers, she bought her ticket five minutes before departure, with cash she'd borrowed from Belle. Even then, to be sure there were no last-minute passengers, she was the last to board. Too much caution was better than too little, she decided.

With her head against the window, she dozed a couple of times for twenty minutes or so. Finally, the bus rolled into Atlanta.

She called a cab from a pay phone in the bus station. She told the driver her destination. He whistled. "That's a fair ways away, ma'am. It'll take a little while."

"That's okay, I'm early."

"Hey, hey, look who's here," said Wade, standing. "Have a seat, Maggie."

By habit, Maggie scanned the mostly unoccupied tables in the small restaurant while Jessie stood up and gave her a hug.

"Sit, sit," said Jessie. "Looks like you're still losing weight. Still running?"

"Yes, of course. But I think it's mostly Aunt Belle's cooking. I'm thinking of sending Violet, our gourmet cook of fried chicken, cream sauces, and cheesecake, to study under Aunt Belle for a couple of weeks when I get home."

"Where's Sandy?"

"He couldn't make it. I came by car and bus with Aunt Belle's help. It was fun." Maggie laughed, realizing it had been. She and Belle talked the whole way about Belle's life with Arthur, Maggie's life with Joel and the kids, and life in general. And today she felt independent, having made a decision on her own and then, with Aunt Belle's help, carrying it out.

"How is the news from home? Is Pookie filling you in?"

"Oh, yes! I can't tell you how happy that makes me. It's so good to get news. It sounds like they're doing quite well. Their grades haven't slipped, Pookie's playing basketball. I...well, I'm beginning to wonder if they really need me."

"Of course they need you," Jessie said. "They're just coping well. Take after their grandmother."

"Let's order lunch," said Wade, "and then we'll talk."

"Yes, please. I'm starved," said Maggie.

"We wanted to see you for a couple of reasons," Wade said after they had ordered. "You mentioned you have been doing more research on that company. North American Development. Find out anything?" Wade asked.

"Look, actually, I've got a printout of what I've learned. Sandy set up a computer for me and taught me how to search for things without leaving a trail that would lead back to him. Or me. I can leave it, and you can look at it when you feel like it."

Wade nodded. She pulled a file folder out of her backpack and handed it to him.

He laid the folder beside him on the table. "Anything jump out at you?"

"Yes and no. NADCO–their corporate headquarters are in New York–is owned and run by three men. I think Sandy told you that earlier. My most compelling question is, do all three of these men sit around and make the decision to kill someone?"

"I would say not likely. Much more likely only one of them. Too complicated and risky otherwise."

"That's what Sandy said."

"Tell me about them."

"I've come up with a short dossier on each of them. Funny thing is, I got quite a bit of my information from the company newsletter. A monthly, and I've read them all. It's PR stuff for employees and very self-promotional, but it gave me a lot of leads to begin my research. You want to hear this now or just read what I have later?"

Wade nodded emphatically as he pushed back his plate. "We still have to order dessert. Now is good." He signaled the waitress, and they each ordered pecan pie, warmed, with a scoop of vanilla ice cream on top.

"I'll start with Alexander Upton, or Chip as they call him," Maggie said. "He's apparently a playboy–doesn't really seem to have much to do with the company. He started out wealthy and is considered, at the age of thirty or thirty-two, depending on the source, to be a very eligible bachelor. He's appeared in *People* magazine and a number of others–the list is in the file. He spends so much time in leisurely pursuits, if you want to call them that, that I doubt he spends much, if any, time at the office. He's listed as a vice president, however. When I called to see if I could set up an appointment with him–"

Wade's eyebrows shot up in alarm. "You did what?"

"No, I wasn't going to keep the appointment. I just wanted to see if I could get one–if he was really going into the office. I didn't see how–"

"You had me worried there. Sorry, go ahead."

The dessert arrived, but Maggie put hers aside so she could put her sheaf of papers on the table in front of her. "I was told he was on an extended business trip. In the next issue of *Rafting* magazine, there was a photo of him rafting down the Zambezi River in Africa.

"When he joined NADCO, ten years ago, they were a much smaller development company, operating out of Newark, New Jersey. Not as prestigious an address as they have now. They put up small apartment complexes here and there. Not long after Upton joined the company, the headquarters moved to where they are now. They did some speculative development in the right places at the right time, apparently–Florida, Colorado, Texas."

"Sounds like Upton contributed the dough and collects handsomely on his investment."

"That's the conclusion Sandy and I came to. I doubt he'd be involved enough to even know what goes on at NADCO."

"Okay. Who else?"

"There's Charles Beauchamp, lawyer by profession, also listed as a Vice President and COO. Can't find out much about him except he graduated from Harvard Law School. Went into a big practice in New York as a junior partner. Was there for ten years, and then he opened a small practice of his own doing estate planning and family law. He was one of three original partners fifteen years ago. Can't find a single black mark against him.

"And last, there's Royal LaCroix. President and CEO of NADCO. He and Beauchamp were undergraduates together at Harvard, graduated the same year. LaCroix went on to business school and Beauchamp entered law school. They were both on the rowing team.

"LaCroix's a pillar of the community. I got all kinds of tidbits about him from the newsletter. He is a deacon in his church, donated a large amount of money for a teen center in his town. At NADCO he started innovative programs like job sharing and flexible schedules for moms and dads. He and his wife host exchange students. When he plays golf, he carries his own clubs. A fitness nut. This guy is a saint."

"Bingo."

"You think he's the one? That's what Sandy says. The perfect profile of a white-collar criminal."

"Sandy says that, does he?"

"Yeah, he says LaCroix–if it is LaCroix–probably doesn't even view himself as a criminal. Justifies his actions as necessary business decisions. And while his business ethics might be in the sewer, he could take on the role of an excellent provider, a terrific boss, and a wonderful humanitarian. But ultimately, even the do-gooding is self-serving."

Wade's eyes were wide open, his eyebrows raised. "I couldn't have said it nearly as well as Sandy put it. You got quite a guy there."

She smiled but said nothing and took a bite of the pie, noticing the ice cream had melted. But, oh, boy, was that pie the best she had ever tasted.

"Well, Maggie, you're doing a great job," Jessie said. "Did you get any sense of the company's history? Any problems?"

"I'm checking out individual projects now. For instance, in Florida, a class action suit was just filed against NADCO. And, in San Antonio, get this. This past year, they had almost finished this huge, multi-million-dollar sports complex. But their plan didn't go smoothly. There was some controversy. It wasn't clear in the article, but the case went to court. A judge was expected to make her ruling, and editorials were saying she would probably rule against NADCO. But she never got a chance. She died two days before she was to announce her decision."

"How?" Jessie and Wade asked simultaneously.

"An accidental death. She fell off a barge on the River Walk."

There was a second of startled silence before Jessie harrumphed. "Now how likely is that? That someone would fall off a boat on the River Walk. And be killed?" She shook her head. "Been there. It's like five feet deep. I don't buy an accident."

Wade nodded at Jessie. "I agree it's very suspicious. Something else I wanted to talk about that's been bothering me. The Archibald wildlife refuge. I keep wondering if they are planning shenanigans around that, as Sam suspected."

"Nothing has come up about it in the newsletter or in any online searches. I think we will have to wait until we get back home to check on that. As soon as we are able, we should, at the very least, take a drive out there, and see if we see anything."

"Agreed. Another thing we wanted to talk to you about," said Wade. "They're still hot on your trail. Every time I mail one of those postcards you write to your family, a week later, someone–same man each time–shows up and flashes your picture around. Jessie?" Wade reached for a photograph that Jessie had just dug out of her handbag and handed it to Maggie.

"Here's what he looks like. Memorize his face. Watch for him. Be ready to duck and run at any moment. Do you understand?"

Reluctant to touch the photo, Maggie held the image gingerly by the edges and studied the face of the man. "He's not the man who killed Sam. This guy's white. And you think he's an assassin?"

"Pretty likely," Wade said. "Doubt they'd send someone who couldn't finish the job if he found you."

Maggie's stomach fluttered nervously. I'm looking at a photo of someone who wants to kill me, she thought.

Jessie reached out and patted Maggie's hand. "Have Sandy memorize his face, too–be prepared for the guy to wear a disguise."

She nodded, picked up her backpack, and slipped the photo in the front pocket.

"Maggie, Wade and I agree you're pretty good at counter surveillance now. You've gained some confidence in staying out of sight, disguising, checking for a tail."

She nodded. As a matter of fact, she was.

"But, as I told you, that's the most dangerous time. People who become complacent tend to drop their guard. Stay alert as if this whole thing started yesterday. Okay?"

"Okay. I promise."

"Now, we've got something for you," Wade said.

From her bag, Jessie pulled out a cellular phone. "We thought it would make communication between us just a little easier."

Maggie took a deep breath before taking it in her hand. Smiling, she held it to her ear. Strange to think that with this instrument, without a cord attached, she would be able talk to the Maxwells. She had read about cellular phones, of course, and had even seen one when she was on a train platform in Boston. A man in a suit had one as large as a brick pressed to his head, and he walked up and down the platform talking loudly, real estate, it sounded like, and she got the strong impression he was trying to impress everybody on how important he was because he had a…well, I guess you'd call it a cordless phone. She had chuckled at the time.

"Finish your pie, and we'll go over how to use it," Wade said.

Maggie practiced for a little while, calling first Jessie's phone and then Wade's. "That sure will make things easier to plan in the future," she said. "I don't know anyone else who has one, though."

"But you can make calls to any landline," said Jessie. "Try it now. Do you know Belle's number by heart?"

"Yes, but she's at the hospital with a friend. I have to plan my trip back to Beaufort. I was going to go to the bus station and then call her from a pay phone to coordinate her picking me up in Charlotte. But, hey, does this make long distance calls? Does it cost a lot?"

"Yes, it does make long distance calls, and yes, it costs. You are signed up with a service provider, and the bill will come to me." He held up his hand to stop her objections. "We'll work it all out at some later date, Maggie. I figure you're good for it."

She gave him and Jessie a hug. "Thank you so much."

"But don't use it to call home, no matter how much you want to," Jessie warned. "Don't give them any breadcrumbs to follow."

Maggie laughed. "No, I know better than that."

"I'm going to go to the post office at Live Oaks next week to pick up your mail," Jessie said. "Oh, I can't believe I almost forgot. Here, I have a few clippings from the Amesbury Times I thought you might want to look at." Jessie pulled a few wrinkled pieces of newspaper from her slacks pocket. "Take care. Be on your guard."

On the bus heading north, Maggie smoothed out the articles Jessie had cut out for her.

The oldest one was dated September 17. *In the city council meeting Monday night, Mayor John Fitzhugh appointed Robert Hoyt to fill the position left vacant by the recent death of Samuel Wiser.*

And so life went on.

Maggie drew in a deep breath and continued to read. The city council voted to move forward on the new mall proposed by the North American Development Company, NADCO. A ground-breaking ceremony is planned for October 10. Construction will begin later that month.

She skimmed. A representative of NADCO, Lincoln Montgomery of New York City, was introduced as Project Manager.

Lincoln Montgomery. She hadn't come across his name before. She read on. *In other business, Otis Oxley resigned as city councilor, leaving a second seat vacant within the last four months. Oxley, owner of Amesbury Stop and Shop, has served as city councilman for...* She skipped ahead. *...due to health problems and increasing demands of his business. The mayor said he will appoint another council member to the board before the next meeting. New elections will be held in the spring.*

Well, well. Had he been forced out, or did he run for the nearest exit himself? Interesting.

She smoothed the creases on the last piece of carefully folded paper dated December 8, a little over a week ago. The newsprint was smudged, but it was clearly Pookie going to the basket for a layup. *Amesbury High Cougars out-play, out-score the favored Manasacook Braves in a Cougars' home game Friday night. Freshman Samuel "Pookie" Wiser tipped the scales in his first varsity game by adding fourteen points.* She blinked back tears of pride.

But Pookie was on the JV team. She read on. *Coach David Martin said he brought Wiser up to the varsity team not only because of his scoring ability but also his outstanding defense. "He has great court awareness," Martin said.*

She fumbled for a tissue and blew her nose. How thrilled he must be. How thrilled she was. But she wasn't there to see his triumph. She had never missed a game in any sport since he started playing baseball at the age of seven.

She was angry to the core. What kind of monster could end a person's life and tear apart the lives of other innocent people? Another surge of anger seized her and burned so white hot she wasn't sure if she wanted justice...or revenge. She thought of the gun wrapped in a sweater in a bureau drawer at Belle's house and then went cold. How had she let her feelings get out of control? That's how people got killed. Anger and the availability of a weapon.

She tried to imagine a real human being in front of her. A gun in her hand. She felt weak and a little dizzy. Good. Comforting to know she was still the same person she had been before she learned to shoot a gun.

So Pookie was on the varsity. She'd bet his latest letter sitting in the Live Oaks post office right now was full of the news. An event to look forward to.

Good news from home.

Chapter 14

Joel sat on the bottom step, looking around. Violet had pulled rank and convinced him and Pookie to clean and organize the cellar. He'd built a bench along one wall so he and Pookie could work on projects this winter. Pookie's 1957 orange Indian motorcycle that he'd found at a lawn sale was in pieces on the bench. They worked on the bike a few nights a week, and it was coming together.

Along another wall, boxes were labeled and stacked in categories. The red and green boxes that held their Christmas decorations rose in front of him. And that was, of course, why he was down here.

What to do about Christmas? If there was one thing his father had bequeathed to him, it was being the "Keeper" of Christmas. But the family had decided to skip decorating this year. Skip putting up a tree. Exchanging a few gifts seemed about right, considering the circumstances.

But, here he was, sitting in the cellar, staring at the boxes, on December 20. Was it the ghost of Christmas past that brought him down here? If there was one time Joel could count on having his father's undivided attention, it was at Christmas. They decorated so much that sometimes Joel felt he'd stumbled into Chevy Chase's Christmas. But decorating was always a "two-man" project, his father said, so the two of them spent all of the weekend before Christmas putting up lights and displays on the lawn. Shopping for the perfect tree together, his father always deferred to Joel on the final choice. They decorated it on Christmas Eve. On Christmas and often the day after, his father was there to play with him, read directions, help him assemble and build. They would even make a snowman outside if there was snow.

Did his father ever know how important those times had been to him? He wished he'd told him.

But what he was thinking now was how important they must have been to his father.

* * *

Maggie and Aunt Belle strolled arm in arm through Beaufort looking at Christmas lights. "Look at that one on the corner," Maggie said. "It's beautiful. I think it's the best one on this block. I like the trend back toward colored lights. For years we did the little white lights. I really liked them, but I think I'm ready for color."

"Sam sure got involved in decorating, didn't he?" Aunt Belle asked.

"In a big way. He wouldn't schedule any clients–took the week before Christmas off. Then he spent days putting up lights. We were the last house in the neighborhood to be decorated, but we were always the best." She chuckled. "You could see the glow of our house two blocks away."

"Oh, my."

"And the Santa thing was a big deal, too. Joel was ten before he was convinced there really wasn't a Santa Claus. Sam would do things like put sleigh tracks on the roof and hoof prints on the lawn. Then on Christmas morning he'd take Joel out to look for signs that Santa had been there. Christmas must have been an important holiday in the Wiser household when Sam was growing up."

"No. Oh, no, it wasn't. Sam didn't tell you? He spent every Christmas with Arthur and me from the time the little guy was a year old. Until he was fifteen."

"His parents spent Christmas here? I didn't know."

Why didn't I? Maggie wondered.

"No, no. They brought him to us and then left for a two-week vacation in Europe. Skiing or whatever. Every year."

"What?"

"My Arthur and his brother Sam Senior were nothing like each other. Sam Senior was a manipulator, a hard man, ambitious–bound and determined to be a success at any cost. He married Lillian Whitehall and her money. Then they could barely bring themselves to talk to us common folk. 'Cept, of course, when they needed to drop their son off so they could take off for Europe. Twice a year–two weeks at Christmas and a month in France, Spain, or Italy in the summer. Every year, winter or summer, they brought back a gift for us, a box of delicate hand-blown glass Christmas ornaments from whatever country they had vacationed in. I have an attic full of them."

"I didn't know Sam had Christmas here. Without his parents." She was appalled that she didn't know.

"We felt so bad for the little guy at Christmas. We loved to have him here, but he let us know by the time he was three that there was no Santa Claus. Lillian had told him so. She let the air out of the magic Christmas balloon. Made for a flat Christmas morning, I can tell you.

"When Sammy was four, we waited to decorate the tree until he got here so he could help. He loved that part. So the next year, Arthur decided to put lights around the porch. He and Sammy. Sam got so enthusiastic, they went shopping for more lights and decorated the garage."

Tears slid down Maggie's cheeks.

"Well, each year the project got bigger, and Sammy was able to help more and more. People started walking by just to see our decorations. Sammy was so proud. At Christmas morning breakfast, Sam and Arthur would start planning what was going to be added next year."

"So that's where the drive came from."

"'Spect so." Aunt Belle squeezed Maggie's arm. "Sorry, dear. The holiday business has got to be difficult enough for you without me telling you this."

Maggie wiped her tears. "Must be hard for you, too."

Belle nodded. As they walked in silence, Maggie wondered how many other painful things Sam had not told her about his childhood. Then she thought of Aunt Belle, who had been a surrogate mother to Sam. She no longer had him or Arthur, yet she faced life with energy and gusto. How did she do it?

"The longing, the grief never leaves you," Aunt Belle said as if she'd read Maggie's mind. "You just get to put them on the back burner and go on. Sometimes it comes to a simmer or even approaches a boil, though, on holidays. I see you boiling a bit, dear. I know the feeling."

Maggie gave Aunt Belle's arm a quick hug. "Hey, let's go get some lights. I have a need to decorate like you wouldn't believe."

"It's a lot of work. Arthur was the one–"

"And Sam was the one. But they've left it to us. We'll call it the Sam and Arthur Wiser Memorial Light Festival."

On the bench was a roll of paper towels. Joel blew his nose and sat down on a high stool, feeling spent.

"Dad, you down there?" Pookie called from the top of the stairs.

"Yeah."

Pookie clattered down the stairs. "I saw the lights on. What's up?"

"Not much. Just came down to straighten things up." He looked at his son who seemed to grow an inch a month and whose intelligent eyes told him he was not buying the story.

Joel said, "I came down to look over the decorations."

"I thought we weren't doing that this year."

"Suppose not."

Pookie walked over to the stacked boxes and opened the top one. "We could put up the pinecone wreath Tildie made."

"No harm dressing up the front door."

"Yeah. So that people won't feel sorry for us." Pookie grinned at him.

Joel smiled back. "Okay."

Pookie opened another box. "What about this garland thing with lights? Why don't we put that around the porch?"

Joel felt a stirring of interest. "Could do that, I guess."

Pookie fidgeted, poking through the remaining boxes filled with decorations.

Joel decided to help him out. "What's on your mind, son?"

"You know the fund raiser for new uniforms, selling trees?"

"Uh huh."

"There's a couple left. They're not big. Kind of scrawny, but...if you think it's not appropriate–"

"Let's go get one."

"Really?" Pookie was already headed for the stairs.

"Yeah. It's the right thing to do."

"Grandma would want us to."

Joel thought, as they trooped up the stairs together, and Grandpa would approve, as well.

"Hurry up, Maggie. It's starting. 1999 isn't going to last much longer!"

"Okay, here I come."

Maggie set a tray on the coffee table in the living room and gazed around the room with satisfaction. "Oh, my, it looks so cozy with the fireplace going. I'm glad we decided to celebrate in here instead of the den."

"Well, the tree is in here. And it's the last night it will be. Tomorrow we undecorate it."

Tiny colored lights glowed from the seven-foot fir tree and reflected off the intricate, hand-blown glass ornaments.

Logs crackled in the small fireplace.

They'd had fun in a competitive bake off earlier in the day. Belle made her pecan pie squares, and Maggie baked the only recipe she knew by heart, Czechoslovakian raspberry bars. They kept out enough for tonight for the two of them and froze the rest for future coffee breaks.

"There's a lot of calories in these things," Maggie said.

"We deserve it. It's the turn of the year, the decade, the century, and a new millennium, to boot. Imagine! We are about to be living in the third millennium."

"Kind of awesome, isn't it? Did you ever think about this, Aunt Belle? When you were growing up, it would turn to a new millennium during your lifetime?"

"I didn't even think of it turning into a new century. It seemed so far away. I was born in 1917, so when anyone said anything about the turn of the century, to me, it always meant from 1899 to 1900. I'm sure no one ever spoke of a millennium."

"Speaking of that, how are you feeling about Y2K?"

"Glad you're here to help me cope when all hell breaks loose."

"It sounds like I haven't convinced you that there will be few problems and nothing that will impact us?"

"Seeing is believing. I think it's a great idea that they will be showing the new year around the world. It starts in the Pacific, you know. So if electricity fails, we'll know before midnight here. Oh, listen, a news bulletin."

The local news anchor said, "The Russian president, Boris Yeltsin, announced today that he is retiring earlier than he had planned. His successor is Vladimir Putin."

"Well, that's sudden," said Maggie. "I don't know who this Putin is. I've never heard of him. I wonder if it will be better or worse."

The announcement was short with relatively little information. The transition had already taken place.

Maggie frowned. "Hmm, a done deal. You always wonder, when it's a country like Russia, if his sudden retirement was voluntary. Sounds like this Putin guy has only been in the administration for four months. A quick rise to power, don't you think?"

"We'll soon see, I'm sure," Aunt Belle said. "Look, ABC is doin' coverage of the Kiribati islands. This is wonderful to see the new year begin in a place so far away."

Maggie smiled at Belle. "See? Everything looks fine there."

"No. Look, they're not using electricity…just torches. So how do we know?"

"The TV cameras and microphone are using electricity."

Belle nodded slowly. "Hmmm, I suppose that's true. Or maybe they have batteries? Anyway, what's so scary, when you think of it, is that we are so dependent on computers. It feels like we, the whole world, and everyone in it is fragile. Everything is controlled by computers. Probably far more than I am imagining."

Maggie picked up a pecan bar. "Yes, that's true and probably far more than I can imagine. But I believe we have technical geniuses throughout the world who are on top of this."

She smiled at Belle and shook her head. "I am amazed that the woman who stares fierce hurricanes in the eye, is now blinking about Y2K." She took a bite. "Oh, my, Aunt Belle. These are delicious. Better than my raspberry bars."

"Look, Maggie. Now they're in New Zealand. Let's see what this announcer has to say."

The news anchor stared intently at the camera. "New Zealand is the first industrialized country we are looking at. New Zealand is like the canary in the mine shaft. We'll know a lot about what's to come for the rest of the world by how they are doing here."

Belle sampled the raspberry bars. "Margaret Wiser, these are wonderful. Better than the pecan bars." She sat on the edge of her chair and watched the screen intently.

The television announcer grinned broadly at the camera. "Reports are coming in from everywhere across the country. Everything seems to be functioning as usual. All normal. All normal here in New Zealand, folks. I'm guessing people from around the world are sighing with relief."

Belle breathed a gentle sigh. "I'm so glad you are with me for this, Maggie. Usually I don't wait 'til midnight on New Year's Eve, but I would have tonight. Hey," she said, taking another bite. "These are really good. And you did this from memory?"

"Yes, it was my signature dessert, alongside the traditional pies, of course, for Thanksgiving. Listen, Aunt Belle. I really want to stay more in touch with you when all of this is over. In fact, last night I was thinking, I mean, would you be willing to come to Maine a couple of times a year? At least? You could come for Christmas through New Year's maybe for a couple of weeks? I've been thinking how I would create a guest room in my house for you. And then, well, it would be a shame not to spend some time in Maine in the summer."

Maggie leaned toward Belle, holding her breath.

"Well, Maggie, darlin', I'd love that! I have a very full life here, but I would love to spend time with you and Joel and the kids. And have a nice change of scenery."

"Done! I'll start planning for it when I get home."

At midnight they counted down with the crowd in Times Square. "Happy New Year, Aunt Belle!"

"Happy New Year, my love." They clinked their glasses of bourbon.

"Oh, wait," Belle said. "Let's be really sure. Just a minute." She went across the hall and into the bathroom. Maggie heard the flush of the toilet.

"It's working. Good to go!" shouted Belle.

Christmas and New Year's had come and gone, and Maggie had not communicated with Sandy. She raised her hand to knock on his door, lowered it, then raised it again. This was silly. Her bruised pride had nearly healed, yet it was still hard to ask for favors. She knocked firmly on the door. In seconds, Sandy stood in full living color, shirt sleeves rolled to his elbows, a newspaper in his hand. He looked startled and then smiled. "Come in, come in. I'm glad to see you. Belle said you went to Atlanta. I've been wondering how the trip went. How're Wade and Jessie?"

"Went fine. I have a photo of my supposed assassin. I got my first genuine letter from Pookie. And then I recently got another one. It had, um, somewhat astounding news. That's, um, why I'm here."

"Then, let's not stand outside. Come on in."

"I wouldn't bother you, but I think I need your help."

"Of course I'll help. What's happened?" He gestured toward the kitchen. "Let's have a cup of coffee."

He pulled out a chair for her, and she sat down. He moved to the counter and picked up the coffee pot. "And?"

"Tildie is apparently pregnant."

He paused, the coffee pot halfway to the sink, taking her words in, his eyebrows raised in astonishment. Finally, he spoke. "Apparently?"

"Pookie overheard her on the phone telling a friend."

He filled the pot with water. "How do you think she's taking it?"

"My guess is not well. Not well at all. She's never wanted a family, not in her whole life. She never even played with dolls when she was little. She has her career plans all set."

He scooped coffee into the basket. "What are you going to do?"

"I want to go back. I *am* going back. I told Jessie and Wade I wouldn't, but I have to."

"You've talked to them about this?" He put the coffee on the stove and turned the burner on.

"Yes."

"And?"

"He said I'd be putting her in danger as well as myself."

"You don't agree."

"I agree it's possible. But so much time has gone by..."

"Four months..."

Maggie was taken aback. Had he been counting?

"...and five days. But who's counting?" he said. "Go on. I'm listening."

"Um, sure, okay. Well, this is my thinking. They're looking for me in Florida and Alabama, following the trail Wade's been laying. Right? They're not looking in Maine. Even if there's an element of danger, I would go home only for a day. Talk to her, help her plan." She frowned, thinking her idea through. "I think I can get into and out of Amesbury without anyone knowing."

"You're sure about this?"

"Yes. You think it's risky?"

"Oh, certainly there's a risk. If Wade feels you can't accomplish this, the risk factor must be high."

But how much risk? At three o'clock this morning, she had finally gotten up and started writing pros, cons, and dangers and how to avoid them. Could she get in and out simply because whoever was looking for her wouldn't be expecting her?

Sandy brought steaming cups of coffee to the table. "How can I help?"

Maggie felt relief. He was willing to help her instead of trying to talk her out of the plan. "This is what I need the most. I'll tell you my plan, and you try to find holes in it."

"Play devil's advocate. Sure, I can do that. First question. What are you going to do for a coat?"

A coat. She hadn't even thought about a coat. What else hadn't she thought of?

"You can borrow my ski jacket if you need it. It'll be way too big, but big is in. But let's back up. Tell me first why you can't talk to her by phone. There must be a way to connect with her. Through letters with Pookie, maybe you could prearrange a place where she can be when you call her. Violet's house? Your office? Angie's house? On this end, you could use Wade's cellular phone."

Maggie couldn't suppress a smile. "Actually, I have my own cellular phone. I almost used it to call you." She watched the astonishment on his face. "Wade," she said.

"Ahhh. Was bound to happen," Sandy said, his eyes crinkling with amusement.

Maggie nodded. "But the overwhelming concern is, I can't get around the fact that any and all of those phones back home are very likely bugged. That would be a colossal breach of my promise to Wade and Jessie. A violation of what we've worked for. So, I'm leaving it here with Belle."

He nodded. "Yeah, I can see that."

"But a bigger issue is that this can't be dealt with in a phone call. Not in any way that would be helpful. In fact, it would probably backfire when she learned Pookie had told me. I know my granddaughter, and I know this has to be approached gently and in person for any good to come of it. Of this, I'm sure."

"Okay. You've convinced me. Let's talk about the details."

"Thank you," she said and felt some tension drain. "I wanted to return home as soon as I heard, but I couldn't go walking up to the house, so I've been waiting until her winter break is over. I know her class schedule. I can catch her at the college."

"Makes sense. How're you going to get to Amesbury? "

"I'm going to take the bus. I just did a test run when I went to Atlanta two weeks ago. It'll work."

Sandy got a pad and pen from a desk in the kitchen and brought them back to the table. "Let's write down the details."

She pulled a piece of paper from her jacket pocket. "I've got a partial list started."

"Good. Okay, have you checked the bus schedules?"

"Yes. I picked up schedules last week. You're sure this isn't an imposition?"

"Let's see. I got a choice between reading Garfield and helping to plan a caper. You win by a cat's hair."

Through the bus window the scenery slipped past, and at dawn Maggie saw patches of snow in the woods that bordered Interstate 95. This evidence of winter developed into snow-covered fields, and she kept track of her progress north by the increasing height of the snowbanks along the highway. The wintry landscape seemed foreign after so much time in North Carolina.

The closer she got to home, the more intensely she imagined her granddaughter's fear and confusion. As soon as she read the letter, she'd known she would crawl on her hands and knees over broken glass to get to Tildie. Now, the longing for this bus ride to be over was immense. Tildie often rebuffed gestures of comfort and concern, but Maggie knew that inside the carefully constructed fortress, her granddaughter was as fragile as an eggshell.

Maggie's pulse quickened when the bus passed by the exit to Amesbury and continued north. She was travel-weary, having already been on the road for twenty-four hours, but she endured an additional two hours and got off in Bangor at three-thirty in the afternoon under a dark gray sky.

Despite Sandy's ski jacket, a blast of frigid air chilled her to the bone. Her feet were protected from the cold only by high-top sneakers and two pairs of socks. From the luggage compartment under the bus, the driver retrieved the gym bag she had taken with her when she ran away from Amesbury. She shouldered her backpack that served as a handbag, grabbed the gym bag, and dashed into the convenience store that doubled as the bus stop to phone a cab.

Fifteen minutes later, she stood at the car rental counter nervously fanning her credit card with her thumb.

"Name?"

Maggie hesitated so long, the bored clerk looked up. "Do you have one?"

"Margaret Wiser." Saying her own name out loud made her feel visible and vulnerable.

The young woman continued filling out the paperwork while Maggie's tension mounted. Was this, after all, a good idea?

"Insurance?"

"Yes."

"Sign here, please. And here. And initial this box here."

The clerk reached for Maggie's credit card. She felt a pin prick of fear. The die was about to be cast. When she was safe in North Carolina, using the credit card had not seemed like a risk. This transaction wouldn't be posted for twenty-four hours. By then, she'd be headed back to North Carolina. Besides, renting the car in Bangor, one hundred miles north of Amesbury, allowed her to lay a false trail–they'd begin looking in Bangor first. Wouldn't they?

Though she used her credit card for the car rental, she'd been forced to borrow cash from Sandy for the bus ticket, which caused frustration at not having access to her own money. But this trip included a plan for solvency. If she could pull it off, she'd have money to repay Aunt Belle, Wade, and Sandy and still have cash to live on for a while.

The wind whipped across the dark parking lot as she jogged to the car, a Volkswagon Jetta. She threw her bags in, started the car, and sat shivering, hands in her pockets, waiting for the engine to warm enough so she could turn on the heater.

In a mall, she bought boots, a hat, and gloves. Now that she was warm, she realized she was starving. At the last bus stop on the trip north, the waiting lines had been so long she had had to reboard without getting a meal. Ahead, she saw Miller's, famous for its miles of salad bars and sumptuous buffets, and drew a sigh of relief. She longed for a glass of wine but rejected the thought and filled up on seafood and coffee. Feeling more adventurous on a full stomach, she paid again with her credit card.

As she drove south after supper, Maggie felt a surge of excitement. She was entering forbidden territory and pitting herself against an unknown enemy. Had she become hooked on the excitement of living on the edge? Was she compensating for a life that had become so predictable and boring that she had almost gone to sleep?

She entered Amesbury, driving along dark roads, and was knocked askew by a sense of unfamiliarity–as if her connection with the city had become so tenuous it had nearly been severed.

She parked in the downtown mall parking lot where most of the small shops were closed, and there were only a few cars in the parking lot.

Against her windshield, tiny snowflakes touched and melted into fine droplets. She didn't need a snowstorm complicating her plans. She tied her hood under her chin, grabbed the gym bag and backpack from the seat beside her, and got out of the car. A fine, silvery snow-mist formed halos around the streetlights.

The Main Street stores were all closed in the deserted downtown area, and there was no one around to recognize her; yet she still felt exposed to view. She crossed the street with her head lowered.

She walked past the front door of Stonefield and Wiser and continued to the alley that would take her to the rear of the building. The alley was a mass of frozen ruts, and she had to pick her way carefully in the dim light.

At the rear entrance, she wondered for the first time if the damn locks had been changed since she'd left. She pulled off a glove, unzipped the parka pocket, and grabbed her set of keys. The security light in the yard was dim, making it difficult to identify which of the five keys on her ring was the right one. She wished for a moment her keys were like Tildie's–arranged in a specific order so you could find the right key by counting. She should have isolated the office key in advance.

She thumbed through them, but her fingers had become numb. She would just have to try each key–but was the key supposed to be right side up or upside down when inserted? She went through the entire ring, trying not to panic. Two of the keys were easily inserted but wouldn't turn.

She started through the keys again, when sensory motor memory took over, and she remembered you had to pull the door toward you and push down as you turned the key. The last key on the ring turned, and she was in.

The sudden warmth brought a rush of gratitude for this shelter. Then exhaustion set in. She'd not had more than four hours sleep in the past thirty-eight. Every time she'd nodded off on the bus, it would make a rest stop; even if she didn't get off, she was awake for several more hours before she could drop off again. Adrenalin must have been carrying her until now. Driving to Amesbury, she hadn't felt tired for a moment. Now she could hardly stand up. She wondered if this was what runners meant when they said they "hit the wall."

With barely enough energy to carry her bag, she walked down the dark hall to her old office. She took a deep breath and opened the door. The same feeling of distancing unfamiliarity washed through her that she had experienced when she arrived in the city.

She staggered to the couch, put her backpack on it for a pillow, and laid down without removing her coat.

When she woke, enough light came through the windows from streetlights so that shapes were defined–but only in blacks and grays. She had a vague memory of waking long enough to remove her coat. She remembered fragments of dreams–someone chased her up and down the aisle of a bus while she tried to solve difficult, nearly insurmountable problems to save the lives of people she didn't know.

She heard a car outside drive into the back parking lot, its tires crunching across the ice. Alarmed, she sat up and pressed the button on her glow watch. Five-thirty in the morning. Surely, too early for anyone to be coming to the office. In another second, she realized it must be Tommy Reed, coming in early to get things started in his coffee shop next door. Tommy's Irish cream coffee and homemade doughnuts had been her breakfast on mornings when she was in too much of a hurry to stop at Hal's.

She had an hour to be out of here before workers on their way to the mill in cars and trucks would begin filling the street. She grabbed the gym bag and headed for the bathroom across the hall, where she could turn on the light without risk.

She happily squeezed toothpaste onto her brush. There had been only one opportunity to brush her teeth during the entire bus trip. She washed her face with steaming hot water, shampooed her hair in the small sink, and dried it with her blow dryer. With a fresh change of underwear and socks, she experienced an enormous sense of wellbeing.

From the gym bag she extracted a tiny flashlight–the kind used to find keys at the bottom of a pocketbook. The one she could have used last night when she struggled to unlock the door–if she had thought about it.

She removed a painting from the wall, and, with the aid of her flashlight, she followed the familiar pattern of the safe combination. The handle turned and the door swung open on the first pull. She found the packet and breathed a sigh of relief.

She brought the accordion folder to her office so she could empty and sort it. A familiar scent caught her attention; she glanced down and recognized the houndstooth jacket that hung over the back of the chair. She snapped on the flashlight holding it close to a photograph on the desk. There, smiling joyfully, was Angie tossing her laughing two-year-old daughter in the air. It was a photograph Maggie had taken during a barbecue in her own backyard last summer.

Yes! Stoney had done the right thing. The logical thing. Angie was doing Maggie's job, making Maggie's office her own. She also felt a burden of guilt lift from her shoulders. With Angie filling her shoes, this place would go on without her.

She pressed the button on her watch again–six-thirty. There were already cars passing by outside. Without turning on the flashlight, she opened the packet and sorted through legal documents, feeling the paper and the weight: the deed, the birth certificates, her passport, until she found the one she wanted. She turned the packet upside down and shook out a key. She slipped the key into her jeans pocket and the document into the gym bag.

Feeling frantic to leave, she shoved the other papers back into the folder, put it back in the safe, and spun the combination lock. She re-hung the painting and took a second to be sure the frame was straight because Angie would notice. She grabbed the bag, checked her jacket pocket for the key ring, and headed for the rear door.

She hesitated before opening it. Dropping her bags by the door, she ran to Stoney's office and picked up a notepad and pen. She jotted down a quick message and looked around, choosing a good place to hide it where only he would find it. Satisfied, she ran back to the door, picked up her bag and backpack, and snapped open the lock. She slowly cracked the door and peered outside. The service area that Stonefield and Wiser shared with four other businesses was empty except for Tim Reid's old rattletrap. She stepped outside and pulled the door closed. Last night's snow had changed to freezing rain–the doorknob–everything–was covered with a layer of ice. Head down, she minced slowly across the treacherous parking lot and down the alley.

A steady stream of cars and trucks, their headlights shining on the vehicles ahead, crawled down Main Street toward the mill in the half-light of the early winter morning. She waited for a small break in the traffic and ran across the road, her mind occupied with the next problem. She had to intercept Tildie at 10:00. Maggie would have to time the meeting exactly right, which meant she had to count on Tildie following her usual schedule. But Tildie was painfully punctual and hadn't missed a day of school in over eight years. Now Maggie had three hours to kill. She headed out of town and north to Waterville for breakfast.

By nine-thirty she was back in Amesbury, and the early morning clouds had disappeared. Every ice-wrapped branch and shrub glittered in the sun. Maggie fumbled in her backpack for her oversized sunglasses and slipped them on. Power lines looked like silver threads looping from pole to pole. Mornings like this, living in the north in the winter, seemed magical.

She glanced at the clock on the dashboard–nine forty-five. She didn't want to be sitting in a high-traffic parking lot for long, but if she got there too late and missed Tildie, she'd have to wait all day and try to catch her as she left. That was longer than she felt comfortable hanging around Amesbury. She already felt exposed driving around familiar streets in the daylight.

The college was now two blocks away. Butterflies. What if Tildie inadvertently gave Maggie away? What if Tildie didn't come to school today? What if Maggie couldn't manage to intercept her? She looked at her watch again. Nine-fifty and a block to go. She pushed the accelerator harder, feeling sure she had misjudged the time. Because the parking lot would be slippery, Tildie would leave herself extra time to walk into the building without rushing. Perhaps she had already arrived at school.

As Maggie pulled in, she scanned for Tildie's car. She drove up one row and down another, looking from right to left, afraid she would miss the car–afraid she would see it and know she was too late.

Finally convinced the car wasn't there, she found an empty space from where she could see all cars that entered the parking lot. She left the motor running. Another set of worries pricked at her. Maybe Tildie's car was in the garage, and she'd gotten a ride from Andrew. Maybe she had the flu. Maybe she had dropped this morning's class from her course load.

A few minutes after ten, she saw Tilde's silver Camry turn into the lot. Tildie was late–late for the first time Maggie could ever remember. She put the car in gear and eased toward the space Tildie had pulled into. Tildie exited the car, shrugged into her backpack, and turned to lock her car with a remote as she hurried toward the building.

Maggie pushed on the accelerator and passed by Tildie, gasping aloud when she realized Tildie's beautiful hair had been cut very, very short. At the end of the row of cars, Maggie came to a stop, rolled down her window, and waited for Tildie to walk by.

"Excuse me Miss," Maggie said loud enough for passersby to hear. "Could you tell me how to get to the administration building?"

Tildie whirled around when she heard her grandmother's voice. Maggie already had her finger in front of her lips as Tildie looked at Maggie in open-mouthed astonishment. Still signaling for silence, Maggie crooked the finger of her other hand–come here.

"I'm a stranger asking for directions," Maggie said loud enough for just her granddaughter to hear. "Point to the administration building."

Tildie took an impulsive step closer, but Maggie held up a halting hand. "Do I have to get back to the main road to get there?"

Maggie watched it dawn on Tildie, and finally she responded. "It's over there." She pointed vaguely, but her face was alert, waiting for instructions. Maggie signaled her closer, and Tildie took a small step and leaned forward.

"Grandma..."

Maggie put her finger to her lips. "Can you skip classes today?"

Tildie's eyes widened, and she nodded emphatically, yes.

"Point again like you're giving me directions. Then walk into the building as if you are going to class and come out on the east side of the quad. I'll meet you in the Methodist Church parking lot."

Tildie straightened; speaking loudly, she gestured. "I think you can get there easier if you turn left here and take a right two blocks down. You can't miss it." Then she turned, and without looking back, hurried into the building.

Maggie smiled for a second before driving off. That was Tildie. Once a course of action was decided on, she would quickly and efficiently carry it out.

As Maggie eased around the parking lot, she realized with a start that her window was still open. How much easier to be seen through an open window. She sucked in her breath because suddenly she felt exposed and vulnerable.

"Today we are indeed fortunate to have with us someone whose unquestionable academic credentials and impeccable reputation have led him to become recognized on four continents as one of the foremost experts in antiquities. During his illustrious career, he has been in great demand internationally as a consultant to museums in the United States, Great Britain, Venezuela, Egypt, and several other countries in Africa for the purpose of guiding and authenticating their collections of historical artifacts. And so, please welcome Dr. Jules Chadwick."

Smiling modestly, Jewel got slowly to his feet, enjoying the enthusiastic applause from both the students, whom he had come to know well, and the couple of dozen visiting guests. Two of the guests were postgrad students from Boston U and Tufts. Others he recognized as assistant curators from various museums in New England. He was pleased with the turnout.

He moved with slow, deliberate grace to the podium. He brought a long-practiced smile to his eyes and let it wander over the assembly until there was a hush.

"First, I'd like to take a moment to thank Dr. Williams," he said, nodding toward the professor who had introduced him, "for his glowing introduction. I must admit, though, if I weren't the only one sitting up here on the dais with him, I'd be looking around to see who he was talking about." Chuckles rippled around the room.

"I'd also like to thank Amesbury College for giving me this opportunity, for these past four months, to share with you a corner of my field that I find particularly fascinating." He deepened his voice a fraction. "And most of all, I'd like to thank the students who have shown an interest in my work, who have welcomed me into their midst, and who have made me feel comfortable here." Students smiled and nodded sentimentally.

"When I first came here in September, I wasn't sure how I would fare among all of you melanin-challenged folks..." He smiled and was rewarded by laughter from his audience.

"And now, so as not to impose on the valuable time of our distinguished guests, I'll get started on this morning's lecture. I call it Antiquing Antiquities, or...Authentic Reproductions I Have Loved and Left Behind.

"The four examples I'm going to show you today represent the most convincing fakes I've come across during my...*illustrious*" ...Jewel sent a self-deprecating smile at Dr. Williams... "career." He paused for chuckles.

"Actually, two of the items I didn't leave behind–I purchased them because I was fascinated by the cleverness of their creators. We'll be looking at photos of the two I have here today as well as detailed slides of the other two. Let's start with the slide show. Could someone hit the light switch? Maybe close the blinds?"

Jewel glanced toward the window and caught the sight of Tildie Wiser striding purposefully, as usual, toward the building. A small compartment of his mind noted that it was most unusual for her to be late. A split second later, he saw the face of the woman Tildie had stopped to talk to and was jolted to the core.

He nodded his appreciation at the students who were doing his bidding, while he struggled to keep his mind on his presentation–filing away the information to be examined later.

Was it possible...?

They sat in the car, watching the incoming tide. The rolling foam gradually slapped higher on the rock-strewn beach, nibbling and melting the ice that had formed during the night.

Tildie had insisted, as soon as she got in the car, that Maggie explain the need for secrecy. As they drove, Tildie listened to the story of her grandfather's death and Maggie's flight in shocked and rapt silence, with only an occasional question. Then Tildie suggested they come to this beach–one of her favorite places to scuba dive in the summer.

"But if it's dangerous," she asked now, "why did you come back?"

Maggie hesitated and took a breath. This was what she had come for, but she hadn't planned how she would start.

"I thought you might need me."

Tildie looked startled and unguarded for a second. She didn't speak.

"I understand you're pregnant."

Tildie gasped. "How did you know?"

"Pookie told me."

"Pookie!" She looked stunned. "*Pookie?* How could he know? No one knows. And how did he tell you?"

"He overheard you talking to someone on the phone. We have a sneaky way of communicating, Pookie and I, that I'll tell you about later. Let's talk about you. This is not a blaming thing, but I have to ask. How did this happen? You have a diaphragm."

Tildie looked at her hands folded in her lap. "I know, I know. Grandma?" Tildie took a deep breath. "Did you ever...well, get swept away? So that you stopped thinking, maybe even forgot where you were?"

A sunny bluff in Bermuda crossed Maggie's mind. "Yes. Once. Maybe twice."

Tildie sucked in her breath, looked sideways at Maggie, and smiled. "It was a rhetorical question."

"You mean you don't exactly want to acknowledge your grandmother has had a sex life?"

Tildie grinned wider. "Yeah. I used to tease you about it, but I guess I don't want to deal with the actual reality."

"Yeah, I heard you rotten kids were like that." She smiled affectionately at Tildie. "Anyway..."

"Anyway, I didn't plan to...I mean I never lose control. Except for this one time I didn't even think of using my diaphragm. In fact, it was a couple of days later before it occurred to me, I hadn't used it. I am so, so stupid."

"You've been carrying this burden by yourself?"

"Yeah, mostly. But now you're here. Everything feels a lot better. But how did Pookie find out? Shawna. He must have heard me talking to Shawna. I...she...I had to tell someone. I thought she might understand. She's an...unwed mother, too. And she doesn't hang around the college crowd, so I felt safe telling her."

"What are your thoughts about being an unwed mother?"

"Well, I'm way past the time for stopping the pregnancy. Funny, as frantic as I was, I didn't even think of stopping it until it was too late. Probably because I wouldn't have been able to go through with an abortion anyway."

"No, I meant you and Andrew must be planning on getting–"

She shook her head. "Oh, no. Definitely not. I mean he probably would–but I won't. We...ah, well, as it turns out, we aren't exactly seeing each other anymore."

Maggie studied Tildie's face. She seemed so defenseless. Maggie's throat constricted. "I'm so sorry."

Tildie managed a weak smile. "Well, you weren't exactly crazy about him."

"Maybe not, but I certainly didn't object to him. I just thought he was a little–"

"Pompous?"

"Stuffy. And maybe overbearing. How does he feel about the pregnancy?"

"He doesn't know, yet. We'd already broken up when I realized. I'm going to have to tell people soon, or they'll start guessing."

"How far along are you?"

"Almost four months. I'm...starting to show. I've been wearing baggy sweaters." Tildie gave her a sheepish half smile. The smile wobbled precariously and then crumbled into anguish. "Oh, Grandma. I can't stand it. This is almost the worst thing that has ever happened to me." A sob caught in her throat.

Maggie tentatively reached across to comfort her. As her hand touched Tildie's shoulder, the last of her granddaughter's control evaporated and tears cascaded down her distraught face. She covered her face with her hands.

Maggie remembered finding an eight-year-old Tildie sitting in the middle of her mother's bed a week after her funeral. Tildie had emptied Miki's closet and drawers and piled the clothing on the bed. She sat in the middle of the pile, her face covered with her hands, crying as if she would die.

Maggie smoothed the hair behind Tildie's ear before she spoke. "Losing your mother was the worst thing that ever happened to you."

Tildie nodded. Maggie continued to stroke her hair until Tildie drew a ragged breath. "Sometimes I still miss her so much. I feel like there's a hole that will never be filled."

"I know. You and your mother were so incredibly close. I used to watch the two of you together–from the time you were born. I had never seen anyone so devoted to a child as your mother was to you. I was amazed...and I envied her."

Tildie blotted her eyes on her sleeve and looked at Maggie. "Envied her?"

"Uh-huh. As a mother, I was too tied up in the everyday grind of earning a living, washing diapers by hand, cooking meals, and trying to be a dedicated wife. But mostly, I was too young–barely seventeen–when I had your father, too young to truly appreciate such a wonderful gift.

"But your mother was twenty-one when you were born–and more than that, she had an inner peace, I guess is the way to put it, that allowed her to focus on the marvel of...well, of you. One day, when you were only six months old, she and your dad were visiting Grandpa and me. I still remember so clearly. She sat cross-legged on the floor near a sunny window with you on her lap. She talked to you, played with you for an hour, forgetting, I think, anyone else was in the room. You finally fell asleep in her arms, but she didn't want to put you down, so she held you for the next couple of hours until you woke up. The wonder and contentment on her face was beautiful to see."

The hungry look on Tildie's face encouraged Maggie. "As you grew older, she seemed to understand what you needed about the same time you were discovering it yourself. The two of you seemed to have an unspoken language. One time, when I was at your house–you must have only been five years old–you came bursting into the room, all excited, almost dancing on your toes. You looked at your mother and raised your eyebrows. She smiled and nodded to you, then said, 'Give Grandma a kiss first.' You did and then disappeared. I asked her where you went, and she said the neighbors had gotten a new puppy and you wanted to play with it. You and she were always doing that."

Tildie pressed her lips together in an effort to control her emotions, but tears spilled over and slid quietly down her cheeks. "I remember that puppy."

"Watching the two of you made me realize how much I had missed in raising your father."

Tildie drew a ragged breath. "Sometimes, after she died, I was angry with her. I needed her so much, and she left me. It was a long time before I could really understand that she couldn't help dying. Then I felt so guilty, and I couldn't apologize to her."

"If it had been in her power, she would have done anything to still be with you."

"I used to hate Pookie so much. I thought that everything was okay until he came along. Somehow, I thought it was his fault. At least he was someone I could blame."

"I know."

"You *know?*"

Maggie sighed. "And I didn't know how to reach you. You wouldn't talk about it. You wouldn't even allow hugs except once in a while from Grandpa."

"I thought no one could feel how I hurt. Not even Daddy. Now, I know he never got over Mommy's death, but I didn't know then."

"Yes, he had a hard time. He did the same thing you did. Locked himself away. I used to wonder if my raising Pookie added to your pain."

"Yeah. Well, I did resent him. He had somebody…you. I had nobody."

Maggie nodded. "At first, I did it because I loved your mother, and I wanted to give her baby the kind of care I knew she would have given him— the way she did for you. I felt almost as if she had entrusted him to me, as if she were somehow asking me to take care of him."

Maggie stared off into the distance at the rolling ocean. "I used her as a role model, at first. And then I started to feel about him the way I knew your mother had felt about you."

She turned to her granddaughter. "And for a long time, I've thought I shortchanged you in the process. I'm so sorry."

Tildie shook her head. "You gave me as much as I let you. I could always tell you loved me, though." She smiled ruefully through tear rimmed eyes. "I must have been a tough nut to crack."

Maggie drew a deep breath and nodded. "Couldn't have said it better myself."

"Grandma?"

"What?"

"I've tried for so long to not think about my mother. Now I can't stop thinking about her. Do you think I could be as good a mother as she was?"

Maggie could see fear in Tildie's face and something else–perhaps a daring to hope. "Oh, sweetie, I have no doubt whatsoever. None. Because of what your mother gave you for eight years, I have no doubt that the maternal instinct she was born with is fully intact inside of you."

Tildie's whole body seemed to relax. She leaned her head back against the headrest. "I have to go home and thank Pookie for sticking his nose into my business. He brought you back when I needed you the most."

"He doesn't know I'm here, and you can't tell him now. At least not at home. It would be better, I think, if neither he nor your father knew I was home. It would be too easy to slip and talk."

"Oh. Yes, of course. I won't say anything. Grandma?"

"What?"

Tildie smiled sheepishly. "If I ever doubted you loved me, I never will again. You risked your life to come talk to me."

"Well, I don't know if it's all that dangerous, but I do want to take precautions for a while longer."

"How long?"

"I promise, one way or another, I'll be back before this baby is born. You can depend on it. I will be here."

"Okay. I'd like to count on that."

"You can."

"Oh, I bet you don't know. You are kind of rich. Grandpa left everything to you."

"What? Are you sure? What about your dad?"

"Dad says he's barely touched what Great Grandpa and Grandma Wiser left him. He said it has like quadrupled since then. Probably more than a million. His retirement fund, he said. He's okay with you getting everything."

Maggie was stunned. "But how? But why?"

"It was the same will Grandpa made out before your divorce. He never changed it." Tildie frowned. "You don't look happy."

"I'm just overwhelmed. I never wanted Wiser money."

"Well, I think it's cool. Like he never stopped loving you."

"But your dad. He must feel..."

"Really, Dad's okay with it. And you can always leave it to him. Several decades from now."

"Your Dad discussed this with you?"

"Yes. We talk a lot. Dad is different now. He pays attention. He talks to Pookie. They're always working on a project together. Right now, he and Pookie are refinishing that antique cradle that's been stored in the carriage house. You remember that? It was in the attic of Grandmother Wiser's house."

"Yes! They used it for Grandpa when he was a newborn. I had forgotten about it."

"It was Dad's idea after I told him I was pregnant. He and I have...great dialogue. We talk about meaningful things. Things that are important to me."

"So that means you talk about the baby."

"Un huh. When I first told him, I was so nervous. I was ready for judgment, condemnation, for a very cold shoulder. But he just reached out and pulled me into a hug and said something like, 'It will be okay. I promise.'"

Maggie caught her breath. The idea of Joel stepping up and being there for his daughter was astounding. It was the best news she could imagine. Something relaxed in Maggie; an anxiety she had hardly been aware of melted like snow on a warm spring day. Joel had become a parent to his kids who had always needed him.

Maggie fingered the ends of her granddaughter's cropped hair. "I wish you hadn't cut your hair."

"I'm going to have a baby–and you're worrying about my *hair?*"

Maggie laughed. "Good point." She pulled Tildie close and kissed her forehead. This was as close as she had ever been to Tildie, and she wouldn't give it up for anything.

The corridors were silent, the offices–having emptied of faculty by two thirty on a Friday afternoon–were dark. The simple lock was easy to open. Jewel picked up his case, stepped inside, and quietly snapped the door shut. He glanced at his watch–5:15. He'd had to wait until the secretaries had left for the day, but he guessed Maggie Wiser and her granddaughter wouldn't return until at least after supper.

At the end of his morning lecture, after the half hour of student crush he had become used to, he excused himself long enough to confirm that Tildie hadn't attended her Constitutional Law class. He was dead sure then that he had seen Maggie Wiser in the car–must have been a rental, and she was still in hiding.

He chuckled now as he opened the case and removed and assembled his .300 Winchester Magnum. The idiot Henry Lee had been tripping back and forth to Florida and coming up empty. Then she drives up, right under Jewel's nose. He would bet money that Lee didn't know she was in town.

284

He would soon, though, when she turned up with a bullet through her head.

Jewel had felt all along his patience and planning would pay off. He snapped the silencer into place; with a gloved hand, he raised the window a few inches. He rolled a chair in front of the window and, spreading his legs wide, settled into it. The bitter cold blasted his face, sharpening his senses. He had a perfect view of the corner of the parking lot where Tildie Wiser's car, one of only two in the lot, sat facing the cement embankment, waiting for her return.

The other car was his rebuilt Nissan 300 ZX. He'd questioned the hassle of bringing it to Maine, but now it seemed inspired.

The Range Rover, the vehicle local folks knew was his, sat outside of his empty apartment–the apartment where the lights were on and the stereo was loaded with five CDs playing just loud enough to be discernible to his landlady, who lived downstairs.

Jewel's pulse quickened. A car slowed and headlights turned into the parking lot.

Chapter 15

The Volkswagen Jetta pulled in on the far side of Tildie's car. Jewel tensed. He didn't care which of the women left first, but, if they moved simultaneously, Tildie's car would become a shield.

Plumes of exhaust billowed from the rear of the Jetta. The women must be saying goodbye. He waited. Finally, through the night scope, he saw Tildie get out of the car, unlock her own with a remote, and get in.

He smiled, satisfied. "Well, well, we meet again," he whispered to the Wiser woman. "Come on, baby." His breath formed in front of him in the cold air. "Come on, your car is running. Back out, now." But Tildie's car moved first. Of course–the woman would wait to be sure her granddaughter's car started. He watched as Tildie backed around and moved toward the parking lot exit.

"Okay, baby, now it's your turn," he whispered as he trained the crosshairs of the scope on Maggie's head.

Maggie was more than satisfied with how the visit with Tildie turned out, but now she was feeling pressure to go–and quickly. Never quite leaving her mind was the fact that she had used her credit card. How many more hours did she have before the danger would become real?

As Tildie's car moved toward the street, Maggie put the car in reverse, swung around, yanked the lever into drive, and pressed on the accelerator. For half a second, her wheels spun on ice, then grabbed the pavement.

As the car lurched ahead, the driver's side window glass shattered, and pieces peppered her face. Terror rocketed through her body, and she jammed the accelerator to the floor.

Her heart pounded wildly as she shot across the open space, careened out of the parking lot, and tried to turn in the opposite direction from where Tildie had gone. But her car slid sideways and into a snowbank on the far side of the street. She pushed on the accelerator as she straightened the wheel.

She was stuck.

Don't panic, don't panic, don't panic, she thought, but she knew she was. She moved the steering wheel back and forth and tried not to push too hard on the gas.

She dropped the transmission into Reverse and rocked the car backward.

Then into Drive. She jammed her foot on the accelerator.

The car swerved out of the bank. But with the pedal pressed to the floor, the car fishtailed the length of the block.

Maggie's thoughts raced as she tried to gain control of the car. It's them. But how did they find me so fast? Wade was right. They want to kill me. They almost killed me.

They could still kill me.

The face of the man in the photograph in her handbag flashed through her mind. Her assassin was suddenly real–a living, breathing human being, intent on ending her life.

She glanced in the rearview mirror. Two blocks behind her, headlights swung out of the parking lot, and a fresh jolt of fear tightened her chest. He was going to chase her down.

She yanked the steering wheel to the right and turned down the next street. She fought to control the car as the rear end fishtailed on a patch of ice. The headlights of the car behind her were no longer in sight, so she turned left at the next intersection. The cold wind rushed through the open window, touching her face, stinging the cuts.

She had to get out of sight until she was sure she had lost the assassin. Think fast. Help yourself. She turned off the headlights to make her less visible.

The only people on the street she knew were the Wheelers. Their house was dark, but, more importantly, their garage was behind the house. She pumped the brakes rapidly. Afraid she was going to miss it, she yanked the wheel sharply. The back end of the car slid sideways as her car shot into the driveway. She let up on the accelerator and turned the wheel to gain control of the car.

Slowing, she pulled up the driveway and behind the house. She nosed up to the closed garage doors and rested her head on the steering wheel. Her heart banged in her chest.

The approaching headlights focused her attention back to the street. She felt trapped in the car, and she sorely wished she had followed Sandy's advice to bring the gun. Too late now. Should she get out and hide in the woods behind the house? Did the dome light come on when you opened the door? Stay put, she decided, unless the car turned into the driveway. She groped for the door handle, holding her breath. She watched as the car passed by the end of the driveway and continued slowly down the street.

When she turned in her seat to watch the progress of the car, she felt something as cold as ice on the back of her head and neck. She put her hand on her head. It came away wet. Startled, she looked at her hand.

Blood.

Once again, a vision of Sam slumped over in his car–his blood everywhere–flashed through her mind. She gritted her teeth to stifle a scream, but a strangled sound rattled deep in her throat and erupted through clenched teeth. She hit the steering wheel with her fist and then hit it again.

Her teeth began to chatter, and she wondered if she was going into shock. An ache had started at the back of her head. Apply pressure. I've got to apply pressure. She yanked several napkins out of the fast-food bag beside her and held the wad to the back of her head. She lowered her forehead to the steering wheel, her throat constricting. Don't fall apart. You have to help yourself.

She checked the napkin; the white surface was dark with her blood– too much blood. Flying glass wouldn't produce this much. She'd been hit by a bullet.

Fighting the urge to drive out of there and rush to the hospital, she pulled her gym bag from the rear seat, noticing, with a start, the passenger window was also missing. She opened the bag, pulled out a towel, pressed it to the spot on the back of her head, wincing with pain. She counted to fifteen and checked the towel. A bloody Rorschach print the size of a saucer had appeared. She felt faint.

She longed for the comfort of an emergency room where a nurse would clean the wound and a doctor would take stitches. But that would make her visible…vulnerable because he'd still be looking for her. She folded the towel, put a clean spot on the wound and counted to fifteen, again. The spot on the towel was smaller.

The danger appeared to be over for the moment, but he was still out there, driving around trying to spot her. She was freezing and couldn't drive the car for long with the windows missing. Then, the solution came to her. She had to follow her original plan–only had to drive a dozen blocks.

With her headlights off and the heater blasting on high, she backed around in the driveway and cautiously pulled out onto the street.

* * *

Parked in a driveway at the end of the block, Jewel saw the taillights glow when she put the car in reverse. He waited until she was two blocks away before he pulled out. He gradually dropped farther back to allay suspicion.

She drove into the business district where traffic was heavier, making it easier to tail her. He was puzzled. He had guessed she would head for the Wiser home, but she parked in front of a professional building. Jewel pulled into a parking place almost a block behind her. The woman, carrying a backpack and gym bag, walked rapidly toward the building. He could wait for her to return, but she might not come back out. She might be going for help or phoning for someone to come to her rescue.

He reached under the dashboard and pushed the button that opened the compartment he'd had built in for a handgun. He removed the .25-caliber Beretta and slipped it into his coat pocket. Without haste, he locked the car door and strolled down the block, not pausing to glance at the shattered windows of the Jetta. He continued on into the building.

The lobby was empty. The elevator doors were closed. He rapidly scanned the directory from top to bottom. Doctors' and lawyers' offices, the Red Cross, the Chamber of Commerce–all offices that would be closed at this time of night. At the bottom of the list, he read Parking Garage LL. Suddenly, the significance of the gym bag hit him, and he sprinted for the stairway.

Maggie had the key ready. She jerked the door open, and the Porsche's burglar alarm went off, sending a shock through her body. She threw her gym bag and backpack into the passenger seat and leaped behind the wheel, yanking the door closed. When she jammed the key into the ignition, the alarm stopped, leaving only a faint echo of a memory. She said a wordless prayer that the car would start.

At that moment, she heard the stairway door slam, and her heart jumped. The face of the man they'd sent to kill her sprung to mind. She turned the key. The engine roared to life, and she sent a mental thanks to Sam for maintaining the car.

The headlights illuminated the cement wall in front of her. She put the car in reverse, released the clutch, and the Porsche lurched backwards. She jammed the car into what she hoped was first gear and let out the clutch. Her tires screeched on the pavement as the car swerved from side to side. She tore through the garage and up the ramp toward the door.

She narrowly missed hitting a tall black man in a trench coat who was running toward her. Seconds later, she burst into the dark night.

The closest path to his car was out of the garage exit. Leaping over snowbanks, Jewel sprinted toward his car, unlocking it with his remote. He nodded as he slid behind the wheel. It wouldn't be hard to track her.

In half a minute, he glimpsed the red Porsche two blocks ahead. Pedestrians turned to watch as the sports car raced by them. The Wiser woman shifted down and turned right.

When he turned the corner, the Porsche was nowhere in sight. He accelerated, and the car leapt forward. He looked left and right as he crossed intersections. No sign of her. She would be headed south. All clues to her whereabouts pointed south.

The question was whether she would attempt to drive the Porsche to Florida or leave it and fly out of Portland. He had to catch her before she reached the Portland exit.

He headed for Interstate 95 with confidence. The Porsche wouldn't be a challenge. Her car equaled his for speed and power, but the Wiser woman was the type who wouldn't exceed the speed limit by more than five miles an hour–maybe ten if she were scared.

Which she was. As she'd careened by him in the parking garage, she looked wide-eyed with fear. Was it because she recognized him? No, he didn't look anything like the man who terminated Sam Wiser. It was because she'd been shot at and chased.

The entrance to the highway was just ahead. He pushed the gas pedal halfway down. The acceleration pinned him to the seat. Usually, he didn't think twice about abandoning a car after a job, but he hoped he wouldn't have to jettison this one.

He pulled onto the I-95 ramp, jammed the pedal to the floor, and careened onto the highway. Ahead was a string of red taillights in both lanes. Friday night R&R people headed for Portland. He flashed back to the traffic in Cambridge when she'd nearly lost him. Not this time, baby. He was too good a driver, and the traffic was moving fast. He slid between two cars in the passing lane. He'd weave through traffic until he caught up with her.

This woman's luck was running out tonight.

She slowed to fifty miles an hour as she turned onto the Congress Street exit ramp in Portland. Two sets of headlights followed her. That didn't necessarily mean anything, but it was impossible not to be paranoid. She sped up, saw a break, and slid into traffic. At the first opportunity, she turned off onto a side street. As she turned, the second car behind her put on the blinkers. Heart thudding, she shifted down, yanking the wheel to the side, and abruptly turned down a side street. And then another and another until she found herself in an unfamiliar residential area. No one followed.

She cruised around looking for a phone booth, wondering if she should have brought her cellular phone after all. Maybe the damage was already done. They knew she was here. She had to call Tildie. On the drive to Portland, it occurred to her that the abandoned rental car would be found by the police. It would look vandalized, and they might find blood. When they checked, they'd find it had been rented by her. A story in the newspapers: Blood found in car rented by missing woman. She had to prevent that. An investigation would mess everything up. But damn, where were the phone booths?

Okay, the woman was heading for the airport, Jewel thought. She'd bypassed the exit that led directly to it, but the exit she did take was still a short hop to the airport. Probably being cautious, checking for a tail. No use wasting time wandering these streets. The terminal was small and finding her there would be a piece of cake.

"Have you got the title?"

Maggie patted her backpack. "Right here."

The owner of Happy Harry's Used Cars looked at her speculatively and then back at the red Porsche. Under the floodlights the little car gleamed like new.

"Mint condition," Maggie said. This was the fourth car dealership she'd tried. The past hour had been a learning experience. Learning the hard way.

Harry nodded thoughtfully, and then looked back at her, calculating, trying to figure out what the story was. Or maybe how much he could take her for. She stared back, meeting his eyes. Sam used to say, when buying a car, "Show no fear." Maybe the same technique worked when you were selling one.

Harry himself had come out of the showroom when she'd driven in, waving aside a salesman. "Harry Rancourt. Happy Harry. We're happy if we can make you happy." He offered his hand. "What can I do for you?" The whole time he looked past her at the Porsche.

Maggie shook his hand and went straight for the pitch. "I want to sell the car tonight. My family needs me in Florida–kind of an emergency–and I know I'm going to need cash to help them out when I get there."

At her first stop tonight, she'd been stumped for an answer on why she was in such a hurry and why it had to be cash. Acting like she'd stolen the car, the man had waved her away and shook his head as he walked back inside. Maggie wondered if he was going to call the police.

"Cash, huh?" Continuing to stare at the car, he scratched his cheek.

"Yeah, afraid so. Normally a check would be okay, but I want to get on a plane tonight. It really is an emergency."

He looked back at her inquiringly, inviting the rest of the story.

"My son and daughter-in-law were in an automobile accident. Serious. I'm going to take care of the children." The story was too close to home; she felt terrible using something that was, in fact, her family's tragedy. Her eyes pricked with real tears, and she blinked.

Harry avoided looking at her and nodded sympathetically. He pulled the inside corner of his mouth into his teeth and chewed on his lip.

"It has low mileage. Only 1250." She'd learned this from dealer number two, who'd stared in disbelief at the odometer.

Harry's head snapped around; his eyebrows shot up. He looked at the car again. "Original? How so? It's ten years old."

She smiled, letting a twinkle come into her eyes. "It's been in storage."

"Oh, well," he shook his head, "then it might not be–"

"It's been run every week like clockwork." Again, she thanked Sam for his compulsive care of the car. "Just not far."

He looked at her with respect. "How much you thinking to get for it?"

"I know how much it's worth. I looked it up in the blue book." She had, before she left North Carolina. "But I'm willing to go lower because I need to sell tonight, and I need cash. If I didn't need cash, I'd have sold it half an hour ago." And this was true. The third dealer would have given her a check, and she'd regretfully driven out of the yard. But there was no way she wanted to stick around until the banks opened tomorrow. She thought she'd shaken the gunman back in Amesbury before she'd picked up the Porsche, but she wasn't taking any chances. In fact, she felt really exposed standing out here under the lights in the middle of the lot.

Hal nodded as if he believed her and scratched the back of his head.

"How much?"

"Seventeen thousand. Absolute mint condition."

He sucked in his breath, but Maggie couldn't tell if it was because the figure was more than he expected or less. Show no fear; she returned his glance steadily.

"Here," she extended the key to him. "Take it for a ride." She knew she was using his own sales tactic on him.

A sheepish grin cracked his face; you got me, his sidelong glance said. She held her breath and continued to hold out the key.

He kicked at a patch of snow, then slowly reached out, but once the key was in his hand, he headed purposefully toward the car.

"Tell, Frank, the guy with the red hanky in his pocket, I'll be right back. We got coffee inside. Make yourself comfortable."

She was happy to get out of the cold and even more grateful to be able to use a restroom–a problem that had been demanding an increasing amount of her attention over the last hour.

The restroom was spacious and clean, but the light over the mirror bleached out her face and made her look years older. Stray hair stuck out around her face from the black ski cap she'd pulled over her head to hide the wound. She tried to loosen the hat, but her hair pulled–stuck to the hat with dried blood. She patted the outside of the cap, which was dry and didn't seem crusty. Good. When she washed her hands, she realized there was dried blood around her fingernails. Oh, Lord. If Harry saw that, he'd think she'd killed someone to get the car. Come to think of it, maybe that was why dealer number one was in such a hurry to get rid of her.

She looked at the hot air hand dryer and realized there were no paper towels. There was nothing in her bag. Finally, with liquid hand soap, she dampened toilet paper, which immediately turned to mush. She scrubbed the best she could around her nails.

She dried her hands, then slumped against the wall, realizing her exhaustion wasn't only from lack of sleep but also from the strain and tension of the last few hours. She thought about her satisfying visit with Tildie today, but it seemed as though it had happened days ago. And tonight, there was still a killer out there trying to find her. Well, she couldn't hide in here all night, though at this moment, doing so seemed enormously appealing–she could rest on the tile floor with Sandy's purple ski jacket under her head.

Even while her body longed to follow through, she pushed herself away from the wall. She had to see if Harry wanted to buy the car. In her backpack she found a lipstick, which contrasted garishly with her pale skin in the fluorescent light, but at least it made her look a little more alive. As she tucked in the stray hair, she steeled herself not to act disappointed when Harry gave her whatever excuse he might offer for not buying the car.

If he didn't, what would she do? Could she find someplace to park for the night where she wouldn't be noticed and sleep in the car? She gathered her strength, stood straighter, and headed out the door.

Harry wasn't around, and she didn't see her car outside. From across the showroom floor, one of the salesmen gestured with his cup of coffee as an offering. If she had coffee now, she wouldn't sleep no matter what happened. Was that good or bad? She decided she needed a lift right now and nodded.

He poured her a cup, put in cream and sugar at her request, and handed it to her. "Nice car," he said.

The warmth on her hands and the fragrant coffee nearly undid her. She longed to be sitting in Hal's diner, inhaling the coffee and waiting for her breakfast. But now she'd settle for a safe haven for even a few hours. Could she risk a motel? She had enough cash left, but would she be trapping herself?

Somewhere she still had to find a phone, call Tildie, ask her to retrieve the rental car, and return it. It didn't matter if the phone was tapped. NADCO obviously already knew she had been in Amesbury. Tildie could make up a story of why the windows were shattered–vandals, maybe.

Before she'd been shot at, her plan was to return the rental car at the Amesbury Airport and take a taxi to Sam's office building to pick up the Porsche.

Then it was no longer an option. On the way down here, she'd considered pulling off the highway to find a phone, but fear kept her foot pressed hard to the accelerator. Before she reached Portland, rational thought clicked in. She had hours, maybe all night, before anyone noticed the car. Now she looked longingly at the phone on Harry's desk. She could reverse the charges.

As she reached for the phone, her car zipped up to the door, and Harry climbed out. She'd make the call later. He motioned to her to join him outside. She tried not to read too much into the fact he was smiling.

He said, "You know, my old man was always telling us boys about the Thunderbird he could of had. Would a been a real sweet deal, but he passed on it. Had a two-year-old and another baby on the way. Thought maybe he'd better get the station wagon. Kept that wagon for twelve years. By then he had four kids. He told me the story again last year just a week 'fore he died. I wanted to go buy one for him, but he had emphysema. Wasn't ever going to drive again. You always hear guys tell you about the deal that got away. Would you go fourteen five? Wife'll kill me, but I don't want to be telling my kids about the Porsche I let get away."

He was lit up like a kid who's just gotten his first bicycle. He wasn't going to resell the Porsche. She felt better about letting the car go. Harry would lavish loving attention on it. Sam would approve. "Deal." She held out her hand, and they shook.

"Let's go into my office and do the paperwork. Don't mention the price to the guys. It's my business how much I pay. Reason I took so long was because I had to go raid my home safe for the cash." He tapped his breast pocket.

When they were done, he asked if he could drive her to the airport. She declined, asking if he could call a taxi. While they waited, they talked about this family in the photo on his desk. He was very proud of his daughter, a gymnast, and his artist son.

Harry walked her out to the taxi. Before she got in, he held her back for a moment. "I feel bad, in a way. I would have gone sixteen thou if you'd insisted."

"Ah, don't feel bad." She climbed into the cab. "I'd have settled for thirteen."

She smiled at his startled face as the cab pulled away.

"Where to?" the cabbie asked.

"Greyhound Bus Terminal."

Once again Maggie stood at Sandy's door. I came to return your coat. Thanks. It really helped."

Sandy opened the door wider. "Come in, sit down. I want to hear all about it."

She told him about the trip, trying just to hit the high spots, but he asked questions, wanting the details, reacting to her story with sympathy, humor, and alarm. She told the selling of the Porsche as a funny story, and he chuckled. But she thought she detected admiration in his gaze.

"And so..." she stood up and pulled a small roll of bills from her jeans pocket. "Here's what I owe you. Monetarily," she added. "I'll never be able to repay you for everything else."

He put up his hand. "Not necessary," he said with some force. "I can't take the money. Don't want to. Can't make me."

She looked at him for a moment, feeling tenderness for this man who was so good in so many ways.

She smiled at him. "Yeah. Absolutely, it is necessary. I've paid Aunt Belle back. Now you. Next week I'll pay the Maxwells back. Please understand it's for my mental well-being. I've been completely dependent on all of you for over four months. My self-image is strained to the breaking point."

"And I seem to remember your self-sufficiency is just a tad important to you." He smiled affectionately. "Okay, if you insist."

He looked at the wad of hundreds and twenties she handed him. "Have you been keeping track?"

"I'm an accountant. Occupational hazard, I guess." She paused, thinking it was time to wind up this visit. "Well...oh, by the way, I've rented my own apartment. I need to put some space between me and Aunt Belle for her safety. It'll be hard for both of us. We've really bonded."

He looked surprised. "Where are you moving to?"

She paused. "Morehead City. Can't remember the name of the street."

"Morehead City," he mused. "Not down the street. Not in town. You're not going to forgive me, are you?"

"Sandy, this is not a reaction to our splitting up, and I'm not trying to punish you. We both have life situations that preclude our having a relationship."

He looked troubled. "Are you really ready to walk away?"

"I don't see any other way. I want to go home. That's where my life is. Where everything I love is."

He looked at the floor and nodded.

"And if you were to uproot and bring your plane and boat to Maine, it would suffocate us both. You'd hate it. We wouldn't survive the move. Better to end it now." She smiled at him. "Just think of our time together as a shooting star–a brilliant flash, and then...phit! It's gone. But not forgotten."

"When are you going back?"

"Wade wants to wait until he and Jessie would normally return so they won't arouse any attention. They'll smuggle me in. I'll have to be in hiding for a while. Something we had hoped wouldn't be necessary. But since this last thing..."

She wasn't able to stop herself from gingerly touching the scalp wound at the back of her head. "Last week of March."

He looked like he was going to say something else, so she stepped closer and kissed his cheek. "Our romance of the century will be the memories that keep me warm in my rocking chair when I'm ninety."

She looked at his distressed face. "Well, okay, they'll keep me warm next week, too." They kissed with a peck on the lips. "Stay well."

"Good luck. And please have someone keep me posted on how things all turn out. Please promise me that. If you owe me anything, it's that."

"I promise." She had almost weakened and told him her address in Morehead City. She was aware of the dull ache in her heart as she walked away.

Jewel valued self-reflection, self-assessment. He learned about the concept in college and had taken time to practice it regularly. It ensured, he'd come to realize, that he didn't go through life without thinking, evaluating, improving. It had been very helpful to him many times in the past years. People usually go through life without pausing to think, to analyze. They don't ask themselves what is working and not working. The unfortunate result is that they get stuck.

He had been so busy since the end of the summer, he'd let the practice fall aside. He picked up his Winchester and removed the bolt so he could clean the rifle. He'd just used it, to no avail, he mused, two days ago. But a clean rifle was a more accurate rifle. It was a routine task, but an essential one. And it gave him time to think.

Often, in these moments, he reflected on his successes, examining them from all sides to see if there was something he could have done better. But it was now time to reflect on his failures. Temporary failures.

Somewhere, months ago, he had strayed from his usual path. "This is just a job. Do not get involved," was a mantra he had always used, and it worked for him. Then, with this job, he departed from that and allowed his ego to take a detour, causing him to do things he'd never done before.

Back to the tried and true. He slid a bore guide into the rifle, soaked a couple of patches in cleaning solvent, affixed one to the cleaning rod, and ran it through the barrel. Then he did it again with the second patch. Once he'd let the solvent sit for a couple of minutes, he switched to a copper brush soaked in solvent. He ran the brush through the barrel ten times–five down and five back. While he had a great capacity to be imaginative, he also needed routines and procedures to ground him.

He soaked a few more patches in cleaning solvent and pondered the past. He had always enjoyed bringing creativity and fast thinking into his work. Had it made him more successful? Maybe. Maybe not. But it definitely brought him more job satisfaction.

He affixed a soaked pad onto the cleaning rod and ran it down the barrel. But had he now mired himself? Become less able to make good judgements? He thought, probably so. Looking back, what would he have done differently? One thing for sure: if the woman had waited one more day before doing her disappearing act, he would have taken her out and been done with it. Collect his money and go home.

She should be dead now. He'd had his sights on her temple. Had he hesitated a split second, allowing her car's tires to find purchase on bare tar? He wouldn't have thought so. But he had missed by a fraction of a second.

He ran two more soaked patches down the barrel, then a couple of dry ones. Finally, he ran an oil coated patch down the barrel, then another dry patch.

Done. He reached for the bolt to reinsert it.

"Ah, crap," he muttered. He hadn't cleaned the magazine or the bolt.

He grabbed a small brush and the cleaning solvent. This is what happens when you rush things. You do them half-assed.

He needed to increase his focus, he decided. He'd invested over four months in this job with little to show for it, but he'd been close. So very close. He had never left a job undone. He wouldn't now. Confidence replaced self-doubt. When the moment came, the job would be all the more satisfying.

Maggie looked out of the window. No MG, yet. She hadn't seen Sandy since they parted five weeks ago. She had reservations about this visit, particularly since it was Valentine's Day, which she hadn't realized when she agreed to see him. Still, she found herself in front of the window, looking for his car.

She had found this gem of a place near Bogue Sound in Morehead City. The second-floor efficiency in a century-old building had a rear fire escape as well as a front entrance. She could see out of the windows on all four sides, which gave her a secure feeling.

But she still had double locks on both doors.

At first, she'd carried the gun in her handbag everywhere, but then she realized how ridiculous that was. What was she going to do, have a shootout in a department store? Instead, the loaded gun rested in the end table drawer, and she mostly forgot it was there.

She had used her mother's maiden name when renting the apartment, so she was now Margaret Miller. She'd asked the landlady to increase the rent to include electricity so she could avoid showing identification to set up service. She didn't have a landline phone for the same reason, but she didn't really need one, anyway. She had her cellular phone, though she seldom used it. She only talked to Aunt Belle and the Maxwells.

And now, Sandy.

She'd had fun shopping for a few pieces of used furniture–a couch that opened into a bed, a chair, a bookcase, and an end table for the television that Belle lent her. The kitchen table was built in–a little thing that folded down against the wall in the compact kitchen. Two chrome chairs came with the apartment.

The living room had a bay window that overlooked the driveway. She often sat reading with her feet on the window seat, watching the street each time she turned the pages of a book. Not good at recognizing makes of cars, she kept notes. Red car with dent, heading south, 11:00 a.m. Shortly, she had a working list of the cars that frequented the quiet residential neighborhood. In daybreak walks, she pinned down where the cars belonged. When a new one showed up traveling west, she watched to see if it returned going east. And would it appear again the next day? She was soon reassured no one was looking for her here, but she continued the surveillance because it made her feel more in control. More engaged. Taking nothing for granted.

Belle had rented a post office box, and the Maxwells had been forwarding Maggie's mail there. Belle checked it once a week and brought her the letters from the family when the two of them had lunch together. Maggie always sat facing the restaurant door, per Wade's instructions, while she read some of the letters aloud to Aunt Belle.

They all wrote now. Using Pookie's address schedule that Wade had created, Tildie slipped hers and Joel's into the stack of outgoing mail at the college. Tildie's letters reflected introspection and insight regarding her pregnancy–everything from the reaction of acquaintances who hadn't seen her in a while, to her father's unwavering support, to her thoughts on the parenting books she read voraciously, to her emotions when she felt her unborn child move. She was healing psychologically, which had a positive effect on her relationship with Pookie.

Pookie's letters contained frequent but oh-so-casual references to a girl named Ellen. She was probably the girl Pookie was interested in when he talked to Sam. Maggie was changing her view of Pookie. He was a young man, not a kid. His letters were punctuated with ambitions that could take him to the other side of the earth. It tore at her that he might not always live in Amesbury, but she saw that Maine was not big enough for him to explore his dreams. The world probably was.

Ever since he was a toddler, he'd brought her treasures to examine: a pink rock, a fallen robin's egg, a favorite basketball card–and eventually his thoughts regarding everything his active mind explored. That's what she would miss–the intense sharing of his life experiences. But when the time came, she'd have to smile and wave goodbye, watch a plane taxi away with its precious cargo, and be happy for him.

Joel wrote mostly about household decisions. He'd changed heating fuel companies, he'd bought a new refrigerator after listing the pros and cons of various types, finally selecting a side by side with an ice cube maker. Maggie smiled thinking that the old Joel could not have been dragged into a discussion on the purchase of a toaster. In each letter he mentioned the kids: shopping for baby furniture with Tildie, helping Pookie with an advanced algebra course. A photo taken by Tildie fell out of one envelope–Pookie and Joel hunched over the old orange motorcycle, Joel with streaks of grease on his face, and Pookie grinning from ear to ear.

Day by day, as she turned this information over, she began to think of this period as a shimmering magical time for her family–a healing time made possible only by her absence.

Though she missed them, she was no longer frantic to get home. A little more time while they learned to become a family wouldn't hurt. The burden of trying to create a family from merely a household was slipping from her shoulders.

Sam was occasionally in her thoughts for brief moments, but she veered away from dealing with anything substantive–there was only so much she could handle.

Then there was Sandy, who had apparently wrangled her address from Belle, to think about. He'd stayed away, but the postman delivered a humorous card to Maggie every day since she had moved in. Finally, she'd agreed to see him. She glanced out of the window as his car turned into her driveway.

He stood in the doorway, looking anxious, holding a bouquet of pink roses and baby's breath in one hand–flowers?–and a white box with red lettering in the other.

She looked at the box.

"Lobstah," he said in an attempt at a Downeast accent. "Maine lobstah. I had them flown in this afternoon."

She looked from the box to the flowers to his face. "You're kidding."

"What, too much?"

She nodded. "Way."

"Okay, give me another chance. Close the door."

He backed into the hall, and she closed the door. In twenty seconds, he knocked again.

When she opened the door, he presented a bunch of green stems–the flower heads were gone. On his face was a goofy, clenched-tooth grin that said, is this okay?

"Much better," she chuckled. "Let me get these into a vase so they'll stay fresh."

She turned away from the door and then back. She looked over his shoulder. "Where're the lobster?"

"In the hall. If we don't eat them, I'll take them home and make them pets."

"We can eat them if you let me pay for them."

He opened his mouth to object, and she cut him off. "You paid for the shipping, which was probably more than the lobster. I'll pay for the lobster."

"Is that your final answer?"

"Yeah. Not negotiable. I still have an insatiable need to be self-sufficient and independent."

"Still?" He brought the box in and put it on the kitchen counter.

She nodded and dug into the cupboard beside the stove. "Here, this is the largest pot I have. I guess we'll have to do one at a time."

"Aren't you ever going to get over this self-sufficiency kick?" he teased. "Most women would have the decency to accommodate and become at least mildly dependent on their erstwhile knight in shining armor."

"Mmm. You need to broaden your expectations of women."

"Just kidding. I'm tense."

"Yeah, me too. Listen, I don't have any butter, but I can borrow some from the landlady. I'll do that while you cook the lobster."

"You sure that won't erode your independence? Me cooking the lobster?" He grinned, but he rubbed his hands together nervously.

She felt a little sheepish. "I have this thing about killing lobster in boiling water. At home I go outside while Joel does the dirty deed. If we're going to have lobster, I think the task of executioner falls to you." She opened the door. "I'm better at butter."

"I have a humane way of cooking lobster, if that makes you feel better," he said. "At least I think it's humane. Haven't actually seen any studies on it. Haven't interviewed any lobsters, for that matter. Makes for damn tender lobster, though."

She paused in the doorway. "Okay. What's the method?"

"I put them in lukewarm water. They're lulled into a false sense of security, thinking they're taking a bath. Then I slowly increase the heat until I warm them to death."

"Okay, I guess that's better. It makes me feel better, anyway. Nevertheless, I'll be in the hallway while you take care of it."

"I bet you don't like killing spiders, either."

"I don't kill spiders. It's catch and release, baby."

When they finished feasting on the lobster, he picked up their plates, took them to the sink, and dumped the cooking water down the drain. The empty lobster shells went into the box the live lobster had arrived in.

His back was toward her. "Have I played my cards right enough so that we can talk?"

She could tell by his voice and the way he moved he was still tense. So was she. They'd made a lot of small talk, but the unsaid things hung there like a fog ready to descend.

"Okay." Her voice was unsteady. She didn't want a scene, didn't want to rehash things.

He turned, leaning against the counter and folded his arms across his chest. "I guess I'd like to start with an apology."

"Nothing to apologize for."

"Yeah, well. There is. When I found I couldn't think of anything but you, I got scared. I was afraid you didn't feel the same. In fact, I was sure of it. I didn't want to hurt again. The pain of losing my wife was almost unbearable. It's much less now, but it's still there. I guess I thought if I took the reins, ended it, it wouldn't hurt. So much. Or at all."

He studied his shoes.

"And...?"

"It was the lame-brainiest thing I ever did. It's been hurting like crazy."

They were silent a moment before she spoke. "I did hold a piece of me apart...kept some distance because I always knew I would return to my life and you to yours–a sad parting but an inevitable one."

"I wasn't as cautious as you. I, ah..." He exhaled raggedly. "I didn't have the foresight to hold back as much as you did."

She tried for a lighter tone. "I've been very happy with my single life. But I like you immensely. In fact, everything about your personality feels like a perfect fit."

He nodded, head still down, and cleared his throat. "Hand in a glove."

"I don't have any answers," she said. "Except to say your wife will always be in your heart."

He looked at her now. "Why do you say that?"

"Because I'm pretty sure we always carry with us those we love, even when separated, whether by death or circumstances. Until we die, I guess."

"You're thinking of Sam."

She nodded.

He looked at her, and she could see anguish glittering in his eyes. Simultaneously, they reached out, clasped hands. Maggie was engulfed in an emotional tidal wave as she stood, and they came together in a crushing embrace.

"Can I stay for a while?" He kissed her forehead. "I think I'd rather lose you later than sooner."

"Can we handle it?"

"We'll find out."

His vulnerability caused some seemingly immovable part of her emotions to crack and shift, and she melted against him. What she wanted at that moment was to be part of Sandy.

"The couch is five steps away," she said.

Half an hour later, she said, "This couch actually pulls out into a bed, you know."

"You're going to let me stay?"

"Posilutely. Absotively."

"Then I guess it's worth opening up the bed."

"Definitely."

Her head was on his shoulder. They didn't move from their embrace. He stroked her hair. "Do you like me better than endive?"

"Much better than endive."

"Do you like me better than avocados?"

"Definitely better than avocados." She smiled up at him. "Give me a difficult one."

"Okay, do you like me better than peanut butter?"

"Hmm. That's a hard one. Plain or crunchy?"

He laughed and patted her hip. "Maggie, I don't know where we're going."

"We only need to know where we've been and where we are. No one in the world knows where they're going. Can we just live each moment as it comes?"

"Okay," he said. "Let's pull out this bed and do some living."

Chapter 16

Lincoln stared in shock at the handwritten names on the page in front of him. Revelation came a second later. Holy shit. How had they missed this detail last fall? This detail that was now mushrooming with implications.

Yesterday, February 28, he had lunch with Roy in Portland. Roy had two items on the agenda.

The project was behind schedule because of a cold snap in January–10 to 30 below for ten consecutive days–and three blizzards in February. Delays were costly. As if Lincoln could do anything about that.

Secondly, and most importantly, they hadn't found the goddamn woman yet. Which, given Roy's edgy behavior, was the primary reason for his visit. If Lincoln couldn't get the job done, Roy said, he had contacts with whom he could solve the problem himself.

In his office later that afternoon, Lincoln had gone back to the beginning. He listened to the tapes of the Wiser household, particularly the day she disappeared. Twice in two days the Wiser woman phoned a woman named Jessie to say she'd be over. The second time was the last time her voice was recorded on the tape.

He stared now at the photocopies of the guest book that had been signed on the day of the funeral. Jessie and Wade Maxwell.

From a drawer he pulled out the Residential Register, running his finger down the page until he found Maxwell, Wade and Jessie, 6241 Orchard Hill Road. Orchard Hill was south of the business district–the same section of town as Maple Street.

He opened a city map, scanned the page. Thinking he already knew the answer did not prevent him from experiencing a bolt of satisfaction when he saw the proximity of the streets. The Maxwells' property must border the Wiser property. According to Mancuso's report, she left in her car to visit them. But that August night she would have walked to their house. And she didn't actually arrive there by car. She drove several blocks and then turned around and came back–it had been some kind of ruse.

He phoned the Maxwell's number with a realtor's "Can I list your house?" routine ready, but the number had been temporarily disconnected. No surprise.

He thought a minute then phoned the newspaper office and asked for the circulation department. "This is Ralph Maxwell. I'm calling for my brother Wade. He wants to know when his subscription is due to start again."

"Wade Maxwell? What's the address?"

"His home address is 6241 Orchard Hill Road, but he's on vacation."

"Just a second."

A minute later the woman was back on the line.

"Mr. Maxwell, you say?" She sounded suspicious. "You're his brother?"

"Yes."

"Why isn't he calling?"

Lincoln took a chance. "He didn't want to make another toll call. I was just talking to him last night, and he asked me to call."

"Well, that's strange. Because his subscription didn't end. We've been mailing the paper to him in Florida."

Of course. Henry Lee had been following the postcard trail in Florida.

"That's why he asked. He hasn't been getting it. What do you have for an address?"

She told him.

"That sounds right. I'm calling him tonight. I'll check the address. Thanks for your help."

"Okay. Call me if we need to change the address. And we'll have to make an adjustment. We've been charging his credit card."

"Sure thing. Oh, before you go, what do you have as a date when you started sending it to Florida?"

She hesitated.

"Just in case he asks me. Save another phone call."

"August twenty-sixth."

"And do you have an end date when it's supposed to be delivered in Amesbury?"

There was a short silence. "Let me check the next screen." She sounded annoyed.

A second later she said, "I'm sorry, that's all the information I can give you." She hung up abruptly.

A week after the Wiser woman disappeared, the Maxwells were getting the local newspaper in Florida. Now that he had all the pieces, it was so painfully obvious that they had left Maine together.

Finally, he had a specific address to send Lee to. He pushed the intercom button on his telephone. "Kathy, bring in the Florida atlas. I'm going to have you make plane reservations for Florida. Need to figure out which airport."

His bet was that in the next few days he'd be reporting satisfying success to Roy. He wanted to be rid of this albatross more than he'd ever wanted anything. He reached for the telephone and dialed Mancuso's cell phone number. Lee was in town, and Mancuso would find him.

Ben Stonefield opened the passenger door, threw his racket and gym bag into the back seat, and slid into Jewel's Ranger Rover. "Sorry I'm late, Jules. A client took longer than I thought he would." He pulled the door shut. "We'll still make it in time."

"Sure we will. No problem. Boy, you guys don't hardly get a break this time of year, do you? We haven't played racquetball since just before Christmas." Jewel pulled away from the curb and headed in the direction of the health club.

"It's crazy from January first until the end of May–could be longer this year."

"May?"

"Yeah, after April fifteenth we do the ones we filed extensions for–which, with Maggie gone, will be more than usual this year. What time is our game?"

Jewel glanced at his watch. "Six o'clock. Still got half an hour. Think she'll ever be back?"

Ben's eyebrows lowered in a frown, and he heaved a sigh. "I figured if she was coming back, she'd have been here to jump in with both feet at tax time. I was hoping she'd stroll in the door on January one, but here it is almost the middle of February." He paused. "I wish she were here. Like this afternoon. This guy comes in for his three-thirty and brings me a box of receipts. Wants his taxes done. He's Maggie's client, and I don't know him from Adam. Seems his wife, who handled the books for his business, died six months ago, and he couldn't afford to hire a bookkeeper, so he's just been throwing the receipts in a box and paying bills without matching up check numbers with invoices. What a mess."

Ben shook his head. "If Maggie'd been here, she would have called the guy after his wife died and got him set up with a simple system and held his hand through the process, and by tax time he'd have been all set. She babies her clients. Me? I don't have the patience. Or the time. I shouldn't even be playing racquetball tonight."

"Angie can't take up the slack? Or isn't she working out?"

"Oh, yeah, she's right on top of everything. In fact, we split up Maggie's clients, with Angie taking seventy-five percent of them, but there are some things Maggie could do as a CPA that Angie can't. Yet."

"And you still haven't heard from her? Maggie?"

Silence. Jewel felt the tension. Holding his breath, he waited patiently for the thing heretofore left unsaid. Finally, keeping his face relaxed, he glanced at the old man and smiled expectantly.

A small grin played across Ben Stonefield's face as well. "Well, I guess there's no harm in saying so now. I told you about the letter she left for me when she first took off in August?"

Jewel nodded.

"Well, last month on a Saturday morning, four, maybe five weeks ago now, I come into my office, I open my box of chocolate cookies, and there on top is a handwritten note from Maggie." Ben's smile broadened.

Jewel adjusted his rearview mirror, glanced over his shoulder, and appeared absorbed with driving. A memory of the Wiser woman almost running him over in the parking garage a little over four weeks ago flashed through his mind. Finally, casually, almost absentmindedly, he asked, "What did she say?"

"Said something like, 'Hurray on the choice for my replacement. You always were a good judge of talent.' She had drawn one of those smiley faces. Then it said, 'I'm okay but can't come back yet. I'm sure you're doing fine without me, though, but I miss you and Angie.' She also asked me to do her income tax." Ben chuckled. "Then she added, 'Happy tax time. Give my regards to the IRS.'"

"Hmm. What do you make of it all?" Jewel reduced his speed slightly to delay arriving at the health club.

"Don't know. Puzzle to me. Her departure came on the heels of Sam's death, but I can't imagine they were close enough at that point that his dying would have thrown her for that much of a loop." Ben paused, looking thoughtful. "Something funny's going on. She added a P. S. 'Don't tell anyone I was in Maine. Very important.' The very important was underlined twice. Don't imagine it matters much if I tell you. You don't even know her."

"Sounds like she's not in Maine, at any rate." Jewel turned to look at a construction site as they drove by.

"Yeah, that's my impression."

Another long silence. Jewel forced himself not to break it.

"Actually, my guess is she left with some friends of hers."

Jewel felt a charge of adrenalin raise his pulse. He turned into the parking lot and scanned for an empty space. Absently he asked, "Someone specific, or are you generalizing?"

Ben shook his head. "Not generalizing. I've long been suspicious that she left with the neighbors who live behind her. They were always close, and they left the same night she disappeared."

Jewel nodded. "Interesting." He got out and pulled his gym bag from the rear seat. "Well, Ben, let's go see if we can't skunk those guys." He didn't need to ask another question. He had missed something earlier.

And he knew what it was.

Sunlight glinted off the Airstream in the Orange Grove RV Park. Thirty yards away, Jewel sat in a rented pickup and watched the Maxwells get into their white truck, buckle up, and drive away. He never should have doubted himself; he'd been correct when he figured out she had traveled out of Maine with these people when he discovered her footprints in the path connecting their backyards. He hadn't turned up anything on previous visits, so the Maxwells, or more likely the Wiser woman, must be clever.

More than he'd given her credit for.

She had eluded him when she disappeared from sight that January night. In the following days he became curious. Whose car was it? Certainly not hers, or she would have known how to not engage the alarm. He used his hacking skills to break into the DMV's files in both Florida and Maine. To his surprise, he found the Porsche had been registered to her, but the title was in the process of being transferred to a new owner. He tracked down the guy–a used car dealer. When Jewel flashed PI identification, the dealer said he had bought the car from a woman for cash at about seventy-five percent of the value he would have expected to pay. She'd had the title with her. Was it stolen? the dealer wondered. Jewel told him not to worry. It wasn't. The woman's husband was just trying to locate her. Where had she gone? To the airport, the dealer had said, headed for Florida.

No, he was dead sure she had not gone to the airport. The Portland Jetport was small, and he had combed it thoroughly. She must have gone by bus. And probably not to Florida because she was too smart to tell her destination to the dealer.

How the hell would an ordinary, number-crunching grandmother know how to disappear from under his nose? Again. But she had $14,500 in cash with her this time. If she were frugal, she could stay underground for some time.

Four weeks ago, Jewel had followed with amusement the flurry of excitement generated by the Three Stooges–Lincoln, Lee, Mancuso–when the Bangor credit card charges came to light. He kept tabs on their investigation but wasn't surprised when it petered out. The woman was way too smart to use her credit card in the city where she was living. And now she had fourteen thousand reasons to not use it at all.

Then he'd gotten the clue from Stonefield yesterday and decided another trip to the RV park in Jacksonville was called for. This morning, Jewel was dressed in worn denim shorts and a grungy blue t-shirt that said Miami Ski Patrol. He'd been parked in an empty RV space watching the Airstream for two days now, waiting for the Maxwells to leave on one of their jaunts.

As soon as their loaded pickup rolled out of the park, he slowly pulled the truck into their parking space and got out. What he'd missed in his previous visits was the bag of trash left beside the driveway. They were methodical and careful, these people. When they left, they had always emptied their trash and put it outside for collection.

Now he picked up the trash bag and tossed it into the back of the pickup. Then, with a gloved hand, he lifted a toolbox from the back of the truck and produced a ring of keys from his pocket. He had found a spare key the last time he'd searched the trailer and made a copy of it.

He inserted the key in the lock, turned it, and was inside. As he had expected, there were no clues. Everything spic and span and orderly. As he had come to expect, they wouldn't have left behind any evidence regarding the woman.

Nothing more to be learned here; he had what he wanted. In his motel room, he spread a small tarp out on the floor and emptied the trash. In forty-five seconds, he found what he was looking for. Torn in miniscule pieces, tucked in a cereal box with discarded junk mail, damp eggshells, and coffee grounds were scraps of a phone bill.

Piecing the scraps together, he saw three outgoing calls to area code 252, exchange 725.

A call to the information operator and two questions filled in the rest of the blanks.

Ten minutes later, he checked out of the hotel.

And was on his way to Beaufort, North Carolina.

Friday morning, at the Orange Grove RV Park office, Henry Lee climbed out of his air-conditioned rental car and got hit in the face with the heat and humidity he'd come to expect from trips to Florida. He showed his identification and asked the on-duty clerk about the Maxwells. Yes, they had a trailer here. They weren't around much. Took a lot of day trips. Or week-long trips. He showed the picture he had of Maggie, but the check-in worker said she'd never seen her. Another dead end? Of course. Lee wiped the sweat from his forehead.

"Oh, there they go now," the young woman said, and Lee watched as a white Dodge pickup slowly rolled by the office. The man at the wheel waved his hand to the check-in worker and pulled out of the park. Lee was back in his car and on their tail in a minute. He wondered if the Wiser woman was in the trailer. Shit! That's what he needed to do. Go back to the trailer and check. But then he'd lose the Maxwells. The RV was small; they probably had her stashed somewhere else nearby and could lead him to her. Besides, it was cooler in the car than it would be searching the Airstream.

He followed them to a festival, where they wandered around eating ethnic food, checking out crafts. In this heat! The woman looked a little familiar, but who could tell. All these aging white-haired people looked the same to him. His best bet was to stay with this couple for a few days. Montgomery would be pissed if this trip turned out to be, like all the others, nothing, and according to him, these guys knew where she was. He mopped his face and unbuttoned another shirt button. He'd rather be in Maine.

Friday morning, Jewel pumped his own gas at a convenience store in North Carolina, gently squeezing the handle to roll the numbers to an even $15. He paid in cash and took off south on Route 70 with rising expectations. The sun was out, the weather was warm, and the day was full of promise. After multiple, fruitless trips over the past six months, on March third, a date he'd never forget, he finally had her cornered–not in Florida, but in good old North Carolina.

He glanced at his watch, estimating another forty minutes to Beaufort, where he would do some exploring. Once he got the lay of the land and spotted her, he'd check out her routine and make a plan. Planning a job was where he could be creative, have fun. Executing the plan, on the other hand, was where he had to think on his feet, be ready to make changes, make innovations on the fly. Always the highest point in any job. Well, maybe except for the actual execution. He laughed. Without a doubt now, this would come together.

When Jewel rolled into Beaufort, though, he was annoyed. Beaufort was a small town. One where people would know each other. One where a new face would be noticed. Blend, he could not. He drove around, orienting himself, creating a map in his head while looking for a place to eat. He picked a hotel restaurant knowing there would be more out-of-towners breaking their fast than locals. Here he could blend. Maybe here he would get a room as a base of operation for…however long it took.

The next couple of days, dressed in Bermuda shorts, a Panthers t-shirt, and ball cap, he carried around a plastic bag full of souvenirs and scanned the tourists and the locals, looking for the woman. One day he carried a plush, stuffed shark under his arm, a present for a child back home. Another day, an alligator. No one gave him any particular notice as he slowly shopped and walked, always scanning from under the brim of his cap.

On the third day, there she was, walking toward him. Sandwiched between her and a man was an old woman who linked her arms through theirs for support. They were laughing. He saw her a split second before she looked at him. Their eyes met, as happens between strangers, and he nodded and smiled in acknowledgement, as strangers do. She returned his smile and then continued a conversation with her companions as if nothing had happened. He stopped to look at a display in the next shop and kept track of the trio in his peripheral vision. They entered a cafe. He was back at this rental car in a minute. Now that he had his quarry in his sights, guaranteed he would not lose her again.

Maggie settled, as usual, into the chair facing the door of the coffee shop. She, Sandy, and Belle were going to grab a bite while they planned their day together tomorrow. She thought about the man she'd just seen. Why did he stick in her mind? There was something familiar about him. Maybe he was a vacationing sports figure, minor movie personality, or local politician whose picture she had seen on a poster? All three unlikely in this small city. She was used to seeing random tourists on the streets of Beaufort, along the harbor. But in March? Not so much.

"That's a splendid idea, Sandy," Belle was saying, and Maggie realized she had missed part of the conversation.

Belle continued, "I haven't been to the Farmers' Market since, well, last fall. They'll be open until one. And then, you know what else I'd like to do tomorrow, if y'all have the time? Take a drive around Bogue Sound."

"Perfect," Sandy said. "I rented the Nissan for the whole weekend."

"I like it," Maggie said. "Atlantic Beach and Emerald Isle...yeah, I like it. Let's do it."

Later that day, Maggie plugged in the Christmas tree lights and the table-top tree came to life. She and Sandy were having Christmas in March to make up for the one they had missed. He'd said he had a small gift for her.

He looked excited but uncertain as she removed the huge bow.

"I thought you said small. This is bigger than a bread box."

"But smaller than an elephant. Go ahead, open it."

She laughed in delight as she pulled the paper away. Luggage–smaller than a full-sized suitcase but larger than the battered weekend bag back in her closet in Amesbury.

"Don't read any expectations into this," he said. "I mean, it's not a message...I'm not, uh, saying you should travel between Amesbury and Beaufort once you get home. I mean I just thought..." he trailed off. "Do you like it?"

"Beats the heck out of a gym bag. I love the color and look at all the pockets! This will be the first piece of luggage I ever owned that will trail behind me." She pulled out the handle and tested the wheels.

"Really?"

"Yeah, I've lusted after one of these since the first time I ever saw one." She walked across the room pulling the bag behind her. "I feel so flight-attendant-ish."

He laughed. "It becomes you. So you're not mad?"

"Of course not. Now I have something for you."

"You weren't supposed to buy me anything."

"I didn't. I've had this since before Christmas. Just didn't find the right time to give it to you." She handed him a gift the size of a magazine and watched him open it.

"Oh, no." He laughed as he flipped through the calendar. On each month there was a different photo she had taken of him during their times together. The last one was of him, upside down in the sail locker, with only his bottom half showing.

"Don't read any expectations into this," she said. "I mean, it's not a message or anything. It's just for posterity."

He laughed and pulled her into an embrace. "Don't start."

"Okay," she said, rubbing her cheek against his neck.

"On second thought," he said, "you can start. How about this? Let's go back to my place. You could spend the night, and we don't have to shock your landlady. She looked disapproving the last time I left in the morning."

"I thought you'd never ask. Let me throw a few things in this suitcase I just happen to have lying around, and it's a done deal."

Jewel had been driving around Beaufort since dawn, but he hadn't found what he was looking for. Now he proceeded slowly around the tidy Morehead City neighborhood in his rented vehicle. Then he spotted what he needed on the next block.

He parked and headed back toward the Black neighborhood, developing a limp and rehearsing his southern drawl on the way. A block from his destination, he scooped up some dirt–rubbed it on his hands and into his faded jeans.

Two Black men were leaning against the hood of a black pickup truck, passing the time of day. Conversation stopped as they watched him approach.

He nodded to the men. "Mornin'."

The man Jewel took to be the owner of the pickup pushed himself away from the truck and folded his arms across his chest. "How y'all doing?"

Already they were suspicious. The color of his skin wasn't going to automatically bring him acceptance in this close-knit neighborhood.

Jewel limped closer. "Jus' fine. Yo' self?"

The man merely nodded.

Jewel walked up to him and held out his hand. "Name's MJ. Matthew Jordan. Friends call me MJ cause they think I look like Mike." He ran his hand over his bald pate and grinned.

Both men glanced at his head and chuckled. The owner extended his hand. "Al Stone. My brother Franklin." Jewel shook hands with both men.

"Nice truck you got there." The truck was about fifteen years old and showed its age, but it was immaculate. And it was registered.

"Ah'm from Piedmont." Jewel used the name of a small South Carolina town he'd picked from the map this morning. Small enough town these men might not have heard of it, but big enough that, on the chance they had, they wouldn't expect him to know Aunt Delia, who grows prize nasturtiums.

"I'm up here he'pin' my sister. She movin' to Mo'head. And ah, well, we's trying to load up everything on one of them little U-Haul trailers. I saw this fine truck here 'while back." Jewel stroked the fender, "And I thought now that would be just the ticket, you know? Havin' a truck to he'p her out."

Al stared at him. Franklin folded his arms, slipping his hands under his armpits. He shook his head, but he was smiling. Jewel could see Franklin was thinking, cold day in hell.

"See, I jus' need it for a day. Have it back by tomorrow. Be willing to pay. I jus cashed my check."

Al's posture softened a fraction.

"Ah, could go…" This was tricky. Had to be enough to cinch the deal but not enough to be suspicious. Jewel shifted his weight, dug at a tuft of grass with his toe, looking hesitant, uncertain. Finally, he nodded like he'd made up his mind.

"I could give you two hunnert dollar. I got the cash right here in my pocket."

Al's body language, a slight nod, a pull of his earlobe, told Jewel he was interested.

"I know it's not much fo' a fine truck like this, but it's all I can go. Okay, two hunnert and fifty. It sure would make life easier makin' one trip stead a driving' back and forth all weekend. Ah'd have it back to you tomorrow. Fust thing in the morning."

"Don't guess I need it 'til church tomorrow morning. Have to have it back by nine."

Jewel counted out a stack of wrinkled twenties, and gave them to Al. "Thank you, brother. Ah'll come to church and bow my head with you and thank the Lord for your kindness."

"Take good care of her. Get a scratch, I'll take it out of your hide." But Al grinned amicably. "Need it now?"

"Yes, sir. Be mighty he'pful."

"Key's in the ignition. 'Member. Nine o'clock sharp. Or my wife will kill me."

"Your truck will be back in this heah yard by nine o'clock. You can count on it."

If the job was clean, Jewel thought, as he drove away, he'd have the truck back as planned. If anything happened that tied the truck to the hit, well, suckers got what they deserved.

"So you're up," Sandy said as she entered his kitchen. "I figured you'd want to sleep in, so I didn't wake you."

From the bedroom, Maggie had smelled the aroma of sauteing onions and green peppers.

"Have you thought of opening a restaurant in your retirement?" she asked.

She leaned against the kitchen counter and watched as he stirred two cans of kidney beans and one of chopped tomatoes into a Dutch oven.

"No, but I've been thinking of entering a Betty Crocker cook-off. One alarm or two?" he asked with the chili spice box poised over the pot.

"Two."

Sandy dumped in some spices, covered the pot, and turned down the flame on the stove. He pulled Maggie into his arms. "Good thing we made up when we did. I'd gotten so disinterested in preparing meals, I was eating out–fast food three meals a day. My blood pressure must have been out of sight. You probably saved my life or something." He kissed her forehead.

"I have to tell you I find a man who cooks very sexy."

"Really? What will it get me?"

"Almost anything you want. Except I don't do high heels and trapezes. Used to–knee joints won't take it anymore."

He chuckled. "My loss."

She pushed back, smiling, loosening the embrace. "Are you going to keep cooking when I leave?"

Releasing her, he picked up a stirring spoon, grabbed the lid of the pot, and dropped it. "Ouch! I didn't think it would be that hot." He turned the faucet on and held his fingers under cold water. "I think Belle will enjoy the ride around Bogue Sound this afternoon."

"Sandy." She moved beside him, put her hand on the back of his arm. "We should talk soon. Wade and Jessie will be here in ten days to pick me up."

"...and while we're out, we can see about fins and a mask for you at that little dive shop." Last weekend they'd flown to Florida and snorkeled in Key West. It was her first time, and she'd loved it.

She turned him around. "You're in denial. About my leaving."

"Denial? The river in Egypt? I thought I was more subtle than that." He pronounced it sub-tel. He lifted her chin and kissed her briefly. "I'll be alright. You have enough to think about without worrying about me." With a potholder, he lifted the lid, stirred the chili, and replaced the lid.

He looked so vulnerable; she felt her heart squeeze. "I've loved being with you, so it's going to be hard, but..."

"Your family is in Maine. Your grandkids need you–both of them. Of course, you have to go back." He grinned at her with a mixture of whimsy and mischief. "I just haven't accepted it yet."

He guided her to the living room and sat down with her on the couch. "Look, I don't want you to spend a minute worrying about me. You need to stay focused on what's ahead." He stroked her hair. "You were nearly killed the last time you went home. We have no reason to believe it will be any safer this time. If there were something I could do to eliminate the danger, I'd do it. But I know trying to keep you here and isolated from your family is not the answer. You have to get your life back."

She nodded. "With Wade and Jessie's help."

"Are you sure you shouldn't go to the police when you get back to Maine? You have more to tell them than you had in August."

She nodded thoughtfully. "Yeah, I've been thinking the same thing. I'll talk to Wade when I see him."

"I know the sun isn't over the yardarm yet, but I sure could use a glass of Chablis. Can I get you one?"

"I haven't even had breakfast yet."

"It's almost lunch time. Somewhere."

"Good enough reason."

He handed her a glass of wine in her favorite stemware they had bought at a glass blowing demonstration and sat beside her.

"So, tell me, Margaret Mary Shaughnessy Wiser. Now that your exile is coming to an end, what have you missed the most?"

"The obvious answers are that I missed all of Pookie's basketball games and that I miss not being there to enjoy Tildie's pregnancy. She writes me about the details, like things she's doing to her room to prepare for the baby, but I want to be there."

"Of course."

"But, at least as much, I miss the connection with Pookie. When we shopped for basketball sneakers or rode bikes, we talked all the time. I know his views on nuclear disarmament, the federal budget for the space program, the pros and cons of carbon fiber bikes, whether or not NBA players should be drafted from high school..." She sipped her wine.

"I can see how you'd miss that. Are you afraid that will have changed?"

She nodded weakly. She had begun to accept that Pookie's relationship with his family would become less and less important. But she didn't want to go home and find the connection already gone.

"You've read his letters to me. Sounds to me like he's still feeling connected."

She took another sip and savored the wine before she swallowed. "Okay. Maybe a benefit that will come from all this is learning that being physically separated from someone doesn't cause the connection to break. Maybe if it is there to begin with, it's always there."

Something flashed behind Sandy's eyes for a second, and then he studied his wine glass. He chuckled. "That would be good to discover. Might save you a fortune in Valium when he goes off to college."

Maggie laughed. "I must sound like a neurotic nut."

"Nope. I like every little nook and cranny of your captivating mind. So, anyway, assuming we've already had our talk about you going back to Maine, let's go pick up Belle."

"Yeah, it'll be a fun day. We can have lunch at the Farmers' Market. And then, well, I've made up my mind that I'm going to listen to that answering machine tape of Sam's voice tonight. I'm not sure why. Maybe I'm hoping I can leave that ghost behind."

At a secondhand store in Morehead City, Jewel purchased shovels and a variety of rakes and put them in the back of the truck, handles out over the closed tailgate.

Then he drove back to the Beaufort house where the people he tailed had gone yesterday afternoon. He had been a block behind them when they parked the Nissan Maxima in front of the house. Then he drove around the block. When he went by the house again, the Nissan was still there. Did the woman live there? Likely, he thought.

But the plaques on the house fronts, announcing the dates they were built, told him he was in a historic district that dated back to the late 1700s. And the very nature of the area, he had realized last night, would make on-going surveillance difficult: Neighborhood Watch signs on every street. He'd gone back to his hotel with the plan to be up and away at dawn.

This morning, the Nissan was gone, but this house was key, he was sure. Now, he parked down the block from the house in his truck with North Carolina plates. He put his head back, pulled his hat over his eyes, and feigned a snooze–a gardener taking a break. Through narrowed eyes he could see no one took any particular notice.

He didn't have to wait long. The old lady he'd seen yesterday with the Wiser woman came out on the porch, and a minute later the Nissan pulled up in front. The woman sprang out of the passenger side and helped the older woman into the front seat. Then she climbed into the backseat behind the driver, the guy she'd been with yesterday. Jewel waited until they were almost out of sight and then pulled out to follow.

He tailed them at a distance for the next four hours. At a fair distance away, he followed them on foot around an outdoor marketplace for a couple of hours and then by vehicle until they returned and left the old lady at her house. Then Jewel followed the Wiser woman and the man to Morehead City to a home near the ocean that had been converted into apartments. When they entered the house, Jewel circled the block, then parked on the other side of the road, down from her house. So she wasn't a grieving widow anymore. An hour later, the man left. Alone. Now it was clear this was where she lived.

He stayed in the truck, knowing he couldn't walk the streets in daylight unnoticed. Even discounting his skin color, his height and bald head would be enough to demand attention in this area where the cozy homes were close together and everyone would know everyone else's visitors. But it was only a couple of hours until sunset.

Darkness was a friend he often relied on.

Maggie pushed the stop button on the tape recorder, grabbed her house keys, and fled down the stairs. She had to walk–get her emotions under control. The impact of Sam's voice, so near, so intimate, so alive, had slammed her to the mat, and she now felt compelled to walk. She gritted her teeth to keep the sounds her throat was trying to make from erupting.

She barely noticed the children rollerblading, the young couple jogging, or the truck filled with rakes and landscaping equipment as she passed. Feeling she was about to lose control and not wanting to be seen crying, she trespassed between two houses to reach the private Bogue Sound oceanfront beach.

Jewel tensed as he watched her bolt out as if the house were on fire. She darted by him and down the sidewalk. He slowly pulled away from the curb and nonchalantly drove around the block. When he got back to her street, she had disappeared. He drove around for a while but didn't spot her. She could be visiting someone–could have disappeared into one of the houses along here. But she'd be back.

And he was ready.

Running along the hard packed sand, she climbed over one private dock after another until she reached a place of comfort–a small sandy stretch of public beach. Out of breath, she dropped onto a rustic, weathered bench.

The sun slid down a peach-colored sky, creating a narrow path on the water like textured gold. A jet left pink contrails in the cloudless sky. How could she feel so much pain when surrounded by such beauty?

A seagull swooped in and perched on an old dock post that stood nearby in shallow water. He became motionless, looking south, the same way Maggie faced. On the other side of the channel, Atlantic Beach, the barrier island that protected the Intercoastal Waterway and Morehead City, was sharply silhouetted–a thin black line against a smudgy pink and gray sky. The horizon deepened to a bright red as the last sliver of sunlight disappeared. Across the channel, the dots of white, yellow, and green lights on Atlantic Beach became a string of clustered bright lights.

Maggie was startled by a sudden movement–the seagull, apparently knowing the show was over, shook its wings and flew away.

As the darkness descended, she took off her shoes, rolled up her pants, and walked into the shallow water, welcoming the cold and feeling the tiny waves wrap around her ankles. Unable to hold back any longer, she allowed bits and pieces of the past to surface.

She waded for more than an hour; by then she knew this ghost wouldn't be exorcized for some time to come. She realized as scenes from her and Sam's past opened like pages in a long-forgotten, black and white photo album–he had loved her. As well as he could.

She wondered for the first time who had taken care of his things after his death. She couldn't imagine his boat, bobbing at a dock, without him. What had become of it? Who had taken care of his clothes? His house? The one thing she could have done for him after he was gone was to have taken care of his things. But she had abandoned him. She sank down into the surf, letting the waves wash around her waist and sobbed until she was spent.

Jewel cruised the area close to her apartment. At dusk, he parked across the street and down one block. He slouched down, pulling his cap lower, and touched the knife in his pocket. After dark, he saw her coming home, three blocks away, on his side of the street. But would she stay on this side or cross the street before she got here?

Earlier he'd disabled the truck's interior light. Now he softly unlatched the door and slid out, closing it with a small click. The street was deserted. He stepped into a driveway and then behind tall shrubbery. If she stayed on the same side, she'd walk right by him. If she crossed sooner, he'd have to follow her into her apartment. The knife was in the pocket of his hoodie–ironically, the knife that he'd had in his hand when she'd inadvertently thwarted his attempt to take out Sam Wiser. But he wouldn't use it tonight, he decided. This job had gotten personal.

He didn't need a weapon.

Maggie was weary, wet, and cold, but she also felt a burden had lifted. She pulled her keys from her jeans pocket as she crossed the street. Just as they came free, she was aware of a movement behind her.

Then an arm wrapped around her.

"No!" she screamed. In an instant, she was dreadfully aware that she had let her guard down, and now all was lost. It dawned on her horribly, all the training was for nothing. Her cry was cut short by a hand clamping over her mouth; the other arm wrapped around her, pinning her against her assailant. The movement triggered a reaction. She stomped her right foot down, with all the force she could muster, on the top of his foot. His hand loosened slightly on her mouth. She bit down hard on his fingers. He yanked his hand back, and she swung her closed-fisted arm backwards, nailing him in the crotch. Gasping in pain, he released his grip on her.

Jolted with fear, she ran between two houses, thinking, this is it. It doesn't matter what I do. I won't escape this time. There was no place to go except the open beach with no place to hide. In a shadow, she flattened herself against a garage wall trying to still the sound of her breathing. She heard nothing, but her skin prickled with the knowledge that he was listening for her. A small door in the side of the garage was ajar, but what if it squeaked when she opened it? And once inside, she'd be trapped. Like she had been in the laundromat. There was an automobile parked in the next driveway. Could she reach it by staying in the shadows of the trees? Crouched, she ran, fell to her stomach, and slid under the car. She listened. No sound, no movement.

Now what? She couldn't go back to her apartment. Ever. She could probably walk to Beaufort, but she would easily be spotted. She looked toward the Sound. No cover for several blocks. Just docks that extended out into the water, the docks she had climbed over earlier when her only problem had been grief.

Anger gripped Jewel. He'd been completely unprepared for her sudden movement and was shocked when she slipped out of his grasp. Except for that, she'd be dead from a broken neck.

Easy, he thought. It's not over yet. He'd learned as he was growing up that anger caused you to make mistakes, kept you from getting what you wanted.

The woman would be running like a frightened jackrabbit. He darted to the truck and grabbed the handgun on the floor. No. He wasn't going to chase her down the beach firing a gun and separating himself from the truck. It was one thing to disappear in Boston and quite another in a small southern town bordering the ocean.

He got into the truck. Well, damn her anyway. What was it with this old lady who'd been able to outfox NADCO and had now gotten away from him? Twice.

And who were these clever old people who had helped her? Either she or the Maxwells had left a trail that led Henry Lee, not to mention himself, on a wild goose chase all over Florida. Probably the old geezers themselves, because it looked, since she had a geriatric romance going, like she'd been tucked away here the whole damn time.

He started the truck. Where would she head? Would she go in the direction of Beaufort where the old woman lived? But to get there, she'd have to go through downtown Morehead City and across a bridge where she would be out in the open. She was too smart for that. Right now, she'd be trying to hide. And if she went toward the ocean, she would run out of beach when she got to the commercial district.

He could pick her up there.

Before that, though, he recalled a small open area where you could walk to the water without trespassing. Worth trying. She'd have to cross there if she were coming down the beach. That would be the spot.

Maggie heard the vehicle start. Then she remembered the truck she had passed just before she was attacked. And she had a vague recollection of walking by a truck on the way to the beach. Could've been the same one–she hadn't paid attention. If she had noted the truck earlier and then seen it on her return, she would have turned down another block and disappeared. Jessie had warned her about letting down her guard when she felt secure. "Stupid, damn fool," she muttered.

The sound of the motor faded in the distance. She inched out from under the car and lay waiting on her belly, muscles tensed, ready to jump. Nothing. Shivering in the chilly night, she cautiously rose to a crouched position. Still low, she moved toward the private dock, dropped behind it, and waited for several minutes. Nothing moved.

Repeating her earlier trek, she scrambled over and around docks, pausing to watch and listen, keeping her head low, running past shorefront homes toward Morehead City's downtown waterfront.

When there were no more houses, she dropped to her knees and crawled through tall marsh grass. Then she ran out of cover. Ahead was a ditch, then a thirty-foot stretch of open beach. To get past the ditch, she would have to stand up and walk a narrow ledge between the ditch and a chain-link fence. There was no sign of her attacker. Had she lost him? There wasn't a movement or sound. No vehicle in sight. And she couldn't lay here and freeze.

She slowly rose to her feet. Stepping on the ledge, she grabbed the fence for support and minced across. Now that she was in the open, nothing to do but run for the grass on the other side.

Two hundred feet behind her, Jewel was just about to give up, thinking she must have headed away from the ocean and back into the residential area, when the lights on the other side of the sound outlined her progress as she ran across the beach. Fast for an old gal.

He waited until she dove for cover in the marsh grass before he jogged to the beach. Still time to catch her before the commercial district.

Maggie crawled on her stomach, not daring to lift her head. Some areas were wet and thick with mud, others littered with beer cans and debris. Ahead was an abandoned building she'd seen before. If she could just get that far...she glanced over her shoulder and froze with fear. The silhouette of a tall man, the faint light of a distant streetlamp shining off his bald head, advanced silently toward her across the small expanse of marsh grass. She had run out of room. She leaped up and ran for the water, scrambling over sharp rocks, timbers, and broken bottles. She didn't feel pain in her hands and knees until she fell forward, and saltwater stung her cuts. She ran in calf-deep water under a high dock. When the water was waist high, she slipped and went under. Coming up, she swam, trying to stay parallel with the cement barrier of a marine repair yard. Further on, a moored sailboat moved gently against its fenders at a wooden dock. She swam into the small crevice where the boat's shape curved away from the dock. Breathing deeply, she clung to the seaweed clad pilings that supported the dock.

She turned away from his direction so her face wouldn't reflect light. Then she took a deep breath, forced herself underwater by pushing against the pilings, and came up toward the bow of the boat, making it less likely he would see her.

She waited, planning to take cover under the dock, holding her breath underwater if necessary. But he didn't come. She counted slowly to sixty.

Then did it again, and a third time. It shouldn't have taken him more than a minute to reach her position.

She counted five more minutes. Nothing. She decided he was waiting for her to make a move when she heard the sound of an automobile.

The vehicle went by slowly. Too slowly. She stayed where she was until it passed. Headlights moved slowly away, down the street–not more than ten miles an hour. Reaching up for the bow line that attached the boat to the dock, she pulled herself up a few inches to look at the vehicle. It was a truck–with landscaping tools in the back.

Ahead, Oceanview Towers confirmed where she was. When the vehicle moved out of sight, she swam until the water became shallow. At the cement breakwater that formed the edge of the public walkway, she was forced to stand because the water was knee-deep and then only ankle-deep. Yet the wall gave her cover from the road. She ran through the water, barnacles and clam shells crunching under her wet sneakers. Suddenly she tripped over a chain and pitched forward onto the barnacles. She didn't feel anything, but she knew the razor-sharp crustaceans had cut her deeply.

A minute later, she saw the statue of King Neptune ahead that advertised deep-sea fishing excursions and knew she'd have to leave the protection of the wall. She waited, listened, and then climbed up on the dock.

Her heart sank when she realized the businesses in this area were closed and dark. It must be at least ten o'clock at night, off season. The police station was in sight, but she'd have to cross the road and an empty lot to get there, and she didn't even know which side of the building to go to or if anyone was there this time of night.

Running from hiding place to hiding place, she reached the Fish Market, remembering there was a public phone on the wall outside. Hearing a vehicle approaching she ducked behind a wooden barrel and watched as the truck neared. It was the same one she'd seen minutes ago. When the truck turned right and disappeared, she ran to the phone and dialed Aunt Belle's.

She answered on the first ring.

"I'm in trouble," Maggie blurted. "Come find me at the Fish Market in Morehead City. It's near–"

"I know where it is. I'll be there quick as I can."

Maggie hung up, noticing she'd left blood on the phone. She retreated behind cover and looked at her hands and knees. Her jeans were shredded, and blood oozed from crisscross lacerations on her hands and knees.

But she was still alive.

And she intended to stay that way.

"This time you've got to call the police." Sandy's tone of voice told Maggie he'd accept no other option. She was standing beside the sink in Belle's bathroom. Beside her, Sandy poured hydrogen peroxide over the wounds on her hands and arms. She watched the peroxide foam in the cuts and carry her blood down the drain.

"You want me to call?" he asked.

"Yes. Please. I guess you're right. Even if this is just a garden-variety mugger, they need to know."

"A garden-variety mugger isn't going to follow you for blocks. You're going to tell them the whole story? Your whole story?"

"Let's see how it goes, first."

Ten minutes later, two Morehead City cruisers sat outside Belle's house. If she was worried about what her neighbors would think, it didn't show. She had come to Maggie's rescue in minutes, not even stopping to call Sandy.

Now, with poise and just a touch of formality, Belle offered the two uniformed police officers their choice of tea or coffee. When they refused, she nodded and sat in her Queen Anne chair, her hands folded in the lap, her sparkling eyes watching the scene with keen attentiveness.

The younger of the two officers, dressed in a freshly pressed dark blue shirt and trousers, was in his early twenties–a handsome Hispanic man named Mendoza. He sat with a pad balanced on his thigh, on the edge of an easy chair, facing Maggie and Sandy, who sat on the couch. The other policeman, whose name was Chapman, stood by the door with his hands folded in front of him. He had short-cropped, wavy blond hair and was pleasant-looking in a boyish, fresh-scrubbed way.

Maggie told them the story while Mendoza nodded sympathetically.

"Well, it's too bad you didn't get a good enough look at the man to get a description," he finally said.

"If he'd been any closer, he'd have killed me." She heard the irritation in her voice.

"Oh, sure. I know what you mean. It's dark, he's behind you. That wasn't meant as a criticism, Ma'am. I just meant that even if we pick up a suspicious-looking character, you won't be able to identify him, anyway.

You don't even know if he's black or white." He sighed and slipped the notebook into his shirt pocket. "The best we can do is drive around town and see if we spot a black pickup. Would be better if we had the make and model. But it's easy to pick out anyone who isn't a resident this time of year–very few tourists. So, we'll see. But thanks for letting us know. We'll be on the lookout tonight." He stood up.

Chapman, who hadn't said anything beyond "Good evening, folks," since they'd arrived ten minutes ago, moved closer to the door.

Sandy cleared his throat and looked inquiringly at Maggie. She remembered the detective from seven months ago, though it seemed like a lifetime, who had sat across a desk from her when she made the decision to confide in him. *Déjà vu.* Sandy continued to look at her. Well, what did she have to lose but her dignity?

"Wait. There might be more to this than a random thing."

Mendoza caught the look between Sandy and herself and seemed immediately interested. He sat down again.

"My ex-husband was offered a bribe." Mendoza's eyes flicked to Sandy as he pulled his notebook out of his pocket again.

"No, that would not be me," Sandy said with a small smile. "Hopefully, I would not be an ex."

Mendoza's eyes crinkled at the corners, and he couldn't suppress a chuckle.

"A bribe, which my ex-husband refused."

"When was that? What's his name?"

Mendoza had a pencil poised over his notebook again.

"Seven months ago–August. Samuel Wiser. In Maine." She watched Mendoza scribble rapidly on the tiny page.

"He turned it down." She took a deep breath and continued. "And the next day he was shot, killed. I was with him."

"In Maine."

"Yes. No, I mean in Massachusetts. I'm sorry."

The pencil stopped in mid-stroke, then Mendoza broke the silence. "That's okay, Ma'am. Take your time."

"He was shot in Massachusetts, just outside of Boston. He was bribed in Maine. I know it sounds–"

"By whom, Ma'am? They catch the killer?"

"No, they didn't really even investigate."

Chapman's tiny shift in posture clearly showed a reaction to what she'd said.

"And why's that, Ma'am?" Mendoza asked. His voice was polite but cautious and formal now.

"Well, they think–they thought Sam was an innocent bystander in the line of fire between two other men."

Chapman shifted again and suddenly developed an interest in the carpet in front of him.

Mendoza put his elbows on his knees. "And you don't think so." The notebook hung from his fingers, forgotten.

"I think it was done that way to look like an accident. Like Sam was killed accidentally. But it looked intentional to me."

"And you could identify the killer?"

"Then, maybe. But now? I'm not sure."

"Did you tell the police about the bribe?"

"Yes. But they didn't seem to believe it was related."

"And you think the man who followed you tonight is your husband's killer?"

"Well, possibly, but more likely, there's a second assassin." Because the man who killed Sam was black, and the man in the photo that Jessie had given her was white. But she didn't say this.

At the door, Chapman pressed his lips together and gave a barely perceptible shake of his head.

"I...see," said Mendoza.

"There've been other things," Maggie persisted. Now that she'd started, she might as well see this thing through to the end.

"What other things?" Mendoza sounded as if he'd like to wind this up and leave.

"A few days later, my grandson was hit by a car while we were bike riding. He only had a broken arm, but he could easily have been killed."

"And why would the killer want your grandson dead?"

"I think I was the target."

"Because you witnessed your ex-husband's death. I see. Did you report it to the police?"

"Yes, but they decided it was just some teenage kids. I didn't tell them I thought it was connected with Sam's death. At the time, I didn't think it was myself."

"I see. Well..." Mendoza sat up and started to put the notebook in his pocket again. He glanced at Chapman who stood up straight and put his hand on the doorknob.

"Wait. There's more. I went back home in January to see my granddaughter, and I was shot at."

Mendoza tipped his chin up, raised his eyebrows. "Oh?"

"I have a scar on the back of my head." Reflexively, she touched the area covered by her hair. "I can show you."

"And what did the police have to say about that?"

"I, ah...I didn't report it."

Chapman moved restlessly by the door. Mendoza caught the movement and shifted closer to the edge of his seat.

"You got shot at and didn't report it? You seek medical help?"

"No. I'd just been shot. I wanted to get away before he finished the job."

Chapman addressed her from his position near the door. "Ma'am. Ms. Wiser. With all due respect, Ma'am, your scar isn't proof of anything. A scar isn't even evidence if you have no way to prove when and how you got it."

Aunt Belle leaned forward and stiffened her back. "Young man," she said indignantly. "I saw the wound myself. I gave her a salve for it."

Sandy gave Maggie's hand a quick squeeze and leaned forward. "I can vouch for that. She had a fresh wound in January when she returned from Maine."

"But you weren't there when it happened?" Mendoza asked him.

"No, but I know Maggie. She's telling the truth." He squeezed her hand again.

"I don't mean to pry, sir, but what is your relationship with Mrs. Wiser?"

Sandy's eyes met hers. "We're friends."

Mendoza nodded. "You're romantically involved?"

Sandy nodded. "What's that got to do with anything?"

Maggie's frustration turned to anger. "Look, I rented a car. The windows got shot out. You can check with the rental company. I abandoned the car, but my granddaughter returned it."

"So maybe the rental company found evidence in the car and reported it to the police?"

"There was only one shot. It grazed me and went through both side windows. I don't think there would've been anything but shattered glass in the car." She paused but couldn't keep the next words from coming out. "It's the same way Sam died. A bullet through the car window."

Chapman folded his arms across his chest but still didn't look at her. "Could the rental car windows have been broken some other way? Maybe vandals? Someone threw a rock? That would be scary."

"No. This is absurd. You think I'm making this up!"

Mendoza didn't meet her eyes. "Well, no disrespect, ma'am, but sometimes, when people experience a trauma? They have to work through..."

Maggie pulled herself to the edge of her seat. "That's ridiculous."

"Excuse me, ma'am," Chapman's voice was not unkind. "Let me tell you what I heard, and you correct me if I'm wrong?"

She nodded, trying to quiet her rapid breathing.

"With all due respect." He looked directly at her for a second, his intelligent blue eyes saying this is going to hurt. "With all due respect, your husband turned down a bribe in Maine. The next day, he was killed in Massachusetts in what looked like a random shooting to the police. And you think a murder was planned–in a twenty-four-hour period–to look like a convincing accident to experienced city police. Your grandson was the victim of a hit and run in Maine. So, you moved to North Carolina–"

"Actually, young man, she's in hiding," Belle said with dignity.

"I...see. Of course. Okay, so you go back in January, and someone has been hanging around for what, five months, to shoot you, using the same MO as when he shot your husband, but this time he doesn't care if it seems like an accident? Or–perhaps you were also caught in the line of fire?"

She was mesmerized by his smooth, reassuring voice. She shook her head.

"No? Okay, then you come back to Morehead City in January, but it's not until March, when suddenly someone follows you–maybe a second assassin–accosts you on the sidewalk outside your home after you take a long walk on the beach–where presumably he could have followed you and taken action earlier and more privately. Someone you can't give any real description of, except you later saw a man driving a black truck, which you also can't give any description of, not make or model."

Now Chapman's eyes held hers and she saw, behind the deceptively youthful face, the shrewd intellect operating. "But he doesn't kill you. You give this professional killer, who you say grabbed you, the slip. Do I have the story straight, Mrs. Wiser?"

Yes, he did. Without benefit of notes. Even Mendoza seemed impressed. Lips parted and eyes wide, he gazed at Chapman with respect; he slipped the notebook back into his pocket.

"Ma'am?" Chapman's voice prodded for her response; his eyes had become gentler but still alight with mental astuteness.

"Yes, I believe you have that right." Her face burned with anger and shame. She pulled herself up straight. "Thank you for taking your valuable time to talk to me. Please note that I am exceedingly sorry I called you. If my friends hadn't insisted, I wouldn't have." She stood. "We won't keep you any longer."

Aunt Belle pushed herself out of the chair with great energy and stepped to the door, forcing Chapman to move. She opened it and stood beside it as if she were saying goodbye to departing guests. Except she wasn't smiling, and she didn't extend her hand.

Chapman gave a stiff nod and strode down the brick sidewalk. Mendoza looked uncertain and apologetic. He turned and said, "Look, ma'am, if you're still worried, don't go out alone at night for a while. It's pretty quiet in Morehead City–Beaufort too–'specially this time of year, but that doesn't mean there couldn't be some unsavory character hanging around." He smiled sympathetically.

She nodded, her face wooden.

"Anything more comes up, call us." He made a polite tip-the-hat gesture and was gone.

The door closed behind them. Through clenched teeth, Maggie let out a frustrated growl. "I will never, and I mean never, put myself in that position again. That was so degrading. They thought I was some neurotic, foolish old woman trying to get attention."

Sandy pulled her into his arms, kissed her temple. "I'm sorry. Calling them was my idea. Maybe what we need to do is take it higher up. Maybe talk to a detective."

Maggie stiffened. "No, Sandy. It ends here. I will not trot from place to place like I'm a dog-and-pony show, trying to get someone to look at my scar. The end result will always be exactly like it was tonight."

"Okay." He pulled her back into his arms. "Okay, you may be right, but there has to be something we can do."

"There is. I'm going home. Tonight, if possible."

Aunt Belle spun Maggie's way. "But Wade and Jessie are coming to get you next week."

Sandy looked at her intently, reading her face. "You mean it."

"Yes. I keep thinking, how did he find me? Something has changed. Maybe something has broken down in our communication system. I'm concerned it had something to do with my cellular phone. Or did someone get to Wade and Jessie? Or maybe Pookie or Tildie? I have to go back and check on them. On all of them."

Belle's forehead wrinkled in worry. "Maggie, I can phone Joel and just casually ask him how everyone is doing there."

"And," Sandy said, "I can track down Wade sometime tomorrow."

"Look, he, whoever he is, found me here. Beaufort and Morehead City are no longer any safer than Amesbury. In fact, less so, now. I have more resources at home. More places to hide. It's time to go. And besides, there is something I can do when I get back that Wade and Jessie can't help me with." She thought of Otis' message after Sam's calls on the answering machine tape.

Sandy lips were tucked into a straight line. He found her eyes and held them. Finally, he nodded and when he spoke, his voice was soft. "Is there anything I can do to help?"

She felt deep appreciation for his unflagging support. "Yes, there is. Can you go back to my apartment and get my gun and my suitcase? I want to be out of here tonight."

"Yes, I can do that. And let's get on the internet. I can find out what planes are leaving the Raleigh-Durham Airport tonight. My plane is ready to go. I can fly you into Raleigh. Where do you want to go in Maine? Portland? Bangor?"

"No. See if we can get anything to Manchester, New Hampshire. If anyone is looking for me, he wouldn't expect me to fly into Manchester. I have a prepaid credit card, so I can rent a car there and drive home. It's only two or three hours. Two, I think."

"I'll have to contact Wade. Tell him you won't be here next week."

"He'll be upset," Aunt Belle warned.

"Don't tell him, please, until he gets here," Maggie said. "Promise me. Just check and make sure they're okay. In case someone is onto them, I don't want to tip anyone off that I'm going." She paused, thinking through her plan. "I won't be able to contact you for a few days because, until I think it's safe, I'm not going to be using my cellular phone, and you won't be able to contact me at all. At least not for a while. I won't know if Wade and Jessie are okay."

And I have to know, she thought. "Here's what I'll do. Tomorrow night I'll phone you, Sandy, from a public phone. I'll ask for Sarah, or any other name–it doesn't matter. If Wade and Jessie are okay, say Sarah is not at home, please call back later. If they are not, tell me I have the wrong number."

The possibility of their not being all right stunned her. A future without Wade and Jessie was unthinkable. That harm might have befallen them because of her was an unbearable thought.

"I'm sure they're okay," Sandy said. "But reassurance will relieve your mind. Listen, there won't be much room for luggage in my plane."

"S'okay. I didn't come with much. Just throw a few things in my suitcase. The gun. I can't take a gun on the plane. Okay if I leave the gun with you, Aunt Belle? Give it to Jessie and Wade when they get here."

"Are you sure you should go back without your gun?" Belle asked.

Maggie smiled. "I'm not planning on going into town with guns blazing. My idea is to be invisible for a while, maybe gather some information."

"Right. Sandy, you go and collect her things," said Aunt Belle, "and then find out what you have to about airplane schedules. Maggie, it's time for another makeover. I picked up a new hair color last week. Let's see what we can do."

Jewel drove the rental car northwest up Route 70 toward Interstate 95. From there he'd drive to Richmond and catch a plane. No use sticking around once the woman had sounded the alarm. Know when to throw in the towel. He had seen the police cruisers outside the house tonight. Morehead City Police.

This was just too unbelievable. He never failed at anything. *Anything.* Ever. He should just chuck the whole damn thing and go back to Boston. He had a life there, jobs waiting for him. He needed a freaking job he could finish.

He took a deep breath and exhaled slowly. He willed himself to relax. He couldn't leave this job yet. It would always nag at him that this lady, this very lucky lady, had outsmarted him. That wasn't going to happen.

Once back in Maine, he would take some time for self-reflection. Perhaps he had become over-confident. Reflecting now, he realized–he should have used the knife.

One thing he knew for sure.

This woman was really beginning to get on his nerves.

Maggie stepped on the wing and pulled herself out of the airplane. She minced toward the back of the wing, turned around, and stepped down on the metal bar that looked to her like a kickstand. By then Sandy was standing beside her and helped her lower herself to the tarmac. He pulled her luggage out of the plane, and they walked silently toward the terminal.

He waited while she purchased her ticket, and he walked her to the gate in silence.

"You're sure about this?" he asked.

"Yes. I'm nervous, but mostly because I don't exactly know how the first few hours will go. Or days. But in my head, I'm already there."

He pulled her close and she sank into him, leaning her forehead on his chest.

"I'll call you from time to time. If it's okay," he said.

She patted her pocket and gasped. "I forgot it! My cellular phone. I forgot it."

"Can't go back now," Sandy said. "You already have your ticket."

He lifted her chin and kissed her on the forehead. "I'll give it to Wade and Jessie. Anything else you left behind?"

A piece of my heart, she thought.

She shook her head. "I'm good."

BOOK THREE

"You Can't Always Get What You Want."

The Rolling Stones

CHAPTER 17

Maggie arrived in Manchester at midnight. She'd been able to sleep for most of the three-hour flight. The rental car Sandy had reserved was waiting.

She was back in Amesbury by three a.m. She drove to Violet's block, parked several houses down, and put her head back to rest. The early March air was cold, and there was still a foot of snow on the ground. Every few minutes she awoke to shift positions. Her hands, wrapped in gauze and tape, ached. The cuts on her knees stung.

Forty minutes later, she had to start the car for warmth. When the heat blasted out enough to be uncomfortable, she turned off the car and fell asleep again. She awoke to a red dawning sky, chilled bones, and stiff muscles. She started the car again, knowing it would be several minutes before it warmed up. She yearned for a cup of coffee.

Finally, at 6:30, she saw Violet's solid figure coming down the sidewalk toward her. She was walking her dog, Wilbur, as she did every morning at this time. Maggie got out of the car and went around to the sidewalk.

Violet saw her, nodded politely. "Morning."

"Good morning, Violet."

Violet stopped short and stared with her mouth open. She clamped it shut. "Oh, my God, it sounds like you, but it doesn't look like you. Lord. Now what did you go and do to your hair? Maggie, is it really you?"

Maggie stepped toward her, and they embraced. Wilbur, sensing this was something to get excited about, wagged his tail and encircled them with his leash.

Violet unsnapped the leash from his collar and commanded him to stay. "I take it no one is supposed to know you're home, or you wouldn't be out here at the crack of dawn, freezing your buns off, waiting for me to come sashaying down the street. And what the devil did you do to your hands?"

"A few small cuts, that's all. Those are the least of my problems. I need a place to get out of sight–a place where no one would think to look for me. So that can't be your house."

"Well, I have the answer to that. My Mom's. She has two spare rooms, and she'd love to have you. Course Dad is getting pretty loony, so we couldn't depend on him not to tell anyone. But on second thought, no one would believe him, would they? How about it?"

"If you don't think they'll mind. Just for a little while until I think of something else."

"Mom'll love it. Why don't I just jump in your car—what's it, a rental?—and put Wilbur in the back. We can drive over there together. I'll go in and explain. Maggie, I can't tell you how happy I am to see you back here. But I wouldn't a recognized you right off. Now that we're talking though, you still look like you. Just a little different. Whajah do? Go to Weight Watchers? That's not healthy. Maybe Mom can put a little meat on those bones. Well, don't just stand there. Let's get going afore we all freeze."

Maggie felt the wind whip at the tears in her eyes. She hadn't realized how much she missed Violet's heartwarming, comforting bullying.

The door of Otis' tiny office was ajar; Otis sat at this desk, his back to the door, tapping the keyboard of his computer. Maggie rapped on the door jamb.

He swiveled toward her. "Come in. What can I do for you?" He stood up and cleared newspapers off a chair near the door. "Sit down."

She sat down, pleased he hadn't recognized her. She was wearing oversized sunglasses. Her dark burgundy-red hair was cropped close in a short shag. On one side the top was gelled so that it stood up in punk style. As the hair got longer across the top, it swooped across one side of her forehead in a wave. Very trendy. And she had, of course, lost thirty pounds.

"I represent NorthCoast Food Distributors." She watched Otis' eyebrows knit in confusion. Did he recognize her voice? "I know it's not your regular day for ordering, but I'm the new rep, and I thought I'd just stop by and introduce myself."

Otis' jaw dropped. He knew. She saw it in his eyes. With a finger to her lips, she lowered the sunglasses. "I'm Imogene Iacocca. You must be Mr. Oxley."

Otis threw his head back and closed his eyes. When he opened them and looked at her, she could see immense relief in them. He passed one hand over his face, looking, for a moment, like he was going to cry. He covered his mouth with his hand, rubbing it from side to side as if to keep the words inside.

Otis finally lowered his hand and shook his head. "I thought..." he began, but Maggie put a finger to her lips and held up her other hand. It might not be necessary to be this cautious, but she was taking no chances.

Otis nodded and began again. "I thought...we already ordered from your company this month." He grimaced and shrugged helplessly at Maggie, looking for direction.

"Actually, you did. You're not due to order until the first of the month. As I said, I just want to stop by and meet people on this trip. Can I give you my card?"

She handed Otis an index card that said, "I have to talk to you. Don't tell anyone I'm home. I'll meet you at Fishing Rock in Ames Park tonight at 9:00 p.m."

Fishing Rock was located beside Manasacook Stream, a small, lazy tributary that cut through Amesbury and fed into the Kennebec River. Generations of Amesbury kids had climbed onto the huge rock to throw a line in the water on quiet summer afternoons.

Otis' eyes met Maggie's, and he nodded.

"Well, it was nice meeting you, Mr. Oxley. I look forward to doing business with you." Maggie rose and put her sunglasses back on.

"Ah, yeah. Good. Me too." As Otis half rose from his chair, he looked like he didn't know if he should extend his hand. He settled for a nod. "Yes, of course. Nice to meet the new sales rep from NorthCoast."

Satisfied with the meeting and exhilarated at having pulled it off, Maggie strode out of the rear door toward the black van she had borrowed from Effie, Violet's mother.

Taking precautions, like assuming Otis' office could be bugged, might not be necessary, but she was going to err on the over-cautious side.

Had he been overwhelmed with relief when he recognized her? Did that mean he thought she was dead? If so, he hadn't gone to the police about it.

When she had listened to the tape of his voice two days ago, she'd been sure he knew or suspected something about Sam's death, but he hadn't gone to the police about that either. Sam was sure NADCO held something over Otis' head. Maggie had been pretty sure it was a threat to expose Otis' tax fraud. Was there still a NADCO ax hanging over his head?

And, if so, when would it drop?

* * *

She sat in the dark behind the wheel of Effie's van and waited. She could be meeting a man who needed to cover up an accessory to murder charge. She didn't think he would harm her himself, but would he have alerted someone from NADCO?

Or was Otis just a coward who didn't report what he knew to the police? Either way, she'd worked up a head of steam this afternoon, but she couldn't let her emotions show if she were going to get the truth out of him.

Her watch showed eight forty-five. A minute later, Otis exited the side door of his house and headed toward his car. She eased the van forward, turned into his driveway, and pulled up behind his car. He looked up, startled.

Maggie leaned out the window. "Can I give you a lift?"

He stiffened in surprise, then composed himself and smiled. "Ah, sure." He climbed into the passenger side of the van. "I thought we were supposed to meet at–"

"This will work better. Let's just ride around."

"Because you don't trust me. I don't blame you, but I haven't told anyone you are here, I promise. I wouldn't do that."

She hoped her smile was disarming as she backed out of the yard, put the van in drive, and moved forward.

"Maggie, you look great," Otis blurted. "Years younger, even. Not that you looked old before. I didn't mean that. But I just didn't recognize you this morning. Where've you been? I thought you were dead."

She pulled the van over to the side of the road. "And why was that?" She turned the key and shut the motor off. This was as good a place as any.

"Well, you know, no one knowing where you were."

She paused for a moment and then said gently, "When did you know they were going to go after me? Try to kill me? Did they tell you?"

Otis' eyebrows shot up in alarm, and he gasped as he turned to look at her. "No! No, no, no. I swear it." He shook his head vigorously, his jowls wobbling.

"But you did know what they were going to do to Sam."

"For God's sake, no! I didn't, I swear to you."

"I listened to your phone message, Otis. Way too late, as it turned out."

"Phone message? What...?" Then comprehension dawned on his face. "Oh. You mean last year. Back...then."

She nodded. "You said something like, 'Convince him to call me right away. It's a matter of...it's very, very important.' You didn't say, 'a matter of life or death' but it came across that way."

340

"I don't really remember what I said. I think I'd been drinking–I don't do that anymore. But I can't really remember what I said." He stared out of the windshield into the dark night.

"You phoned to warn him. To ask me to warn him." She stretched the truth. She believed the call had been a last-minute attempt to warn Sam, but Otis hadn't used those exact words.

Otis rubbed a hand across his eyes as if he were trying to recall the moment, then he shook his head.

"Otis."

He turned to look at her.

"You know what's going on."

"No."

"A minute ago, I asked you if you knew they were going to try to kill me."

He nodded, looking at her.

"You didn't ask who 'they' were. Because you know."

His face crumbled. He turned toward the night outside of the windshield, blinking his eyes. She waited. Finally, he drew a ragged breath. When he spoke, he didn't look at her.

"Maggie, I am so damn sorry. When I heard Sam was killed, when I heard it on the news, I thought it was all my fault. I still live with that every day. I was the first one that those bastards contacted in Amesbury. I welcomed those guys with open arms. I did everything they asked me to do."

"NADCO."

He nodded, still staring, unfocused, out at the street in front of them. "When I realized it was a dirty operation, I wanted to pull out. Especially when Sam dug in his heels and wouldn't go along with them. But they had something on me–"

"You were skimming money to avoid taxes."

His head snapped toward her. "How did you know?"

"That's not important, but for goodness sake, how did you ever get in this pickle with your business in the first place?"

"In the beginning, I cut corners a little bit. It was easy in those days with the mechanical cash register. I did it to keep the business going.

"I didn't think I was ever going to be successful at anything in life. Then, when old man Higgins said he'd sell the business to me, his little gold mine, he called it, I thought it was my big chance. When you're pulling pizzas out of the oven, running the cash register, and seeing all the money pouring in, you do think it's a gold mine. Turned out, he was in real trouble. There wasn't enough coming in to pay the creditors. He was on a cash-only basis with his suppliers. And that was the only deal they'd give me. Cash on the barrelhead. So, I cut corners to keep it going. When I pulled money out of the register to pay for supplies, I didn't report it as income. I was only going to do it until I got the business back on its feet."

"Which you did. And very well."

"Yeah, but then, as business got better, I could see ways to make it grow. Add to the menu, then add to the building. I kept skimming because it seemed like a good business investment. I wasn't spending it on personal stuff, and I got really good at it after a while. I showed enough profit to get a loan to add the supermarket but kept back enough to pay for some of my supplies with cash, which gave me more elbow room to enlarge and improve."

"So you've been doing this the whole fifteen years I was your accountant?" Maggie was horrified to think she hadn't caught on earlier.

"Oh, yeah. And before that. I started to measure my success by how much I could hide rather than how much profit I showed. When I had to change to electronic cash registers, it was more of a challenge. But I figured out how. Then I started to take it for granted that I could get away with it. Well, there's always that fear that you can't in the back of your mind, but I had gotten away with skimming for so long and nobody had caught on. Not you, not the frigging IRS. Somehow those NADCO bastards found out."

"And they kept you involved in their plans."

"Yes. But I didn't know they'd kill Sam. Honest to God."

"But afterward. Afterward, you sat on information about his murder to avoid tax fraud charges?"

"I didn't know for sure they had murdered him. I only suspected. I just didn't know what to do. Then, on the day of his funeral, they stuck a gun in my ribs and told me to go for a ride with them. I thought they were going to finish me off because I knew too much.

"They drove down the old County Road. Used to be the old road to Lewiston before they put in the Interstate. You know it?"

She nodded.

He continued. "Then we turned off that road and went down a narrow, beat-up paved road, then a dirt road–a logging road. Fairly new."

Otis folded his arms across his chest and squinted, remembering. "They hadn't bothered to keep me from knowing where we were, so I thought for sure I wouldn't be coming back out. But I still kept trying to place myself and think about the geography, in case, by some miracle, I got away. Then I realized we must be on the Archibald Estate. The wildlife thing?"

The Archibald Estate, again. Maggie nodded.

Otis said, "I soon realized someone had used the road for logging in recent years. The big stuff, the timber, had been removed not too long ago. The woods were thick with a lot of young saplings filling the gaps. After a while, we came to this logging camp."

He ran his hand over his head. "I was thinking, 'This is what happens to those people who seem to drop off the face of the earth.'"

"I can imagine how scared you were," Maggie said. She surely could.

He nodded vigorously, his double chin quivering. "We got out–"

"Who was with you?"

"Guy named Lincoln Montgomery and another tough looking guy named Mancuso. He had the gun, but Lincoln Montgomery, I hate that sleazy bastard, he was in charge. We went into the cabin. Maggie, I was scared shitless. But all they did was bring in a tape recorder, and this guy, this Mancuso character, plays a tape for me that's been doctored up. They had recorded me at different times when we met, and then they must have put bits and pieces together somehow. It sounded so incriminating. Like I knew in advance Sam would be killed and like I told them where and when they could find him. But I swear to you–"

"I believe you." And she did. Otis didn't have enough imagination to think up this story. "You believed you would be accused of being an accessory to Sam's death if you reported it to the police."

"They told me the money they gave me–okay, the bribe, I might as well be honest–would look like a payoff for services rendered."

"Two hundred and fifty thousand dollars?"

"How did you know?"

"I saw it on your bank statement."

"Then you probably saw I spent some. I bought a new car. That was really dumb. It makes me really look guilty. And, I had to pay taxes on the money!"

Maggie stifled a smile, thinking how much that must have hurt.

Otis said, "And that's when I realized they weren't going to kill me. They set me up so I wouldn't tell anybody."

"And so you didn't."

"Maggie, if you'd been as scared as I was, if you thought someone was going to kill you, and then you got a reprieve, you'd have done the same thing. Kept your mouth shut."

"But you have to talk now, Otis. There have been three attempts on my life. And I saw the killer deliberately aim at Sam. They didn't believe me, but with your testimony—"

"No! What are you thinking? I can't. Now I *am* an accessory. After the fact. Don't you see that? Now I *would* go to jail."

"But I can't get my life back until the police put these people behind bars."

"Don't ask this of me. I've changed my life now. The day after those characters hijacked me, Stoney called me in, talked to me. Said he was taking over some of your clients until you came back to work. He'd figured out what I was doing with the books. He said it could be jail time. Lectured me for an hour, but I guess he didn't have the heart to report me. He said he'd settle for supervising my books. Now I have to turn all my register tapes over to him. And I have to pay a little more in accounting fees, but it keeps me honest. Since that day I haven't even wanted to dip into the till. I'm walking the straight and narrow path now."

"You won't help me."

"So help me, if you go to the police, I'll pull up stakes and disappear. Gone. Look, going to jail is not the worst thing that could happen. Because of what I know, they'd fucking kill me."

Maggie had no doubt about that. She sighed. "Okay. Without your cooperation it won't do me any good to go to the police. So, I won't."

Yet. She thought for a moment about Otis' skittishness and made a decision.

"If, at some point, I have enough information that I think I can go to the police, I'll contact you first, and you can decide then what you want to do—be with me or run. I'll promise this in exchange for you not telling anyone I'm back."

Otis nodded. "Okay. That's fair, I guess. More than fair."

"Just confirm one thing for me. This whole thing was about the mall, right? Because Sam blocked the building of the mall?"

"That's what it looks like. They expect the mall to be ready for occupancy by fall. But there's more than that, I think. I overheard them talking one night. They're planning on taking over the Archibald Estate, no one knows about this yet, and developing it into a big-deal, fancy pantsy hotel, golf course, and million-dollar mansions." Otis held up a hand. "Don't ask. I don't know how. I swear, Maggie. I just want to stay out of everything, and you should too. There's just no overestimating how dangerous these people are."

"You have never been more right about anything."

"You're worried about her, aren't you?" Jessie asked. She was behind the wheel of the pickup heading north from Virginia. They had arrived in Beaufort at two in the afternoon planning to visit and stay overnight. After Belle told them the story, Sandy loaded Maggie's possessions into the Airstream, and Wade and Jessie were on the road an hour later with Jessie behind the wheel.

Wade rubbed his forehead like he was trying to wipe away his concerns. "Yeah, it's been over a week since she left here. No way to contact her." He shook his head. "See if she's still alive. Won't know how to find her...assuming she knows to stay in hiding."

"Oh, she does. She just had a refresher course. Scares me just to think about it. Maybe she'll be watching for us. She's a smart cookie."

Wade squinted in thought. "Yup, she is. But, Jess, she doesn't have any—okay, okay, she doesn't have *much* experience in dealing with those ruthless bastards."

"I know. I did the best I could, but she's still a lamb among wolves."

"Professional wolves. Had to be professional. And relentless. How the hell else did they find her in North Carolina?"

"It had to be through us. The kids didn't even know where she was."

"I keep thinking that." He paused. "I was really hoping it would have ended way before this–that they'd stop looking for her. Then we bring her back, with protection. Let them see she's no threat. Just went on a vacation. But they never stopped looking, all the while planning to eliminate her when they found her."

Head bowed, he massaged his temples with one broad hand. "Aw, shit, damn and piss." The words were soft, discouraged. "We did something wrong somewhere along the line." He turned toward her. "Then we lost control. She took it right out of our hands. I hope to God she doesn't..." He gazed out of the side window.

"Pay for it with her life? I don't think so. Look at what she's handled already. She's earned her stripes. You need to trust her judgment."

"What choice do we have?"

"None at this point. What's next?" Jessie asked. "When do we get home?"

"If all goes well, by six tomorrow morning."

"Okay. Let's get food to-go at a rest stop and get back on the road."
He reached over and put his hand on her arm. "Thank you, darlin'."
"So, back to my question. What's next?"
"Gotta take the bull by the horns, I guess."
"Which means?"
"How the hell do I know?"

The only bad thing about Maine was you couldn't smoke in restaurants, Arturo Mancuso thought. Not that Lincoln would let him smoke while he was eating anyway. Henry Lee, just back from Florida, had come straight from the Portland International Jetport and joined them for dinner at Felipe's Restaurante de México, known as Fleep's by the locals.

"I'm telling you," Lee said, "she was never there. I show her picture to the RV park manager. He says he never saw her. I knock on every trailer door. Nobody seen her. Not now, not never. I even go into town and ask around at every restaurant, every goddamn stinking little store. *Nada.*"

Lee banged his fist lightly on the table. "For days I follow the old geezers here, there, everywhere. They don't never meet her. They just poke around like tourists. I swear, they don't know nothin' about the Wiser woman. No connection with her. And yes, I did break into their RV when they was away on one of their jaunts, and there was no sign of another person living there. It was so clean you could hardly believe anyone lived there. But the only clothing and personal stuff was for the old folks. I don't know what else you want me to do."

Mancuso saw the boss's shoulders slump. This was not the news he wanted. On the way to Portland, Montgomery had told Arturo he was sure Lee would have a report that was going to make them all happy. So, the boss had had some information he hadn't shared with Mancuso. But it hadn't panned out.

"There is a connection. I'd bet my life on it," Montgomery said. "So where are the Maxwells now?"

"On their way back to Maine. Driving. Should be here soon."

"Who are the Maxwells?" Mancuso asked.

Montgomery's jaw tightened before he spoke. "Neighbors behind her house, live on Orchard Hill Road. They whisked her away right from under your nose. They've been in Florida all winter. Now they're returning. Even if she's not with them" –he looked at Lee– "and I'm not convinced she's not. They know where she is, Artie."

Arturo nodded. "Okay, surveillance on them?"

"Around the clock. Bug their house. Increase surveillance on the family. And especially watch the kids. She'll make contact with them first. I'm sure of that."

As the line moved closer to the Order Here sign, Maggie watched Angie inch forward. This was the second day she'd sat in a small booth at Reid's Coffee Shack watching Angie pick up donuts for the office of Stonefield and Wiser.

Maggie slid out of the booth and browsed at the glass front donut case, standing behind Angie. "I hear they have great glazed donuts here," she said.

Angie froze and then slowly turned toward her.

"Of course, they also have terrific Bismarks," Maggie said, smiling into Angie's incredulous eyes. She thoughtfully tapped her forefinger against her lips, still smiling. She nodded toward the donut case to indicate Angie should go ahead and order. Maggie strolled back to her booth in the far corner and watched Angie's elegant figure as she paid for the donuts, then turned and searched for Maggie. She raised her eyebrows in question, and Maggie beckoned her over.

She couldn't help giving Angie a smug smile as she slid into the booth. Angie stared at her with a quizzical, raised eyebrow. Then smiled in amusement. "There's no question, girl, that 'do' has got to go." Then her expression darkened. "Where in the blankety-blank have you been?"

"I can't tell you the whole thing now. I can't sit here that long. Don't tell anyone, not even Stoney, you've seen me. Okay?"

Angie nodded, her shrewd eyes scanning Maggie. "You want to borrow some of my clothes? They'd fit."

Maggie chuckled with delight. "My gosh, you might be right. But I don't need much right now. Thank you, anyway. Listen, I want to talk about two things. First, it's getting near tax deadline."

"Tell me about it. I'm working twelve-hour days."

"Is there any way I can help you? Answer questions? Without a computer I can't do actual returns."

"God, Maggie, if you only knew how many times I've said, 'If I could only ask her about this or about that.' I feel like I'm doing this job blindfolded."

"Make a list of questions. I'll stop here each morning at 6:30. If I can't answer them right away, I'll take them with me and have answers the next day. Will that work?"

"Lord, Maggie, you are literally the answer to my prayers."

"Now I need a favor."

"Don't tell me. You want me to get you a Bismark."

Pookie slipped his arm into the sleeve of his suit jacket and groaned. The sleeve stopped inches above his wrist. He'd grown since he'd worn the jacket to his grandfather's funeral seven months ago. Well, he didn't want to wear it anyway. Maybe just a shirt and tie would do. He hung the jacket in the closet and grabbed his black dress shoes. Now if they didn't fit...damn! They didn't. He looked at his sneakers. Naw, that wasn't going to work.

He charged down the hall and into his father's room. His father was tying his tie in front of a mirror.

"Dad, do you have a pair of shoes I could wear?"

In the mirror he could see his father's eyebrows raise in surprise, but he only said, "Yeah, look in the closet. I don't know if anything will fit, though."

That had been Pookie's thought also. He found a pair of brown wingtips, slipped his foot in, and wiggled his toes. Startled, he looked at his father. "They fit."

His father looked pleased. "The only thing is, they're brown. They don't go with navy."

"Doesn't matter. No one will look to see if I'm color coordinated. You ready, Dad?"

"Almost."

"I'll go check on Tildie."

His sister's door was open. She was bent over, holding onto the side of her bed, trying, unsuccessfully, to look under it.

"Can I help you find something?" Pookie asked.

"Oh, yeah, if you could, Sweetie. I kicked my shoes under the bed by accident. I could get down on my hands and knees, but it's too hard to get up."

He nodded, thinking, that's the third time she's called me Sweetie. But it's better than Twerp.

"No problem," he said. He still wasn't used to seeing his athletic sister's bulky, awkward form. He retrieved a pair of sandals and handed them to her. "You need a jacket?"

"Nope. All set." Tildie looked at him closely, then sat on the bed and dropped the shoes to the floor. She worked one foot into the sandals. "You're anxious to get going, aren't you?"

"Yeah, well, it's quarter to two. Gotta move. We should be there before two."

She wedged the other toe in. "Boy, are these tight. My feet must be swollen."

He considered making the ultimate sacrifice–helping her get her shoe on to save time–but he didn't have to.

"Okay, I'm ready." With one hand, she pushed herself from the bed into a standing position. "What're you waiting for, Twerp?"

Well, it was good while it lasted, Pookie thought.

He stuck his head in his father's room as they went by.

His father was buttoning his suit jacket. "I'm coming, I'm coming. Relax, we'll make it."

"Okay, but it won't work if we're late."

Ten minutes later, in front of St. Mark's Cathedral, they pulled up behind a limousine. Across the street, in a park with a bandstand in the middle, two children walked around the railing, arms out for balance. Pookie smiled, remembering when he'd done that as a kid after Mass on Sunday mornings.

He scanned the far side of the park to see if he might spot a tail. A car with tinted windows had already pulled into a parking space. A Nissan, he was pretty sure. Very sporty, and not like most of the cars you'd see around Amesbury. No one had tinted windows. He scanned the row of parallel parked cars in front of the church. There was another car with one man sitting in it. He didn't get out, and as Pookie watched, the man lit a cigarette. Strange.

On the sidewalk in front of the church, smiling people milled around, brushing wrinkles out of their clothing, chatting. Pookie jumped out of the back seat, opened the front passenger door and extended his hand to Tildie, but he kept the Nissan in his view. No one got out.

She grabbed Pookie's hand and laughed. "Brace yourself. This is getting more difficult every day."

Pookie and Tildie waited while his father parked the car halfway down the block. Still, no one got out of the Nissan.

People began filing into the church for the wedding. As his father joined him and Tildie, he made sure they were among the last to enter the church. The family in front of them turned right and went up the four steps to the sanctuary. Pookie turned left, and followed by his sister and father, descended the six steps to the church basement. They walked rapidly across the hall, passing under the white honeycomb bells that hung in the center of the room where, half an hour from now, the bride and groom would dance the first dance.

They entered the kitchen, where Effie, Violet's mother, waited surrounded by trays of food encased in plastic wrap. She catered just about every wedding and most of the funerals at St. Marks.

Pookie probably knew Effie better than anyone else in his family. Violet used to take him grocery shopping when he was a kid, and they'd stop at Violet's mother's house. Effie's kitchen smelled like vanilla or fresh baked bread, and she always had a mouthwatering snack ready for him.

Now she stood near the rear door, her blue eyes lit with excitement. She handed his father a ring of keys and whispered, "Good luck."

As they exited the rear door, Pookie glanced at his watch. They had three hours to get back here. Just outside the door was Effie's battered, black van that she used to haul around mountains of sandwiches, salads and pastries.

Pookie briefly touched Joel's sleeve. "There were two cars I didn't recognize parked out front. No one got out. While you get Tildie settled, I'll walk down the back driveway and see if the coast is clear."

At the end of the driveway, the residential street was quiet–not a car in sight. He motioned, and his father backed down the driveway and out onto the backside of the block. Pookie yanked open the door and jumped in.

He slammed the door. "Go."

Angie pulled a jacket on her three-year-old daughter and looked at her watch. To Maggie she said, "They should be here in a few minutes. We're out of here. We're going to visit *our* grandma, aren't we girls? Be back in a couple to take you home. Well, not home, but you know what I mean."

"Why don't you stay?" Maggie asked. She was looking forward to this, but she'd been nervous since she woke up this morning.

Angie raised her eyebrows. "Are you kidding? You haven't seen your family in over seven months. I don't think so. Come on, ladies. Auntie Maggie has some catching up to do."

Angie and the two girls were out the door and gone. Maggie heard Angie's car disappear down the country road. Her tension increased with every breath. It had been so long. They had all changed. And they were a close family unit. She was now an outsider. What would they say to each other?

She heard the van rumble into the driveway. By the time she got to the doorway, Joel was helping Tildie out while Pookie stood by. Pookie looked up and saw her in the doorway. He waved self-consciously, a lopsided grin on his face.

Then, Tildie looked up, saw Maggie, and screamed, "Grandma." She ran toward Maggie with Joel trying to keep up and hold her elbow. Tildie threw her arms exuberantly around Maggie, the most emotion she'd ever seen Tildie display.

"I'm so glad you're here. I couldn't wait. I just couldn't wait."

She finally released Maggie and was replaced by Joel, who gave his mother a quick hug then said, "Next time you decide to leave, would you please ask permission first? We'd have all turned you down, though. Man, it is good to have you back. Let's get inside. There isn't much traffic on this road, but we still shouldn't hang around out here."

Maggie glanced at Pookie, who was still standing by the van, looking as shy as she had ever seen him. She knew how he felt.

"Coming, Nick? Angie and I fixed a huge lunch–enough for an army." He had been signing his letters to her as Nick.

"Enough for an army? Then barely enough for Pook...Nick," Tildie said, laughing.

Pookie gave a sheepish grin and walked stiffly toward Maggie. He did not look ready for a hug. As he approached, she was amazed at his height–and his shoulders were broader. The Wiser jaw was now evident in his face. He had metamorphosed into a young man–one who was still not quite comfortable with his growing body.

Maggie sensed that Pookie needed to keep some distance between them. Okay. Little by little. They had the rest of their lives to work it out.

"Pook-Nick," she said, glancing Tildie's way. "Now why didn't we think of that before?"

"Yeah, sounds like a Russian spaceship or something," he said.

Maggie opened the door and led them inside. "Let's eat."

Angie had been right about making this visit a luncheon. While they filled their plates from the buffet and settled around Angie's kitchen table, they caught her up on news, telling her about the major events they'd experienced, supporting the stories with funny trivia. The mood was light and joyful. Maggie didn't spoil it by telling them she'd had another life-threatening event.

At the end of the meal Pookie said, "I'll help you with dishes, Grandma."

"Great! Let's go sit in the living room, Dad." Tildie said. "Before we get drafted to help."

"I've enjoyed reading about your games," Maggie said, when Pookie joined her at the sink. "The newspapers and your letters."

"I can't believe I'm a starter. Seems funny playing with the big guys."

"You must be as tall as most of them."

"Yeah, well, you know what I mean. The rest of the team are juniors and seniors–mostly seniors. But they're pretty cool with it. There's this one guy who's been helping me with defense..."

And there they were, talking just as if no time had passed. He finally got around to mentioning his friend Ellen.

"Does she go to your games?" Maggie asked.

"No, she's on the girls' basketball team. But we talk about our games. She's cool."

"I can't wait to meet her," Maggie said. "What does she look like?"

"Let me show you." He dried his hands on a towel and pulled from his shirt pocket a photo that he just happened to have with him. There were six teenagers sitting on the floor around the coffee table in Maggie's living room. A board game was open on the table. "Dad's old Axis and Allies game. We found it in the basement. This is Ellen."

She was sitting next to Pookie and grinning at the camera–a wholesome, attractive brunette with an engaging smile.

"She's pretty, Nick. And from what you've said, she's smart, too."

He put the picture back in his pocket. "Straight A's."

"Who took the photo?"

"Tildie." He cleared his throat. "She's, ah, been pretty cool, lately."

"Nice change, huh?" Maggie smiled up at Pookie.

"You can say that again."

Pookie turned away and plunged his hands into the dishwater to open the drain. "Are you really home for good?"

"Yes. Here in Amesbury. But you realize why I can't come home yet, don't you?"

He nodded. "It's okay...as long as you're back here. And then, pretty soon, you will come home, would you say?"

"I hope so. I'll work out a way we can visit until I can come home. Probably no bike rides for now, though."

"You think when they tried to run us over, they were trying to get you?" His voice was tense as he busied himself with rinsing the soapsuds down the drain with the sprayer.

"'Fraid so. You were right."

He nodded. She could tell he still had something to say. She waited.

"Grandma, I am glad you're back. You don't know." There was a quaver in his voice.

"But you've had a lot of time with your father. And sister."

"Yeah, and that's been great. Really great. But it's just, well, it's still kind of empty without you. You know what I mean?"

"Yeah. I know what you mean."

"Hey, listen. If you promise you'll only go away for vacations, we've got something for you." He looked at his watch. "We'll have to hurry. We've got to get back to the church. I'll be right back." He dashed out of the kitchen, through the living room, and outside.

In the living room, Tildie and Joel looked at the door expectantly. Pookie came back into the living room with a big, wrapped package and put it in front of Maggie.

"Late Christmas present," Tildie said.

Maggie pulled away the paper from a large suitcase–a matching piece for the one Sandy had given her.

"Oh, my. It's beautiful. This is wonderful. And it *matches*…but how did you know?"

Pookie's face took on a teasing look. "We collaborated with that old guy, Sandy."

"Oh, my. I'm overwhelmed. I know I'll use it a lot." And she did suddenly know she would not let Amesbury pull her into a rut. She would travel. With matching luggage. She laughed. "Thank you all, so much. Thank you, Pookie…sorry…Nick."

"Okay, folks, we gotta go," Pookie said. "We've only got fifteen minutes to get to the church."

He gave Tildie a hand, pulled her out of the low couch, and herded them to the door. Maggie exchanged amused looks with Joel at Pookie's taking the leadership role.

Joel and Tildie each gave Maggie a quick hug and kiss and headed for the van. Now Pookie was ready. He enveloped her in a bear hug. "Take care, Grandma. Stay safe. See you soon."

And they were gone.

* * *

Jewel drove back to the garage where he stored the Nissan. What a waste of time. He had been sure something was up. He locked the garage and walked to his apartment. He'd heard Lee and Mancuso discussing it on the phone. Mancuso thought it was funny that the family made a big deal about the wedding and talked about it quite a few times, but they had never received an invitation in the mail. Maybe it had been handed to a member of the family. But none was found in a search of the house, not even in the trash. Mancuso thought that was strange. So did Jewel. He knew Mancuso was planning on checking it out, so he decided to do the same. The family arrived, dressed up for a wedding. They went into the church, they came out of the church, and then drove home. What was he missing? Was he overthinking this?

Effie slipped the army jacket over her husband's arm and up over his shoulders and straightened his tie. Though his shoulders were rounded now, it still fit pretty well. She thought of the many times he had worn it proudly in every Amesbury patriotic parade, the fourth of July, Memorial Day, and more than a few Veterans Day ceremonies.

He'd slipped in and out of the past more frequently this year. Still, her heart squeezed in happiness every time he looked at her over his cup of coffee and said, "You make the best damn coffee in the world, Effie, my darling."

This morning, he was firmly in the past. "Come on, soldier. It's time to move out," Effie said.

PFC George Lizotte looked around, puzzled. "But it's still light out. We never move until dark. What's going on?"

"We're moving the troops closer to the front earlier tonight, so we'll be in place when night falls. Climb in the jeep, Private," said Effie.

"Makes sense." He yanked the jeep door open and climbed into the passenger seat. "Wait! Sarge, you have to wait. I forgot my M1."

"It's okay, Private Lizotte, our weapons are in back."

George nodded. "We hit the mountains tonight? I heard we're headed for..." George searched his memory. Damn. This was important. What did they call it? He worried for a moment–his memory wasn't what it should be. Then it came. "El Alamein."

"Right you are. Sharp."

Whew! He'd pulled that one out. As they bumped along, he compared the terrain of North Africa to his native Maine. Sure was some different. Who would have believed a Maine boy, born and bred, would end up fighting for his country in North Africa?

Funny. He'd hardly even heard of the place, and now it seemed more real than his hometown of Sherman Mills.

"Why're we stopping here?" he asked. The jeep was backing up to some sort of building.

"Got to pick up a few more men." The Sarge climbed out of the jeep.

Effie Lizotte looked at her husband as she closed the van door. "Stay put, soldier. I'll only be a minute." At the rear of their van, she opened the double doors and nodded at the passenger in the back. Then she looked toward Jessie and Wade Maxwell's house.

Jessie waved to Effie as she descended the front stairs and headed for the van.

Wade followed. "Hey, there, Effie. Looks like maybe this spring weather is here to stay."

"Looks like it. Thanks for pitching in to help me. I needed a few more muscles than George and I have, if you roll us both together."

"I'm not up to much lifting, but Jessie here is as strong as a horse. And stubborn as a mule."

"Hey, hey!" Jessie reached the van first. "If we're talking stubborn, I think the first fifty people I ask would say 'mule' is Wade Maxwell's middle name." She smiled at Effie. "Glad to help. Where're we going?"

"Not far. Why don't you climb in among the sandwiches? I got a couple of bench seats in there."

"Okay. Wade, you go first so I can give you a boost," Jessie said.

"Smartass," Wade retorted.

Wade glanced into the rear of the van as he reached up for a handhold. Maggie got a charge out of his startled glance. Using the strength in his arms, he propelled himself into the van with more force than she would have guessed he could muster.

"Whoa back. Look what we have here." His eyes twinkled with merriment. He lowered his weight onto the bench seat across from her. He tipped an imaginary cap at her. "Well done, ma'am."

Jessie plunked down beside Maggie. "As I live and breathe."

The van doors clanged shut. Effie went around and got into the driver's seat. George turned to look at the passengers in the back.

"Hey, Wade, old man. How've you been?"

"Not bad, George. Yourself?"

"Pretty good for an old timer. How about a game of checkers later?"

"Done."

George turned back around and started a lucid conversation with Effie. Maggie still hadn't become used to his slipping in and out of reality. She was in awe at how easily Effie handled it. "It must break your heart when he does that," she'd said to Effie when she first went to stay with them two weeks ago.

"It did the first year. It was hard–and scary–when the man I'd always leaned on, kept leaving me to live in the past. But you know, now I thank God every day that at least he's happy. I've visited the nursing home he'll have to go to when I can't take care of him anymore. Some of the people there are violent or so frightened they cling to the walls. I think of his form of illness as a blessing."

"Maggie," said Wade. "I have to hand it to you. I didn't know how we were going to find you."

"We were afraid you would call us or just come by," Jessie said. "We figured our house probably wasn't safe, and we were right. Wade found four bugs."

"Didn't want to remove the devices and tip 'em off we're on to them, but I was a might bit worried."

"I thought that could be the case," Maggie said. "I still don't know how they found me in Beaufort, but somehow they connected you with me."

Wade nodded. "I think so too but haven't figured out how, as yet. I have to say, you look a little different than when I last saw you."

"Becoming," Jessie said dryly.

Maggie patted the spiked hair. "Aunt Belle disguised me. And it's working, I think."

Wade leaned forward with his forearms on his thighs. "What have you been doing since you got here? Do you have a lead on anything?"

"I do have a couple of things to tell you."

"It'll have to wait," Effie said from the front seat. "We're here, and you two want to at least look like you're helping."

"Why're we stopping, Sarge?" George asked.

"Rations, Private. We have to unload rations for the men at the front lines."

Maggie stayed put while Jessie, Wade, Effie, and George carried trays of little cakes and finger sandwiches into the church basement.

When they were finished and back in the van, Wade's face cracked into his characteristic smile. "Okay, Maggie, shoot. Oh, sorry. I understand you don't believe in shooting."

Maggie looked at Jessie, but Jessie shrugged. "I told him you were nervous, that's all. And I told him you said you would never shoot anyone. Even in self-defense."

"And you're never going to have to. Take my word for it. Just a precaution." He stroked the sides of his mustache.

"But first, we have to get you a new cellular phone with a Maine number. I don't know for sure, but I have a feeling it was our phones that gave us away. Maybe somebody found a phone bill in the trash? Can't figure out how. We were careful not to leave our trash in the trailer whenever we left. Anyway, let's start fresh. I'll have one for you by tomorrow. Jessie and I have new ones."

"Yes, I had the same feeling that the phones somehow gave us away. Funny, last year, I couldn't imagine ever owning one. Now I've gotten so used to a mobile phone, I can't imagine not owning one. It's been difficult to skulk around and make contacts without a phone. Should it be in your name for now?"

"I think that's wise," Wade said.

"And second?" she asked.

"Are you ready to carry the PPK again? Belle gave it to us to bring home. It's in my gun safe."

Maggie nodded. "Yes. Before the last attack, I felt silly carrying a gun, but now I'm ready to lug the damn thing everywhere. I don't plan to use it, but I'll carry it right here." She patted the large fanny pack around her middle. "We better talk quickly. We're almost back."

"I'll just keep driving around," Effie said. "Go to it."

An hour later, they pulled into the Maxwells' driveway. "I think we've got a good idea here," Wade said. "Give me some time to think on it, fill in the details."

"Need some help, Sarge?" George asked as Effie opened the door.

"Sure would appreciate it, Private. Why don't you let these KP men out of the truck?"

Wade gazed speculatively at George for a long moment as he got out of the van to come around back. "Hey, Maggie. What did you say that guy's name is who runs the NADCO show here in Amesbury? Montgomery?"

"Lincoln Montgomery."

"Hmm. I think I'm getting a brainstorm. Let's talk again in a few days."

The van doors opened, and George saluted. "General. Welcome to North Africa."

Wade returned the salute. "Thank you, Private Lizotte. Much obliged."

Wade nodded at Maggie as he departed. "Keep the faith, lady. We'll get through this."

CHAPTER 18

In the Appleton building, Kathy Omsbury had a small office and no assistant, but she was still the executive secretary of the Amesbury branch of NADCO. Making the transition from New York City to Diddley Poop, Maine was the hardest thing she'd ever done. Only the generous pay raise made the change worthwhile. She hoped she wouldn't be in this burgh much longer, though. Five days a week was way too long to leave her boyfriend, Justin, on his own. Men could get so restless. But yesterday, Mr. Montgomery hinted they would be going back to New York soon. She couldn't wait to get back to her old position. And Justin.

The glass outer door opened, and an old man shuffled in. Kathy took in his baggy work pants held up by suspenders and inwardly rolled her eyes, but she maintained a professional demeanor. She'd get rid of him in short order.

"Yes, can I help you?"

"I'm here to see the general."

"The general. Do you mean you wish to see Mr. Montgomery?"

"That's him. General Montgomery."

"No one can see Mr. Montgomery without an appointment. And I'm afraid," she said as she pretended to look through an appointment book, "I'm afraid he's not going to be free for three or four…"

"I must speak with the general. It's urgent and top secret."

"…weeks." Okay. She had a fruitcake on her hands. She never dealt with anything like this in New York. Frontline receptionists dealt with crackpots. She'd been part of the inner sanctum. "You'll have to leave." Her hand moved casually and slowly to the phone while she tried to decide whom she'd call.

The door flung open, and an elderly woman hurried into the reception area. "George, there you are!"

The white-haired woman strode to George and took his elbow. "It's okay, Private. We can go home now."

She turned toward Kathy. "I'm Effie, his wife. I can take care of him."

Kathy was weak with relief. "Thank you."

"He's mostly harmless. Most of the time. He was just getting his medication changed. Down the hall with Dr. Alexander. The psychiatrist. We'll be going now."

Effie made coaxing noises, slowly turning the man around. Suddenly, the door flew open again, banging back against an end table.

"Be careful!" Kathy said. Too sharply–she had to get a hold of herself.

A disheveled woman with white hair piled on top of her head looked frantic. "Please help. My sister Violet has fallen, and I can't get her up."

"I'll call 911," Kathy offered, reaching for the phone again.

"No, she's not injured. And she damn sure can't afford an ambulance, young woman. I just need a hand to get her to her feet. Now please help."

Kathy looked hopefully at Effie.

Effie smiled at Kathy. "I'd be glad to help. Will you just look after George, here, for a minute?"

As if. "No, that's okay." Kathy nodded to the newcomer. "I'll help you." She scurried from behind her desk. She wasn't going to be left alone with the nut case. She glanced at the old woman tugging the man's sleeve. They shouldn't be in here alone.

"We're on our way out, young lady," Effie said. 'I've got everything under control. We'll be right behind you."

On tiptoe, Effie whispered into her husband's ear. "Private Lizotte. You must get the message to General Montgomery before Mussolini catches up with us. That's his office, in there."

George charged forward, grabbed the door handle and flung open the door.

The man behind the desk jumped to his feet. "What the hell?"

George saluted and waited for a return salute. Effie moved up beside George. "At ease, Private." Looking at Lincoln Montgomery, she tapped her finger to her temple and tipped her head discreetly toward George.

Lincoln Montgomery's dark eyes widened with anger. He looked beyond them through the open door, evidently wondering how Ms. Peroxide had let them get by.

"Sorry to interrupt. The Private here has just had a spell, and we had to get his medication changed. At the psychiatrist's." She tipped her head back toward the open door. "Down the hall."

"Well, get him out of here."

Effie had already seen everything she needed to know, but now her back was up, and she was inclined to be less obliging.

"Would really help, sir, if you saluted him."

"What?" Lincoln looked incredulous.

"Salute him, young man. He'll be more likely to leave without a fuss if he completes his mission."

Lincoln glared at Effie, his jaw clenching noticeably. She smiled and looked calmly back at him. She could see the anger on Lincoln's face fray toward indecision. He probably doesn't know how to salute, she thought.

She pulled a smart salute. "Like this."

Looking self-conscious, Lincoln hesitantly put his hand to his eyebrow.

George saluted again. "Private Lizotte, Sir. I've got a message for you, Sir. Top Secret. From Major Richards. Right here." He pulled a piece of folded newspaper from his shirt pocket and handed it to Lincoln.

Lincoln leaned across his desk and took the paper reluctantly, as if it were covered with a virus.

"Thank you, ah..." Lincoln's eyes strayed toward Effie, looking for guidance. He was a man used to being in control, and he was going to hate the memory of this moment, she thought with satisfaction.

"Private Lizotte." Effie grinned innocently. "Just dismiss him, Sir."

"What?"

"Just say, 'dismissed, Private Lizotte.'"

Lincoln brought his hand awkwardly to his eyebrow again, this time trying to look more business-like. "Dismissed, Private Lizotte."

Beaming, George snapped a salute, did an about face, and marched from the room. A wave of love for her husband washed over her, and tears threatened to spill. Coming back into her office, Kathy watched, mouth open, as Effie joined her husband, and they marched by and out of the door.

The elevator door slid open. Jessie and Violet, grinning from ear to ear, were waiting inside. Effie nodded at her daughter as George stepped in and turned to face the door. They rode down in silence and dispersed on the sidewalk, Violet turning left, Jessie crossing the street, and Effie and George turning right.

Effie patted George on the back affectionately. "We've had enough K-rations, Private. While we're on leave, let's get some good home cooking. How about a hamburger and some fries? You've earned them."

He certainly has, she thought. Mission accomplished.

* * *

The owner of Pelletier's Realty and Management beamed at Wade across the desk. "So, you going to start up a business, Coach?"

"I'm not your coach anymore, Rick. You can call me Wade." Ricky Pelletier had been his go-to pitcher when Wade coached Little League a couple of dozen years ago.

"Right. Of course. So, you're interested in renting an office in the Appleton Building, Mr. Maxwell?"

"Wade. Unless you want me to call you 'Ricky.'"

"No, sir. Rick is fine. So..." Rick frowned, squinting as he looked out of the window. "I don't think I can, sir. Can we settle for Mr. Maxwell?"

Wade chuckled. "Sure, Rick. And to answer your question, I'm thinking about opening a consulting business. Just askin' around to see how much it's going to set me back. Heard you had a couple of empty offices on the fifth floor."

"Yeah, that's right, but the elevator only goes to the fourth. The owners don't expect I'll ever be able to rent them, so I could give you a bargain. But there's the stairs..." He looked doubtfully at Wade.

"How much?"

"How many people will be working there?'

"Oh, one or two. Why?"

"Just thinking about water and sewage costs. You have to pay for your own electricity. What do you think about four hundred if I don't have to clean it up? It hasn't been occupied since I took over management five years ago. There's nothing up there but dust, and there'll be plenty of that."

"Speaking of cleaning, do the tenants make their own arrangements?"

"No. For security reasons and to avoid having two or three cleaning companies rattling around the building at night, we contract with one. If you're interested in the service, we bill you monthly. By the square foot."

"We'll do our own cleaning. That reminds me of another question. What about security?"

"There isn't much. Both entrances to Appleton are locked at 8:00 p.m. when Dr. Lester's last patient leaves. I also have a man, Ray Tibbetts–we call him Tibbs–who checks the building twice a night. He has a key, goes in and checks all floors. One tenant has a suite on the fourth floor. They put in their own security system. They used Morissette Locksmith, if you're interested."

"I'll think about it. Do the tenants have keys to the entrances?"

"Oh, sure. Have to. Some nights people work late at the office. Come in after supper to catch up. That sort of thing."

"Rick, I don't have to look any further. Can I give you a check for two months?"

"Two months' rent is good. You sure you don't want to go look at it first?"

"No. I'm sure it'll do. Might stop by in the evening."

"Sure, Coach. Let me get the keys for you.

"It's for a good cause," Wade said.

Jim Sedgley wiped the sweat from his forehead with his sleeve. "I don't know why I'm even listening to you, you son of a gun. You're going to get me in a pile of trouble. No, I can't do it. Opening locks is how I make an honest living."

"I'm not asking you to break the law. I just need a little information and the loan of some equipment."

"Yeah, sure. So you can start a new hobby."

"Right. Listen, I've told you our story."

"And you have my sympathy."

"Budge a little on this, Jim. These are bad dudes we're talking about. You don't even have to be there."

"Well, I won't be. Wife and I are taking off for Colorado to visit the grandkids."

"There you go. But you'll help me out."

"Yes, dammit all. But I'm telling you, you rascal, if I get into trouble, you're putting my grandkids through college."

Wade picked up his folding cribbage board from the passenger seat of the pickup and got out of the vehicle. The sign in front of the VFW said Cribbage Ev ry Satu d y Nite. The last "y" hung at an angle. He didn't bother to lock the truck's doors. If a bug were going to be planted, it would have been done by now. He and Jessie didn't talk about anything but daily life and world news when they were in the truck.

He entered the VFW but avoided the bar and hall, where a dozen or so guys were already playing cribbage. The hallway that led to the restrooms ended in a door that opened onto a service alley. With his hand on the doorknob, Wade hesitated. He'd done a dry run last week; it had gone perfectly. Still, his plan would go down the tubes if a tail spotted him sneaking out the back.

He opened the door a crack. A Ford Escort sat in the alley with Violet behind the wheel. She nodded; the coast was clear. He was worried, though. Violet was sharp, but she wasn't a pro. Any tail following her would be.

Wade slipped out of the door and into the car. He placed his cribbage board on his lap. "Looks like we're good to go."

Violet nodded, causing sprits of red hair that had escaped from her bun to bob up and down. "I did just as you said. I think I'm getting the hang of this." She eased out of the alley and into the quiet street.

Wade watched the rearview mirrors as Violet followed his directions. After two minutes he said, "Okay, we're clear. Let's go get Jess." Jessie had left the house ten minutes after him in their old, faded red Chevy pickup truck, which they hardly used except to take the lawnmower and snow blower for repairs.

A few minutes later, they pulled into the rear of the Congregational Church. Organ music emanated from the church, and choir voices lifted in exultation. Jessie was waiting in the shadows. She hopped in the back seat of the Escort, and they rolled down the driveway into the residential street.

"Mighty pretty singing back there, Jessie," Violet said. "Would have been better with your voice added, of course. How long is choir practice, you say? I reckon you practice longer when you're gettin' ready for Easter."

"Yeah, usually it's an hour, but tonight it's two. Let's step on it. I want to get back there before anyone leaves, sees the pickup, and wonders why it's there, since I didn't come to practice."

Violet accelerated. In another minute, they were behind the Appleton Building. Wade used his key, and the three entered the building from the back door.

The elevator was in full view from outside the building, so they took the stairs. Jessie had no trouble since she walked two miles a day for exercise, but Wade gasped for breath trying to keep up with her. A wheezing Violet arrived last on the fourth floor.

Maggie was waiting in the stairwell. Wade stopped to catch his breath for a second before stepping out into the hall and waving the women to stay put.

Before tonight, his team, consisting of Jessie, Effie, and Violet had scoped out the building. No one took notice as they shuffled along the hallways gathering data—what hours each office kept, when Tibbs, the security guard, made his rounds, when the cleaning crew came in, and, more importantly, who worked late.

He stopped in front of NADCO's outer door and opened his "cribbage board." Inside the box was a set of fifty tryout keys that he'd borrowed from Jim Sedgley. As rapidly as his stiff fingers would move, he selected keys and tried them. He also had his old pick set with him, but his skills had deteriorated, and the tryout keys would probably be faster. The lock was a common one, and the twelfth key turned in the lock.

He turned to the stairwell door and nodded. Maggie, Jessie, and Violet dashed down the hall and into the dark office.

Wade locked the outer door behind them with the dead bolt. Maggie and Violet stood back in the shadows, but Jessie stayed next to the door, where the upper glass panel of the door allowed her to peek out and see the elevator and stairwell entrance.

The lock on the inner door was going to be more of a challenge. After twenty-five tries, he lost patience and pulled out his pick set. He was losing precious time. He removed the tension wrench and favorite pick from the black leather case. He slid the tension wrench into the keyhole and inserted the pick beside it. Applying sight pressure on the wrench, he manipulated the pick. "I should be able to get this in a minute or two. Little rusty."

Wade's attempt with a third pick was successful, and the cylinder turned. "Showtime," he whispered. He opened the door, activating the motion sensor of the security system NADCO had installed. He had thirty seconds to deactivate the alarm. The LED readout said System Activated. Jim had given him nine numbers to use. Jim was friends with Frank Morissette of Morissette Locksmith, who'd installed the system. They covered for each other, and they each knew the code the other used for installations.

Using the keypad, Wade typed out the code, hoping Morissette was still using the same one. He slipped and got one number wrong. He started again.

"Twenty-one seconds," Jessie said.

He forced himself to go slowly.

"Twenty-eight seconds. Twenty-nine."

"Done," Wade muttered.

The LED read System Deactivated.

"Nothing to worry about. A second to spare," he said.

"We weren't worried, love," Jessie said.

Wade rolled his eyes. "Yeah, neither was I."

The four of them were in the dark office in seconds.

From a canvas bag Jessie carried, she pulled out a stack of black construction paper that unfolded into a three-foot by six-foot mat. Wade retrieved the masking tape. Pushing aside the drapes, he noted the car parked half a block away.

Pookie and Tildie waited inside Tildie's car. The kids had wanted to help, and Wade figured it would look natural for a couple of youngsters to be sitting in a car outside a pizza shop. They were thrilled to be lookouts watching the front door, armed with a new cell phone that Wade had provided for them.

He stretched to hold the black paper over the window while Jessie taped it.

Wade pulled the camera out of the bag. It was much smaller than the one he had used years ago for the same purpose.

"I'll take the right side of the desk," Jessie said. "Violet, you take the other. Maggie, get yourself over here with that itty, bitty spy-type camera."

Maggie had already burned one roll of film practicing for this event. She fished the camera out of her fanny pack.

Wade took photos of the room with the Polaroid from every angle, each time laying the prints on the seat of the couch, letting them develop as he took the next.

Jessie examined the contents of the drawers, deciding what was important. She guided the women in placing documents on the desk, photographing them, and putting them back exactly the way they found them. Paper clips were removed and carefully replaced in the dents they had left in the paper. Jessie removed staples, put them in her pocket, and, after the pages were photographed, re-stapled into the old holes.

Glancing over his shoulder, Wade caught Maggie's look of incredulity as she watched Jessie re-staple the pages. "Pretty good, huh?"

Maggie nodded without taking her eyes off Jessie's fast-moving hands.

"The desk is done except for the locked drawer," Jessie finally announced.

"Okay. Let me pick it. The good stuff will be in there."

Maggie's cellular phone suddenly beeped, freezing all of them for a breath-holding instant. Wade looked at Maggie and nodded. She pulled the phone from her fanny pack and pushed a button. "Yes?" Her body was stiff with tension.

They were all tense, their eyes were riveted on Maggie except for Jessie, who had moved to the door with her hand hovering over the light switch. Maggie nodded and said, "Thanks. Yes, everything is okay." She ended the call and put the phone back in her pack.

"Pookie says to check the window. There's a slice of light shining out."

Wade moved rapidly to the window, locating the problem. Jessie was instantly beside him tearing off a long piece of masking tape, helping to pat it into place. When he turned around, he could see Violet, eyes wide-open, still rigid from the scare. "The last sixty seconds was a drill," he said. "Should a real emergency occur, please drop to the floor and cover your head with your arms." He grinned, and she relaxed.

The desk drawer lock yielded easily. The women got busy again. "How much longer?" he asked Jessie.

"It's a hanging file folder drawer, and it's packed. At least fifteen minutes—maybe twenty."

Wade roamed the room, moving pictures aside and then realigning them carefully. "We're still in our timeframe for getting you back to the church."

"How much longer we got?" Jessie asked.

He glanced at his watch again. "Half an hour."

"Minus five minutes for traveling and five minutes leeway so I don't meet anyone coming out of the church."

"That gives us twenty minutes. Can you do it?"

"Do we have a choice?" Jessie asked, chuckling.

Wade moved to the wall opposite the windows and moved an Ansel Adams print.

"Bingo," he said softly. "A wall safe. By the looks of it, it hasn't been here for long. The painter's caulk looks to be on the newish side."

Jessie looked at him, and he shook his head. Safes were not his forte. When he'd been twenty-two years old and in the OSS, he'd been part of a team assigned to break into foreign embassies when the United States government suspected they were being used as a base for espionage. He had run the camera and watched in awe every time an experienced safe cracker opened a safe in less than three hours.

"We'll have to come back. I don't care what we find in the desk, the safe is here for a reason. We need to get inside."

Jessie nodded, her hands flying to unfasten the documents. She handed them to Violet, who placed them for Maggie. As soon as Maggie took the photo, Violet handed the documents back to Jessie. She refastened them and placed them back in the drawer.

"Time?" asked Jessie.

Wade looked at his watch. "You have to be done now, Jessie, my darling. Violet, you take Jessie to the truck behind the church and come back and get Maggie and me. Jessie can't be late, and we still have a few things to do here. We'll meet you later at the back entrance."

Jessie nodded. She and Violet hurried out of the office.

He put the Polaroid camera in the canvas bag and took out a soft, white cloth. He wiped the file cabinet, the chair, the fronts of the desk drawers, and the shiny desktop methodically and thoroughly. The women's prints would still be on the documents because it would have been too difficult to handle the paper with gloves in the amount of time they had. If he did his job well enough, no one would have a reason to suspect the break-in, so they wouldn't be dusting the documents–or anything else.

He put the chair back behind the desk that Violet had shoved out of the way. Then he picked up the Polaroids and studied each one. He repositioned the chair, compared it to the snapshot. Then he repositioned articles on the desk that Jessie had pushed back to make room for them to work.

Out of the canvas bag, Wade pulled the folding vacuum cleaner that he used in his Airstream. He plugged it in near the door and vacuumed the area behind the desk. "Taking the footprints out of the rug. There were hardly any when we arrived."

When he finished the entire floor, he laid the vacuum by the door. "Let me look at the photos once more." He estimated the exact amount the drapes had been pulled when they entered the office. "Okay, I'm going to the windows. Shut off the lights and come help me. Walk where I do."

They worked together to pull off the blackout mats. Wade adjusted the drapes. He nodded for Maggie to return to the door. "Remember, take the same path. We'll make the approximately the same amount of footprints that were here when we arrived."

Wade stopped to think through a mental checklist to see if he'd forgotten anything.

He shouldered the bags and headed for the stairwell. All in all, seemed like a successful evening, but they'd know more when the photos came back. No doubt, though–they'd have to go back in. They'd need Jim.

Then he remembered. Staggered by the enormity of his own stupidity, he turned around and reentered the office. In the inner office, he tapped in the code. The LED read System Activated. He wiped for prints, relocked the doors in much less time than it had taken to open them.

Wearily, he headed out, wondering what other mistakes he might have made.

Chapter 19

Along with hundreds of taxpayers who had come to voice their opinions on next year's school budget, Wade and Jessie made their way into the junior high auditorium. Not far behind them might be a tail.

Inside, Wade caught Violet's eye and nodded. Slowly, he and Jessie made their way across the back of the gym until they got to the bleachers that lined the wall. Wade pointed toward the center of the bleachers and waved as if to have someone save them seats. As the throng pressed forward, Wade and Jessie allowed themselves to be nudged back beside the bleachers, toward the door that led to the locker room.

Pookie was waiting for them inside the door. He guided them through the boys' locker room and a maze of corridors that made Wade wonder how the kids found any place in the building without a map.

"Here it is," Pookie said. "The band room. I hid here until Mr. Languet locked the door at 3:30, and then I unlocked it."

Wade held up his hand, and Pookie slapped a stinging high five.

"Good job, Pook. Sorry…Nick."

Jessie smiled and produced a twelve-inch Subway sandwich and a can of Pepsi from her canvas bag. "Glad to see you're putting your intelligence to good use."

"Thanks. I'm starving! I'll eat this as soon as I come back with Violet. How long are we staying?"

"We have to leave when the shindig downstairs is over," Wade said. "Cars can't be sitting in an empty parking lot. You have any problem with someone tailing you?"

"Well, he's not a problem." Pookie looked satisfied. "Guy thinks he's a mountain bike champ, but hah! I can beat 'im. I'm glad the weather warmed up so I can give this guy a good workout."

He unwrapped his sandwich and took a male adolescent-sized bite. After he swallowed, he said, "Guy rode back and forth in front of the school for two hours. I just did my algebra homework, looked out once in a while. Must have been almost five o'clock when he goes up to the field to check. When he was out of sight, I ran out, got my bike, and brought it inside. You should have seen him when he came back and saw my bike gone. He bounced the front wheel of his bike up and down so hard you'd have thought the tire would have come right off the rim." Pookie demonstrated the action. "Then he threw the bike on the ground." He grinned lopsidedly.

Wade chuckled. "A little put out, you say? And then?"

"He left."

"Imagine he headed for your house, hoping he'd pick you up there. Proud of you, boy."

Pookie bit off another huge hunk of sandwich, then rewrapped the rest. "Gotta go. Be right back with Violet," he said through a mouthful.

Jessie opened her canvas bag, pulled out several large brown envelopes, and handed them to Wade. "Too bad Maggie can't be here."

"Yeah, the van being in the shop for repairs put her on a real short leash. Probably for the best, though. Won't worry about her as much. Maybe that table over there? I'll pull over three chairs."

They set up a work area, and Wade divided the photos into three piles. The door opened, and Violet, Pookie, and Maggie walked in.

"Well, if that ain't a shit-eatin' grin, I don't know what is. Now how in hell did you pull this off, Margaret Wiser?" Wade asked.

"I phoned a cab."

"What?" Wade was stunned.

"Had a cab pick me up behind Dick's Market–the store down the corner from Effie's."

Pookie grinned from ear to ear. "I told her to have him leave her off behind the school near the cafeteria door. I put a wedge in the door so she could get in." He settled into a chair by the door, unwrapped his sandwich and took a sip of Pepsi.

Wade shook his head. Well, why not? It could work. Hell, it did work. He knew she walked to the store along the railroad track that ran behind Effie's. She didn't have to come out on the street until she got to the corner. And she'd earned the right to be here.

"Your idea?" he asked her.

"Sort of." She shrugged. "I was pacing the living room floor a couple of days ago. I think I was distracting George from his movie because he looked up and said, 'You want me to call you a cab?'" She laughed. "Then I thought, why not?"

Wade guessed he'd have to get used to her doing things her own way. He nodded. "Well, all right then, let's get to work. Pull over another chair, Maggie.

When you're done with supper, Pook, why don't you throw your bike in my trunk? You can go home through the backyard."

Pookie nodded. "I'm gonna go finish my homework in the locker room. I'll be back in an hour?"

"Two's okay," Wade said.

Pookie nodded and left with the rest of his sandwich.

Wade turned toward the women. "Jessie and I've been over all of the photos. Let's look through 'em while I tell you what we've found."

An hour and a half later, Maggie tapped her pen on the pad of white lined paper she'd filled with notes. "By the looks of it, once they have the mall started, they're planning to divide up the Archibald Estate and sell a third of it to a developer. But they don't own the land yet. No one even knows it's up for grabs."

She looked closer at her notes. "The foreclosure sale is coming right up. May eleventh. Today is April eighteenth. Less than a month to go."

"No, the sale is May tenth. Says right here in this letter from the bank." Jessie shuffled through the photos and pulled one out. "May tenth at eleven a.m. at the bank."

Maggie found a photo in her stack. "This clipping from the newspaper says May eleventh at ten a.m. A typo?"

"Hot damn!" Wade said. "Under these circumstances? No. Appears like an error, but I think it was deliberate to be sure no one showed up to give a competing bid."

"I wish we could be there to give a competing bid!" Maggie said. She tapped her pen lightly on the notepad. "Wait, why can't we?"

Wade nodded. "Suppose we could. How much they asking for a cash down payment?"

She thought of the money from Sam's estate. "Ten thousand. I can do that." Hell, she could buy the land outright and rename it the Samuel Wiser Wildlife Refuge.

"Sounds like a plan," Wade said. "We'll talk over the details later."

Maggie nodded. "What do you think about this letter from Roy LaCroix to board members of NADCO, copied to Lincoln Montgomery?" She looked at Wade.

"Refresh my memory. What's it say?"

"It talks about plans to develop the refuge acreage once the mall is close to completion. 'We are certain that NADCO will be…'" she ran her finger across the photo, skimming. "Yada, yada...here it is... 'we anticipate

372

a groundbreaking in August.'" She looked up. "August? They would still have to have testing done, get the permits, get electricity out there...and they don't own the land yet."

Wade shifted in his chair. "No problem. I think this outfit knows shortcuts."

"Otis was right," Jessie said. "Everything he told Sam was right. The mall was only part of the plan."

"You know what I don't get," Violet said. "With one of the mills closing last year and everybody needing jobs, these people could have pulled this off without having to bribe anyone."

Or murder, thought Maggie.

"Except for two things," she said. "They needed to move forward on the mall, and then Sam got in their way."

"We can do something about that, can't we? With all this stuff?" Violet asked.

Maggie met Wade's eyes. He confirmed what she suspected.

She shook her head. "There's nothing here–absolutely nothing illegal. It confirms our suspicions, but there's nothing that says, 'Bribe Otis Oxley and kill Sam Wiser.'"

"But what about stripping land they didn't own of timber?"

Maggie shook her head in frustration. "That wasn't NADCO. From what Otis said, that was done a couple of years ago. He's been on that land in recent times. He said the biggest trees are gone, and the forest is filling in with saplings."

Wade nodded. "They're just taking advantage of a situation that already existed. Would sound like good old entrepreneurial savvy to most folks. But I keep wondering, just curiosity–how this piece of land ever got mortgaged." He met Jessie's eyes and she nodded. They'd talked about this. "I might be able to find out. Won't change anything if I do."

"But the effing date of the auction is wrong," Violet persisted.

Maggie shook her head. "Maybe they are messing around with the auction dates so they'll be the only bidder, but if that comes to light, nobody can prove it wasn't an honest mistake, a typo in the newspaper."

Violet banged her fist on the table. "So, we do all this for nothing, and them bastards, they get away with it!"

"Nope. We're going in again," Wade said. "There's a safe. They got more. We just gotta go get it."

Jessie turned toward Wade with a raised eyebrow.

"Jim Sedgley," he said.

"But will he do it?"

"Oh sure. He'll jump at the chance to one-up me."

All I have to do is talk him into it, Wade thought.

Lincoln watched as United flight 1704 rolled to a stop at the Portland Jetport. Roy LaCroix strolled into the waiting area, looking bigger than life. By way of greeting, Roy clapped Lincoln heartily on the back. "So, Lincoln, I hear you still have snow on your golf courses."

"In patches." For a moment, Lincoln was grateful for the late spring. Otherwise, they'd be hauling clubs across a fairway instead of having lunch.

Lincoln navigated the heavy traffic around the Portland Mall and parked in front of a small Italian restaurant. They were seated and their orders taken before Roy spoke again.

"On the tenth of May, the land will be ours. I want to be there myself. I'll fly in the night before and meet you at the bank. The purchase should be–but isn't–the last hurdle."

Roy meant the woman. Lincoln was sick to death of talking about the goddamn woman.

"We're getting closer," he responded. "Increased surveillance, wider surveillance. But surely you can move forward, regardless."

LaCroix picked up his fork and traced around a pattern on the placemat. "Let me tell you a little story, Lincoln, about loose ends.

"Years ago, oh, maybe twenty years or so," Roy said, "Mary, my wife, learned to knit. For her it was a labor of love. By then we knew we would not be having any children of our own, so she lavished all this maternal affection on her nieces and nephews." Roy paused to look at Lincoln to be sure he was attending.

Lincoln nodded, thinking, if he has a goddamn point to this, why doesn't he just get to it?

"She took them to the zoo, made mittens for them at Christmas. One time she knit Conner, her favorite, a red sweater and gave it to him for his fourth birthday. Conner did what kids do. He found this one tiny dangling thread and pulled. Mary blamed herself because she must not have tied off a piece of thread–I guess you call it yarn–exactly right.

But it must have amazed the little bugger that this thread kept getting longer and longer. And he pulled it until the entire sweater was unraveled to his armpits. One little thread, Lincoln. That's all it took."

Lincoln got the point. "But Roy–"

Roy held up a finger. "No buts. You are the one who did not tie off the thread correctly. And if this comes unraveled, we lose everything– a healthy return on the investment, not to mention the loss of the capital we've already invested."

Not to mention a possible indictment for bribery–and murder, Lincoln thought.

Their meal arrived, and the waitress disappeared. Roy placed his napkin in his lap and leaned forward. "I don't mind telling you, Lincoln, this is driving me nuts. You think she's in Maine, but there still doesn't seem to be any end in sight. No closure. No resolution."

Roy picked up his fork and knife and began eating his veal parmesan. "If you are able to resolve this matter satisfactorily by May tenth–that gives you two weeks–you can return to your old job in New York, but with a better office. The lights of Broadway. Central Park. The effing Yankees, for chrissakes. Beats the hell out of Butthole, Maine, doesn't it?"

Lincoln looked up to see if LaCroix meant it.

"However, if you aren't able to," Roy continued, "NADCO will give you an early retirement–and forget the severance package. Maybe they'll be hiring at the mill. Or" –he gazed around the restaurant, then pointedly back at Lincoln– "who knows? Maybe this place is hiring. Busboy or something."

Roy calmly took a bite, dabbed his mouth with this napkin.

"Eat, eat, Lincoln," Roy said. "Keep your strength up. You're going to need it."

Wade rapped gently on the partially opened door.

"Come in."

He stuck his head into the office and grinned.

"Coach," Eliza said, smiling.

"Liza," Wade nodded, entered the office, and settled into the chair in front of her desk.

She must be, what? Twenty-eight now and assistant manager of the Amesbury Savings and Loan. Her silky, light brown hair was pinned back behind her ears but waved softly to her shoulders. She sure looked more grown up than when he had first met her.

She had been fifteen when she strode confidently up to him as the first Little League practice of the season was about to start. Her ponytail swung back and forth from the back of her ball cap.

"I'd like to help you with the team," she said. Her chin lifted a little, as if to ward off his objection.

Wade could see a couple of the dads lean forward to see what was going on.

"Any experience?" he asked her quietly.

"I'm the pitcher for the softball team." And then, as if she wished she didn't have to, she added, "I've been playing baseball with my brothers since I could hold a bat."

Wade picked up a bucket of balls and a bat and handed them to her. "Warm them up," he said, nodding toward the players in the field, and then stepped back and watched.

For twenty minutes, Eliza tossed balls in the air and hit them to the players scattered around the outfield. Some were pop flies. Some were grounders. She was very good. When the practice was over, Wade walked her toward the dugout within earshot of where the moms and dads were watching practice.

"I'm glad you could make it," Wade said, loud enough for the parents to hear. "I was afraid you weren't going to."

Light shone from Eliza's brown eyes. "I won't be late again," she said.

She had the team's respect from the first practice. She had the grudging respect of the parents who, by the end of the season, were crediting her hard work with the team as part of why the Amesbury Falcons Little Leaguers made it to regionals that year.

She continued to be the assistant coach until she graduated from high school.

And now, here she sat as assistant manager. Wade felt a satisfied smile tug at the corners of his mouth.

"So, Coach, what brings you here?"

"I just want to confirm that the bidding on the Archibald foreclosure sale is on May tenth. At eleven."

Eliza laughed. "Yes, it is. But you could have gotten that information in a phone call. What's up?"

Wade brushed the underside of his mustache with his forefinger and grinned. "Well, now, I do have something on my mind, but you probably can't help me."

"So, we're done here? Or how about you tell me what this is about, and I can tell you if I can help you."

"Okay, fair enough. What I'd like to know is" –Wade shook his head– "how in the blankety-blank did that property come to be in a position where it's being foreclosed on? I always thought it was legally designated as a wildlife refuge. I don't want to put you in an awkward position. I'm not asking you to breach confidentiality."

Eliza shook her head. "It's not confidential, but—sensitive. The bank would prefer it not to become public knowledge. It's an unfortunate situation that we'd like to get past and not shake consumer trust."

"Your decision about whether we discuss it, Eliza. Your call."

She inclined her head toward the ajar door. He got up and closed it.

"I will ask you not to let the information leave this office."

Wade nodded. "Of course."

"In the early 1990s, you probably remember, the savings and loan banks got themselves into trouble. Lenders were reckless, and in many cases, committed fraud. A lot of bankers around the country went to jail."

"But not around here?" Wade asked.

"Correct. In Amesbury, it wasn't bad, no, but the bank manager at the time, Martin Ebsen, was careless about real estate investment requirements. In many cases, loans were grossly under secured, and he couldn't give away money fast enough."

"I don't remember anything coming to light back then," Wade said.

"No, we lucked out in almost all cases. But, then Ernie Archibald came in for a loan. He and Marty went to high school together. Both played on the basketball team. Probably made it easier to play fast and loose with the bank's money. On the loan application, Ernie said he wanted to make improvements on the land. Dig a freshwater pond for the animals. Fencing, I don't remember what all else. Ernie put up the land–it was legally his, that he inherited it from his grandfather–as collateral to secure the loan."

"But wasn't it actually, officially, a wildlife refuge? There's a sign at the opening of a trail. I've seen it."

"It's been a while since you've been there, then. The sign is now rotting and overgrown. And it's not a trail head any more. It's a logging road. And the sign appears to me as if it were handmade, probably by Ernie. Maybe to show good faith to his grandfather before he passed? We don't know, but Ernie never did anything to make it official. He doesn't appear to have contacted any private, state, or federal agency to make it happen. It remained privately owned by Ernest Archibald. Until the bank owned it."

"Aaah. I see. But all that was a few years ago, right? Wade asked. "Why is this foreclosure happening now?"

"When it comes to light that Ernie defaulted on the loan after a year or so, Martin himself makes some unsuccessful attempts to find him, like calling mutual acquaintances, checking with neighbors, and eventually skip tracing, with no luck. But he's dragging his feet on this, and time goes by. Now it's spring of 1998, and Marty drives out to the estate, hikes in, and finds out it's been stripped of all the mature timber. Quite a lot of it on four hundred acres, I would guess."

Eliza smiled ruefully and shrugged her shoulders. "I had just started working here, but I remember it well. He looked physically ill when he came back that afternoon. He came into my office, sat down, and put his face in his hands. Finally, he looked up and said, 'Eliza, I screwed up. I think of myself as an environmentalist. But I lent him money so he could freaking strip the land.' Marty didn't come in to work the next day, and there was a letter of resignation on top of the file on his desk.

"It took a while to hire another manager and a while longer for him to get up to speed. The Archibald property wasn't his first priority. When he got around to it and was trying to decide what to do about this fiasco, somehow word got out that the property might be for sale. A company contacted him…"

"NADCO, by any chance?"

"Ah, you've heard of them. They said they'd be interested in buying the land for more than the original mortgage. Bob, that's the new manager, said we would go through the usual foreclosure process. NADCO asked him if he could wait until spring to start the procedure, and Bob said that wouldn't be a problem because he had enough on his plate. He told them, though, the bidding would be open to the public. No guarantees they would be the successful bidder."

"What a shame about stripping the land, though," Wade said.

"Not as bad as you might think, in my opinion, anyway. There are still stands of tall pines and oaks, just not as mature as what they took out. There are small maples filling the gaps. Maples grow fast. So do pines, for that matter. In another generation, you won't really be able to tell. Well, except for the stumps they left." She grinned and shrugged.

"Sounds like you've been out there."

"Yeah, my husband and I take the kids hiking almost every Sunday."

"Okay, so removing the timber is not a tragedy yet, but what if a new owner clear-cut the land and developed it, let's say put in housing, a golf course, a hotel, that sort of thing."

"For this girl, that would be an environmental tragedy. Yes."

Wade found himself deep in thought for a minute. "I have a friend who might be interested in acquiring the land and keeping it natural. I believe she will be putting in a bid."

"I sure would like to see that happen."

He stood up and offered his hand. "It's been great talking to you, and thank you for sharing the information. It will go no further."

Eliza chuckled. "You can share it with Mrs. Maxwell, of course. Tell her I still remember the butter pecan cookies she used to bring to practice."

"I will. Good to see you again." He moved to the door.

"Wish you were still coaching. My twins, a boy and a girl, will be old enough to try out for Little League next year."

"Well, now, that's something to think about," Wade said. "Could I get you to volunteer?"

"No way! I'll be one of those pain-in-the-ass, involved parents who will yell suggestions to you from the bleachers."

"That'd be okay. I'd be listening." He tipped his hat to her and left. The information she had given him didn't help their situation much, but at least the blanks were filled in.

Wade surveyed the cafe as the hostess approached them. Jessie had just finished reading the specials that were posted on a chalkboard inside the door. Wade could see where one entree had been erased from the middle of the list–sold out, apparently.

"Jessie, honey, what do you say we try to get that table over by the window?" He turned to the young hostess.

"Just two?" she asked, looking past them as if someone were standing behind them. Wade looked. Nope, no one there.

"Yes, ma'am. But..." he leaned toward her, tilting his head to make a special appeal. "Could we have the table for four over there by the window? My wife would like that one. Would that be okay?"

The hostess nodded curtly, power walked by a table for two, continued on to the table for four, placed the menus at each place, and left without a word.

"Friendly young thing," Wade drawled. He pulled out Jessie's chair to seat her. "Still being followed. I didn't want to say anything in the car."

She sat down. "That's why you took the longest route I ever did see, to get here?"

"Yup. Not much doubt. That means they've got us made." Wade took the seat across from Jessie. "See that white car across the street down in front of the camera shop?"

Jessie leaned forward, looking down the one-way street. "Uh huh."

Wade nodded. "So, we still can't go near Maggie."

There was concern in Jessie's eyes. "What are we going to do? This can't go on indefinitely. You don't think they already know where she is?"

The waitress approached.

"Can you tell us the specials?" Wade asked.

The waitress rattled off four.

"What about the one that's erased?"

"That was broiled scrod."

"Yup, that's what I'll have."

The teenager's eyebrows shot up, and she opened her mouth to speak.

"Just kidding," Wade said.

Jessie tsk, tsked, shaking her head. "I'll just have the baked haddock special."

"It comes with a salad and fries. What kind of dressing for your salad?"

"French," Jessie said.

"I'll have the same here but make my dressing blue cheese. And would you mind putting it in one of those itty-bitty cups on the side?"

The waitress looked at him for a second to see if he was pulling her leg. Deciding he wasn't, she said, "Sure," good naturedly and took the menus Wade and Jessie handed her.

Jessie looked at him with a twinkle in her eyes. "About Maggie. Do you have anything in mind?"

"Well, yes. I been thinking on it while we drove around. These people are tipped to us. It's only a matter of time before they make a few connections and know where Maggie is. It's time to move her."

"But where? When?"

"It's May. I think the snow is off the camp road. I'm going up there later this afternoon. I'll open up the lake house, turn on the gas."

"Won't you be followed?"

"Nah, I can lose the guy as easy as I lose my socks. Then we'll move her tomorrow. Sound okay?"

"I don't know. It's so remote. There won't be anyone else out there for another month. She wouldn't have anyone to run to if there were trouble. She'd have to have food. There's a lot of canned goods left from last summer, but she'd need fresh stuff."

"We'll do grocery shopping this afternoon. There's no way whoever is following us would know about the lake house. She'll be safer there than anyplace else I can think of."

"Okay, but I'm not comfortable with it."

The waitress returned with their salads.

"We're in a hurry, so you can bring out the main course anytime," Wade said. "When you get to be our age, you gotta do everything fast so you get as much living in as you can."

The waitress grinned good-naturedly. "Want dessert at the same time?"

Jessie chuckled. "Now you wouldn't want to be offering dessert to an old geezer whose arteries are crackling with plaque, would you?"

"We have a chocolate mud pie topped with whipped cream. Guaranteed no fat."

"Sold," Wade said. "In a to-go box. Jessie, honey, remind me to tip this lady well, will you?"

When she left Wade said, "After lunch, let's stop at the hardware store for some tools to make things right at the lake house. Then we'll swing by the store to pick up the groceries. I'll leave you off at home, and then I need some time to lose that tail before I head for Route 1."

"I hope you know what you're doing, Wade," Jessie said.

He reached across the table and squeezed her hand. "Me, too."

Lincoln Montgomery had nearly choked when he heard the conversation at the next table. His back had been toward the old man and woman, and he'd dismissed the conversation about being followed as the delusions of a paranoid old coot–until he heard Maggie's name mentioned. An electric shock coursed through his body, and he became very still, filtering out the murmurs of lunchtime conversation and the clink of silverware on china.

He didn't know if he'd even eaten the rest of his lunch, though he tried to go through the motions so he'd look natural. Deciding he'd heard everything of value he was going to, he left the restaurant before the old couple.

Now, in his car he dialed Mancuso on his cell phone.

"Go ahead," Arturo answered.

"Artie. Meet me at the office in ten minutes."

"But what about–"

"Don't worry about it." Lincoln pushed the off button and disconnected. Funny, he'd spent all that money, hired the people who flew around trying to find her, and he'd found her himself—practically in his own backyard.

He drove back to the office in five minutes. He took the elevator to the fourth floor and entered the NADCO suite of offices. Kathy looked startled as he walked through her office; she realized he was smiling.

"How was lunch, Mr. Montgomery?"

"Excellent." He couldn't even remember what he'd had.

In his office, he leaned back in his seat and grinned. Finding the Wiser woman was quite a coup, and he might as well enjoy it.

Mancuso came through the door a few minutes later.

Lincoln sat up, resting his arms on his desk. "We got her."

"What!"

He steepled his fingers and nodded slowly, allowing a small smile to appear.

"Where is she?"

"Actually, it doesn't matter where she is right now. What matters is where she'll be tomorrow night. And she'll be a sitting duck, you might say."

Lincoln filled Mancuso in on his lunchtime eavesdropping activities.

"I can't believe the old bastard saw me," Mancuso said. "He must be ninety years old. Well, sure as hell, I can't tail him now. Not in that car anyway."

"You don't have to tail him at all. Get a hold of Henry Lee...you can, can't you?"

Mancuso nodded. "Yeah. No problem."

"Have him pick up the old man when he turns on to Route 1. The guy is apparently still sharp, so Lee'll have to be on his toes. He can find out where the lake house is today. Then tomorrow night, when she's alone, he can take her out."

"Still have to look like an accident?"

"The best outcome is where she disappears without a trace. No body. No evidence. But I doubt Lee can pull that off. So, yes, if there's a body, it damn well better look like an accident."

Lincoln was satisfied. He was back in the game, and it was through his own efforts—being in the right place at the right time.

Across the desk, Mancuso's smile lifted his jowls. "Been a long road, but we're finally there, Boss. How the hell do you suppose they pulled this off? Was it the old couple who hid her all this time?"

"Of course it was." He thought about his discovery when he listened to the tape. "Strange how you overlook the simplest and most obvious things. It was a lot of smoke and mirrors."

"But Boss. Who would a thought? They're just a couple of old farts waiting for their bones to cave in."

Lincoln nodded thoughtfully. "Makes you wonder. Who are these people?"

Henry Lee parked his car down a side road a hundred yards from the lake house. The old geezer's car was parked further up the primary road but still visible from here.

He got out of the car and gently closed the door. He'd cross the dirt road and go into the woods behind the two-story house that must belong to the old guy. The woods didn't bother him. He'd been in Nam. He could make a silent path through the woods with the best of them.

He came out on a bluff behind the house, where a few spruce trees gave him cover. There was some sort of shed halfway down the hill between him and the house, but there was no reason to risk leaving his cover to get to it. He sat on the cold ground and settled down to watch.

The old man carried what looked like a bedroll from his truck to the house's back door. Two bags of groceries, two more trips. He pulled out a key ring and inserted a key. Looked like it wouldn't turn. He tried another, yanked on the doorknob. The old guy was going through every key on the ring. No luck. Lee smiled and shook his head. Must be getting senile.

The old man looked around, first over one shoulder, then the other, like he hoped someone would pop up with a key. Then he stepped around the corner to the back of the house and over to a weathered bulkhead. He pulled a two-by-four from under the handles and lifted one of the doors.

Lee laughed silently. The old guy had been looking around to be sure no one saw his secret entrance.

Once inside, the old man unlocked the side door from inside and brought in the bedroll and bags of groceries. He stayed in the house for twenty minutes, during which he opened two upstairs windows. To air it out, Lee guessed.

When the old man came out of the side door, probably the kitchen, Lee thought, he walked around the corner and closed the bulkhead doors, jamming the two-by-four under the handles again. Must be to keep animals out, Lee surmised. It sure as hell wasn't going to keep out intruders.

The old guy slowly made his way back to the truck and left.

Lee waited for ten minutes to be sure the guy wasn't coming back for something he'd forgotten. He descended the slope and stayed near the perimeter to check out the front of the house, which faced the lake. A small dock extended into the water.

At the rear of the house, he entered, as the old man had, through the bulkhead. Ten minutes of recon inside, and he knew exactly how he would do the job. And it would be an accident.

In all the months he'd been looking for her, he'd gradually concluded that if he found her, he was going to have to subdue her, hit her on the head, and dump her somewhere.

But this was so much finer–something he never could have imagined until the situation presented itself. She'd never know what hit her. Sticking around for this job was certainly going to pay off in more ways than one.

Tomorrow the old guy would bring her out here. He'd wait until dark.

He guffawed. "The better to see you disappear, my dear."

Water splashed on Pookie's feet and legs as he powered through the puddle that hadn't looked that deep heading toward it. Now his jeans were wet and cold. He steered around the next one. It had rained during the night, but this morning was sunny. Cold though. Letting go of the handlebars and coasting, he snapped the front of his letterman's jacket closed, then put one hand in a pocket. May mornings were warm enough if you were shooting baskets but still chilly for bike riding.

He wondered if Wade had thought about that when he came up with this idea. Pookie had just gotten home from a date last night...yeah, he guessed he could call it a real date. It was the first time he'd gone someplace alone with Ellen. He thought about sitting in the dark theater beside her.

They took turns holding the popcorn, and three times their hands accidentally touched. Each time it was like an electric shock. He thought she might have felt the same thing, but he couldn't be sure. His heart beat hard, and he couldn't think about the movie. He wanted to look at her, but he didn't dare.

Then she put the popcorn box on the empty seat beside her and put her arm on the armrest between them. With his heart hammering, he slowly placed his arm beside hers, careful to leave space between them. Maybe she wasn't thinking about him.

But maybe she was.

He tried concentrating on the movie and realized he must have missed something. Then Ellen shifted in her seat and their arms touched from elbow to wrist. His heart lurched as their hands suddenly entwined. He could hardly get his breath. He never saw the rest of the movie. It seemed like the only thing he could think of was how tightly they were holding hands.

He walked her home, and they held hands all the way while they talked about school and what they were going to be doing in the summer. When they got to her house, he didn't know what to do. It seemed like he should do something, but kissing her seemed way, way out of the question. In the awkwardness, he finally said, "Well, see you later," then turned and galloped off her porch. And down the street.

He had gone three blocks before he noticed where he was. He decided to work on his motorcycle in the carriage house for a while. He wanted to think about what had happened.

He'd just pulled the carburetor off when Wade slipped into the carriage house. As soon as Pookie saw him, Wade put his finger to his lips to signal "quiet," then beckoned him outside. By moonlight, he followed Wade to the woods, where they sat on a log. Wade told him what he needed him to do to help keep his grandmother safe. The plan seemed risky, but Wade said this was the best way.

Pookie had his doubts.

But the plan was in motion.

Pedaling hard, Pookie maneuvered the mountain bike through the park, down an alley, across the street, and through another alley. The guy who sometimes followed him on a bike was never around this early, but even if he was, Pookie could outride him.

Once Pookie had known for sure that he was the object of surveillance, he'd seen it as a challenge. He and his mountain bike had found paths he hadn't even known existed. Now, there wasn't a path, driveway, or alley in the city he didn't know. It never took him more than five minutes to lose the guy.

This morning he came into Effie's yard along the railroad tracks. When he was little, he'd explored every inch of this yard while Violet visited with her mother. The bushes became his hideout, and the willow tree his fort.

He leaned the bike against the inside wall of the garage, went through the breezeway, and up the steps to Effie's kitchen.

"Come in," George said when Pookie knocked. In the kitchen, George was pouring coffee at the counter. Maggie and Effie sat at the table, Maggie in pajamas and robe, Effie in a nightgown.

"Hi, Honey," Effie said. "I declare, you grow like a weed. Aren't you half a foot taller than you were last week?"

Pookie grinned. Effie always said that. But lately, it seemed to be true.

His grandmother held out her arm. He bent to kiss her cheek, and she gave him a squeeze around the waist. "Can we fix some breakfast for you?"

"No, I already ate. I came to take you away." He smiled at her, picked up a piece of toast that looked like no one was going to eat, and spread some jelly on it.

His grandmother's eyebrows raised. "Away? Where? Why?"

Pookie signaled wait a minute; his mouth was full. They all waited, watching him. He realized he should have explained before eating the toast. He took a glass from the cupboard, remembering when he was so short he had to stand on tiptoe to coax a glass out with his fingertips. He poured orange juice from the pitcher on the table and washed down the rest of his toast.

"Wade says it's time for you to move. He's got a plan."

Pookie sat down in an unoccupied chair. He pointed to the pile of home fries that was the only thing left on her plate. "Are you going to eat that, Grandma?"

"It's all yours." She handed him the plate. "Do I need to get ready now?"

Pookie nodded, speared three pieces of potato, and popped them in his mouth. Darn. Now he couldn't answer immediately. He chewed, swallowed, and drained his orange juice.

"Un huh. You're going to take my bike–I brought it. Not as comfortable, but better for now–and ride the heck out of here." He grinned at her puzzled look. "I mapped out the way. With Wade's help, I can get all over town without anyone being able to follow me. So can you."

"I'll go get dressed. Do I have to bring anything?"

He nodded. "Whatever will fit in your fanny pack and backpack. I'll get the rest to you later. Is anyone going to eat that bacon?" There were two strips left on a plate in the middle of the table. No use wasting them.

Effie handed him the plate. "I can fix you breakfast."

"No. I ate before I left. This will be fine." The bacon was crisp, the way he liked it. He put the slices together and ate them both at once. Effie poured the rest of the juice into his glass.

It didn't take his grandmother long to get ready. He handed her his letterman's jacket. "It's cold."

"No, you'll need it."

"I'm walking, so I won't be cold. You'll feel it while you're riding, though. Besides, with the jacket on, you might look like a boy. Well, sort of."

She put on the jacket and fastened the snaps. "Now, did Wade say why I have to move?"

Pookie adjusted the bike seat to a lower position. "Un huh. He's being tailed, and he thinks it's only a matter of time before they make the connections and start looking for you here. I wasn't so sure about you riding around in daylight on a bike, but then I realized, with the helmet and sunglasses on and my jacket and my bike, no one would know it was you anyway." He handed his grandmother her bike helmet.

"And you're sure about where I'm supposed to go? I don't know if it's a good idea."

"I wondered about it, too, until he explained it to me. He's got it all fixed up for you. The only thing is, the timing has to be right." Pookie looked at his watch. "It is. You have to leave now."

After she snapped the strap under her chin, he handed her a piece of paper. "Stick to the River Road. No one will see you there. Just before the bridge, there's a bike path that goes through the woods for a while, and then...well, it's all there on the map."

She looked over the map and nodded. "Okay. When I get near the bridge, I'll look at it again. Did Wade sound...well, did he sound...worried?"

"No. This is just a safety measure. No one knows where you are now, and he wants to keep it that way. I put your toe clips on the pedals, but I can take them off if you don't want them."

"That was thoughtful. No. I've gotten used to them. Leave them on. As long as I can get my feet in."

She swung her foot over the saddle of the bike and slipped her foot into the clip. "Feels good."

"Here's your backpack." He held the straps while she slipped her arms through.

"Okay, looks like I'm ready. You've got a long walk ahead of you. Wish we could have had both bikes here."

"It's only three or four miles. I'll run. It's good for training."

"Okay, well here goes." She pushed down with the top foot, and the bike started forward.

"Grandma."

She stopped, putting one foot on the ground. "What?"

He didn't know what, exactly. He just needed to say something.

"Um...do good. Be safe."

She grinned, gave him a thumbs up, and then wobbled across the lumpy ground and out of the yard.

He had to admit he really liked all the excitement of playing spy, or whatever he should call it. But he'd feel a lot better if his grandmother's safety weren't in the middle of it all.

CHAPTER 20

Lee doused his headlights as he turned onto the camp road and waited for his eyes to adjust before continuing. He pulled into the side road he had used yesterday.

Staying under cover, he checked the front of the house again. Nothing moved; the only sound was water lapping quietly against the sand. Not a boat at the dock, not a light along the shore.

Staying in the meager fringe of woods, he circled stealthily to the rear of the house. The tool shed offered closer cover than he'd had yesterday. He lowered himself to a small pile of firewood stacked beside the shed and watched the back of the house.

The lights were on in the kitchen, but there was no movement. Upstairs, a light was also on, and soft music floated out of the open windows. He waited, patiently watching both floors, and soon the woman passed by the upper window, her shadow falling across the sheer curtains. He formed a gun with his fingers, pointed it at the second-floor window, and said, "Gotcha."

He pushed himself into a standing position, brushed off the seat of his pants, and ran in a crouch to the back of the house. When he had replaced the two-by-four yesterday, it was just far enough so it would come out soundlessly. He opened the right-hand bulkhead door and, leaving it open, descended into the blackness of the cellar and switched on his flashlight.

As soon as the man was out of sight, Wade whispered into his walkie-talkie. "He's in." He stepped quietly out of the tool shed door and darted across the back lawn to the bulkhead. Heart pounding with exertion and tension, he closed the right-hand door, climbed up on the slanted bulkhead door, and peered cautiously into the kitchen window.

He asked himself once again, had he made a mistake in judgment? Did he think he was still forty and could pull off something like this? She was younger than he, but would she be able to handle her part?

He was about to jump down and tear open the kitchen door, gun in hand, when he saw the intruder–the man he knew was the assassin from the photo Jessie had taken of him in Florida–back out of the tiny bathroom and go to the kitchen stove. The man opened the oven and turned on the five gas jets–four for the burners and one for the oven.

Then Wade got it, and his insides lurched. Could he wait until the man reentered the cellar? Not more than a few seconds.

The man opened the door that led back to the cellar. From the kitchen side, he flipped the bolt lock on the door, took a step down, and closed the door behind him. The lock snapped closed.

Wade jumped down, closed the bulkhead door and jammed the two-by-four under the handles. He ran around the corner, tore open the kitchen door, and ran through the house shouting, "Get out of here! The house is going to blow! Run!"

As he started up the stairs, Jessie appeared at the top. Running as if she were sixteen, she scrambled down the steps. Wade already had the front door unlocked.

He grabbed her hand, and they ran outside, across the lawn toward the water. Halfway to the lake, his knee gave away, and he fell to the ground. Jessie pulled him up, and with his arm around her shoulders, they hobbled to the shore.

She didn't ask questions. She let go of him and yanked the underbrush aside. Grabbing the dinghy rope, she shoved the boat into the water.

Wade stood knee-deep in the lake. He grabbed the boat and held it steady against his thighs. Jessie climbed in, and Wade hauled himself aboard. Jessie pulled on the oars.

"We need the motor!" Wade said.

Jessie let go of the oars, turned around and twisted the wing nut that controlled the gas. Holding onto Jessie's shoulder, Wade leaned across her, grabbed the starter cord, and pulled with all his strength. The engine roared. Jessie slid the throttle to full speed, and the boat leapt ahead. Jarred by the movement, Wade dropped to a sitting position, straddling the wooden seat.

They were a hundred yards from the shore when the house blew up.

Jessie stopped the acceleration, and they sat there for a while at idle, the dinghy bobbing hard on the steep wake caused by the explosion. Minutes passed as they watched the remnants burn.

"He in there?" Jessie finally asked.

"Yup."

"How did it happen?"

He could hear a siren far away. That quick.

"We need to get out of here right now. We don't want to be answering questions on this side of the lake. Let's go quietly. Can you row us across, lady? I don't think I can put enough pressure on this leg to do much good."

Jessie slid the throttle to the off position, turned the gas off, and tilted the engine so the prop was out of the water. She dug the oars deep in the water and pulled; the little boat slipped forward. They were quiet for a couple of minutes.

"There we were," Wade finally said, "ready for anything we could think of, including a fake body in the bed and a bulletproof vest for you, and he decides to blow you up."

"Blow Maggie up," she reminded him.

He nodded. "Right. I'm sorry Jessie. Your pretty little house is gone."

While she rowed the boat toward the middle of the lake, he turned, and they watched the flames finish what was left of the house and saw the headlights of the first emergency vehicle enter the camp road.

"Not going to worry about it, Wade. Just glad we both came out alive. How'd he do it?"

Wade turned back toward her, noticing hair had escaped from her bun and fallen, framing her face–a sight that always gave him a lift. There was a light sheen of perspiration across her skin from the effort of rowing, though she didn't look as if she were overexerting. Maybe for the millionth time, he was aware of his extraordinary good fortune to have found Jessie. The other half of him that fit perfectly. How close had he come to losing her? In fact, both of them could be dead right now, with nothing for the medical examiner to even scrape up. He wasn't ready to relinquish life yet. He needed time with Jessie like he needed air and water.

"Wade?" She continued to row–something she did so well that the only sound as they dipped and raised was water streaming off as she feathered the oars.

"He must have turned the pilot light off on the kitchen stove. Maybe when he was here yesterday. But the water heater in the bathroom was on. So all he had to do tonight was make sure it was still on, then turn on the burners on the kitchen stove and let the gas pour out. The house was small and tight as a drum. Wouldn't take long to fill up enough to be ignited by the water heater's flame."

"And he didn't get out because you had locked the bulkhead doors."

"Yup. And he locked the kitchen door to the cellar before going down, probably hoping the lock would be found intact in the debris, proving the house had been locked from inside. Showing it was an accident."

"Well, we said we wouldn't do anything to him unless he showed intent to kill."

"If it had been in the movies, I'd have subdued him outside and forced him to testify against whoever hired him. But I couldn't see myself running through the woods after him, shaking my fist."

"You had your gun."

"Still do." He touched the butt of his 9mm under his jacket. "Didn't want to use it unless I had to. Getting old, Jessie. Getting old and soft. You know, while I sat there in the shed, I was thinking we're out of our minds to be attempting this. We're not in the prime of life, not middle-agers anymore."

"Speak for yourself, old-timer. If I'm as young as I feel–not a day over fifty."

"We're going to have to put on a good act when the police come to tell us our summer home is gone," Wade said.

"That's the easy part. I will feel terrible. The hard part will be telling Maggie what we did."

"Can't do it. Ever. She wouldn't be able to handle it. No way, no how. And better she stays cautious. We need to assume NADCO will replace this guy. But at least we distracted them long enough to get Maggie moved to a safer place. They were going to stumble onto Effie and George's involvement any day now."

Multiple sirens wailed in the night, and the headlights of more vehicles darted down the dirt road toward what used to be their summer retreat.

She stopped rowing for a minute. Leaning on the oars, she watched the activity across the lake. "Easy come, easy go," she said softly.

"We'll rebuild this summer."

"Let's make it a one story, modern log cabin with big windows, this time."

"How about a deck?"

"I always wanted a deck." She started to row again.

Jewel often watched as Lee scurried around town like a lost puppy. He seldom followed because it seemed that Lee didn't have a clue what he was doing.

But today, as Jewel sat in a diner with a rare sirloin in front of him, Wade Maxwell drove by and turned onto Route 1.

Interesting.

Even more interesting, the missus was not with him. One always went with the other. Except, apparently, today.

Forty-five minutes later, Jewel was about to tackle a homemade blueberry pie when Lee's rattletrap Caprice went by and also turned onto Route 1.

Seeing one of them? Nothing to get excited about. But two of them, with Lee sniffing at Maxwell's heels?

Jewel dropped a twenty on the table, ran to his Range Rover, and sped along Route 1 until he saw Lee in the distance. Probably nothing to it, he thought. Then again, why not check it out?

Fifteen minutes later, Lee turned into a wooded road and disappeared. Jewel cautiously pulled in and saw Lee's car a hundred yards or so ahead, bouncing over the rutted dirt road. When Lee veered onto a smaller dirt road, Jewel decided to follow. He continued on slowly, rocking over ruts and splashing through puddles, hoping his Rover would not raise any attention. The lake was on his left, and a two-story house was on his right. He glanced at a nearby sign. The Maxwells. However, the old man's truck was not in sight. Further along, the road split, the left way going straight ahead toward a boat launch; on the right, the road curved up and around the plot of land the Maxwell house was on. And there, a few yards away, was the Dodge Ram, tucked into the woods so well he almost missed it.

Interesting. Very interesting. He soon found a small side road and tucked his vehicle behind a stand of pines.

He got out of his car and slowly made his way through the undergrowth toward the house.

He found a small ledge to sit on where, undetected, he could watch the side of the Maxwell house. As darkness fell, he saw no movement at all. Along the lakeshore, it was whisper quiet.

Then the house exploded in a massive fireball.

The blast rocked Jewel back, but he scrambled up and got back to his vehicle. He waited until the emergency vehicles bounced and rocked down the rutted dirt road, sirens blaring. He waited for two more hours, but Lee never returned to his car. Likewise, Maxwell did not come back to his truck. Jewel would bet half a year's salary that Lee, at least, was history.

Was the Wiser woman still safe and sound someplace? He would bet the other half she was.

* * *

The rooms were cavernous, with high ceilings and enormous old-fashioned casement windows–the kind Maggie remembered from elementary school. When she'd arrived this morning, she'd opened the door with the key that Pookie had given her. Sunlight streamed through the windows, giving the two rooms a cheery look.

She'd had misgivings when she realized she was going to be one floor above NADCO in the Appleton Building. Yet Wade's plan made sense. No one would believe she could be hiding in the same building. And since the elevator only went to the fourth floor, why would anyone go higher?

The first thing she looked for was a bathroom, regretting during her bike ride the second cup of coffee she'd had at breakfast.

Everything metal in the bathroom was made of bronze, even the sink's faucet handles. Cost had not been a concern when this place was built, and the decor probably hadn't seen any changes since the 1940s.

The flush worked, but the sink had only cold water. She shook her hands dry. She had to start a list of things she'd need for the next week or so–like soap and towels. In the second office, she found a cot with a red sleeping bag on it. She picked it up and smelled it. Ah, April fresh. Jessie. In the first room, she found an old swivel chair with wooden arms and a matching oak desk. There. Now she had a table and chair for meals.

Beside the door she had entered, she found two bags of groceries: canned fruit with pop-open lids, cereal bars, and canned meat–camping food. At lunchtime she'd be happy, but she didn't want to live on this stuff for long.

Across the rear parking lot was a string of stores. From the west windows, she could see a Dollar Store, a hardware store and–a coffee shop.

Back in the bathroom, she looked at her reflection in the mottled mirror over the sink. She had brought along her cover-up foundation, which Belle had given her to hide her freckles, in her backpack. After applying the makeup, she colored her lips with a burgundy lipstick that did nothing for her skin or eyes but matched her hair. Sort of.

She tied a green scarf around her spiky hair and knotted the material behind one ear–a jaunty style she'd never worn before. She chuckled, thinking that before this all happened, she hadn't changed her hairstyle in a dozen years, and now she'd changed color and style so many times in the past months that she'd lost track. She put on the large, squarish sunglasses and was ready to go.

The hardware store had a two-burner electric stove that she carried across the parking lot and into the building. She rested in the stairwell of the third floor thinking if she weren't already in shape, she would be shortly.

At the Dollar Store, she bought two towels and two face cloths, cleaning supplies, a pillow, and three paperback books.

The clerk was polite but distant, taking no special notice of her. And why should she? Because, Maggie reflected, the whole world wasn't looking for her–only a few people.

She spent the rest of the day cleaning her space. The room with the desk would be the kitchen, and the second room was where she would sleep. She raised the lower window sashes to let air flow in, freshening the rooms and cooling them of the heat that slowly built during the morning. She had a lunch of Vienna sausages, a cereal bar, and applesauce.

In the late afternoon, she went back to the Dollar Store to buy a saucepan, a mug, instant coffee, cream, sugar and a box of plastic forks and spoons. She'd be all set for breakfast. At the coffee shop, she bought a pastrami on rye for supper. She headed for home. Home, loosely defined.

After supper, she began to feel uneasy. She was essentially okay with spending the night. She'd noticed each room had a deadbolt–she could secure herself behind two locks. But she'd turned on the overhead lights, which gave the place a chilling, ominous feeling, especially as the day's light disappeared, and the night, with its hidden eyes, dominated the rooms. She stood by the window toward the river and realized all the buildings were no higher than two stories. On the fifth floor, she would be safe from prying eyes.

She fastened her fanny pack around her waist again. She'd have to make one more foray before the stores closed for the night. She was really tired now that she thought about it. Time to use the elevator. The building was as quiet as a tomb–there certainly wouldn't be anyone around on a Saturday night.

At the hardware store, she bought two table lamps and carried them back to the building. She took the elevator to the fourth floor and walked to the fifth.

On the fifth floor, she pulled open the stairway door and held it with her hip while she picked up the lamps and swung them into the hallway outside her lair. Then she stopped short.

Through the glass of the front outer door, she could see light spilling from the second room doorway. She knew she'd left it off. Her first instinct was to run. But where would she go? Riding her bike down the street at night, she'd be conspicuous. Could it be Wade or Pookie? But wouldn't they have called her on the cellular phone to say they were coming?

She'd locked the door when she left. Hadn't she? Maybe not. She wasn't sure, now.

She slid the lamps into the stairwell and stepped back into the hallway letting the door close silently behind her. She moved into the deep shadows of the long hallway, leaned against the wall, and sank into a sitting position. She slowly unzipped her fanny pack, knowing, but not believing, the noise wouldn't penetrate to the second room.

Slowly, reluctantly, she lifted her gun from its resting place in the bottom of her pack. Think. She'd work her way down the hall into the black shadows and wait, gun drawn. If someone was in there–well, okay, someone *was* in there–she'd wait him out. Eventually he'd leave, and she could watch him go. He'd never see her back here. Even if he did, she'd have the gun ready if he pulled one out. And then what? Would she shoot him? She couldn't imagine it. Was there a Plan B?

She was almost beyond the door when the light coming from the second room altered, as if someone had moved in there. She leaned forward to peek. There, someone crossed by the door. A man.

She waited until he passed by again. She pushed herself to her knees, then jumped up and dashed to the outer door.

Was it Pookie? Wade? Jessie? They were the only people who knew where she was. Weren't they?

A killer?

She took a deep breath. Then another.

No use in putting it off.

Holding the gun against her leg and leaning against the wall, she reached out and rapped on the glass.

Sandy's startled face looked toward the door.

She yanked the door open. "Oh, my God, what are you doing here? Do you know I might have shot you?" She flung herself at him, and they were in a crushing embrace.

"I notice you are armed. And dangerous? Would you really shoot that thing?" He kissed her forehead.

"Honestly? I'm sure not. I can't even begin to imagine it."

He released her. "Well, that's an...interesting look." He touched her hair. "That's what I like in lady friends. Variety. Especially when they're all you." His eyes crinkled with delight.

"Really? Well, I was thinking of making this my permanent look."

"I love any look as long as you get your freckles back."

"Freckles on demand. Kinky."

He glanced around the empty room. "Looks like you're making yourself comfortable in your sumptuous new digs."

"Uh huh. But why are you here? I'm not complaining. Actually, I'm thrilled. But..."

"Well, I thought you might need research done on NADCO and I... No, that's not it. I just wanted to hear your voice. I was going to call, and then I decided I'd fly up and hear it in person. I promise I won't get in your way, and I won't stay long. In fact, I'll leave tonight if you want me to. Go find a motel. If they're all full, I'll pull up a slab of concrete and sleep on the street. May in Maine. It could work."

"They're a little touchy about vagrants around here. You can stay, but we'll have to talk about who gets the cot and who gets the floor. You said you flew up? Your plane?"

"I started this morning."

"But how did you know where I was?"

"Wade."

"Ah. Wish he'd told me. I was scared out there. Listen, have you eaten? Are you tired?"

He reached for her hand and pulled her close again. "Not tired at all. You?"

She leaned against him, her face near his neck; the feel of his arms and the smell of his skin were both comforting and beguiling. And compelling.

"Not in the least bit tired. Listen, I know of a motel with a queen-size bed."

"And I have a rental car outside."

"Let me get ready." She put the gun back in her fanny pack. "I'm ready."

Other than a brief visit to the office this morning, Lincoln had been at home near the phone all day. Pleasant anticipation built as the day wore on. Mancuso would be reporting welcomed news any minute now. Lee had told Arturo the job would be done after dark tonight.

Lincoln looked out the window. It was sufficiently dark.

A few minutes after midnight, the sound of the phone ringing gave him a sharp thrill.

He grabbed the phone. "Yes?"

"I need to come over," Mancuso's gravelly voice rumbled over the line.

"Why?" They occasionally met at Lincoln's apartment. But a meeting was not planned for tonight. Lincoln glanced at the clock. Wasn't tonight anymore.

"I have news," Mancuso said. "Ain't good."

Alarmed, Lincoln blurted, "What?"

"On the phone?"

"No. Come over."

The boss yanked open the liquor cabinet, took out a bottle of bourbon, and banged it down on the bar. Then he paced the length of his living room and back, the bourbon apparently forgotten. Arturo Mancuso would a liked to remind him. He needed a drink. Or three.

Lincoln turned toward him. "How did you find out?"

"Police scanner went nuts."

"You have a police scanner?"

"Who don't? Keeps me from getting bored. I almost shit when I heard where all the commotion was."

"But how do you know he's–"

"I went out there. His car was parked on a little dirt road off to the side, unlocked."

"You think he was in the explosion?"

"If he wasn't, why didn't he come back to his car? I waited around with the other onlookers until they got the fire out. They found a body. Male."

Montgomery stopped pacing, lost in thought. He looked sick. Shock, Arturo thought. He looked longingly at the bar. He needed a drink. So did the boss. Ignoring protocol of the past, he walked to the bar, grabbed the bourbon, and poured a healthy dose for Montgomery, over ice.

He handed it to the boss and made one for himself. Fuck the ice.

Montgomery finally took a sip, then sat down on the sofa. His arms rested on his thighs, the drink held in both hands between his knees. Arturo sat across from him and watched him. This is what I like, he thought. A boss who falls apart when things go wrong.

Montgomery finally looked up at Arturo. "Only one body."

"Far as they can tell. They'll be there all night. Might come up with something else by daylight. She mighta been in there too. Don't know." Don't think so, Mancuso mused.

"Who the hell," Montgomery's voice was almost a growl. "Who in freaking hell are these people?"

Arturo had been wondering that himself.

"The old man?"

"I got a report as soon as I got back in town. She, the wife, left in the afternoon. Drove away. He wasn't in the truck, so the tail stayed at the house with him. Far as he can tell, the old coot never left. I can't see him pulling this off, anyway."

If the boss had been in shock, this seemed to jolt him out of it. He straightened up and glared at Arturo. "Oh, really, Artie? Oh, really. Well, we wouldn't have thought he could pull off her debut disappearing act either. Dragging our asses over half of Florida when she was never even there!"

Montgomery's jaw clenched several times before he took another drink. The boss seemed lost in thought again, and Arturo was inclined to leave him there.

Finally, Montgomery spoke. "They led us down the garden path. That's what they did. I don't fucking believe this."

"You think it was planned by them?"

"The lunch that day. They leaked the information to me, and I bought it." Like a baseball pitcher winding up, Montgomery pulled his glass back over his shoulder and let it fly. It smashed against the far wall and shattered, leaving a splattered wet mark on the wall. The bourbon ran down in rivulets.

"I want a tail on her, too. The Maxwell woman. Round the clock. Change tails every four hours. I want everyone fresh. Continue surveillance on him. I'd bet my money that the old guy gave your tail the slip."

Mancuso started to speak but caught a look from Montgomery and closed his mouth. Not much point in defending his guys. The boss was right; someone had screwed up somewhere.

And if the boss looked in the mirror, Mancuso mused, he might get his first clue who it was.

"What I want to know, more than anything else in this goddamn world," Montgomery said, pounding a fist into his hand, "is who *the freaking hell* are these people?"

Maggie paced, then, annoyed with herself for being agitated, sat down. A minute later, she was pacing again. Wade had called Sandy and asked him to meet for coffee a couple of blocks away. Wade had news for Maggie. Was it good or bad? She didn't know.

Finally, half an hour after Sandy left, he was back with two steaming cups of coffee in paper cups and a newspaper folded under his arm. She knew, as soon as they made eye contact, he was bringing significant news.

"Let's sit over here," he said and put the coffees on the desk.

"Is it bad?" she asked.

"I guess it depends on your point of view. *I* think it's good. For *you*. Very good. It's not all that great for Wade and Jessie, but they're handling it far better than I would have thought. In fact, it seemed like they were in a celebratory mood."

"Sandy! What is it?"

He unfolded the newspaper and laid it on the desk. She looked at the headline. *Explosion Kills Intruder*. There was a photo of the remains of a house she wouldn't have recognized except for the context of Sandy meeting with Wade and Jessie.

"Is it their camp at the lake?" she asked. It had to be. She would have known if it were their house.

"But they're okay, right? You just met with Wade."

"Yes, they're fine. And they're already thinking about what kind of house they will replace it with. The good news for you is that Wade knows that that man, his name was Henry Lee, was your assassin. The police are still working on identifying him, but Wade and Jessie got several good looks at this guy when they were in Florida. Jessie took his picture, remember."

"But he was not Sam's assassin."

"No, Wade and Jessie think, and I agree, that man is long gone. Disappeared as soon as his job was done. So, no justice there."

"Okay, but how did *this* happen?" She gestured at the newspaper. "Did Wade see this guy here in Amesbury?" she asked as she worked through the implications.

"When I met with Wade and Jessie, they were still not in agreement about whether or not you should be told the whole story. Jessie won out. She has a great deal of confidence in your resiliency. Wade doesn't want your opinion of him to 'go sour' as he said."

"Just tell me!" She was exasperated.

Sandy took her hand in his and began. She could feel her eyes open wide; her jaw hung in disbelief. She was horrified by the account. Only

Sandy's repeated reminders that Henry Lee had tried to kill her, helped her to accept the awful truth.

"What a horrible way to die," she said.

"But it was exactly how he planned for you to die. And, if not for a speedy Wade, Jessie would have died."

"Yes, I see. Okay, I get it. I can handle it. You know I hate violence, but I don't love Wade any less. But wait! Does that mean I don't have to be afraid anymore? I don't have to hide?"

"Not so. Wade was adamant. NADCO cannot know your location."

She nodded. "That makes sense. But their lake house! They loved that place! All of this because of me."

"No, all of this because of NADCO. They have no ethics, zero morals...but they do have sleazy, incredible, narcissistic greed."

She nodded. "LaCroix and Montgomery are despicable. They are the reason Sam is dead. We have to get those bastards and make sure they are behind bars— and suffer. For a long time!"

Sandy nodded and squeezed her hand. "Wade's working on a plan right now."

"You know what I think about your idea, Wade?" asked locksmith Jim Sedgley. "You can take that idea and..."

They had been driving around in Jim's van for fifteen minutes. Wade thought he was close to convincing Jim. "We almost got these guys. Where's your sense of justice?"

"You don't seem to realize. I'm bonded for a million dollars. I lose that, and I sure as hell can't make a living."

"You won't. If we got caught, I'd say I told you it was my office, and I needed a lockman."

"So, I tell the police that I unlocked a door that had NADCO lettered on it, disarmed a security system, and opened a safe all because my old buddy said he, what...he suddenly owned the company? If that's the level of your thinking, count me out."

Wade knew he was halfway there. "Jim, haven't you ever wanted to? Isn't part of your job's appeal, knowing you could if you wanted to?"

"Mind your own business. And the answer is no."

"I know you have the keys to most of the banks in town, and I know you're the best safe man around, and I also know you wouldn't do anything like that.

But, Jim, these are bad guys. Murderers. Here's your chance to satisfy an itch and take the bastards down at the same time."

"What part of 'no' don't you understand?"

"Fine. I'll just have to do it myself. No way to sugar coat it. I'm the best there ever was."

Jim laughed. "How many years since you cracked a safe? Just because you got lucky with the try-out keys and pushed a few buttons to disarm the alarm, that doesn't make you a goddamn safe cracker. Not even a mediocre one."

"I bet I can crack that baby in four hours," Wade said.

"A Mosley?"

"Yup."

"Anybody knows what they're doing, could do it in three. Two and a half."

"No way."

"Done it myself. Had to open one over in Bowdoinham. Two hours, twenty-seven minutes."

Wade snorted. "Child's play. I could beat your time."

"In your dreams, buddy."

"Nope. In reality. You against me. Winner gets bragging rights. Forever."

"Bragging rights," Jim snapped. He massaged his forehead, then looked at Wade. "Where and when?"

"Appleton Building, tomorrow night. You go first."

A big grin spread across Jim's face. "You son of a B. I knew you were going to talk me into this. What took you so long?"

At 8:00 p.m., Wade moved the bread maker and raised the pantry window. He'd left Jessie in the living room sitting near the window playing an audio tape they had made of themselves a couple of weeks ago–an evening of Wade and Jessie watching TV, having a snack. On cue, Jessie would get up and move around so she matched the sounds on the tape.

He was behind schedule, but he didn't want to call Maggie and tell her until he was away from the house. In the pantry, the old wooden window that never got opened slid up with ease because he'd tested it–sprayed it with silicone. But it wouldn't stay up–the counterweight must not be attached. He needed something to hold it up. He grabbed boxes of macaroni and cereal and jammed them under the window. They didn't hold the window completely open, but good enough.

He tossed couch cushions, pillows, and a comforter out of the window to break his fall. He extended his game leg out of the window and then, sitting on the windowsill, he swung the other one out, but somehow, he snagged the boxes, dumping them on the ground. The window slid down, hitting him on the back, causing him to lose his balance and fall to the ground. The window slammed loudly behind him. Old reflexes took over. He tucked and rolled, ending up sitting in the middle of dry pasta and corn flakes.

Piss, shit, and damn, he thought. They're likely to come investigating the noise. He scrambled to his feet, ignoring his aching knee. He scooped up the boxes, cushions, and blankets and hid them in the shadows of the trees twenty feet away. He stood behind a spruce tree and watched. Sure enough. A crouched figure walked stealthily around his house. He walked like he'd been here before.

When the figure disappeared around the front, Wade pulled out his cell phone to call a cab.

Maggie and Sandy lay in an embrace on the double air mattress he had bought the day after he arrived. In the now dark room, he could barely see her. He traced the line of her bare shoulder to her elbow, then back to her neck. A day hadn't gone by since Sandy arrived that they hadn't made love at least twice. One day they had stayed in bed all day, talking, loving, and talking some more. They were finally getting up to cook breakfast when Sandy noticed the sunlight shining through the west windows. They'd stayed in bed all day. They had talked about everything under the sun with intensity. Well, not everything.

Their relationship was strictly off-limits. Neither of them wanted to do anything to break the spell.

It was the same with them today. Anything but the relationship.

"Do you like me better than jellybeans?" she asked him now.

"I can make this really brief. I like you better than my Cessna."

"Woosh. I'm impressed." She stretched luxuriously, then rolled against him. "But not the boat, huh?"

"Hmm. I'm thinking. I'm thinking." He traced her ear, then her jaw. "Maybe I'd better spend the next twenty minutes evaluating."

She looked at her watch. "Mmm, but we don't have time. Rain check? We have to be ready for action soon."

"I am ready for action now."

"You are always ready for action."

"Do you see that as an asset or a liability?"

"It's only a liability if we starve to death," she said. "Or if we're late for an appointment with a safe. You know we don't even have to be there tonight. But I feel like I must. It feels like..." She thought a minute. "You know what it's like? When children are sick, you feel you can't take your eyes off them for a minute, as if by the sheer force of your total attention, you can make them better? It's like that. I have to be present and watching so everything will be okay."

"I know the feeling." He grinned at her. "I'm that way when I'm watching the Panthers."

"You don't think I'm silly?"

"Nope. I myself have been the beneficiary of your power to focus."

She sat up and looked at his tousled hair and teasing eyes, and her heart squeezed with tenderness and pain. "Sandy, you know this–you and I–will be over soon."

"Shh." He put a finger to her lips, then gently pushed a lock of hair behind her ear. "But we're not over yet."

Wade came out of the woods on the road below the surveillance vehicles. Getting around in the woods was harder than it used to be. He looked at the luminous hands of his watch. Eight-thirty. He was pushing their window of opportunity. He wanted the operation to be over before the pizza shop closed so Pookie and Tildie wouldn't draw attention parked in front of a closed store. Now he wished he'd told them to start without him. Why did he think he had to be in the middle of everything? Maggie, Sandy, and Jim could handle the job without him. You old coot, he thought. Don't know when to move over and let the next generation take over? He limped to the corner, wondering if the cab had already come and gone.

* * *

404

Do you want any pizza?" Pookie asked Tildie. Wade had told them to order some food and sit in the car, eating. They'd been sitting here for an hour, and he was starved.

"No. You go ahead." Tildie rubbed her stomach. "I can't eat right now."

"Are you still having those fake labor pains?"

"False labor. Uh huh." She closed her eyes and put her head back on the headrest. "It'll go away soon. It always does." She suddenly jerked her head forward, her face wincing in pain. "Ow, ow. This one's really getting me."

"Hey, you sure you're okay?"

Tildie took a deep breath. "Yes. I'm okay. Go get your pizza."

"Okay. Lemme call Grandma first to see if they've started. It's eight-forty."

"Don't you dare mention the labor pains. They'll stop in a minute."

"Okay." Pookie dialed his grandmother's cell phone.

"Hi," she said when she answered.

"Hi. Just wanted to make sure you had your cell phone on."

"It's on."

Pookie knew they were trying to keep conversation to the minimum, but he added, "And to see how things are going on your end."

If she asked how things were going on his end, he was going to tell her, whether Tildie liked it or not.

"Okay. But the star of the show isn't here yet. Got to get off the phone in case he's trying to call. Talk to you later." She disconnected.

Pookie thought for a second, then decided he might as well be thinking about the whole thing while the pizza was baking, so he got out of the car, glancing back at Tildie, who seemed just fine after all.

Maggie and Sandy heard footsteps coming up from the third floor as they waited on the fourth landing. Jim Sedgley blinked, looked startled, and flushed when he saw them.

"Are you Jim?" Maggie asked.

"Yes, ma'am. You know I don't usually do this. Where's—"

"Wade. I don't know. I thought he'd be here already. I'm Maggie, this is Sandy.

Jim appeared to be in his late fifties. He had hazel eyes and a round, cheerful face that made him look like he would break into a smile any second.

"So, folks, what do we do now?" Jim asked.

"Well, I don't think we should be hanging around here," Maggie said.

"Okay, where's the office?" Jim pulled on latex gloves. "Not that I'm nervous or anything, but my prints are on file from my old Navy days." He stepped into the hall and fished a tension wrench and pick from a leather case. In thirty seconds, he had the NADCO office door open.

They hurried in, shrinking back into the shadows of the outer office. In whispering voices, Sandy and Jim traded one-liners about breaking and entering, but Maggie remained silent, frequently looking at her watch, worrying about Wade. She was beginning to fear the worst, when he tapped on the door. He shrugged sheepishly as Jim let him in.

"How the hell did I get the impression you were the leader here?" Jim asked. "What? D'you stop for a second cup of coffee?"

"No. I stopped twice to take a leak. Only one of us here has a seventy-year-old prostate," Wade said. "Okay, let's get at it. The next door should be duck soup."

Jim was on his third pick when he wiped sweat from his brow. "Jesus Christ, Wade. I thought you said this door would be easy. This isn't easy."

Wade moved away from the wall he was lounging against, but Jim patted the air, waving him back. "I'll get it. I'll get it. Don't worry. It's just giving me a little trouble."

"For the record, it barely gave me any trouble. And you know how good I am."

"Yeah, the opposite of good."

As Jim fussed with the lock, he dropped the pick. It pinged when it hit the floor. He grinned, shrugged, and bent to pick up the tool–then leaned closer to the lock. "You know, this is a newly installed lock. Hasn't been here long enough to get one scratch on it."

"What! No way," Wade said.

"Yeah. This probably isn't even the same goddamn lock you opened."

Jim fished in his case and got out another pick. "Should only be a couple of minutes."

Maggie saw Sandy involuntarily look at his watch. She felt the same way.

"Got it." Jim pushed the door open. Maggie grabbed the bag that sat at her feet and followed Jim in. She immediately went to the window. Pookie and Tildie were in the car up the street. She taped the blackout mat into place and turned on the light.

Wade took the painting off the wall. "Here's the safe. Let's hope there's more than a slush fund in here. If I'd had your tools with me the last time, I might have gotten lucky."

"Don't take luck, you doofus. No wonder you were always so bad at this. Takes skill."

Wade grinned at him. "Of which you have a lot."

"I've been known."

"Well, pull out the stops."

Jim pulled a stethoscope out of his bag and put the earpieces in his ears. He placed the diaphragm near the combination dial.

"Just like in the movies," Maggie said.

"Yup, except in the movies it only takes twenty seconds. In real life, a minimum of three hours," Wade said.

"It's a Mosler. More difficult than most," Jim said.

"How does this work?" Maggie asked.

Wade crossed his arms and leaned against the wall. "Inside the lockbox there are three wheels–one for each number. All safes use only three numbers in their combinations. He's going to manipulate the dial, listening for the drop zone of each wheel. When all three wheels are lined up, the gate will drop. Then he'll move the dial back to zero, turn the handle to retract the bolts, and voilà!"

"That doesn't sound like it would take too long," Maggie said.

"Wade, you guys are going to have to stop your yapping if I'm going to hear anything." Jim turned to Maggie. "But to answer your question, ma'am. When I come up with the numbers, I have to find out which number goes with which wheel. They have to be in the right order. If everyone will settle down now, I'm aiming to beat my personal record. I want to open this up in two hours."

Wade whistled long and softly. "Game on."

Arturo Mancuso was making the final rounds for tonight. After he checked with his surveillance team and made notes, he would call Montgomery with the no-news-as-usual report and hit the sack. These long days and short nights were getting to him.

With a lot of difficulty, he'd talked Montgomery into suspending the reports to him between the hours of midnight and six a.m., despite Montgomery reminding him that that was the time period that the broad had disappeared.

Mancuso had pointed out everyone they were watching was sleeping then. The surveillance guys could stay up all night, but he, Mancuso, needed to sleep. Montgomery never slept, he decided. Goddamn vampire or something.

He pulled up behind the Dodge that Dusty Sheffer was sitting in, got out, and strolled to the passenger side of the car. He opened the door and lowered his weight into the car. He shook a cigarette loose and lit up. "Hey, Dusty. Howzit goin'?"

"A big fat nothing. This is the most boring detail I've ever done. What the hell are two teenagers mixed up in that calls for this kind of weight? Jesus, I'm so sick of watching them go to school, come home from school. Eat pizza."

"You're getting paid and pretty damn good. If you don't want the job, I can find another walking, talking stiff."

"Hey, no, man. I'm just tired. You get tired of doin' nothin'."

"Yeah. That's why I'm always doin' something." Mancuso pulled out his notebook. "So, what have you got for the last four hours?"

"The first couple a hours they was inside the house. The last hour and a half they been sitting up there in her car" –Dusty motioned toward Matilda Wiser's silver Camry– "talking, eating pizza. Same as a few weeks ago."

Taking a long drag, Mancuso looked at the rear of the car a block ahead of them on the other side of the road. It was parked a block away from Lincoln Montgomery's darkened office building. He let out the smoke slowly. "This same pizza joint?"

"Yeah, they got video games and stuff. A lotta kids go in and out all night."

A coincidence? Mancuso chewed the inside of his mouth. "You say a couple of weeks ago?" He held the cigarette between his second and third fingers and started thumbing through pages in his notebook.

"Or three, maybe. I dunno. The days run together. Doesn't seem important. Does it?"

Mancuso located the note. "Three weeks ago. I got your report by phone that night. I didn't ask you for the street address, so I didn't know it was here."

He made up his mind. "Stay with them until you hear from me." He got out of the Dodge, threw his cigarette butt on the sidewalk, and ground it out with his foot. Now he was really interested in what the surveillance team on the Maxwells had to report. But first he'd call the boss.

Lincoln answered on the second ring. "You're early."

"Yeah, I want to run something by you."

In a few short sentences, Mancuso explained.

"What do you want to do?" Montgomery asked.

"We need to stop by the other surveillance unit, but I wanted to check with you first since you're closer."

"Come by my place. I'm going with you. I'll be ready by the time you get here."

"I'm already here. I'm outside your building."

"I'll be out in two."

Mancuso pulled up behind the surveillance vehicle that was parked a hundred feet up the road from the Maxwells' house. Something was up. He could feel it. Lincoln leapt from the car, and they both approached the driver's side of an old, beat-up Toyota truck. A second vehicle, a black ten-year-old Plymouth, was parked almost out of sight another hundred feet beyond. The driver of the Toyota said there had been a loud noise from behind the house at eight-forty.

"We investigated, but it wasn't nothing. Then the old fogies watched TV. Just like a lot of nights."

"What did they watch?" Mancuso asked.

The man mentioned an early evening show.

"You're shitting me, right?" Mancuso said.

"Just a TV show, Artie," the man said. "No big deal."

"Just a TV show, he says," Mancuso groused, looking Lincoln's way. "Yeah, moron, but on the wrong freaking night!"

He turned to the tail. "Have you actually seen either of them?"

"Sure. The woman went into the kitchen to make a snack. Came back. I can see her right now in the window."

"Can you see him? When was the last time you saw him? Think."

"Don't have to. Got it right here. Um, the last time we saw him was when he went in the house after they went shopping."

"Stay on the job until I tell you otherwise." He turned to Montgomery. "They're outfoxing us. Playing a tape that makes it look like they're both there."

Montgomery nodded. "That's how they shook the tail when they wiped out Lee. Let's get over to the Appleton Building. Something may be going down."

May be? Arturo thought.

Maggie, Sandy, and Wade sat in silence, hearing only their own breathing.

"One hour and fifty-three minutes," said Wade.

"What are you, the town crier?" Jim asked. Two minutes later he turned and beamed at them. "Okay folks, think I've got it."

Jim reached for the handle. Riveted, Maggie held her breath. What if there was nothing in the safe? What if there was no more proof than what they already had–which was nothing. Maybe NADCO had caught on and moved any evidence that existed. Sandy squeezed her hand.

Jim pulled the safe door open and stepped back, motioning Wade forward with a flourish. Wade reached in and pulled out two large, orange zippered bank bags, a video tape, and a small notebook. She watched him feel around in the safe. That was all there was.

Maggie's heart sank. Now what?

Wade glanced at her. "Hold on, Maggie! What were you expecting? A signed confession? Let's see what these things contain."

Wade laid the bags and the video on the desk and opened the notebook. He pulled his glasses out of his shirt pocket and settled them on his nose. He skimmed a page, turned another, and continued reading. He leafed several pages along and read again. Several silent minutes went by as his finger led his eyes down the page.

Then his face relaxed into the most high-spirited, jubilant grin she had ever seen.

He met her eyes.

She saw triumph.

Maggie's spirits lifted as Wade skimmed the pages with increasing excitement. "I think we've got 'em. We've got LaCroix!" Wade grinned at Sandy. "You said it would be him."

"Sure wish we could photocopy this–damning as hell–and put the book back before they knew it was gone. We could show the copy to the police, and then they could find it with a search warrant. But we'll have to take this thing with us–don't dare take a chance it will still be here. But the jig will be up when Montgomery finds it missing, so we might as well take everything."

Wade handed Maggie the journal. "Here, read this entry."

She read aloud. "Date: October nineteenth, Place: Central Park, NYC. Present: myself and R. LaCroix. Subject of meeting: Elimination of M.

Wiser." Maggie looked up and met Sandy's startled eyes. Jim looked aghast. Wade nodded, a grimace settling on his face. She read on. "After some discussion regarding letters and postcards received by the family from the Wiser woman and estimating how much it would have cost her to stay underground since she disappeared on August 17, R. LaCroix said he had recently given orders to his contract killer to dispatch the woman as soon as possible. He said he had instructed the hit man to place her body in a swamp in Florida, hoping she would be there long enough so that she could not be identified. I objected strenuously, but R.L. threatened to frame me for her disposal as well as the elimination of SW if I spoke out."

Wade thumbed through cash in one of the orange bank bags. "Don't let it get to you, Maggie." He then turned to Jim, who was standing with his hand on the top of the open safe door. He clapped him on his shoulder. "Hey, old man. You lucked out again."

"You think so, huh? Next time, I'll stand around and watch you open the damn safe." But Jim was grinning, pleased. He wiped his forehead once more with his arm. "So, we gonna get outta here now? I'm getting a little antsy."

"Yeah. It's a mistake to hang around congratulating ourselves when the job is done. Take the cash bags and tape with you, Jim, will you?" Jim dropped them into his tool bag. "We'll see what they're all about tomorrow. The video could be interesting. Better take the journal, too."

Maggie's phone rang. She handed the journal to Wade and pulled out the phone.

Pookie cleared his throat. "Uh, Tildie says I shouldn't be telling you this yet, but I think the baby is coming."

Maggie could hear the panic in his voice. "What's happened?"

"This thing happened..."

Maggie could hear Tildie talking to him in the background.

"She says her water broke."

"Is she in pain?"

"Yes, off and on. Seems like more on, right now."

"Okay, Pookie. It's going to be okay. Let me talk to Tildie."

Tildie's voice came on sounding remarkably unflustered. "Don't worry. I can drive to the hospital. The contractions are eight minutes apart, and the hospital is only five minutes away." She chuckled. "Gives me something to shoot for."

"How long are the contractions?"

"About two minutes."

"I'm coming right out. Don't move. I'll drive you."

411

"You can't. The seat is wet."

"Tildie, don't move."

"Okay." Her voice sounded weak now, and Maggie suspected she was having a contraction.

Maggie shut off the phone and turned to Sandy. "I've got to go. Phone the hospital to tell them we're coming."

She moved toward the door.

CHAPTER 21

Mancuso pulled up behind Tildie Wiser's Camry, got out, and double timed it to the rear door. He yanked it open and slid in.

He put the gun barrel to the boy's head and held out his hand for the phone the girl held. Her eyes were wide with fear. Good. Maybe it would keep her from being stupid.

Montgomery strode down the sidewalk toward his building.

"Just stay nice and quiet, and nothing will happen," Mancuso said to the kids.

Like wooden Indians, they didn't move a hair. Down the block, he watched Montgomery unlock the front door and enter the building.

Maggie headed toward the outer office, feeling an urgency to help Tildie.

Walking beside her, Jim looked pleased. "Well, that went well."

"You saved the day," Maggie said. "The journal is the proof we need. Still have to figure out what to do with it."

"Kill the lights," Wade said. "Time to retreat. We'll be right behind you, Maggie."

Sandy hit the switch, the office went dark, and Wade pulled off the window mat and looked outside.

Maggie was nearly out of the office when Wade whispered, "Someone's coming down the sidewalk. It's Montgomery!"

Jim looked stricken. "Jesus, what do we do?" His eyes darted from side to side.

"He just entered the building," Wade said. "From the lobby to here, Maggie, you think a minute?"

"About twenty seconds."

"We can't make it to the stairwell. Get in the washroom." He pushed Jim toward the bathroom in the outer office.

"But we didn't close the safe. He'll know. He'll find us."

"Got no choice."

In the tiny bathroom that held only a toilet and sink, they flattened themselves against the walls as far from the door as they could. Sandy moved Maggie into a corner, turned toward her, and shielded her body with his.

They heard the outer door open, then the inner door slam. Resting his weight gently against her, Sandy bent to whisper in her ear. "Tell me if we have sex. I wouldn't want to miss it."

That eased her tension, and she leaned her forehead against his chest, drawing comfort from his strength.

A moment later, the inner door slammed so hard, Maggie wondered for a second if it were a gunshot. We're going to be killed, she thought. I'll never see Tildie's baby. Oh, God, poor Tildie and Pookie. This is going to be awful for them. She tensed and waited. But there was no more noise.

They waited silently for a minute until Wade whispered, "I think we'd better take a look."

Maggie gasped. It might be a trick. When the door opened, the man could be standing there with a gun. And they were unarmed.

Her mind clicked.

No. They weren't.

"Wait," she whispered. Moving Sandy back, she unzipped the pack and pulled out her gun. For the first time, the weapon didn't feel like an enemy. In the blackness, she reached out for where she knew Wade was, located his arm, and put the gun in his hand.

"Damn if I didn't know this would come in handy," Wade whispered. "But you hold it. If I go down, you won't have any defense. Promise me you'll shoot. It's the only way the rest of you will survive."

Her breathing was constricted as she held the gun in both hands, the way Jessie had taught her. She couldn't decide–should she take the safety off or not? She sensed Wade near the door, heard the knob turn. Then rattle. Wade grunted as he pushed on the door. "Something's wedged against it. Probably a chair under the knob. It'll probably give if we keep pushing on it."

"Let me see what I can do," Sandy said.

She heard the impact of Sandy's body against the door and Wade's yell of pain. The door opened abruptly. The outer office was empty.

Her relief was enormous. Then she saw Wade on the floor, holding his knee with both hands. He shook his head from side to side. "I got in your way."

Sandy looked horrified. "It's bad, isn't it?"

"Just one knee. I have another one," Wade said. He rocked back and forth, his face wracked in pain. "Maggie," he said, his breathing labored. "Go tend to Tildie. Be careful. Use the stairs. Go out the back and circle around to be sure he's not waiting outside for you."

He looked up at her and gave a sheepish shrug. "I think I'm sidelined. Listen, however this turns out, we were never here. Sandy, can you get an old man out of here?"

Jim squeezed out the door, tool bag in hand. "I'm gone. I got a living to make. I can't do it from jail. I hope you all understand."

"Always knew you were the kind to cut and run. Guess that tells us who the better man is," Wade said.

"No, it tells us who the smarter man is. See ya, folks." Jim pushed open the outer door and walked rapidly to the stairwell.

Maggie looked at Sandy. He nodded. "I can get him to the ER. Go take care of Tildie."

Anxious to get to Tildie, she chose the front exit, pushing the panic bars. The door flew open. She ran down the middle of the street toward the car, but even before she got there, she knew something was wrong. The driver's door was open. In a few more steps, she saw the car was empty.

She looked up and down the empty street, realizing even as she did, it was useless. They weren't walking to the hospital. They'd been taken.

She thought of news reports about missing children–bodies found days or years later. She ran to Tildie's car, awash in her own culpability. She had left Maine to protect her family, yet when she'd returned, she'd allowed them to take part in dangerous activities. Now they were in mortal danger.

The keys hung in the ignition. In the passenger seat, the cell phone lay discarded.

She should call the police. But she would be a long time explaining everything. Even if the police believed her, which was a long shot at best, it would take time to find out what car Montgomery might be driving, for surely it was he who took the kids. Would the police start looking for the car, or would they go to his house and see if he were there? If they decided to do anything at all.

Suddenly, it occurred to her where they might be. She punched in the numbers to Wade's phone. Sandy answered.

"They've taken the kids. They're gone. Call the police. Wade will know what to tell them."

"Okay. Are you coming back in? We've made it to the lobby."

"No, and I'm not waiting. I'm taking Tildie's car and going after them. I'll let you know what's going on–where I am–where the police can come to...if I'm right."

"Jesus, Maggie, don't go alone. Let me come with you."

"No. Stay with Wade. Call Jessie. She should meet you at the hospital."

She started the car, pulled a U-turn, and accelerated down the empty street. Glancing at her phone, she dialed with her thumb. It rang four times before a sleepy voice answered.

"Otis, this is Maggie. I'm coming to pick you up. Five minutes. No time for questions, and don't call anyone. My life depends on it. Yours, too."

The Pontiac's speedometer was at sixty as the car careened around the corner of the deserted, winding country road, Lincoln Montgomery at the wheel.

Mancuso knew the road. He'd never driven more than forty on it. "Might want to take it a little easy on this road, Boss. Potholes all over the place."

Montgomery didn't answer. Finally, he nodded, and the vehicle slowed to fifty. "You said they had a phone. They must know the old lady's number. Get it."

Mancuso sat sideways in the front seat so he could hold his gun on them. He turned to look at them now. The girl bent over, her face in her hands. The boy, he could tell, was giving the situation his full attention.

"Okay, kid. You heard him. What's the number?"

He could see the boy thinking it over. He glanced at his sister, at the gun, then nodded. He told them the number.

"Dial it," Montgomery said.

Mancuso punched in the numbers and listened. "Busy. I'll try it again in a minute. Want me to try dialing the kids' phone? The one they was using? It's still in the car, on the front seat."

Montgomery glanced at Mancuso, looking startled.

The boss wouldn't have thought of it himself, Mancuso realized. Helluva thing when the person most afraid was the guy in charge.

Montgomery nodded. Mancuso waved the gun at the kid and raised his eyebrows.

The kid made eye contact with him. Not a wiseass look. But one that told him the kid's brain had not shut off.

He pushed the numbers as the kid gave them to him. "It's ringing, Boss."

Montgomery extended his hand for the phone. Mancuso heard someone answer.

Montgomery smiled. "Ms. Wiser, may I say it's a pleasure to finally talk to you–especially under these circumstances. I have your grandchildren with me."

Mancuso couldn't make out her answer, but it was short.

Montgomery said, "I believe you have some things that belong to me. Some things that you and your friend took from my safe. Okay, then. Here's the deal. We exchange your grandchildren for the items you stole."

After a second, Montgomery continued. "No, you cannot talk to them. You will have to trust they are okay because, literally, I am in the driver's seat. I'll make this simple."

He gave her precise directions to the meeting location, then said, "You have half an hour. Come alone, be on time, and bring the items. Any mistakes, you'll find your kids in a ditch. If you find them at all." He ended the call and handed the phone to Mancuso. "That's how you do it."

Mancuso thought about the conversation for a minute. "Not to be nosy, Boss, but what's she got you want?"

"The diary. If the shit hits the fan, and I'd guess it's about to, I need the diary to plea bargain with. I can put that sonovabitch LaCroix away for the rest of his life, and I will walk."

Lincoln had bragged about the diary awhile back. The first thing Arturo Mancuso thought now was that the diary wouldn't protect him. Was Montgomery planning on hanging him out to dry? Unless he made a clean escape, Arturo Mancuso would be behind bars.

Again. No fucking way he was going to let that happen.

"Boss? That might, ah, get you out of the woods on the past stuff, but now you got kidnapping charges you're looking at. Ain't nothing gonna get you out of that, far as I can see. Unless..."

Lincoln turned toward him. Arturo could see panic in his eyes.

"So, I figure you must be planning to get rid of the evidence." He nodded toward the back seat. Both kids stiffened.

Too bad about them, he thought. They're probably okay kids. Their tough luck to get in the middle of this friggin' mess.

"Whatever it takes," Montgomery said. "I have to get the diary. And the money. Then I'm gone."

Mancuso wondered how much had been in the safe. Montgomery always peeled hundreds off a large roll when he gave Mancuso the weekly payroll to distribute, and there was never a shortage of money for unexpected expenses. Could a been hundreds of thousands of dollars in the safe. Now he was sure the boss intended to keep it all.

And leave him holding the bag.

Which wasn't gonna happen.

So, he'd play along. The woman brings the diary and the money. He takes care of the woman and kids, then Montgomery. He dumps the bodies in the well and leaves with the cash. In Maine, he can live simply and cheaply. The money in the cash bag would probably keep him comfortable for the rest of his life. He just had to get his hands on it.

"Good plan, Boss."

Otis was waiting in the shadows when Maggie drove in. He slid into the car.

"They have the kids. From what Montgomery said, they've taken them to the camp you told me about," she blurted. "Tildie is in labor. We've got to go get them."

Maggie started backing out of Otis' driveway.

"Wait, let me go back for my gun," he said. "My .308. It's leaning against the wall." He opened the door and slid out without waiting for her to stop. She slammed on the brakes.

Otis reappeared immediately and climbed back in the car with a rifle. "I had it outside with me. Didn't know what was going on. Figured if my life was going to be in danger, I wanted to be prepared, but I didn't want to scare you by holding it."

She backed the car rapidly out of the driveway, turning sharply onto the street. "Which way?"

"The quickest way to the County Road is by the river, then take a right. I'll show you from there. How'd they get the kids? She's in labor? I didn't realize she was due yet."

"She's not. She'll be eight months next week."

"But why'd they take the kids?"

"Because I have something of theirs."

"That damned cabin," Otis muttered. "It's the logical place to take them. It's out of the way." He paused. "For a reason."

The car bumped down a rutted road. Pookie held Tildie's hand. Every few moments her body stiffened, and she squeezed his hand so hard he had to keep himself from yelling, but she never made a sound. For some reason, this gave him more courage. He was not going to let anything happen to them.

As far as he could tell, only the big guy had a gun. And would use it.

Only fifteen minutes had gone by since the little guy talked to his grandmother. One thing was getting clearer–they might not have another fifteen minutes before Tildie's baby would be born. What the hell was going to happen then?

The car hit another rut, knocking them sideways. Tildie sucked in air and gripped his hand.

Pookie watched the man with the gun. He was big, like an old wrestler who'd gained a lot of fat. But he was probably slow. Everything about him looked slow. And Pookie was sure he couldn't run. He'd seen guys who were fifty years old who didn't stay in shape–like coaches, sometimes–try to run. They could barely lift their feet and were only good for four or five strides.

The guy was probably still strong. Pookie wasn't going to overcome him and take the gun away. Just have to be ready for whatever might happen. Maybe quickness and speed would help.

"Turn's coming right up. Better go slow," Otis said. "There, that's it."

Maggie pulled in, but two car lengths later it was obvious this trail didn't go any further.

"Damn! It's hard to tell in the dark. There are so many of these little openings along here where hunters park their trucks. Go a little farther."

Maggie's nerves were on screech. She was getting physically closer to the kids, she was sure, but they couldn't spend all night combing this ten-mile section of the road, yard by yard.

Every wasted minute, the kids' lives were in rapidly increasing danger. Every wasted minute brought Tildie closer to having the baby without help in God knows what horrible conditions.

She accepted that the baby, born out here in the wilderness ten miles from a hospital and one month early, might not survive. But losing Tildie and Pookie was not something she would accept.

"They need the kids," Otis said. "They're not going to harm them until they see you have nothing to negotiate with. Even then—"

"Why do you say 'they?'"

"Lincoln Montgomery wouldn't be able to pull this off without help. His henchman Mancuso will be with him. Think about it. Could he drive a car and keep Pookie from attacking him?"

"Yes. If he had Tildie in the front seat threatening her with a gun."

"Maybe so. But I can't imagine that weasel Montgomery having the balls unless he had some muscle with him."

"So, we're up against two of them."

Otis repositioned the rifle in his lap. "'Fraid so."

"Nervous?"

"Nervous is when you have to give a speech. Get caught in a speed trap. Misplace your wallet. Hell, I'm scared to death. But I'm not letting that stop me this time. If I hadn't been such a coward, Sam might still be alive."

"And you might be in jail."

"Couldn't be much worse than what I've been going through. I can't bring Sam back, but I'll die, if I have to, to save his grandchildren."

"I'd rather you stay alive and save the children—not die trying." She glanced at him. "Okay with you?"

He looked sheepish. "Sorry for the rhetoric. But Maggie. I'm here. I'll do everything I can. Hey, that bend in the road looks familiar. No, this isn't it. Keep going. We've got to be there soon. God, I hope we haven't passed it."

That thought sent Maggie into fits.

"No, wait. We did pass it. Right there, just now. Go back. I know this is it. I remember that fallen oak."

Maggie slammed on the brakes and backed up.

"Okay," he said, seeing the half covered-up sign. "This is it. The road itself must be two miles long, and it's a lousy road. Still has skidder ruts. But maybe you'd better drive with your lights off anyway. No use tipping them off."

"Phone Sandy again. Tell him the turnoff is about five miles and six or seven tenths from the County Road intersection."

She pulled into the logging road and shut off her lights. All she could see was total blackness outside of the car. "Our eyes will adjust. We'll have to wait a minute," she said.

"I wish we had another gun."

Maggie patted her fanny pack. "We do."

Sitting behind the man with the gun, Pookie scanned the area. The car was stopped in front of a log cabin. The driver was on the porch, unlocking the door, using the car headlights to see by.

The big guy held a gun on them as he slowly backed out of his seat. Pookie realized the man was taking him seriously. They could wait a long time for him to make a careless move.

The big guy motioned to Tildie. "Okay, get out. You first." She reached for the door handle and opened the door. She had just stopped having a contraction; it would be a few minutes before the next one. Her hand was across her stomach as Tildie slowly pulled herself out of the car.

"Come around on this side," the man said.

She walked around the back of the car.

He motioned Pookie out with the gun. "Okay, now you."

Tildie came around to Pookie's side of the car. He opened the door a little, knowing he'd have to wait for Tildie to pass before he could open it all the way.

Suddenly she clutched at her belly and doubled over. Screaming through clenched teeth, she went down. Mancuso reflexively reached out to grab her.

Pookie shoved his door the rest of the way open, slamming hard into Mancuso's arm. The gun went flying.

Tildie scrambled to her feet. Pookie pulled her toward the rear of the car away from the headlights. His arm in front of his face, he dove into the woods, pushing branches aside, pulling Tildie behind him.

He heard the man on the porch shout, "They're getting away, you fool!"

"Not for long," Mancuso shouted. "Come help me find the gun. They won't get far in the dark. Turn the car around and aim the headlights toward the woods. You got a flashlight?"

"In the trunk."

"I got the gun. They're in the woods. That way."

Pookie and Tildie pushed through the brush. Two gunshots exploded in their direction. Tildie fell to her knees saying, "I'm okay," as she went down. Pookie helped her up.

"Keep going. You gotta keep going," he whispered. "This is our only chance." She staggered forward.

"Turn the car around," the gunman shouted. "They can't get far. The woods are too thick."

Pookie heard the car start. He helped her up, wondering if she could still walk. She could, small halting steps. But they could still move, make forward progress.

The headlights helped. They weren't pointed exactly in their direction, but the light spilled over enough that he could tell they were going downhill. The ground suddenly fell sharply away. He stumbled, lost his balance, and they both went down to the sound of cracking branches.

"They're over that way," the little guy shouted.

Pookie grabbed Tildie's hand and whispered, "Sit. Try to slide."

They scooted silently. A few yards later, his foot hit something hard. Feeling it with his hands, he realized it was the upended root of a tree that had fallen.

He pulled Tildie behind the root shelter. "Shh. We better stay here. If we make any more noise, they'll find us."

They heard two more shots, but they didn't sound any closer than the last ones. He put his arm around Tildie. Her body heaved and tensed with pain, but she didn't make a sound.

Maggie and Otis heard the shots. She screamed, "No!" and pushed the accelerator harder. The car bounced off the ruts and slid sideways. She yanked it back onto the road, pulled on the headlights, and accelerated again.

"Oh, my God," Otis moaned. "No, no. Don't let this happen."

Everything Lincoln had accomplished funneled down to this moment of crushing clarity. He was going to lose. LaCroix would go down too, but Lincoln's safety net was gone. He didn't have the journal; he didn't have the kids. He could try bluffing the woman, but it wouldn't work. Whoever she was, she was a hell of a lot smarter than he'd thought. She and the old couple had outsmarted them all.

He should've taken off as soon as he found his safe empty–could already have been halfway to Boston. And if he left now, he'd be in New York before the cops knew where to look for him. Just get the money he had stashed away–not go back to his apartment, not here, not in New York.

Take Mancuso or not? Lincoln had the car keys in his hand. He could drive away. He heard the man crashing through the woods. "Artie! Artie. Come on back. We have to talk."

Mancuso came out of the woods. "Let them stay until daylight. We can find 'em then."

"Get in the car. We're out of here. Know when to fold 'em. I can give you enough money to get wherever you want to go."

Mancuso jumped into the car. He hadn't wanted to kill those kids anyway. "Let's go, Boss."

The contractions seemed to last forever now. Just when she thought this one wasn't going to stop, it let up. Weak with exhaustion and fear, she pulled air into her lungs, then went limp, dreading the next contraction.

Her brother whispered in her ear, "Is the pain gone?"

She nodded.

"I don't think you can go any further. The last two shots were way over to the right. They're going in the wrong direction." He paused. "Can you, are you able to keep quiet?"

She nodded, but she didn't know if she had the strength left.

Above them the car started.

"Listen," he whispered. "They must be leaving. One of them, anyway." Half sitting, he cradled her head and shoulders. His voice sounded scared and helpless. "I don't know what to do," he said.

Neither did she.

"Maggie! Turn off your lights. I saw something."

They plunged into darkness again. Uphill to the left, headlights shone through the trees, bouncing up and down over the rough terrain.

Maggie forced herself not to dwell on what might have happened to the kids. She stopped the car. "Otis, get out and into the woods. Have your gun ready."

Otis scrambled out of the car with remarkable speed for so large a man. "Good idea. You, too, on the other side."

Maggie nodded but didn't move. She heard branches snapping as Otis gained the small bank beside the road.

Pookie had heard two car doors slam and the car pull away. The danger from the thugs was over, but now the baby was coming. There was no way to stop it.

"You'll have to help me get my pantyhose off," she gasped.

Every fiber of Pookie's body wanted to run away. Run and not stop. He had not been this scared of the man with the gun. Because all hope had not been lost. He'd known if he kept his head, he might find a way to get them out alive.

But now there was nothing he could do. He was afraid Tildie would die.

"Come on, Twerp!" she growled. "Help me!" She tried to struggle to a sitting position.

"I can't."

"Then don't. I'll do it myself." She pulled at her skirt and tried to locate her waistband.

Pookie backed away.

"I'll get help." He stood up, looked around, and knew if he went uphill, he'd get back to the camp. Maybe there was a telephone or something.

"No time. I need you…" Then she let loose with a long, wrenching animal sound that terrified him.

He dropped to his knees. He helped pull off the panty hose.

"Your coat," she gasped. "Put your jacket where the baby will come out."

He peeled off his jacket. He slid it between her legs, bent at the knees. "Ready."

"Me too," she groaned.

* * *

424

Maggie watched the headlights get closer. She unzipped the pouch and pulled out the gun, grateful for Jessie's instructions. She slid her finger against the trigger guard. Her left hand rested on the car's headlight switch.

The approaching car careened toward them. When it turned the corner, she pulled on the headlights, popped open the door, and dove to the ground. She crawled into the brush and turned in time to see the other car crash into a tree on Otis' side of the road.

Maggie kneeled and pointed her gun. Her hands and arms trembled–her whole body shook. A large man with a gun in his hand got out of the car. He walked forward on unsteady legs, shaking his head as if to clear it. Blood trickled down his forehead. He put his hand on the fender and bent to look at the front of the car, which had buckled around a tree.

The flash of light and boom of a gunshot tore through the forest. The big man fell to the ground, clutching his leg, screaming in pain.

"Get out of the car, Montgomery," Otis yelled to the other man.

The driver's door opened, and the abductor of her grandchildren slowly got out of the car with his hands in the air.

"Don't give me an excuse to shoot you, asshole," Otis said. "Put your hands on the hood and don't move."

Maggie stood up, her gun still pointed in the direction of the men, and walked carefully toward the car, her feet testing for ruts and bumps as she moved.

"Maggie, this guy's gun is on the ground over here."

Lincoln Montgomery spun his head toward her, his face incredulous.

"I'm not taking my eyes off either of these characters," Otis said, pointing his gun at Lincoln Montgomery. "Can you get the gun, Maggie? Don't pick it up. We need to preserve fingerprints. Just in case."

Just in case he's killed the kids, she thought. She pointed her gun at the injured man on the ground and circled to the front of the car.

"Just kick it away. We'll get it later."

"What did you do to my grandchildren?" Her voice came out like a growl.

"We didn't harm the kids," Montgomery said. "I stopped Mancuso. I wouldn't let him kill them."

Mancuso held his leg. Blood ran down his hands. He glared at Montgomery. "So that's the way it's going to be. Don't bet on it. You're not the only one who has information to plea bargain with. Fucking pansy asshole."

"Maggie, you gotta go find the kids," Otis said. "I don't want you to do it alone…"

In case of what I might find, she thought.

"…but I've got to stay here hoping one of them tries to escape."

She nodded and kicked the gun into the underbrush.

"That's far enough," Otis said. "Now, drive ahead up the road and find those kids. I don't think it's far."

She slid into Tildie's car and dialed 911. She drove while talking to the dispatcher. She told him Otis was holding kidnappers at gunpoint. One was wounded. Send two ambulances. Her granddaughter was going to need one.

"Oh, God, let it be true," she prayed. "Let them still be alive."

Pookie heard a car coming. They were coming back. And Tildie couldn't keep from making noises anymore. What could he do? The car stopped. A door slammed.

"Tildie! Where are you?" his grandmother shouted.

"Down here. Down here. Hurry. Tildie's having her baby. Hurry!"

He saw a flashlight beam swinging around above them.

"Down here, to the right."

Tildie groaned again.

"Hurry!" Pookie shouted.

Maggie ran, pushing branches to the side. She fell, got up, fell again. Finally, she crawled in the direction where she had last heard his voice. When she next heard Tildie's cry, she was close. Maggie swung the flashlight toward the sound.

Pookie stood up, waving her on. "Here!"

When she arrived, Tildie's face was pale in the darkness; her eyes were huge.

"Grandma," she gasped. "I can't do it." The words turned into a groan.

Maggie crawled into position at Tildie's feet. "Yes, Matilda Wiser. You most certainly can." She handed the flashlight to Pookie. "Hold this." The beam wavered. "Pookie! Hold the light still."

Tildie's groan tore from her throat through clenched teeth.

"I can see the head," Maggie said. "If you push hard, it will be over in a minute."

"No-o-o. I can't," Tildie gasped.

"Breathe. Pull in a deep breath. More. As much as you can. Okay, now push!"

Suddenly the top of the head became a full head, followed by one shoulder, then the other, followed by a very tiny baby. A very wet baby.

A whole and complete baby.

"Okay, almost done," Maggie said.

"Is she okay?" Tildie asked.

Maggie cleared mucous from the infant's nose and lifted her. The baby shuddered, then opened her mouth and gasped, pulling in air for a lusty cry.

Leaving the jacket under Tildie, Maggie pulled her own sweater off over her head and wrapped it around the infant, wondering if it were possible this tiny slip of life could survive. There was more to do. She tried to remember anything she had read that would give her a clue.

"I need something to tie off the cord."

"My pantyhose? If we had something to cut them with."

"My pocketknife," Pookie said.

His hand, with a jackknife in it, appeared in front of Maggie. The baby cried, but not as frantically. It was a beautiful sound.

"Find the pantyhose, Nick."

"Here. I've got them. Cut 'em how?"

"In small strips. I only need two."

The flashlight beam, dimmer now, wobbled as he cut through the nylon.

Maggie was afraid to bring the bundle of baby and sweater any closer to Tildie. There was dirt and dead leaves everywhere. She was terrified for Tildie's life. She was sure mothers who birthed their babies in these conditions seldom survived.

She laid the baby down between Tildie's legs. Pookie handed her a circle of nylon.

"Perfect," she said. "Hold the flashlight here so I can see." She tightly tied off the cord between Tildie and the baby. She tied the second strip of nylon six inches below the first. She'd read about a taxicab birth where the driver just put the baby on the mother's stomach without cutting the cord and drove to the hospital that way.

"Hand me the knife," she said.

In the distance, sirens wailed. There will never be a sweeter sound the rest of my life, she thought.

"Pookie...I mean Nicholas. Nick, will you go up to the road and guide them down here?"

427

Her grandson stood up.

"Nick?"

"What?"

"You did a terrific job."

"Yeah, he saved our lives," Tildie said.

"But thanks for showing up when you did, Grandma."

"Wait, before you go, hand me the flashlight. Let me take another look at the baby. See if there is anything else I should do."

He handed her the flashlight. She unwrapped the edge of the sweater to gaze at the sleeping infant.

"Tildie?" She could hear the question in her own voice.

"I was going to tell you, Grandma. As soon as things calmed down."

"Well, I know now, honey."

"What?" Pookie asked.

"Nothing important. Help's on the way, Pookie. Go get them. Take the flashlight."

Maggie peered again at the infant, now totally absorbed in sleep. She was incredibly beautiful, even in her wrinkled infant skin. Maggie lifted the infant's tightly balled tiny fist. The baby's hand jerked back, but she continued to sleep. Maggie pulled the sweater across the top of the child's head so that only her tiny, precious face was visible. Preemies were put in incubators. If she could keep the child warm long enough, was it possible she would live?

"Is she going to make it?" Tildie's voice was strained, but she wanted the truth.

"She looks fine. She seems to be breathing okay. But I'm not going to kid you, honey. This is a bad situation. She needs to be in a hospital. You do, too."

The siren was just above them now, then the noise stopped abruptly. A red light swept through the woods, was gone, then returned again. Doors opened and slammed. Above shouting voices, she heard Pookie's voice, strong and forceful, giving directions. A spotlight shone in her direction. Flashlights bobbed. More than one. Then it sounded like a herd of moose crashing through the woods...profoundly welcomed.

CHAPTER 22

The only sound in the hushed, dimmed hospital corridor was the cardiac monitor. It was four in the morning; Maggie stood alone in front of the window, watching the small bundle that was her great-granddaughter. The baby's brown skin and silky black hair poked out from under the pink knit cap. Every time the heart monitor beeped, she willed the tiny rib cage to move. And move again.

The pediatrician had given her a good chance. "Even at five weeks early, she's a good bet," he'd said.

As Maggie's anxiety receded, admiration for this fragile infant took its place. Human beings are miracles, she decided. This precious child was fighting to live.

Maggie turned toward the nurse, who had just appeared at her elbow. "I just gave your granddaughter something to help her sleep, but she'd like to see you before she goes out." The nurse smiled. "She said you'd be standing here."

Maggie took a last look and sent a prayer in the direction of the sleeping infant.

From the end of the corridor, Jewel watched the woman walk away from the brightly lit nursery. He strolled up to the viewing window, nodded, and smiled at the nurse. She smiled back, and then, based on his skin color, she walked to the incubator and wheeled it to the window for him to view the tiny scrap of humanity that lay sleeping inside. She smiled broadly, expecting him to be overjoyed as he laid eyes on the wrinkled infant. Jewel obligingly smiled back at her and then focused, as he knew he should do, on the infant.

Whenever he experienced this moment, and there had been four in the past ten years, he was appalled that human life began this way, in supreme weakness and dependency and disturbing ugliness. He had only checked in to confirm they were his, and then, having no interest whatsoever in their lives, he had never checked back to see how they were doing. This would be the same.

He walked away, his mind already on the things he still had to do before he quit this burg.

* * *

Tildie was hooked up to an IV. An antibiotic dripped into her bloodstream as, no doubt, did the sedative she'd been given.

As soon as she saw Maggie, Tildie blurted, "Is Daddy here yet?"

"No, honey. I talked to him half an hour ago. He's chartering a plane and should be in town in a couple of hours. He's coming straight here from the airport."

"Good. Grandma, did you see her?"

"She's incredibly beautiful. And she has a lot of hair, just like you did."

"Thank you for getting there in time. You saved us both."

Maggie stood beside her and smoothed back her hair. "In January, I told you I'd be there."

"Little did we know..." Tildie shook her head and smiled ruefully.

"...where there would be," Maggie finished.

"Grandma?"

"Uh huh?"

"About the father..." Tildie looked uncomfortable.

Maggie grinned. "He's the man who...the man you thought you were in love with?"

Tildie nodded and sighed. "I really did think so. The whole thing hit me like...like a tidal wave, I guess. I had no control."

"That's not a bad thing, necessarily," Maggie said, thinking it would be good for Tildie if she lost control once in a while.

"Yeah, but in this case, while I was thinking I was in the middle of a love affair like no one else had ever had, he was..." The words caught in her throat. She grabbed a tissue from a box beside her bed and blew her nose.

"Dating someone else?"

"Several someones. He's a professor–"

"Oh, Tildie."

"Well, an adjunct professor. Temporary. It seemed different, you know? He was just a visitor. We told ourselves the rule against faculty and students fraternizing didn't apply to us. We were very careful not to be together in public."

"Was he married?"

"Who knows? He said he wasn't. But it turned out while we were dating, he was also seeing someone in administration–the assistant dean of students."

"I see."

"Who is married."

"Ah."

"And since I stopped seeing him, he started dating another student."

"My heavens."

"And another professor. Who knows if he told the truth about anything."

"Can I guess…you don't feel in love anymore?"

"No. Not at all. I just feel stupid." Tildie pursed her lips and twisted her mouth to the side, trying to get her emotions under control. Finally, she darted a peek toward Maggie. "It's so embarrassing to say this, but I was such a sap." She looked chagrined. "You know I've never been a pushover before."

"I'm sure. But you can learn from your experience."

"You're okay with this? With Samantha?"

"Yes, way more than okay. You're naming her Samantha?"

"After Grandpa. You okay with that?"

"I'm okay with that, too. And I can't wait to hold my beautiful great-granddaughter."

"The nurse said I can go into the nursery tomorrow. Today, I mean. When I wake up. She said I should touch her as much as I can. To help her thrive."

Tildie had the mystical expression of joy on her face that reminded Maggie of Tildie's mother.

Maggie said, "Do you think they'll let me in, too? I can spell you when you get tired."

"Probably. Ask at the desk. We can do a tag-team thing." Tildie's eye lids were getting heavy. "I can't seem to stay awake."

"Go to sleep. I'll go watch her for a while."

Tildie reached for her hand and squeezed it. "Tell Pookie thanks for saving our lives, too. Samantha and me." And she was asleep.

In the dim room, Maggie said a prayer of thanks for Tildie's life and then responded to the magnetic pull of the nursery, where a tiny life waited for her.

At seven in the morning, Joel, swathed in a blue mask and gown, stood alone beside the incubator and watched his granddaughter's tiny rib cage move so slightly he wasn't always sure she had taken a breath. Falling back on childhood training in a religion he no longer practiced, he prayed fervently that this infant would live.

Tildie had become so maternal–glowing with happiness in her final months of pregnancy–he couldn't imagine how she would survive the loss of this child.

As instructed by Tildie earlier, he opened the incubator door and gently placed his fingers on his granddaughter's arm.

She moved and stretched, and her hand flexed open. He quickly slipped his finger next to her palm and her tiny fingers closed over his. His chest heaved and his throat constricted. He pulled in a ragged breath and exhaled slowly. Awash in feelings stronger than when he had first viewed his own two newborn babies, he looked at every fine, minute detail–from the wisps of black hair to the unbelievably tiny fingernails. Suddenly, he was aware of the vulnerability of this child, who had left the safety of her mother's womb too early, and he knew he'd move heaven and earth, if he could, to protect his granddaughter. In reality, there was nothing he could do but stand beside her and pray.

"Welcome home, Joel. She's a beauty, isn't she?" His mother, who'd gone to the cafeteria to talk to the police an hour ago, was at his elbow. She was also dressed in a gown and mask.

"She..." He cleared his throat. "She is a lot like Tildie when she was born."

He grinned at his mother, and then realized she couldn't see anything but his eyes.

"Imagine, me, a grandfather at my age," he said.

He could tell by the laugh lines at the corners of her eyes that she was smiling back. "Yeah, it kind of catches you by surprise, doesn't it?"

"Been there, huh?"

She nodded. "Do you want me to spell you for a while?"

"No, but thanks. I'll just stay a little longer–until Tildie comes back. She went to rest for a couple of hours. I'm thinking I'll stay all day and through the night, take turns with her. They'll give me a cot. Do you mind?"

"Not at all." His mother patted his arm. "I wouldn't deprive you of the joys of grandparenthood for a second."

She stood on tiptoe, and he lowered his cheek. She found an uncovered spot and kissed him through her mask.

"What do you think she's going to name her?" he asked.

"Samantha, she said."

Sam, after his father. He nodded slowly. Yeah, her name was fitting and right. His father would be proud.

After his mother left the nursery, he leaned close to his granddaughter. "Okay, Sammy. It's just you and me right now. Let's breathe together until your Mommy comes back."

* * *

At eight a.m., Maggie walked into Wade's room, one floor below Tildie's. Sandy, looking weary, leaned against the wall with his arms folded across his chest, talking to Wade.

Sandy smiled at her. "And here's the lady, now, looking as fresh as a daisy."

"Yeah, sure." Maggie laughed, looking down at her filthy, mud caked jeans– the same ones she'd been wearing when she knelt on the ground and delivered Tildie's baby. She still wore the zipped-up jacket the emergency medical technician had leant her. Until the woman had bundled Maggie into it, she'd forgotten she was wearing only jeans and a bra.

On the way to the hospital in the ambulance with Tildie and the baby, she'd phoned Sandy. He was already at the emergency room with Wade, who had broken his fibula, and they were putting a cast on. Sandy told her they wanted to keep him overnight for observation.

Sitting on the side of the bed, now, with a thin hospital blanket across his lap, Wade buttoned the top of his dress shirt.

"They aren't keeping you?" Maggie asked.

"Guess they need beds more than they need a crusty old coot like me to give 'em a hard time."

"Not true," said Jessie, shaking her head but smiling. "He's leaving over their objections."

"It's the tenth of May," Wade said. "Got places to go, things to do. Not gonna miss today's shenanigans. How're Tildie and the baby?"

"Both fine. Tildie is more content than I've ever seen her. She'll be going home tomorrow, but the baby will have to stay for a while. I'm sure Tildie will be here almost around the clock until she can bring her daughter home."

"That's wonderful news," Jessie said.

"Sure is," Wade said. "Hey, the cops talked to you yet?"

"Yes. For the last hour, in the cafeteria."

"How'd that go? Pull up a chair."

"No, I'm fine. Went well. I gave them the short version of events. Otis' bribe, Sam's death, Pookie's bike accident, my running away and hiding, and then coming back for Tildie. I told them I was sure NADCO had Sam killed and was equally sure they wanted to eliminate me. The detective I talked to was Alfie Sandborn. We were in physics and algebra classes together in high school. It's easier talking to someone you know and who knows you are a solid citizen. He really listened, took lots of notes, asked questions to clarify points. I think I had tears in my eyes because he believed me.

"I told him I had been living with a relative out of state, so NADCO couldn't find me, but then I came back to be with Tildie in her last months of pregnancy. I was living in the Appleton Building, thinking it was the last place they would look for me. Tildie went into labor, so she and her brother drove to the building to pick me up on the way to the hospital. But when I went out, the kids were gone. I guessed it must be Montgomery who'd taken them. I said I'd heard about the cabin from Otis and decided to go there."

"How do you think Otis feels about your mentioning him to the police?"

"He was already involved. He was still holding a gun on those guys when the police arrived. I think he was ready to talk. I gathered, from the questions they asked me, that Otis had a lot to say about his suspicions regarding Sam's death."

Wade lifted his shirt collar and wound a tie around his neck. "Probably you left out our break-in. Jim'll appreciate that."

Sandy moved beside Maggie and put a hand on her back. "Do you want me to hunt him down and get the diary? What'll I do with it?"

Wade extended his hand toward Jessie, and she placed his trousers in it.

Wade nodded to Sandy. "Go lock yourself out of your car. Call Jim for help. Tell him you were talking to me last night, and I recommended him as the best locksmith around. He'll get the message and show up with the book and the money."

Maggie said, "Tell him to hurry, since today's the day for the Archibald Estate sale. I want to buy the land myself. Be nice to use Montgomery's money. Poetic justice, I'd call it."

"What irony," Jessie said. "She buys the land out from under NADCO with their own slush fund. I love it."

"I don't think you can buy land with cash. In bundles of hundreds," Maggie said. "But the account that Sam's money is in, I mean my money, is in the same bank where the sale will occur."

"Well, all of you need to skedaddle," Wade said. "I gotta get my pants on. What say we all meet at the bank at ten-thirty? Jessie, honey, will you hand my crutches over here?"

"What'll I do with the book and money?" Sandy asked. "Bring them to you?"

"Not going to work. As soon as we are done at the bank today, Jessie and I are heading for New Hampshire. We're looking into replacing the lake house with one of them fancy, glass front, log cabins."

"Well, that's moving really quickly," Maggie said, "Don't you want to take a few more days and think about it?"

"Nah. We've got a lot of living to do and a short time to do it in. There's an open house today and tomorrow at a company in New Hampshire."

Jessie nodded. "They sell plans and kits, and we want to browse. There's nothing more we can do here to help. We'll be back in a couple of days to visit Tildie and Sammy."

"Meanwhile, we still have to decide how to handle the evidence and money," Sandy said.

"How about plant them at Montgomery's house?" Maggie asked. "If they haven't searched there already."

Wade's eyes lit up and his face crinkled in amusement. "There's the ticket. One more job for Jim. And he'll have to do it. To get rid of the goods, he'll have to break into Montgomery's apartment and leave them there this very morning. Unlikely the police have gotten a search warrant yet since he's confessed. Tell Jim what to do."

"Okay, children, out of here," Jessie said. "If we're going to do this, we still need to go through all the rigamarole of signing out."

"Can I assume I'm no longer in hiding?" Maggie asked.

Wade's face cracked into a wide grin. He met Maggie's eyes. Behind the merriment, she could see something else. Relief, maybe, and some kind of closure. "Yeah, I think it's safe to say everything is copacetic. No more skulking around corners. No more false beards and mustaches–"

"Or red hair."

"Or red hair. Been a long, hard road, but I think you're liberated."

"Home?" Sandy asked Maggie in the hallway.

"Yeah, I need to go home–my real home. I need to change. You can lock yourself out of your car in my driveway and call Jim from my house."

Then it hit her. She hadn't been home in nine months. She was actually going to walk through the door of her own home. And, happy day, none of her clothes would fit.

* * *

435

They all wanted to be there with her–Wade, Jessie, Sandy, Violet, Effie, and George. They arrived in the bank parking lot at 10:45. Maggie had the urge to link arms and advance on the bank as one, marching to triumphant music–the theme of Rocky, maybe.

While Maggie made out paperwork on a clipboard, they all sat in a waiting room until the bids would be taken.

The door from the corridor opened. A tall, distinguished, gray-haired man walked in. It took a second for Maggie to recognize him from the grainy photos in the NADCO newsletter.

He glanced around, obviously looking for someone and dismissing their group as having nothing to do with him.

His handsome face twisted into an expression of annoyance. Then, remembering himself, he quickly slipped into an expansive smile.

"Morning, folks. Nice spring day out there, today."

"Sure is," Wade said.

The others nodded and smiled. Maggie stared at him. This man, with his expensive suit, carefully styled hair, and phony smile, was responsible for Sam's death. And her exile. She stared openly at him, hoping he'd look her way.

He finally did turn and glance at her the way people do when they feel they are being watched. He automatically smiled and gave a tiny nod. Maggie poured all of her anger into her eyes.

He flinched and looked away in confusion.

To Maggie, it was an infinitesimally small triumph, but it felt so good.

She looked up when the outside door opened again, and two men entered the room. Maggie nodded to Detective Sandborn.

He glanced around the room. "Royal LaCroix?"

"Right here." He looked relieved as he stood up. Extending his hand for a handshake, he advanced toward the men. "My business associate isn't here yet, but maybe we can begin the preliminaries without him."

The detective didn't respond to LaCroix's extended hand. Instead, he held up a badge. "Mr. LaCroix, we'd like you to accompany us down to the police station. We need you to answer a few questions for us. It won't take long."

"What is this about? I have an important business matter to take care of right now."

Royal Lacroix scanned Maggie's group, consternation on his face, as it dawned on him, they might all be there for the same reason he was–to bid on the property.

"Your business will have to wait, Mr. LaCroix."

He was almost a head taller than Detective Sanborn, and now he pulled himself more erect. "No. I don't think you understand. I am refusing to go with you right now. I will not risk this business deal."

"I understand you have a Lincoln Montgomery working for you?"

Roy stiffened. "Yes, he's our project manager." LaCroix's glance darted nervously at Maggie. She continued to stare but added a mischievous grin. He did a perplexed double take.

"We arrested him a few hours ago," Sanborn said.

"For what possible reason?" He sounded indignant. He was going to bluff it through, Maggie thought.

"Kidnapping, for one."

LaCroix looked thunderstruck. This was clearly not on the list of things he might have guessed at.

"What?"

"Yes, sir. And we need you to come with us. Just for questioning at this point."

"But..." He glanced nervously around the room again. "I have things to do."

"Yes, sir. And so do we. At the police station."

Roy LaCroix's shoulders sagged. "I really must speak to the bank manager first."

"Okay, we can do that on the way out." The detective held open the outer door.

"Wait." Maggie jumped from her seat. With three long strides, she was in front of LaCroix.

"I'd like to introduce myself," she said, holding his gaze. He started to offer his hand. She kept hers at her sides. "I hear you've been looking for me. I'm Maggie Wiser."

There was only a split second of confusion, and then he looked at her in horror as if she were a coiled snake in striking distance.

She smiled broadly. "I'll see you again at your trial. And your sentencing."

She stepped aside. Detective Sanborn gestured for LaCroix to pass through the door then turned at the last second, acknowledging with a nod the assembled group. "Maggie, folks. Sorry about that. Have a good day."

The door closed, and there was a golden moment of silence while they savored the scene they had just witnessed.

"Glad I was here for *that* exit, stage left," Violet said.

"Safe to say there won't be any competing bids," Jessie said, smiling at Maggie.

Wade nodded, a lopsided grin on his face. "Safe to say, everything is hunky-dory."

Sandy took Maggie's hand and glanced at her. He stroked the back of her hand with his thumb. "Nice touch, Margaret. And I wish you many more triumphant scenes."

George spoke up. "Any truth to the rumor that General Montgomery might surrender?"

"Doesn't matter, private," Effie said. "The war is over. We won."

After the bank accepted her bid, Sandy drove her to the police station, but the detectives were busy with Montgomery and LaCroix. Tomorrow would be soon enough for her formal statement.

Back at home, she fell into bed and slept for four hours. Sandy had gone to Wade and Jessie's house to see them off on their trip to New Hampshire. When Maggie awoke, she realized she hadn't had more than a sponge bath in days. She headed for the shower.

A sharp memory of the last time she'd stepped into this shower caught her unaware. She'd been getting ready to go to Cambridge with Sam. Sam, who'd been alive and now was dead. But at least his killers would pay. She didn't believe in capital punishment, but she hoped Roy LaCroix spent the rest of his life in prison–and she hoped it would be a long, long, miserable life.

After the shower, Maggie borrowed slacks and a top from Tildie's room. When she went downstairs, Sandy was sitting on the couch reading a blue and yellow tri fold pamphlet. He looked up, smiled, and briefly held up the glossy paper before tossing it carelessly on the coffee table.

"Now you *do* look as fresh as a daisy. Bet you *feel* better, too."

"Immensely. What've you got there?" she asked, nodding toward the pamphlet.

"Oh, well, it's just…nothing…um, maybe this wasn't a good idea, but I, um…took a few extra minutes to stop by the airport to see if they give flying lessons there. I was curious. We can just throw this away," he shrugged. "Don't pay any attention to it."

Maggie laughed. "You are *so* obvious despite your *so* convincing nonchalance. Wade and Jessie get off okay?"

"Happy as clams and excited about the possibilities of rebuilding out at the lake."

"Ready?"

"Where're we going?"

"To the hospital."

Pookie stood in front of the nursery, holding hands with a girl. He was talking while she looked at Pookie in awe. Maggie assumed the girl was Ellen.

When she got closer, Maggie could see that Tildie was in the nursery, standing beside the incubator, her hand lightly on Samantha's chest.

"I was pretty sure the gun was loaded," Pookie was saying. "But I had to do something. Probably a good thing it was dark, or we wouldn't have gotten away."

"But you were so brave," the girl said.

"Nah." Pookie looked embarrassed. "Anybody would have done it."

Then he noticed Maggie and Sandy and smiled, his eyes dancing.

"Hi Grandma." He hugged her and shook hands with Sandy. "I told her–this is Ellen, Ellen this is my grandmother and her friend Sandy–I told her all about what's happened."

Ellen smiled at Maggie. "I'm glad you're back and okay. I think Nick really missed you."

"Thank you, Ellen. I'm happy to meet you. Pookie–excuse me–Nick has told me a lot about you. Listen, I could order pizza for supper tonight. You're invited if you'd like to come."

Ellen nodded. "Thank you, Mrs. Wiser."

"Ah, Grandma, if you don't mind, could we skip tonight?" Pookie's eyes were both pleading and tinged with guilt. "On Friday nights, we all, the whole gang, go bowling and then have pizza at the bowling alley. You don't mind, do you?"

She had just gotten her family back, and now Pookie was running off with his gang. Then she imagined the fun Pookie would have relating his recent adventures to his friends. She felt Sandy's reassuring hand on her back. She stifled a sigh.

Pookie looked at her. "I don't have to if you want me at home."

"Go with your friends. You need it. We could even say you earned it. We can do something over the weekend. You go and have fun."

With his eyes, he telegraphed his gratitude to her.

"Something else." Pookie looked a little sheepish. He took her arm and steered her several yards away from Sandy and Ellen. "The guys were going to stay over at Doug's tonight so we could jog and shoot baskets in the morning."

"Of course." But something else was the real reason he had moved away from the group. He looked at the floor. "Um, thanks for...you know. For, ah...for showing up when you did. For finding us." He darted a quick glance at her and then back at the floor. "I don't think...well, the baby...I couldn't have...you know. Whew! You'll never know how glad I was to see you."

"Yeah, I think I do know. I wouldn't have been able to deliver a baby when I was fourteen. You did a terrific job. Keep this thought–you saved the lives of your sister and your niece. Not to mention your own. For which I will always be grateful." She gave him a quick hug. "Now, go have some fun. I'll see you tomorrow."

He kissed her cheek and headed back toward Sandy and Ellen, who were admiring the baby in the nursery.

"Nick?" Maggie called.

He turned.

"Sometimes it may come out as 'Nicky.' Can you live with that?"

"Sure can." Then he gave a thumbs up.

"You need to be alone tonight," Sandy said with his usual perception. They were just finishing a meal at a picnic table outside of Subway. He rolled his sandwich wrapper into a ball and put it into his empty Pepsi cup.

"Yeah. I need to commune with my home. I...I want to spend time with you, but I'm not ready to have you...stay over. You know what I mean?"

"Uh huh. It's a turf thing. A boundary thing. I understand."

"Yeah, boundary–not turf. I just need that space."

He smiled. "Except that the size of your space doesn't end with your house. I think it might extend to the Virginia border."

She smiled back, meeting his eyes. "Well, maybe to Rhode Island."

He snapped his fingers. "Shucks. And just when I was thinking of moving to Boston."

"You know I have to live here. I'm home."

"Never any doubt in my mind."

"So, what do we do?"

"Nothing. My line is, 'can I call you sometime?' I get three hundred free minutes on my cell phone."

"Okay. And my line is, 'I'd love that.'" She felt a catch in her throat.

"I might ask you for a date. Not sure yet."

"I might say yes. Can't be certain." She felt a tear run down her cheek.

He handed her a Subway napkin. "I'd be flattered at this display of emotion, but I think it might be that you haven't slept in something like thirty-six hours."

She smiled, trying to get the tears to stop, but they seem to have a life of their own. "I took a nap." She mopped her face with another napkin. "But how would we date?"

"I happen to have shuttle transportation between Beaufort and Amesbury. But no set schedules, no commitments. I'll call, and you can say yes or no."

"And if I call?"

"Same thing."

The water works, which had almost stopped, freshened and flowed. "I seem to have sprung a leak."

"I wonder why. Let's see–for months you've dealt with uncertainty every day–you've been separated from your home, your family, you've been worried about them, worried about a possible rift between you and your grandson, you've been afraid for your very life on a number of occasions, not to mention afraid for their lives, you've been dealing with the violent death of someone to whom you were very close for most of your adult life, you've watched your nemesis begin the process of incarceration, you've delivered a baby, and you've feared for the life of the mother of the infant, as well as the infant herself. Hmm. Have I left anything out?"

She grinned, but foolishly the tears continued.

"Could be you did."

"Oh. Yeah, not to mention being in and out…and in and out…and possibly in again, of a relationship."

She nodded.

"Okay, so your body is telling you something. Catharsis is good. Go with it. They have plenty more napkins inside."

"No, I think I'm done for now."

"Okay, let me take you home, then."

"You don't mind? I'm too tired for a hotel room tonight."

"Furthest thought from my mind. Well, not quite the furthest." He smiled, took the wet napkins from her hand, and picked up the debris from their lunch. "I'm going to get a room for myself tonight here in town. You get a good night's sleep at home, and we can have breakfast before I take off tomorrow."

"Sandy?" What did she want to say? I think it's possible I love you? Not trusting her judgment when she was this tired, she said instead, "You are more of a wonder every day."

"That's me. Wonder Man. Just remember that the next time you need a tall building leapt."

Suddenly, the last residue of tension broke inside her, and a delicious relaxation spread through her limbs. She closed her eyes and felt the warmth of the sun on her back.

"Okay, Wonder Man, let's get me home before I fall asleep right here."

"Happy to oblige. You've earned it."

Jewel snapped the locks on his last piece of luggage. He scanned the room to see if he'd left anything behind. He noticed the cheap photo album some students had given him as a going-away present. He laughed aloud. Small college, small town life—both a first for him. What a trip. Students and faculty flocked to him...were putty in his hands. He'd enjoyed toying with them to see how far they'd go in their adoration.

He sat down and flipped past the pages documenting his field trip experiences to the loose photos he'd slipped inside the back cover. There was a smiling photo of every woman he'd had an affair with. He fingered the one of Tildie Wiser–his first conquest in Amesbury.

He chuckled again. In a couple of months, there'd be another similar birth, and possibly a third a little later. Well, at least he'd provided some color for Amesbury. He put the album in his briefcase. Yes, the trip had been worth the price of admission.

But things were wrapping up quickly. After the explosion last week, he'd discovered the old man was alive and uninjured. Lee's body had been identified and his car towed. The woman still had not shown up, but he had been sure she was in Amesbury, well tucked away. Then, this morning at

Hal's Diner, the place was abuzz with the information that Maggie Wiser had delivered Tildie's baby. He had already stopped by the hospital, glanced at the infant, knew it was his.

Things were coming to a close, so he'd driven the Range Rover home today and taken the train back. It was past midnight, when he clicked his briefcase shut, picked up the other two pieces of luggage, and headed for the Nissan parked outside.

There was only one stop to make on the way out of town.

Jewel had never before made a sound when entering this house. But he'd never entered when the woman was in residence–the woman who'd now left luggage carelessly strewn in the hallway near the cellar door. He regained his balance and waited in the shadows, breathing slowly, listening. No sounds. He'd wait for five more minutes before moving, just to be sure she was asleep.

Maggie picked her head up off the pillow as she woke from a light sleep. Had she heard a noise? She sat up and slowly reached for the gun she had placed on her bedside table. She listened to the silence. Nothing. How long would it be before she relaxed—before she stopped scanning her environment for danger?

The assassin was dead. She had to remember that. She lay back down. If she'd heard something in her sleep, it was probably just that nocturnal raccoon rummaging in the trash can. She knew it was silly to be concerned.

Nevertheless, the gun now lay beside her thigh where her hand would quickly find it. In the quiet, she sensed, rather than heard, something. What was it?

Jewel looked around the living room and was transported back to the day he had first entered this house. *Déjà vu*, sort of. Not exactly the proper definition, but in this reality, he suddenly felt he'd been here before for the first time, only minutes ago.

As he stood there, realizing his breathing was becoming rapid, he tried to slip into a meditative state. And then the pictures of his last eight months slid into place, one by one, like a slideshow. He remembered his thoughts on that day about this job and what he should do. He couldn't fault himself for his decision to stay and check things out.

He should have been clearer in his thinking though: the woman was just a job–not even that. A possible job.

But what had happened after that? He had entangled himself in this drama. He had become fascinated by the events and had risen to the call of a challenge. Each step, he now realized, made it easier to stay engaged. It *had* been the challenge, mostly, that had kept him here. The challenge provided by...yes, by the woman. He could see his mistake in getting involved, in letting it become personal.

But now something has changed, he acknowledged. Quite drastically. He *wanted* her to simply be an object to be removed. That's the way it worked. But....

Maggie eased out of bed with her gun in her hand and stepped into the hallway. Feeling silly, knowing she was overreacting, she glided silently down the carpeted hall toward the other bedrooms. Peering in each open doorway, she shook her head. She was being ridiculous. Turn around and go back to bed, she told herself. But, she'd come this far, she might as well continue. The gun was heavy in her hand.

What was different? Jewel wondered. He searched his mind, tried to be as honest with himself as he could. What, at this very moment, had changed?

It was–could it be? He'd been bested by someone he'd underestimated all along. And think about it...*she was never his contract.*

Face it. Admit it. She had *bested* him. Yes, she had been lucky when he missed his sniper shot in January, but then, as he gave chase, she had eluded him. Not only had she dropped from sight, under his nose, but she had also sold the car and then disappeared without a trace.

Then, in Morehead City, she had escaped from his grasp and gotten away. He had sighted her on the beach shortly after, but then she'd disappeared again. And managed to get back to Beaufort without his seeing her.

Now it appeared she and her cohorts had engineered the arrest of Lincoln Montgomery and LaCroix and, if the story were correct, had delivered Tildie's infant in the woods at night. That story, he was sure, would become a local legend.

And he was now prepared to just pop her in her *sleep*? He stiffened. His self-respect went deeper than that.

Maybe, just maybe–he had, what–respect for the woman? Hard to say for sure. He'd had respect for so few people. He thought about it. Yeah, maybe.

Maggie was at the end of the hallway and considered turning around and going back to bed. But I've come this far, she thought, so I might as well finish. Then she realized the safety was on. If she encountered an intruder, it wouldn't do any good to have a gun. Feeling absurd, she, nevertheless, took the safety off. She smiled thinking how she would tell this story to the Maxwells when they got back. In her right hand she held the gun; with the left, she held the handrail and silently descended the stairs.

In the kitchen, Maggie stiffened. Had she heard another sound? She slowly worked her way through the dining room with the gun firmly in her grasp.

He took the silencer off his gun and slipped it inside his pocket. He picked his way through the luggage, opened the cellar door, and slipped inside. He descended the stairs without the benefit of light.

She stepped into the hall thinking, this is silly. The doors are locked. How would an intruder even get in? Then with a shock, it occurred to her that not all the doors *were* locked. A shiver of awareness and alarm swept through her.

As she caught her breath, she swiftly reached out and turned the lock on the cellar door. She was dead sure the bulkhead was not locked. They would have to padlock it in the morning. She shook her head. How careless they had been!

At the bottom of the stairs, he heard the click of the cellar door lock and smiled. The end of an era. He switched on the tiny flashlight he carried and picked his way across the cellar. He stopped and glanced at the antique cradle, newly refinished. There was a pink bow on top and a card. It said, "Welcome to the newest Wiser."

He put the flashlight away and exited the cellar.

Stepping around her luggage, both old and newly acquired, she entered the living room. She switched on the light and, noticing the pamphlet Sandy had left on the coffee table, picked it up. This time last year, she reflected, she would have thought the idea was ludicrous. But now?

Now, maybe she *would* take flying lessons. She slid the pamphlet under her arm, turned off the light and headed up the stairs to her room.

She glanced at the clock. One-fifteen. Good. Six more hours of delicious sleep.

She slipped into bed and closed her eyes, sleepily thinking about how they would renovate the house so that Tildie and Samantha would have rooms next to each other, and they would create a guest room for Aunt Belle.

Then, making a decision, she put the gun in the bedside table drawer. She vowed to empty it of ammunition in the morning and give it back to Wade and Jessie. This family would have a child in the house now, and there would be no guns.

She lay back down on the pillow, and as she drowsily closed her eyes, somewhere off in the distance, she heard a car start. She felt a relaxing peace, deeper than anything she'd known for a long time, and fell asleep.

THE END

Acknowledgements for the dream team of *No Loose Ends:*

To appreciate the dedication of the members of my "team," I need to explain how long *No Loose Ends* was a work in progress. I started it in 2000. Yes, this is why it is set in that time period. In this twenty-three year stretch, it was finished, more or less, three times. During this time, I also completed and published my first book, *Never Leave on a Friday,* and started my third–working title: *Homeless in Honduras.* While I'd like to offer this as an excuse for not working on *No Loose Ends,* I can't. Life called me in so many different directions, and, let's face it, I'm easily distracted, always throwing myself into whatever needs doing at the moment.

The people to whom I am profoundly appreciative and indebted, in order of appearance:

Dorin Zohner - My late husband believed I could write this book before I did. After I took a creative writing class, we walked daily and talked through the characters and plots and ran many "what if" scenarios. It was great fun, and his support is what kept me thinking about the trouble my characters were in and how they'd get themselves out of it. He had his private pilot's license, so he helped with the airplane scenes. He would be relieved and beyond happy that I finished it, finally.

Pam Ames - Over twenty years ago, she and I took a writing class together, formed a critique group, and became friends. Through the years and several versions of *No Loose Ends*, Pam has been there, reading and critiquing from cover to cover. She is an excellent editor and proof-reader with amazing patience and tenacity, and she has a good ear for language. Because she was also an assistant DA, she brought to this book a specialized knowledge of police procedures and crime scenes. Thank you, Pam.

Detective Sergeant (ret) John Gould - When I decided Maggie needed to learn to shoot, I realized my gun experience, which consisted of target practice with my dad using a .22 rifle off our back porch when I was twelve, was not going to do it. So, I walked into the Waterville Police Station and asked to speak to someone about learning to shoot a handgun. I expected to be dismissed with a head shake and a chuckle, so imagine my surprise when Detective Gould graciously agreed to teach me. We used an outdoor shooting range, and he brought two handguns (like Jessie did for Maggie) to choose from. I had the same experiences that Maggie did, including, in spite of Detective Gould's warnings, a scraped and bloody thumb joint. As soon as the lesson was over, I went home and wrote the scene. The accuracy in this scene comes directly from John, and I want to thank him profusely for sharing his expertise.

Many years and two more versions of the book came and went because, for various reasons, it was shelved. It wasn't until the final version was a couple of months from completion that my son Mike (a major member of my team) mentioned that he was acquainted with John on Facebook and sent me John's contact information. Now happily enjoying retirement, John responded to my inquiry and said he'd be willing to look at my work. What a valuable and knowledgeable resource he has been. I started with showing him a version of the "crime scene" scene and, while being supportive, he responded with extremely valuable information. This emboldened me to show him additional scenes like the "escape" scene and the "police station" scene, which he also critiqued and improved. He also has extensive knowledge of guns, being a competitive shooter, which he generously shared with me. Thank you, John. I couldn't have done it without you.

Michael Shepherd - My son Mike has been my most dedicated supporter and most valuable critiquer, without whom this book would never have been finished. Many times, he encouraged me to take it out of mothballs and continue. And I would. Until the next mountain or molehill appeared in my life. Never giving up, he would nudge me again. And again. He lives almost a whole continent away from me, so we did it all on the internet, texting, emailing and facetiming, sometimes several times a day. He has been so generous with his time, attention, and talent. He travels for his job, and many times the texts and emails would come from the airport waiting area, the tarmac, or a foreign country.

Further, he wrote, for my consideration, a couple of scenes that appear in *No Loose Ends*, almost exactly as he wrote them. They are the poolhall scene from Yabo's point of view and Sam's scene of regret, both of which I immediately incorporated, and they are among my favorite scenes.

Mike has a great sense of humor and takes rejection well, always with a laugh or smile emoji when we disagree on a scene, so he was an excellent collaborator.

In addition, Mike's finely tuned feel for characterization and motivation caused him to frequently ask, "Why?" This is the most valuable service one can offer an author: to understand a character's motivation, and *No Loose Ends* is a much better book for Mike's involvement. Times ten.

Garrett Shepherd - Garrett, another son (I have five), was a supportive critiquer and had valuable information to add to Pookie's high school sports career. He shared other sensitive observations that were dead on, much needed, and appreciated.

David Bennett - A classmate from high school, Dave has done a lot of sailing, including trans-Atlantic, on his private yacht, so I asked him to check my sailing scene to be sure I remembered how to "come about."

Marilyn Wheeler - An exercise buddy and friend, Marilyn happened to mention she had done proof-reading in a former job, so, in spite of her misgivings, I twisted her arm into working on the manuscript. She was indeed helpful, and it came at a time when I was having doubts, so she was an energy booster. A couple of her "why" questions caused me to rethink and rewrite a couple of scenes. She also brought her laptop to my house so she could teach me how to use Google Docs in editing mode, so I could pass that information on to someone else. (Turns out being on the receiving end of the edits is different from creating edits.)

Carol Sturtevant - When I play with words while writing, punctuation and sometimes grammar fall, willy- nilly, by the wayside. So, I really needed Carol. She was first, my Spanish teacher. When I needed someone to correct my Spanish in *Never Leave on a Friday*, Carol agreed. She was excellent, of course, but I quickly realized she was a pro at punctuation and grammar (she is also an English teacher), so I asked her to do that as well. Then she moved away, but I still had her contact information, so a few years later, I begged her to work on *No Loose Ends*. Though her teaching schedule was full, she asked me for a sample of the book, so I sent her Tildie's haircut scene, and she said, "Yes." I think of Carol as the punctuation expert and much, much more. It's exhausting to read text word by word, looking at and correcting punctuation and usage, but she kept her shoulder to the wheel and powered her way through the book. I consider her a friend and a fun person to have breakfast with.

Diane Durrell, RN Retired - Another exercise buddy, Diane agreed to read and correct the baby delivery scene. Yes, I have given birth, but that doesn't tell you what is happening outside of your body, and your kind of preoccupied at the time. Thank you, Diane.

Cory Shepherd - Anyone who read my first book, *Never Leave on a Friday*, will be familiar with my youngest son, Cory, who at the age of 16, sailed the ocean blue as a crew member with my husband and me for a year. Pam, Mike, and I knew, after reading *No Loose Ends* multiple times in its various forms, weaving in new scenes here and there, that we would no longer be able to pick up continuity problems and inconsistencies. We desperately needed fresh eyes, and Cory, in spite of being ridiculously busy with work and family, found the time to squeeze in reading the book. It's fortunate that he is insanely dedicated and can power his way through difficulties because he read it on a device that didn't give him page numbers and which began each reading session at the beginning of the book, so he had to scroll through to find wherever he had left off. And it's a good thing for me that he did. He quickly unearthed a couple of significant issues that had to be addressed. In the eleventh hour. When the book was done. Almost. And his enthusiasm for *No Loose Ends* was a huge energy boost when I really needed it. Thanks, Cor.

Dustin Shepherd - My grandson, who has lived with me for twenty-eight years, patiently listened to me talk through plot and character issues and gave me valuable feedback and encouragement. Then he stepped up to the plate and, to my great relief, took my Google Docs documents, changed them to Word, and uploaded the book, in all its many pieces, to Amazon–no small feat! I am so grateful.

Dave Fymbo of Limelight Book Covers - Thanks to Dave, who created the cover and who proved to have the patience of a saint. He is highly skilled and was tireless in his dedication to creating the cover that I fell in love with. I was picky and changed my mind more than once, sending him back to the drawing board a number of times, but he kept assuring me we would keep going until I was satisfied. And I certainly am!

Tomasz Wachowski – To my brilliant and talented website designer whose latest endeavor is redesigning my website to include *No Loose Ends*, thank you!

To all five of my sons and the grandson I raised, I hope you recognize yourselves in Pookie's scenes. It has been the joy of my life and a privilege to be your mother and grandmother.

To the entire team who invested their time and effort to help me finish this book, from the bottom of my heart…thank you. The idea that Dorin and I started many years ago would have never been more than a sadly forgotten manuscript that never saw the light of day. Now, thanks to you, it's complete.

And on to the next one!